THE SEVEN RAZORS
OF OCKAM

THE SEVEN RAZORS OF OCKAM

Roger Ormerod

This first world edition published in Great Britain 1997 by
SEVERN HOUSE PUBLISHERS LTD of
9–15 High Street, Sutton, Surrey SM1 1DF.
This title first published in the U.S.A. by
SEVERN HOUSE PUBLISHERS INC of
595 Madison Avenue, New York, N.Y. 10022.

British Library Cataloguing in Publication Data

A CIP record for this title is held at the British Library.

ISBN 0 7278 5280 9

Typeset by Palimpsest Book Production Limited,
Polmont, Stirlingshire, Scotland.
Printed and bound in Great Britain by
Hartnolls Ltd, Bodmin, Cornwall.

Preface

This story is based on an incident that occurred some time ago at a location I cannot recall. I never did hear the outcome. If, therefore, I have inadvertantly embarrassed or offended any of the real participants, I offer my apologies. If the outcome in any way resembled my imaginary reconstruction, possibly my condolences would be more in order.

This book is therefore dedicated to the original winners.

R.O. 1997

Chapter One

Monday, 4 September

His belly resting against the inside of the extensive plate-glass window of the mayor's parlour, Bert (Slasher) Harris, the incumbent mayor of Ockam, stared out pensively. The view was not unpleasant as it encompassed the new concourse as well as the modern council office block to his right, and offered the full benefit of the terraces, the landscaping, the statues and the convoluted steps up to the offices. At 8.50 a.m., with the council staff hurrying to another Monday, it should have presented, to a retired man still two years short of sixty and in possession of most of his faculties, an invigorating prospect, even gladsome. But Bert Harris was frowning, and he saw nothing of this.

His attention was focussed on the building facing him from the far side of the concourse. Ask anybody in town their opinion of this building, and you'd get a single rude word in response. Ask the proposed demolishers, and they'd say they couldn't wait to get at it. Even the preservationists would shake a sad head and mutter such words as 'offensive' and 'ugly'. It was a Victorian block of red, smoke-blackened brick with massive mullioned windows, through which light had long since ceased to make the effort, and with a wide, balconied portico, supported by flaking and wearied columns and surrounded by a low, crumbling balustrade.

1

This was the old Town Hall. Above its wide entrance, and now nearly undecipherable, had been carved, in the arch provided for it, the town motto. As this carving has by now become completely beyond recall, it is possibly best to record it here for posterity.

ENTIA NON SUNT MULTIPLICANDA
PRAETER NECESSITATUM

Ask anybody in Ockam what this means and nobody will be able to tell you. Or will refuse to.

It was not at this motto that Bert was staring, it was at the balcony above it. He was not hearing the clatter and scramble of scurrying workers in the concourse and the repeated agreement that it was bloody Monday. He was hearing cheers; whistles; screams; even a bugle. He was again standing there on that balcony with the swirling and tightly-packed mass below him, on what had been the site of the open market before it became the concourse. There wasn't one cobblestone of that venerable surface without a foot on it. There was not one mouth that wasn't shouting his name. Slasher Harris! Slasher Harris! The cup was digging into his right shoulder, left arm raised, waving a salutation to right, to left, to centre, while the whole town throbbed to the cries. Slasher Harris! Slasher Harris! He lived it again, a time when the balcony had not been in its present crumbling condition, when he, Bert (Slasher) Harris, captain and centre-forward of the Ockam Cutters, had brought the FA cup to his home town.

There! he thought. "There!" he muttered. And it was as though a great weight had been lifted from his mind. A decision had had to be made. Slasher Harris had achieved one. That day, the day of the cheers and the adulation, had been the pinnacle of his life. It had also been thirty years before and Bert Harris was consumed by nostalgia.

2

He would relive that day. He would stand once more on that balcony with the swaying sea of pink uplifted faces below him, and again he would receive the electric jolt of self-satisfaction that had carried him forward – then gradually faded. Once more he needed stimulus. From there he would make the draw.

Bert Harris had been asked to make the prize draw for the raffle that was expected to supply a new dialysis machine for St Mary's Hospital. To him, now having had six months of experience on the job, it would be the most interesting mayoral duty to date. And he would make it from his balcony.

There was the most gentle and discreet of coughs behind him. To Bert, so deeply concentrated on another time, another place, it was like a clap of thunder. He jumped and he turned.

The town clerk, Llewellyn Pugh, was standing there, as he did every morning at this time, waiting to give the mayor the details of his day's programme. His instructions. As there was rarely anything for Bert to do, this absorbed very little time. But Llewellyn Pugh was punctilious about this. He'd been the town clerk for twenty years, he'd seen them come and he'd seen them go, but to each he'd extended the same solemn courtesy. His opinion of mayors, as a collective noun, had not been recorded as it would probably be unprintable, but nothing of this ever entered his voice or his expression.

"Good Lord, Mr Pugh," said Bert breathlessly, "you didn't half give me a shock."

"I'm sorry, Mr Harris. I only wanted to tell you there's very little on today. You'll be showing the regalia to the members of—"

"I've made a decision." Bert moved away from the window. The room brightened as he was a hefty man and had obscured a lot of light. He brought his beefy palms

3

together with a decisive slap. "I know where we're going to do it."

". . . and get yourself photographed with the leading lady in the production of—" Pugh was blandly plodding on.

"There!" cried Bert, waving grandly towards the window.

"What?"

"The balcony of the old Town Hall."

"What is?"

"On Saturday week."

Pugh gave it up. He asked wearily, "What are we talking about?"

"The raffle draw on Saturday week, my dear chap."

Pugh hated being anybody's dear chap. Slasher Harris, no more than one of those weird footballing types, wasn't going to condescend to an MA, FIAI, FIAC, FIS, and one other he couldn't bring to mind.

"A raffle draw is not on your schedule of official duties, Bert," he pointed out, dropping the formality abruptly.

Bert waved a hand impatiently. "It's a favour. It's extra-something."

"Marital? Mural?" Pugh's eyebrows were the best raisers in the business.

"All they want is me and the old chain."

"I'm sorry." Pugh bent his head. "That will not be possible."

"*What* will not be possible?"

"For you to wear the mayoral chain. Only on mayoral duties—"

"Oh, come on. Don't be a fusspot."

"I could not permit it."

The mayor pointed a finger. He clearly remembered his remark to the referee at Molineux. "Now listen to me, you tight-assed—"

The raised eyebrows caught him. Pugh's never-raised voice added, "Especially for a raffle."

4

"What's the matter with raffles?"

"I do not approve of gambling."

"You'd approve of a dialysis machine if your kidneys conked out."

"My kidneys," said Pugh with dignity, "are—"

"All right. All right. Forget it. Forget the damned chain. It's a ton weight, anyway."

Clearly, Bert Harris thought this was the end of it. But no. Pugh clung doggedly to the nub of the situation.

"There was mention of the old Town Hall balcony."

Bert drew a deep breath. "I am going to make a raffle draw on Saturday the sixteenth day of this month, and I intend to do it from that balcony."

"It's not on."

"Then you can make sure it is."

"It is not part of my duties, and the building facing us, that monstrosity over there, it's been condemned. You cannot, therefore, use it."

Bert thought of things more suitable for condemning. "Please make the necessary arrangements." After all, who was the mayor around here?

"The borough surveyor—"

"Pff!"

"The police—"

"Pff!"

"I thought it was going to be done in the football grounds," said Pugh in a fit of inspiration. The man was an ex-footballer, wasn't he? Nostalgia. The old turf beneath the feet. That sort of thing.

But Bert, having already considered exactly the same thing, had decided he wouldn't be able to face it. The turf without a ball at his feet? Never! Turf and a football had been as one to Bert. Why else had they called him Slasher? Because he'd slashed his way through the defence, that's why. He had become a legend. Those fabulous runs through the whole gamut of eleven men, the ball, it seemed, attached to his boots! It was said that he could pass the ball, observe it would be intercepted, and withdraw it from the air. As though on elastic. Many there were who would swear to this. When properly primed with the local brew, they would swear they'd witnessed it a dozen times. And now – he couldn't even see a damned ball if it was at his feet. Apart from that, there had been the uncomfortable feeling that on the soccer pitch he would this time be playing to a limited number of supporters, and he'd always played to packed terraces and stands. No . . . he couldn't face it.

"Unsuitable!" Bert dismissed it. "The balcony, that's the place." And the concourse would be packed, even with a poor turnout.

"The regulations—"

Bert was losing his temper. "Bugger the regulations."

Town clerks live by, with and for regulations. Pugh drew himself up to his full height, which was a mere five-eight, and inflated his meagre chest. "I will send the borough surveyor to see you. And the police and the chairman of the raffle committee."

"Send the Girl Guides, if you like."

"Pff!" said Pugh, who didn't see why the mayor should monopolise it. Then he left sedately, with dignity, closing the door with a gloved hand.

"Send 'em all," Bert shouted at the closed door.

He was now even more determined. Something of his former glory had entered into him. He had performed at his best when the opposition was strongest, when the odds were highest, the objective least obtainable. Hadn't he scored, personally, from pick-ups way behind the halfway line, those final two goals that had won the cup in the last five minutes? Clean, solitary runs, they had been.

"Send 'em all," he repeated, squaring his shoulders and trying to draw in his belly.

Which Pugh, outside, conscientiously proceeded to do. He squared his narrower shoulders and headed directly for his office and his phone. He didn't know, never having seen Slasher Harris on a soccer pitch, that once his mind was made up the mayor was not to be thwarted.

Having taken a solitary and restful coffee in the executive dining room, Bert Harris turned his thoughts to more pleasant tasks. His ladies were due at ten o'clock, a special lot this morning from Philadelphia. He knew exactly what they would wish to hear, and Bert was always pleased to stand amongst a group of adoring females and do his stuff. He didn't know that they were adoring; he had to assume it. So at five minutes to the hour, he was standing beside the display case, which was set in the centre of the upper floor walkway and ten yards from the mayor's parlour, where he would take them for refreshments afterwards.

They were no different from any other group, but he assumed that, being Americans, they would wallow in his prepared (by Pugh) history of Ockam's past, because Ockam had begun its life's work long before the first settlers had confronted their first Indians.

After the initial introductions and having shaken twenty hands, he produced his gold key to the display cabinet. The mayor's key was gold-plated – the duplicates held by Pugh and the chief security officer were common steel, insofar as Ockam steel could be decribed as common. The wealth of the town and district had grown from its very uncommonness. Opening the cabinet, he drew out the mayoral chain and draped it across his chest.

"It weighs a ton," he told them jovially. "That's why I got this job. They can't find many men big enough to stand it."

Laughter there. Almost as good as the cheers from the terraces.

Then he displayed the gold-plated axe-heads. "One left-handed, one right-handed," he explained solemnly, though they looked identical. "Why's that?" was always the inevitable question, thus allowing him to say, smacking his lips, "These are the famous one-cut executioner's axes. One-cut Ockams, they called 'em. The technique, I'm told, required a twist of the wrist – so, one for left-handed headsmen, one for right-handed."

"Oo . . . oo . . ."

He then showed them the mace, a fine example of local craftsmanship in silver and gold. He waved it around, but they'd seen maces before, and were visibly unimpressed.

And then – the final item in the showcase – the Ockam Razors. These were in a silk-lined case, leather-bound, on the outside being the imprinted gold motto of the town in the original Latin. As Bert didn't know what this meant he skipped over it and opened the case. On the inset plate inside the lid were the words: 'Presented to the town of Ockam on his retirement as Mayor by Professor Julian Packman, 1958'. Bert didn't know the explanation for this, either, but he could and did tell them that the seven razors symbolised the philosophical principle of William of Occam, who'd lived in this town from 1270 to 1349, this principle being known as Occam's Razor.

This was a complete fallacy. Everybody knows that William of Occam lived in the other Ockham, in Surrey. But no one had ever challenged it, and nobody did this time. So Bert sailed ahead, explaining that Ockam's history relied on sharp edges and sharp points, and that these seven razors were the finest example in the whole wide world – a rash statement to make to twenty American ladies, but again unchallenged – of the classic open razor, and that they'd been sold in sets of seven, each with a day of the week engraved on its rear edge, it being assumed that a gentleman who could afford such luxuries would assuredly shave on Sundays as well as the rest of the week.

Here he would always run his hand over his own beautifully smooth chin and take a deep breath.

Then, that over, he would launch into a history of the town and its outlying districts. Regrettably, his account also contained inaccuracies and it would be as well to record the truth.

Ockam, let it be admitted, had always been an arms centre from the early days when the first caveman discovered a globule of metal in the ashes of his fire. From that time weapons were made from this hard stuff, beginning with large globules on the end of a leather thong. But greater things were to come. Metals became the lifeblood of this small village, which, by the Middle Ages, had become a sizeable sprawl of neighbouring villages. It was here that the finest swords were made and their fame soon spread to far distant parts of the country. Barons would trek here for an Ockam broadsword. Kilted and bewhiskered Scots would fight their way south – for Ockam is right in the centre of England – wearing out two claymores in the process, and all for one good Ockam claymore, the Scots being thrifty. By this time it was possible to have your broadsword or claymore fitted with a personalised handgrip in gold and silver filigree. The Ockamites were even then alive to every possibility of profit.

Soon, rival barons would make the journey, accompanied by their footsoldiers and serfs etc, all to be equipped. While the necessary fitting and testing and balancing was going on the two or more factions would live together peacefully, separating only to journey home and to meet later in order to slaughter each other in distant parts with their new Ockam weaponry.

Throughout history Ockam itself has been free of such strife. Nobody attacked Ockam. It was too precious and its expertise in too much demand.

There was a certain advantage in living so far from the sea;

invaders rarely reached this area. Occasionally a tattered and distressed band of Swedes or Norsemen might find their way there, but by that time they were too exhausted for rape and too bored with pillaging. These settled and married. No legal problems were presented to them; the word refugee was not mentioned.

Very soon, so comprehensive had become the range of Ockam's goods, that Princes and Earls turned up with their armies – even the odd King or two – to be rekitted for the next war. There was nothing that couldn't be supplied. Knights and their retinues were measured and fitted with armour in one district which was guaranteed to resist any arrow ever made. Their bowmen were equipped with arrows tipped with the recently perfected hard metal which was guaranteed to puncture any armour yet made – this in another village. In the first district the knights were invited to test the end product by having arrows shot at them. For this test the older soft-tipped arrows were used. Result: satisfaction. In the other district a similar offer was made, but this time to test the new hard-tipped arrows. Squires who had outgrown their obsequiousness were invited into their sire's secondhand armour. Result: the loss of one or two squires. In other words, complete satisfaction.

Lighter, leather protection could be supplied in another district for the bowmen, in yet another the bows and arrowshafts. It is said that Robin Hood journeyed here, leaving Maid Marion to entertain the Sheriff of Nottingham, and here bought his special, accurate bow, purchased with the proceeds of robbing the rich. Little John bought the largest and strongest bow they ever made. Nobody dared ask him to pay for it.

It was all hustle and bustle. The town grew to encompass the surrounding districts. They are still there as parishes. Arrowvale, Axe Edge, Armour Crossing – the creek where the knights were invited to test the waterproofing – Tannin

Reek and Link Green, where chains were fashioned, from the small mesh for chain mail to the huge links for anchor chains. Chains were ordered by royalty for the Tower of London.

There was never a time when the town of Ockam was silent and still. Busy, busy. And rarely was there a time when opposing factions were not camped, quite peacefully, in the surrounding countryside. The Ockamites were never morally concerned with supplying arms to both sides, even when one side was ours and one theirs. This became known as Ockamodating, later to become corrupted into accommodating. This distortion no doubt came about because the citizens of Ockam had no necessity to learn how to read and write. Only to count.

In 1414 a French contingent journeyed across the Channel and north from Dorset in order, they claimed, to acquire the famed new penetrating arrowheads. In fact their purpose was to display the latest ultimate deterrent, the crossbow. The new arrowheads were for their bolts. This is probably the first-known use of psychological warfare, as the journey had been made purely for the purpose of intimidation. Or, as the French put it, to scare the *culottes* off the *bâtards Anglais*.

What is not generally known is that the battle of Agincourt in the following year was won at Ockam, as the Ockamites palmed off on the French their soft-headed arrowheads, as used for testing armour. This story is probably apocryphal, as it is a fact known worldwide that the English, and especially the Ockamites, are too sporting to perpetrate such a dirty trick. In support of this they will show you their bowling green on which, they claim, cricket was invented, when opposing teams became disenchanted with each other and hurled their bowls at their opponents' heads, thereby establishing the basic principles. But they did not, it is admitted, give the new sport a name.

This deficiency was later corrected by Sir Francis Drake

when, on hearing the Spanish fleet was so close, also hurled a bowl, this time at his caddy's head. Historians claim this to be apocryphal, as Elias Proot, in his pamphlet 'Carrying The Cannonballs For Drake', states that Drake's remark was "Friggit!" But this was later corrupted to cricket and any suggestions that Drake was calling for his frigate can probably be discounted.

Be that as it may, the fact remains that Ockam really came to prominence with its axe heads, whereas, had France won at Agincourt, it might have been guillotine blades. In fact, M. Guillotine did purchase blades from there, but for his own domestic use. In Britain it was beheading. Not a pleasant experience, this, at the best of times. It required, therefore, the best axe heads available. And beyond all dispute, the Ockam one-cut axe heads were supreme. Headsmen from all over the country journeyed there. It was an important issue for them as their kings or queens always liked a non-messy job. Once a headsman began to require two, or even three blows, he'd had it. In practice, he was for the chop himself. Next man in, so to speak. And by then, having been messed about so much, the axe would be blunt. So . . . one-cut Ockams it had to be, until the advent of the rope.

Ockam then began rope-making.

Ockam had it all, and continued to have a good portion of it in the following decades, progressing to cannon to field guns to tanks, from small arms to middle-sized arms to big arms. Until gradually it all slipped away. Who wants armour-piercing arrowheads? Who needs headsman's axe heads or hangman's ropes? And where have all the wars gone? Abroad, that's where. The once almost solid black smoke clouds that hung over the area – thus giving rise to the term Black Country – have long since drifted away, to reveal that there is a sun up there. The town has wilted, having to fight back with different and radical projects, and in full sunlight.

This then is the background to the incidents to follow. The townspeople are derived from countless generations of fire-hardened and fume-toughened ancestors. They are not easily swayed, are perhaps somewhat cynical and there is ingrained in them, from the times of Ockamodation, a basic sense of fair play.

Such a man was Bert Harris, by this time just finishing his history of Ockam. It may not be the true history, but that's not his fault. Bert Harris was an honest stalwart of Ockam, and gave value to the ladies from America. He then took them into the mayor's parlour for tea and buns, and got rid of them just in time to face the onslaught.

There were two police inspectors, one borough surveyor, one borough engineer, one town clerk, and the chairman of the committee promoting the charity draw. Bert Harris faced them blandly. Damn it all, he was The Mayor. But they had come in a mood demanding capitals to their titles.

"That building," said the borough surveyor, "has been condemned."

"Tcha!" said Bert. "There'll only be three of us."

"All the same," put in the borough engineer, "that balcony's ready to collapse."

"Shore it up," Bert advised him. "That's it, old chap, you'd better shore it up."

Inspector Masters (Traffic) said, "I'd have to block off Council Road." This ran between the gloomy face of the old Town Hall and the concourse.

"Block it then," Bert told him. "It'll only be for half an hour."

"And how," demanded Inspector Arkwright (Riot Control), "am I going to contain them if they get out of control?"

"Out of control!" shouted Bert. "What d'you mean – out of control? *I'll* be in control."

"Hmph!" said Cartwright.

"But Bert," put in Arthur Moreton, his good friend from schooldays, but now representing the raffle committee, "we've advertised it for the football pitch."

"Time for—"

"And we were going to have the Ford Escort there and the BMW bike, and all the other stuff."

"It's all on the tickets," Bert pointed out.

"But . . . the advertisement, Bert! Why d'you think these prizes have been offered? Not out of their kind hearts. It's business. Advertisement. Listen to reason, Bert."

"I want to do it there!" Bert Harris said, stabbing a fist in the general direction of the old Town Hall. Then he slipped a notch and challenged fate. "If I can't do that, you can get somebody else."

And Llewellyn Pugh, always prepared to be fairminded, and realising that Bert Harris was the most prestigious mayor he'd ever had to lead through a term of office, put in, "There isn't anybody else."

Thereby rising several degrees in Bert's estimation.

They all thought about that. The truth was that they knew there was nobody else who could be persuaded, bullied or bribed to take it on. They looked at each other, looked at their feet, and they agreed.

The stage was set.

Chapter Two

Tuesday, 5 September
to
Friday, 15 September

Nothing worth recording happened during the next eleven days, apart from a minor exposure which barely qualified as indecent. The two borough men laboured at their tasks, the two inspectors of police worried, the chairman of the raffle committee, Arthur Moreton, grew noticeably thinner, and the town clerk moved around like a ghost. At one time he reached the point of wondering whether to fake a robbery in order to keep the mayor's fingers off the mayoral chain.

As the names of the eventual winners are now a matter of history, there seems no point in making any secrecy out of it, so here they are, in order of seniority:

> Ada Follett, 72, widow.
> Lucifer Hartington, 65, bargee.
> Arthur Moreton, 58, factory owner.
> Lucinda Porter, 45, a sick lady.
> Paul Catterick, 38, civil servant.
> Esmeralda Greene, 36, teacher.
> Charlie Pierce, 22, unemployed.

Ada Follett was the widow of Eric Follett and as such was a woman of distinction. It was still, even eight years after his death, good for a free pint of milk stout round at the Plucked Goose on any evening she wished to go there. As she had this desire every day of the year, Ada was well supplied, and only one glass brought out the best in her, or the worst, depending on your temperament. If you want a good laugh, buy Ada a milk stout. But you'd have to endure her screaming hoots, her poke – later in the evening, if you're still buying – a forthright punch in the shoulder, and her blue jokes which had more than once threatened her with banishment from the premises.

This was not a serious threat. Bill Fisher, custodian of the Plucked Goose, knew that she pulled in the customers and a good laugh always makes people thirsty. Oh . . . and you'd have to endure, when she became maudlin at about her seventh glass, her talk about Eric.

She was invariably there with her lifelong friends, Connie and Floss, who occupied the houses each side of Ada. It was impossible, in Chamois Street in the parish of Tanner's Reek, not to become intimate with one's neighbours. Only one brick's thickness separated them, in a long row mounting up the hill to the old foundry at the top, which had been the employers of all the men in the street, except Eric Follett. It was possible to conduct a conversation through those walls, which is why the Chamois women all had loud and piercing voices. The houses ran, front to back: pavement outside, front room, rear room, kitchen, coalhouse, outside toilet, blue brick yard, back fence, canal – and that was it. Intimacy was the keynote. Ada didn't need to shout to her friends when setting off to the Plucked Goose – open her front door and they'd pop out like Smarties. These three, together, were enough entertainment for a full evening.

They had each moved into these houses on marriage, fifty or so years ago. Their husbands had worked all their lives at the foundry, except Eric Follett who'd been at Weldless Tubes, so naturally the three husbands used strong language as daily conversation. To the three widows, it was a legacy.

But Ada was the star turn and her eminence grew from her husband. Eric had been a slinger. *The* slinger. Nobody else would do the job, or wanted to try. You could say the factory relied on Eric. They cosseted him, watching anxiously for evidence of colds or flu, but Eric was a man of steel. He was never ill. He was treated as royalty by the management who knew that if it was not for Eric they would have to install prohibitively expensive machinery. In fact, after he retired the factory lasted only three months. Coincidence? Perhaps.

Eric had his own shower stall. He had a personal and continuous flow of orange juice, he had a helper who mopped off the sweat during those odd moments when the extruder paused for a breath, to light his cigarette, to hold out a glass of orange juice. The helpers, too, were difficult to find; it scared them rigid. Eric had his own parking slot in the executive car park, his name on it. He was spared the indignity of clocking in and clocking out. But he was never late, arriving punctually on his bike, which he left leaning against the nameplate: Mr Eric Follett. He was worth a fortune to Weldless Tube.

They didn't pay him a fortune, though. He was never one to ask for more. His shop steward promised an all-out strike, but Eric always shook his head. "I'm all right, mate. All right."

Which meant he could visit the Plucked Goose every evening with Ada and buy his ten pints of bitter and four glasses of stout for Ada, and not feel the pinch. Eric required a large quantity of liquid, and huge meals, to sustain him.

What he did was stand between two machines, ten feet apart, stripped to the waist and with a pair of three-foot pincers in his hands. The machine at his one side extruded eight separate white-hot, two-inch tubes of steel, each a second or two behind the other. The other machine received these on rollers and transported them for further treatment. The difficulty was that, being white hot and in a flabby condition, the tubes writhed like demented and evil snakes as they reached the air, and it was Eric's job to catch them in his pincers and guide each one on to the rollers, then turn in time to catch the next before it entwined itself around him. One miss and he would be in danger from the one he'd missed, and from the next one, sneaking up behind him. He never missed.

Strong men have fainted, just watching. His helpers had to work in shifts. It was two hours per delivery, half an hour to reload the feeder, then on to the next two hours. Eric never missed.

They tried him in the local cricket team, both as fielder and batsman. He was hopeless. Give him a pair of pincers and he never missed a ball. But pincers were not permitted, as it wouldn't have been cricket. Especially when you're batting.

He retired at sixty, still a big, strong and terribly healthy man. In six months he was dead. It was his nerves that went. He couldn't stop himself from glancing over his shoulder for the next white-hot tube. Ada tried to interest him in the garden.

"What garden?" he asked.

"You could get them bricks up in the yard, dig it over—"

"Nah!"

"Grow some flowers, Eric."

"Nah!"

"You're a lazy pig. Why don't y' rent an allotment?"

Which he did. This he dug completely in two hours, then he couldn't think what to do next. It all seemed so unnecessary and what with the twitches . . . He shrugged and went home. Life had lost something. Even at the pub

18

. . . what had been ten satisfying pints dwindled to six, then to four. His body didn't need it any more. He wilted, he lost weight, he had a nervous breakdown.

Then he caught a cold. He didn't know what it was. It turned into influenza. He was baffled. Then to pneumonia. In hospital they tried oxygen. Perhaps a few lungfuls of furnace fumes and a fanning with a red-hot length of tube would have been better.

Then he died. No fight in him at all. His burial was attended by leading dignitaries of the town and three hundred friends. His grave is marked by a pair of three-foot pincers bearing a cross-piece of two-inch tube.

Ada was bereft. At the Plucked Goose he was terribly missed. He'd never said much, had sat there a stolid mass of humanity, and occasionally had smiled. But he was missed.

Weldless Tube gave Ada a good pension, which fortunately continued after the demise of the firm. She was a long while recovering her former spirit and *joie de vivre*, but in that tiny frame of hers was all the toughness and resilience of her Eric.

It was in the Plucked Goose that Ada bought her ticket for the raffle organised by the 57 Club – the 57 Battleaxes they called themselves, in full. Her friends Connie and Floss also bought tickets. But these two were lucky; the draw just missed them.

Lucifer Hartington lived on a converted longboat, which he had moored on the canal in close proximity to the Buckled Arrow. Little was known about him. The police are continuing their enquiries. He was a person of no fixed address, in that he would, from time to time, unhitch his home and travel to the next pub along the canal.

This travelling presented some difficulty as the engine

had long since ceased to putter, but he had discovered that he himself could, by pulling hard and long, move his barge. Slowly and with immense effort, this was. But he could not at the same time steer it.

However, he always stayed long enough in one spot to establish a rapport with the locals, sufficient to call on their help. Half a dozen would do. He was popular in the pub, but not vastly so. He was not one of your hail-fellow-well-met types. Rather, he was quiet, joining in where necessary, never hesitant in his calling for fresh rounds, and he was inoffensive. His clothes had a certain elegance but were never pressed. He always wore a tie in the evenings. But apart from the fact that he objected to being called Lucy, nobody even knew his full name.

He was sixty-five years old at this time, but years of facing inclement weather, winters and summers, had hardened him into a nutty brown colour, his face creased, though most likely because he smiled so often. The rumour was that he'd spent all his life on a barge, though Lucifer seemed an unlikely christian name for a bargee. Certainly, up to recent years, the canal had been heavily used by the surrounding industries, interlinked as they were and each supplying the others with their necessities. But Lucifer never revealed his background.

When the tickets were going round the Buckled Arrow, he bought a couple, just for the laugh of it. Reading the list of prizes he asked, "What on earth would I do with an Escort XR3i, whatever that means? Drive it up and down the canal?" General laughter. "What about a BMW motorbike! The towpath for that. Or two thousand quid's worth of kitchen equipment! They couldn't get a cooker through the doorway." Roars of laughter. "And an electronic typewriter. That's for me. Run it on batteries, I suppose. Heh! Here's an electric lawnmower. Just the thing. I could keep the canal banks trimmed. And here's a set of suitcases. What the devil would I do with suitcases? If I go anywhere, I take my whole home with me. And one of those walking radios with headphones! I've got a good battery set inside."

He bought the tickets just to help out with the dialysis machine. Later, he had to do some more thinking, because it's never a good idea to laugh at fate.

Arthur Moreton we have already met as the chairman of the organising committee for the raffle. Strictly speaking, he had no right at all to be in the list of prizewinners. None of the committee was supposed to buy tickets. It would "look funny" if he should win.

But Arthur had sold forty-five from a book of fifty, to workpeople in his own factory. Ashamed to return five unsold, he'd bought the rest himself. No harm in that, surely. Secretly, he'd been ashamed that his workmen and women had not demanded more, but it'd been the devil's own game to sell forty-five. On the shopfloor he was, at that time, something of a *persona non grata*.

Arthur Moreton was the sole owner of Moreton Milling. It wasn't a public limited company, it was all his. He'd built it up from nothing, starting in a shed with cast-off machines from a larger firm, on a deserted patch of derelict ground. There was not one machine on his shopfloor that he couldn't operate, so he knew what he was about. As a boss he was popular. His work force was 123 on the shopfloor and 23 in the offices. He was content with this. He could run it all himself, whereas he knew that if he expanded he'd be separated from the working heart of it by production controllers and sundry other executives. As it was, he'd always been confident he could cope with anything.

Only one thing stood between him and pure happiness, only one because there was only one union involved. But Kenny Scott was worth a dozen ordinary shop stewards when it came to sheer cussed stubborn stupidity. Take a dozen doses of bile from any of a dozen others and you had Kenny Scott. A dozen open and receptive minds, a dozen reasonable thinkers; there was not one iota of any of these that touched Kenny. He faced life with a snarl and a bitter tongue. One couldn't blame him, Arthur always admitted, considering his home life.

So they'd fought over the years. Win some, lose some. Kenny Scott had seemed, at least, to draw some small measure of satisfaction from their battles. Until the question of equality hit them both between the eyes.

It was ironical that in this Arthur and Kenny reversed roles. Arthur was all for equality of pay for his ladies. He was not merely willing to introduce it, but had been urging it for some time. He knew which machines were too heavy for women, which not. It was not a matter of sex, it was a matter of strength. His shopfloor workforce consisted of seventy-eight men and forty-five women.

But Kenny Scott hated women. He hated them with a virulent and poisonous loathing that had gone way beyond all reason years before. As a collective breed, women were the very dregs to Kenny Scott. And who could blame him if they'd met his wife and his two daughters? Arthur simply wished he wouldn't bring his hatred here to his factory. He even wished – though this was no more than a fleeting thought – that Kenny would stay at home and send his wife in his place. But Arthur had then met his wife. No thanks. Not again.

On the question, therefore, of equality, Arthur and Kenny clashed again, but now it was Kenny who was against it and Arthur for. Arthur rarely lost his temper, but this time he came very close. He pointed out that he could incorporate the change in his payroll and *then* Kenny could argue about it. Kenny said in that case he'd have the men out. Arthur doubted it. Kenny said just watch him, then.

So Arthur gave it more thought, quietly and during long walks in the evenings along tree-shaded Crécy Drive with his red setter. Then, casually, he dropped the information that Kenny was opposing equal pay for women into the delicate ear of his private and very confidential secretary, knowing she would confidentially pass it on to her friend Polly in production control, who would whisper it as a secret to her friend Esther on the shop floor, operating a tapping machine. Then he waited.

What they did to Kenny in the ladies rest room was unspeakable. Arthur paled when he heard it. The following day, when Kenny was able to manage the stairs, he appeared in Arthur's office and whispered that he had thought it over and now agreed.

That should have been the end of it but Kenny had savaged his mind for revenge. A week later he arrived with a demand for higher piecework rates for the Lasco vertical millers and the Fischer multi-headed lathes.

This was a poser, Arthur thought. His factory milled, drilled, tapped and partly assembled components for carburettors, and more recently for fuel-injection systems. His main machines were these Lascos and Fischers. They were operated solely by men. To agree to higher rates would put the women back almost to where they'd been before and Arthur couldn't afford a tit-for-tat progression. He cursed. He procrastinated. He couldn't see how he was going to resolve it.

He was in this state of tension and indecision when he was appointed chairman, by his fellow fifty-six members of the 57 Club, for the raffle draw. He confidently took a book of fifty tickets to the factory. As he was his own boss, he invariably had no one to turn to. This applied not only to the matter of decisions, but also to the question of who was going to tote these round the shopfloor. The shop steward would have been the obvious man, but they weren't speaking.

The men rejected his advances. Kenny had got at them. The women welcomed him as a friend. He sold forty-five to his shop-floor ladies, and was left with five on his hands.

It was therefore partly because there was not one man's name on any of the stubs that he bought the other five himself.

It was a big, almost tragic, mistake.

Lucinda Porter was a sick woman. In fact, she believed she was dying. Already there had been one small attack. It was not outwardly apparent and she made every effort to hide it. In the ordinary routine of her life she would have had no difficulty in this because, ever since she had moved into 3C, Foundry Street, in the parish of Link Green, she had lived a very secluded life. Her trips out of doors had always been no more than rapid dashes around the shops. At first there had been no outward signs of her illness, pain not displaying itself, but they were so clearly a matter of scuttling out and scuttling back that they attracted the attention of her neighbour in 3B on the floor below. This was Madge Fenwick who spent most of her time sitting at her window overlooking the street.

This had been going on for several months, and if it seems that Madge's behaviour was equally strange for a young woman, sitting so much at her window, this is easily explained by the fact that she did her work there. Madge Fenwick was writing a novel. It was her first novel, obviously, as any experienced writer would have told her that to sit at such a window was non-conducive to concentrated thought. The book was progressing very slowly, she would have admitted, but not, she would protest, because of the constantly changing scene in the street below her, but rather because her typewriter was missing one letter. The E. Which any typist knows is a crippling disability. Es abound. When you have to write in every one by hand . . . well, you can see she was handicapped.

Madge was twenty. She was a bright and intelligent girl, and you would wonder why she had been reduced to the level of writing a novel in a scruffy little bed-sitter on the second floor of a house that should, frankly, have been condemned years ago. She had one or two O levels, but no As. She could use the correct fingers on her machine, but was not sufficiently qualified for a post as secretary or even plain typist. I mean . . . what could she do?

The difficulty was that her father had died when she was a child, so that she and her mother had become strongly attached. During her mother's long illness she had been willing to forego the progress of her education and training, but on the death of her mother she was made to realise that she couldn't remain alone in a council house with three bedrooms. She was offered a flat in a high-rise complex. She shuddered away from it. Hence the cheapest room she could find, and the prospect of living on what the Social Security people would allow her. The poverty trap.

She was not the sort of young woman to sit back and let it happen. She therefore thought around and in the inaccurate belief that one novel ought to set her up for life, she'd bought a typewriter and set about to write one. Then she had discovered that there was an incentive scheme that encouraged initiative.

So she took along a first chapter and a summary of the plot, and was awarded £50 a week in order to complete it. This seemed an easy task. A novel in a year! Easy – if it hadn't been for an ancient Royal lacking an E and the so-very-tiring search in her mind for words that also lacked it.

It was not surprising, therefore, that she worked at a table in her window. Her limited finances also limited her activities. She was not in a position to go out on the town, or to buy the necessary clothes in which to undertake it. But she was not depressed by this. She was a buoyant young lady and could withdraw into the limited extent of the possibilities on offer.

But it did seem to her, gazing through her window and watching the couples strolling the street in the evenings, that one basic element was missing in her life. A boy, a man – something male, anyway. There had been no end of this tribe hanging around at one time, because she was five feet four of very shapely female indeed, with flaming red hair and dancing eyes. In fact, they'd queued up. Two or more had fought over her. But looking after her mother had restricted her social activities for four whole years, during which she had simply lost touch. At first her friends visited, but the young feel restricted and uneasy in a house that contains illness. Now, with her mother gone, the whole social scene had changed. Friends from school now had babies; some were even married. The boys were now young men, full of get-up-and-go. And mainly they'd gone. She now realised that she was missing something in life.

Then she met Lucinda Porter on the stairs. Her neighbour from above. It was at once evident to Madge that Lucinda was unwell. Two flights of stairs with two full shopping bags seemed too much for her. She even seemed to be in pain.

"Here, let me help you with those." Madge spoke almost instinctively.

"You're very kind."

At forty-eight, Lucinda looked closer to sixty. At the time of this first meeting she was at the stage of hospital visits for tests, but already her skin was showing a faint grey tinge and her features were pinched. Madge stayed for a cup of tea. Lucinda was, if anything, even more lonely than her younger neighbour.

"You're from the room below, aren't you?"

"Yes. That's right." From this window, Madge could see

the view was just the same as from her own, but more elevated.

"I can hear you tapping away."

"I'm writing a novel." Madge was still brash enough to claim this rather than admit it.

"How exciting. You must come up some evening and read me some of it. Two heads, you know."

"Oh – I couldn't!"

"Why not?" The smile was so very soft, contained so much yearning, that Madge bit her lower lip and merely nodded.

She was trapped again.

The very fact that she'd thought so spontaneously in this way brought a faint blush to her cheeks. In some way it was a reflection on her mother. But in the following second she was flooded with the whole gamut of the emotions involved. She saw a lonely and sick woman and she was an expert in dealing with such people. She saw somebody perhaps even more restricted in her connections than she was herself. And she saw a friend. Yet at the same time there was, tinging away inside her, a spark of protection for her novel. It was personal; it was a secret. She couldn't possibly share such a thing. Could she?

A week later she was doing exactly that. They joined together in laughter over the situations in which they could involve their heroine. It was clear that what had started as a tragic love story was going to be a comedy of errors after all. Where had all the serious social comment gone? And Madge had taken charge of Lucinda. She now spent more time in Lucinda's room than in her own, and after all, Lucinda did seem well supplied with a few luxuries, such as very easy armchairs, a large TV set and an extensive hi-fi combination with simply dozens and dozens of CDs. All Lucinda's room lacked was the typewriter. It sat idle in Madge's room.

"Get the words down! Get it down!" Lucinda would

say. "Scribble it down so that it's captured. Type it all later."

They really enjoyed throwing their heroine into rather hairy escapades. During that long and extended summer, when the window remained open, their laughter illuminated the drab street, until there came a day when Lucinda went in for X-ray tests and was not allowed to return. Madge, the expert, had known it had to happen. Nevertheless, it hit her hard.

She transferred back to 3B all the bundle of her own personal items that had drifted up to Lucinda's room. Lucinda, aware that somebody had to be able to bring to her her own things, when required, had given her the key to 3C. Madge spent long hours at the hospital.

And Madge, more lonely now than she had been before, found herself back in her own room, pecking once more in frustration at the Royal, and still with no social life, unless you care to count the friends she acquired in Lucinda's ward, where she wrote letters for them or ran errands. It was Madge who took the raffle tickets round, the hospital being the obvious place where one might unload tickets in aid of a dialysis machine. Madge bought a couple herself, Lucinda a whole bookful of fifty.

But of course the friends in Lucinda's ward were all female and now there was even less time to go out and search for company of the opposite sex. During the times she was back in her room, she wondered idly whether, if she sat very still and allowed fate to take a hand, such a person might come knocking at her door.

Things like that only happened in books, in silly, romantic and happy books, such as the one she was trying to write.

Didn't they?

Paul Catterick was thirty-eight and a bachelor. He is perhaps the most difficult to present, being, as anyone in his office would tell you, a nonentity. There was no visible personality to him at all.

He was a supervisor in the office to which Madge had applied for her initiative grant. It might well be that he was the officer who had processed her application. Ask her and she wouldn't remember. Paul went through life like that, a blurred image in the mind's eye.

"Paul . . . Paul? Who's he?"

"Oh, you know, that biggish chap with the sort of empty look. Doesn't say much. You know!"

"Can't say I remember."

That was Paul Catterick. He ambled through life leaving no wake behind him, no wash, no foghorn blasts as warnings. As he was thirty-eight it had to be assumed he would become thirty-nine, but it would be with no assistance from himself.

There seems so little to be said of him. Where he lived – what on earth does that matter? Personal habits? It is recorded that he arrived at work punctually and left on time. He did his job without imagination, but with critical accuracy. That which is writ, so shall it be. And with Paul it was. To the last depressing and uninspired letter.

Sometimes, for a thrill, he changed his brand of tobacco.

He had, in all his years, never had to face a crisis. It's unlikely he would have recognised it if he had. For such a man to buy a raffle ticket was to be taking a step into the unknown.

He was ill-prepared.

Esmeralda Greene was a schoolteacher at a private and somewhat advanced boarding school for girls from the age of eleven to sixteen. Gels, she called them, her gels. And that about expressed her sense of possessiveness. She was the physical culture and advanced mathematics professor at the Boadicea School for Young Ladies, since renamed Boudicca, which had been founded, it was claimed, in AD 62, to train young women in the handling of chariots and sundry finer points in the use of the mini-sword, a special weapon pioneered in the district for the shorter in stature and the nimbler of arm. Esmeralda had had the sense to insist on living out. Although chariots were no longer on the curriculum, she brought her gels to such a pitch of physical development that it couldn't help but lead, she knew, to a certain amount of energetic and boisterous – or rather, girlsterous – activity in their spare time, when she preferred to be elsewhere.

Esmeralda, bearing such a pleasant name, could have carried it off only if she herself had been even reasonably good-looking. She had a certain firm and rock-steady personality, which was critical to the performance of her duties, and a firm and shapely body, much trained and disciplined. She favoured trouser suits and hefty shoes, and she favoured a short and somewhat bristly hairstyle, which, had she allowed it to grow, might have been a splendid flow of auburn hair. She was forthright, she was commanding, and rarely did she smile.

Outsiders, rashly visiting the school on prize-giving days, could understand this outlook.

She loved animals. This, she felt, was a weakness, but she couldn't help it. To offset this flaw in her personality, she hated men. There had never seemed to be one particular man on whom she could lavish this, so the hatred was generalised – men as a group. It was a healthy attitude that she attempted to instil into her gels, who, in most cases, had fathers who'd been only too glad to get them off their hands for five years and were thus not averse to complying with teacher's wishes. Younger men, now . . . ah, those illicit trips into town on dark and murky evenings . . . perhaps teacher was missing something.

On hearing that the raffle was organised by men – what else could the 57 Battleaxes be but a chauvinistic club? – Esmeralda bought ten tickets, if only for the pleasure of watching what balls-up men would no doubt make of it. In this she was amply rewarded.

But behind this she couldn't help thinking what a dash she would make grasping the wheel of something brisk and requiring taming, such as an Escort XR3i. Even a BMW motorbike. Yes, that even more so. How the gels would drool if they saw her, in leathers and crash-hat, astride such a bike! She didn't consider beyond the first two prizes. She was a woman of supreme self-confidence.

She just knew her ticket would come up.

Charlie Pierce was twenty-two, close enough to his schooldays to remember that he'd not, at that time, made a significant mark. For some reason that he could never understand, the teachers never seemed to touch on any subject in which he was even remotely interested, and when it came to tests and exams he was never asked anything for which he had the remotest idea of an answer. Clearly, they didn't know their jobs.

Physically, he ought to have been a success. Even at a very early stage he showed adequate growth in all directions. He didn't lack in enthusiasm when it came to sports. He might have made a good runner but always there was something that seemed to go wrong. A shoe might fall off because he'd forgotten to tie it, or he would run into a tree, this a considerable accomplishment on an open sports ground. Once he ran into, and over, the headmaster. Another drawback was that he was unable to remember whether "go" came after one, two or three, or even four. On long-distance runs, where this didn't matter, he always got lost and hours were wasted looking for him.

Later, free of the restrictions of school, he indicated a fair ability with a football. Slasher Harris, though well before his time, was his hero, his father having filled him with the legend. Clearly, as Slasher had demonstrated, the secret was that the words "foot" and "ball" were connected. Charlie practised this until he reached the perfection of being able to run with the ball apparently stuck to his feet, and continue to do so in spite of obstructions. But unfortunately he never learned how to get rid of the damned thing. People on his side, who should have known better, were never where they ought to be, even, sometimes, were heading in the opposite direction. The goalposts were never where they'd been when he started. He was therefore advised to try rugby, but it wasn't played near Ockam. So he was at a loose end.

Work therefore faced him, but nobody had yet perfected a machine he could handle. Destroy, yes. Handle, no. Shopkeepers in town, who might have allowed him behind a counter, soon showed him the door. Even then he had difficulty finding his way out.

As a chucker-out at disco halls he showed promise, but at the same time revealed a basic weakness. Somewhere in his ancestry a seed had been sown and Charlie reaped the harvest. It was a severe handicap, but he couldn't shake off a stubborn feeling that the female of the species was delicate and fragile. Touch them and they would disintegrate, like that stuff in the china shop where he'd tried for a job. Disgusted and frustrated ex-girlfriends would willingly testify to this. It therefore became demonstrated that, although he could handle two men at the same time, women had him beaten. Screaming viragos, intoxicated with pot and noise and psychedelic lights, he treated with gentle and gallant respect. Two of these, and they travelled in pairs like policemen, could completely unman him. Though he usually recovered in a couple of days, he was nevertheless sacked.

Believing he could do no harm with a bass broom, an unsuspecting factory took him on as a sweeper-up. He became an artist at this, even polishing the boots of the machine operators as they worked. But again his eagerness to be helpful let him down. Show him a crate in an awkward position that the fork-lift trucks couldn't reach and Charlie could lift it, and did. The foreman swore he'd said, "This way a foot." Not *on* his bloody foot. Faced with a choice between a revolt of foremen and Charlie, the management reluctantly allowed Charlie to go.

He was – let's be honest – inadequate. His mother, and mothers always see their only sons through a rose-coloured cloud of steam, described him as soddin' well useless.

So, similarly handicapped as was Madge by a shortage of cash, Charlie had his dreams. But Charlie's dream was of himself astride a motorcycle. Not any crummy little 125 or 250. He had to admit he'd look stupid on such a thing. No – he yearned for a man-sized bike, so that when he saw that a genuine brand-new BMW R80RT was the second prize in a raffle, he sacrificed a couple of pints at the Crooked Claymore to invest in two tickets.

Eleven days having elapsed during all this, the raffle was due to go ahead. It was Friday, 15 September. The weather forecast for the following day was "set fair". Bert Harris, outwitting the town clerk, had captured the mayoral chain and smuggled it home, thus giving Llewellyn Pugh a fit of the collywobbles, and Tina, the mayoress and his wife, was at home practising with the rotating drum which was to be used for the draw.

"Looks like being a good day for it," said Bert, staring out at the stars.

The trap was set.

Chapter Three

Saturday, 16 September

The concourse was packed. Bert Harris, resplendent in his best suit and the mayoral chain, stood on the balcony and beamed down upon them. Beside him was the drum, a contrivance made of fine wire mesh so that it could be rotated with its handle and the raffle stubs would be seen to be tossed around satisfactorily. Through a hole in the end, Tina would reach inside and extract them one at a time at his call. She, too, was appropriately attired in a flowered dress and flowered hat, which was already indicating a tiresome tendency to misbehave in the growing breeze. Behind Bert was Llewellyn Pugh, impounded for the job. He complained that it was no part of his duties to field the winning stubs. Nobody listened, but to himself he had to admit he didn't think he dared allow Bert Harris a free run at it without supervision.

No more than three people were allowed on the balcony. The borough engineer had done his stuff, the portico being supported with enough ironwork to prop up the tower at Pisa. From the mayor's parlour window, had anybody been there, it would not have been an inspiring sight, the mayoral metalwork being quite outclassed by the borough engineer's. No longer was the town's motto visible.

This was a pity, because it exactly covered what was now to take place.

At precisely 3 p.m., as scheduled, Mayor Bert (Slasher) Harris blew into the microphone and tapped it with his finger, as he understood to be standard procedure. The roar and the two heavy thuds drew attention to him, for the two loudspeakers, borrowed from the concert hall next door and now standing each end of the balcony, were bigger even than Bert himself. He looked outwards and downwards.

It was not as he'd anticipated. These were not the red, sweating, roaring, cheering and happy faces of thirty years before. These were white, tense, unremitting and frighteningly silent faces. Bert swallowed. He went straight into the preamble that had been written for him; the required plug for the 57 Club, the reference to the dialysis situation at the hospital, ". . . fortunately raising a sum in excess of expectations . . .", and the absolutely vital advertisement plugs for the seven dealers and shops who had supplied the prizes.

"Gerron with it," somebody shouted. "Bloody old fool!"

Bert glared. There was laughter. It was not right, not right. An estimated 2,500 faces waited for him to gerron with it.

"I shall," Bert boomed with massive dignity, "conduct this draw in the established way used at beauty competitions."

This was because he had often been asked to invigilate at these. He therefore knew how to build up the tension. But behind him the town clerk, who had also participated in similar entertainments, gave a sudden start and muttered, "But Mr Mayor . . ." His thin face paled.

"My wife will now draw the first ticket," continued Bert happily.

Tina spun the drum vigorously. When it stopped, she thrust her hand in through the hole and drew it out holding a screwed-up ball of paper. The stubs had all been mangled in this way, over painful hours, by fifty-seven rheumatic

36

and arthritic pairs of hands, the belief being that it obviated the trouble involved if two were drawn together. Tina therefore offered a tiny pea-sized screw of paper to Bert, who to heighten the suspense pretended to have difficulty in unravelling it. He dropped it. Pugh moaned. But it was safe. Bert raised his head, waving it in triumph and applied himself to the mike again.

"The number," the speakers blared, "is C2943, held by a Mr . . ." He peered. ". . . a Mr Paul Catterick, who wins the seventh prize, a Sony Walkmaster radio with headphones."

Standing on the steps of the Square Roundshot, Paul Catterick had been staring, stunned, at his winning ticket. At first. Now he stared, stunned, at Bert. The *seventh* . . . "Heh!" he managed to croak, even he being stung into emotion.

But this was the only sound. No cheers, no jeers. Silence. The citizens of Ockam were absorbing it. Something had gone awry. It was not yet clear exactly what that was, but . . . something.

Bert, too, was aware that something was wrong. They were silent. Why were they silent? But . . . the show must go on. Bert handed the stub to Pugh, who was transfixed, gobbling. Yes, gobbling, Bert decided. Why didn't the fool concentrate on what he was doing?

But meanwhile Tina, who sensed that a certain urgency had intruded, was vigorously rotating the drum, sticking in her dainty hand and extracting another paper pea. This Bert managed to unfold without incident.

". . . the sixth prize . . . a set of suitcases in Samsonite, to . . . I think it's Esmeralda Greene."

Esmeralda, her eyes also fixed on the ticket in her hand, gave out an eek of excitement. She'd got the bike! The bike! Then she registered the words: a set of suitcases.

"Heh!" she said, but much louder than Paul had managed. "What're you talking about, you old fool?"

"Yeah!" agreed Paul, from ten yards away. "Gone out of your mind, you have."

These remarks were clearly heard, there being such a breathless hush over the concourse today. Then it broke. There was a rumble indicating discontent. It was a frightening sound, like the first hint of a landslide somewhere up there. Bert stared around. What was the matter with them? Where were the happy faces, the cheers – the admiration?

He handed the stub to Pugh, who said in an intense whisper, "But you can't *do* this."

"Nonsense!" said Bert. "I'm doing it, aren't I?"

"Oh Christ!" said Pugh. It was, in fact, a prayer.

Standing beside his car, which blocked off one end of Council Street, Inspector Arkwright (Riot Control) dived inside his door for his own microphone.

But putting his head down and ploughing through it, as he'd done through so many defences, the mayor proceeded.

"Number T . . . that's T for trouble . . . 8753 . . . Mrs Ada Follett, the fifth prize, an electric lawnmower."

"Just what I wanted," cried Ada, thereby halting for a minute or two the outcry. Her friends Connie and Floss echoed this sentiment.

"Good old Ada!"

"That's a fair treat."

Because, get right down to basics, what would Ada have done with any of the other prizes? What – come to think of it – was she going to do with an electric lawnmower?

Ada, Connie and Floss clapped their hands. They linked arms and would have performed an impromptu dance, had they been able to move a foot in either direction.

These three ladies doubtless saved the day. To Bert it was a reviver, that one tiny nucleus of enthusiasm. He was able to hand back the stub to Pugh with the remark, "There, you see, you old grumbleguts." And the crowd, who'd thought – were almost certain – that something had gone wrong, and now saw that something had, in fact, gone right, were quite flummoxed. "Hooray!" they murmured, though without obvious conviction. They were prepared to see what happened next.

"Ticket number G6949, held by a Lucinda Porter, wins the fourth prize . . . an Olivetti electronic typewriter."

This was clearly more like it. Those of the crowd who could count now realised that the ticket drawn out fourth had copped for the fourth prize. All, therefore, was as it should be. There was a concensus of opinion that they couldn't have heard right, earlier on.

And Madge Fenwick, clutching in her left hand her own two tickets, in her right Lucinda's fifty, broke quietly into tears. Her own were G6948 and G6949, Lucinda's G6950 to G6999. One out. Lucinda was one out. And what a thrill, what an excitement it would have been for Lucinda, whose spirits had been so low in the past week, to hear that she had won *something*! So Madge quietly wept.

But the rest of the crowd cheered and happiness rested upon them for the whole of one minute. Then it all went wrong again.

For the fifth draw, the mayor, gaining confidence, made a comic gesture as he held the stub in front of his eyes. He even got a laugh. Singular. Bert leaned forward over the balustrade to acknowledge it and dislodged a foot of parapet, which landed on the laugher's toe. More laughter, this more sincere. The borough engineer hid his face with his arm.

Bert glowed. He felt he was getting to them. Behind him, Tina, having several degrees more of sensitivity and detecting the mood, hissed at him, "Get it over with, you big clummock."

So the mayor raised his head. "Number five ticket," his voice boomed out, bouncing back from the surrounding buildings: Ticket . . . icket . . . ket. "The number is . . ." Dramatic pause. "L for leather . . . 7529."

Charlie Pierce was leaning against one of the rust-stained reinforced concrete statues – the one called Enterprise – looking not unlike it. He was in a state of numb bafflement. Four of the seven prizes had been announced, which, his learning told him, was beyond the halfway mark. The motorcycle had not been mentioned, although it was the second prize. This, he could not understand. Had he come to the wrong raffle? But no – the gibbering idiot on the balcony had named the prizes, and there had definitely been mention of a BMW R80RT. The 797cc job. There had! So it hadn't gone yet and there was still a chance. And the goof had just mentioned a number very like the one on the ticket in his hand. He blinked at it again. Exactly like. In fact, the same.

Charlie stiffened. He was now indistinguishable from the statue.

"A two thousand pounds complete new kitchen layout," boomed Bert Harris, "which goes to . . . er . . . er . . . Mr Charlie Pierce."

A what? thought Charlie. Kitchen what? Where was the bloody bike? "Hold on!" he bleated. "Heh you . . . bloody hold on."

They'd already got a fully-equipped kitchen at home. Eight feet by five it was. You couldn't have got any more in it to save your life. One more saucepan and the cat wouldn't be able to get to his cat door.

There was, by this time, a positive and generally accepted realisation that this raffle was not being conducted in a proper manner. A groan pulsed through the crowd.

"Hold-bloody-on!" bellowed Charlie.

"That's right, son," said an old man, waving his stick, "you tell 'im."

Which Charlie did, advancing from his statue and moving

forward in a straight line, his bulk producing a ripple of movement that provoked the mayor into a more energetic procedure.

Inspector Masters (Traffic) began to supervise the dismantling of his barriers, feeling that the traffic, if only foot, would shortly become brisk. As part of the obstruction was Inspector Arkwright's car, a certain amount of disagreement arose. Later, it was to be alleged that it was on this spot that the fighting began.

The mayor handed back the ticket to Pugh, who'd not moved, not said a word, for the past couple of minutes. Like a slot machine, he accepted it. Tina thrust another ticket into Bert's hand. "Hurry it up, love." He grimaced at her. Love?

"Ticket number . . ." he paused. There was a menacing swaying below him, red faces now, exactly as he'd longed for, but not from happiness and joy. "Ticket number six," he pressed on, "is P7429. A BMW motorcycle won by Mr Luci . . . Luci-something Hartington."

In the hush, Lucifer was heard to state, quite positively, that he was a monkey's uncle, and what-d'you-know. Charlie Pierce howled out, "That's mine. Mine." He was now halfway to the front.

"No it isn't," screamed Esmeralda. "It's mine . . . mine—"

Lucifer Hartington turned, raised his fingers gripping the winning ticket, and called out, "Pardon me, madam—"

The rest was drowned by a roar from the crowd. In vain did Bert appeal for order, the speakers hammering out something like a thousand decibels. Pugh appeared with authority at Bert's elbow. He held up his palm for silence. Somebody threw a half-eaten apple at him. White, he retreated.

Then Bert retrieved a little of his past glory. He went to the parapet, raised both arms and flinched not at all as the various projectiles flew past him. It was an everyday occurrence to him – had been, rather, an every Saturday one. He waited. The tumult died. There was silence until, with dignity, he returned to his duties at the mike. Cleared his throat. Shakily accepted the final – thank God – pea.

"The seventh ticket . . ." He paused, almost afraid to say it, "is for the premier prize, a Ford XR3i . . . number B9248, to a Mr Arthur Moreton." Then he held his breath.

In the car park of the 57 Club, which is in Gunfire Street only a quarter of a mile downwind from the concourse, Arthur Moreton clung to the roof of his Rover 213. The distant speakers reached their message to him, hollowly and mockingly. Having a good memory he had no need to consult any bit of paper. It was one of the five tickets held by himself. The name was his, too. So rapidly will the mind work in moments of crisis that he'd visualised every possible embarrassing variation in the miseries that loomed ahead, even before he got the door open. Then he drove like a fiend through the town, heading for Chain Mail Crescent, where his son Richard lived with a wife and two children. It was possible he could be persuaded or bribed into using his second name, so far never used, of Arthur, and claiming the Escort under that name. Certainly, he needed a new car.

Arthur – our Arthur – would have been too far away, even if he'd waited, to hear the comments of Kenny Scott. He would, however, have heard the outcry that arose after ten breathless seconds.

To the crowd in the concourse it was clear that the draw had at last finished and that it was now too late to deny that the whole thing had been a mockery. Or words to that effect. The concerted bellow of disapproval was heard at distant Crécy Manor, the site of Esmeralda Greene's girls school.

It was now that breeding came into its own. The seed of generations of hard men, tempered in the baths of steaming oil, their lungs hardened from shouting through fumes, was germinated in the new men of Ockam. Generations, too, of

42

suffering and smoke-kippered women were to be found in the present ladies of Ockam. And shared – equality not an issue here – was the mercurial sense of fairness and decency that arose from several hundred years of carefully balanced neutrality. They knew what was right and what was wrong. And a wrong had been perpetrated before their very eyes. With a concerted rage they raised their voices, and with a concerted movement they advanced on the old Town Hall.

At this time they embodied the very essence of William of Occam's dictum: *Entia non sunt multiplicanda praeter necessitatem*. It was in their blood. They did not chant these actual words, roughly translateable into: Entities are not to be multiplied without necessity. But they were, individually, each in favour of the spirit of the thing. There *was* necessity, an urgent one. There *was* an entity: his honour the mayor, Bert Harris. And far from wishing to multiply him, they were agreed in an intention to divide him, into as many portions as practical.

They surged forward. Bert, Tina and Pugh retreated. They ran – Tina losing her hat – towards the far reaches of the empty and echoing building, whilst behind them they heard the destruction of the borough engineer's scaffolding and the subsequent collapse of the portico which subsided with a rumble and a cloud of brick dust, thus reducing the cost of its subsequent demolishment. Beneath the rubble, the speakers played on, the mike undeterred, in a replay of the chaos. It amplified the approaching howl and whine of police cars and vans, all loaded with riot shields and impatient coppers, so that the crowd was diverted and turned to face the oncoming and promising fray.

From a shattered rear window the three fugitives climbed and ran and ran. In the end Pugh had no breath left to say a word. Quietly and furtively Bert searched out his car and drove home with his wife, a changed man.

Behind them the battle commenced.

Left isolated by the onrush, six people stood undecided. Charlie had no interest in riots; his was a solitary fight against fate. Ada and her two friends, counting as one entity, found they now had room for their little dance. Lucifer Hartington lit a cigarette and stared at the sky, wondering how he would get his motorcycle onto the barge and in the doorway of the Square Roundshot, Esmeralda Greene and Paul Catterick were talking together. It was an historic meeting.

And all by herself was Madge, who'd by now realised what had happened. She had, due to her friend's increasingly shaky hand, filled in all the fifty counterfoils of the full book with Lucinda's name and address, and, finishing with her own two, had absent-mindedly written in the same information.

She had won and she had lost.

Chapter Four

Sunday, 17 September
to
Saturday, 23 September

On Sunday the town square, which was actually circular, was strangely busy. Usually it would be empty, the church bells arousing little more than a trickle of worshippers. This day there were several scattered groups, heads close, plotting. At this stage there was no concerted opinion as to the objective of these plots. The mayor, yes, but how and in what way, no.

Quietly, out of uniform, Inspector Arkwright (Riot Control) drifted around, sniffing for possible trouble. Inspector Masters (Traffic), released from hospital and told to take it easy, also prowled. He was investigating the theft of two loudspeakers, an amplifier system of unlimited power and a microphone. It was not so much the catching of who'd done it, but rather, as a matter of interest, discovering how it had been done from beneath several tons of rubble in the middle of a riot. Strictly speaking, this was CID work, but he felt it as a personal problem.

The mayor sat in his den at home, a small room full of two armchairs and football trophies, and listened sulkily to his friend – likely to be former friend – telling him what he thought of him. Arthur Moreton used shop-floor language. He'd pleaded for some action from Bert, to start again, to do it all over again . . . anything. But both of them knew it was too late. It was fate definitely accomplished. Now . . . if, as seventh prize, Arthur had won the Sony Walkmaster, he could've given it to Kenny Scott and curried a bit of favour, and perhaps, if Kenny had worn it at work he might have been diverted from his evil schemes. As it was . . . Arthur could visualise Kenny, sitting full of dinner, smiling in the sleep of an afternoon's relaxation.

Which was exactly what Kenny Scott was doing. Kenny had it all worked out.

Charlie Pierce was standing in front of the show window of Arrow Motorcycles in Fletcher Street, where *the* bike was displayed. There was a sign, in case no one had realised, that this was the second prize in the raffle draw, and setting out fully its delights. Fifty horsepower, 797cc ohv engine, flat twin, shaft drive, maximum speed 105 m.p.h., 35 m.p.g. It was, to Charlie, the absolute end. From now on, nothing less would be possible to aim for. He walked away moodily to locate the particular section of the canal where, the list in the Saturday night's paper had indicated, lived Lucifer Hartington.

He was sitting on his deck in a deckchair, being put to its correct use, and still wondering how he was going to get the bike aboard. By this time, Lucifer had realised that he'd always wanted to own a motorcycle. It – this desire – had been hidden away in his subconscious mind. Subliminal, wasn't that the word?

"Mornin'," said Charlie.

"Mornin'. Come aboard, son. Wasn't it you got the kitchen?"

"Sure did."

"Your wife'll be pleased."

Charlie stepped aboard. "No wife."

"Mother then. Got a mother, I suppose?"

Charlie grimaced. "Yeah. Sure have. An' she ain't pleased."

"No? A new kitchen – she ought to be."

"We already got one. Eight by five. Stick two thousand quid in there and we'd have to leave home."

Lucifer eyed him with a hint of amusement. "Trade it in, then."

"How's that?"

"Get your voucher from the Town Hall, go to the place and ask for the cash instead."

Charlie sat with his knees drawn up, his chin on them, and stared at his sneakers. "I could do that, I suppose. It's the bike I wanted though."

"I guess you would." Lucifer's eyes ran over him. "You'd just about fit it a treat."

"That's what I thought. Here . . . you wouldn't care to swap? I mean, mine *was* drawn before yours."

"That which is first shall be last, and that which is last, first."

"What's that mean?"

Lucifer stuffed his pipe. "I don't know. But it was my ticket that won it."

"So you wouldn't care to swap?"

"That was the impression I wished to convey."

"Oh well—"

"It was worth a try," said Lucifer approvingly. "You could cash yours in and buy one."

"What! Some buzzing, whining little horror! I'd look an idiot on somethin' like that." And besides, he *wanted* the BMW.

Lucifer slapped him on the shoulder. "Never mind. Come and have a drink."

"Got no money."

"I've got money. Come and have a drink. And if you've got no money, how would you buy petrol?"

Charlie flashed him a grin. It didn't show itself often, but it was worth waiting for, having been lurking there and maturing for ages. "I might haveta get another job."

"There you are then."

And they went to have a drink together, while Madge was hurrying into the ward with a fistful of flowers and saying, even before she reached the bed, "Did you hear, did you hear? You've won a prize."

Her smile was wide, because the Ward Sister had warned her there'd been deterioration.

"I heard, yes." Lucinda reached out a hand. "What lovely flowers."

"It's the typewriter."

"I know. Sit down, Madge. The flowers can wait a minute. The nurse'll bring a vase, you'll see. Tell me what happened."

"You'll never believe it . . . such a shambles. And there was fighting."

"You're quite unmarked, dear."

"Not *me*, silly."

"And what do we have to do," asked Lucinda, "to acquire this treasure?"

"I, on your behalf, will go to the Town Hall and collect a voucher and take it to the shop."

"Very good. So now you won't have to worry about Es."

"It's yours."

"But you can have it."

"Oh, but I couldn't!"

Lucinda fingered the sheet. She knew Madge inside out by now. A very proper and correct young lady, this was. Clearly, the typewriter had to be for Madge, but Lucinda would have to meet her halfway and make it acceptable.

"Then if it's mine," she said, "you shall collect it for me. If you need a taxi to get it home . . ." Home! she thought. Heavens, what next! " . . . you must charge it to me. Then you can set it up in my room and use it there. How's that?"

Madge bit her lip. By this time she thought she knew Lucinda through and through. She was clearly a lady of some distinction, who had 'come down in the world'. It would make her very happy to find herself in a position of distributing largesse to the less well endowed. Madge did not think this in any cynical way; it was simply how life happened to be. And in any event, Madge knew the pleasure of handing out presents. If it made Lucinda happy – if anything could – it was clearly Madge's duty to comply.

"Oh!" she cried. "May I? That would be just fine. Thank you."

And after all, it *had* been her own ticket that had won it. So both of them were pleased with the outcome.

As, at about the same time, Ada Follett was similarly expressing herself.

They were in the Plucked Goose: Paul Catterick, Esmeralda Greene, and Ada. This was what Esmeralda had been planning with Paul in the doorway of the Square Roundshot. "We three," she had said, "must get together."

Paul had not been able clearly to see why, though he was sufficiently intrigued by this bristling and forceful woman to wish to see her again. If she'd only do something about her hair . . . oh, never mind, he thought. Esmeralda was clearly a woman to throw advice back in his teeth, possibly accompanied by a fist.

They had therefore, together, hunted out Ada's terraced house, and invited her for a drink. Ada wasn't going to refuse such an offer, although her friends Connie and Floss were not invited. So there they were in the snug, Ada with a milk stout, Esmeralda with a gin and lime, and Paul with a pint of bitter, his pipe going well, and sitting back with quiet, contained amusement.

"We three," said Esmeralda, plunging straight to the nub of it because it was eating her away from inside, "are the ones who've copped-out."

"Copped-out?" asked Paul, raising his eyebrows. "And you a teacher!" Which Esmeralda had already confided to him. "A lady teacher."

"What does it matter what sex I am?"

"Oh it does, dear," said Ada, patting the back of her hand.

"And don't call me a lady," went on Esmeralda briskly. "I'm a woman."

"Of course you are," Ada agreed comfortingly. "Don't fret."

"I am *not* fretting. And if this . . . man . . . here has anything against women partners, then we might as well finish this right here."

"We are twin souls," said Paul, beaming at Ada, meaning Ada.

Ada eased her empty glass towards him. "I'm sure we are."

"*Have* you got anything against women?" demanded Esmeralda, staring at Paul, wanting to get it straight.

He sighed. "I'm a supervisor in a social security office, in charge of a staff of twelve. All young women. I spend the best part of my life with women."

"And you don't like that?" Esmeralda asked suspiciously. "You do not communicate with them on a psychological and spiritual level?"

"I love them all," he declared quite honestly, safety being in numbers. "And we communicate on a level we all understand." By this, he meant that the language would have shocked Kenny Scott, if he'd known Kenny Scott.

"And I've no doubt they all love you," said Esmeralda sourly.

"That has not been made clear," Paul admitted. In fact, they teased the life out of him.

"All this talking," complained Ada, "is making me dry," so Paul called 'em in.

When they were all supplied again, Paul turned to Esmeralda politely. "Did I gather you were trying to make a point?"

"How very perceptive of you. Yes, I was. Has it occurred to you that out of the seven winners there are only three women?"

"Hadn't thought about it. But it couldn't have been even-stephens unless we had a neuter in our midst."

"Funny! Ha! And of the ones – we three, who have . . . er . . . lost out, two of us are women!"

"So you are. Well, I never noticed."

Ada winked at him. Paul remained solemn. "But if," he continued, pointing his pipe stem at Esmeralda in what she felt to be an offensive masculine gesture, "if the draw had been done in the right order, then those who'd copped-out would be three males, and of the top three winners two would be female."

"Exactly!" said Esmeralda, who'd lost him halfway through. "That is exactly what I mean."

There was a short silence, broken only by Ada sucking in her stout. She sucked her lips for added effect, and said, "What *do* you mean, dear?"

"I mean we've got to do something about it," Esmeralda declared.

"Such as?" asked Paul with patient interest.

"It has to be illegal or something."

"Illegal or not, it's done."

"And you're happy to sit back, when you might've had an Escort XR3i right this minute!"

"Tomorrow. It's Sunday."

"It's all the same."

"No it's not. It's how life is. The luck of the draw. Fate. I might not be alive tomorrow."

Which, thought Esmeralda, is perfectly correct, buster, if you go on like this. "It's just not right!" she burst out.

Ada again patted her hand. "There, there. It's no good kicking against the pricks, as my Eric used to say."

"*Did* he!" said Esmeralda, leaning back to get a good look at her. "Did he indeed!"

"An educated chap, your Eric," Paul observed mildly.

"Oh, he was. A lovely man. You can be sure of that. Clever. He could tell any beer within thirty miles with a blindfold on. Not that he ever *went* thirty miles. Mind you, I could never see why anybody'd want to kick 'em."

"Kick the . . . oh, I see," said Paul, barely smiling. "He must've meant the pricks from the arrows of outrageous fortune."

"That's probably it," Ada agreed.

"Can we just get back—" Esmeralda tried.

"And of course the slings," Paul enlarged on the theme, and he beamed a large smile at Ada. She'd go down a treat at the office, he decided.

"Yes, those too. He wore one of those."

"Will somebody please tell me what the hell we're talking about!" Esmeralda demanded.

"Eric's truss," Ada explained. "When he was at work. He had his own private shower, too."

Paul lit his pipe which had gone out during this exchange. He decided he was enjoying himself.

Esmeralda said, "Can we get to the point at issue?"

"Oh yes," said Ada. "We ought to do that." And Paul nodded thoughtfully.

"The point is: that mentally-crippled apology for a mayor drew the tickets in the wrong order. In the reverse order. That's to say," she enlarged, forgetting that she wasn't in the classroom, "he started at the end and worked forward."

"Or the front and worked back," Paul suggested.

"That then. And there just *has* to be a law about it, somewhere."

"Why?" Paul persisted.

"Because there's a law for everything."

"I wouldn't say that," Paul observed quietly. "Not everything. There're too many laws for some things, and none where they're needed."

"Enlarge on that," Esmeralda snapped.

"There's no law for instance, no actual law, that says you've got to drive on the left-hand side of the road."

"That's because they do."

"Not," Paul pointed out, "on motorways."

"It is not *needed*," Esmeralda told him sharply.

"Exactly." And Paul contemplated his beer.

Esmeralda was a patient woman, she considered. With young gels one had to be. But there were times when her restraint was sorely taxed. "Will you kindly explain that deep remark – exactly."

"It is not needed, as you said. Perhaps it is assumed that with raffles the first ticket drawn *is* the first. No law needed. The whole thing boils down to the fact that it hasn't previously been put to the test with a mayor like Bert Harris."

"My Eric knew Bert," put in Ada.

They stared at her. She nodded. "Same school, but Eric was older. My Eric always said this about Bert: 'I'll always say this about Slasher,' my Eric said, Slasher being what they used to call Bert Harris, 'I'll always say this about Slasher – that he's as good up the left wing as the right.'" She stopped, thinking. "Or the middle, I suppose."

"Are we talking about the same thing?" Esmeralda asked distantly.

"Ada," declared Paul solemnly, "has put it in a nutshell. Ada sees it clearly. The fact is that Bert *would* drive on the wrong side of the road if the mood took him. Or the right side equally, that being the left, or the right if you're talking about—"

"Will you please . . . stop!" Esmeralda cried.

"We only wished to make the point—"

"The point is that the mayor acted outside the law," Esmeralda declared tersely. "And I am here today to suggest we see a solicitor about it."

"My father used to say," Paul said gently, "that the law is like a mad dog; don't put your hand out to it unless you're absolutely desperate."

"Nonsense! If you know what you're doing, you can . . . why the hell're we talking about dogs?"

"I would not advise taking it to court. And on what legal grounds?"

"On the grounds that when you buy a raffle ticket you rely on the assumption that your ticket will be there, to be drawn, for the first prize. That! And six of those tickets were not *in* it when the draw for the car was made."

Esmeralda was pleased with this. She'd thought it out herself.

"In that case, all six would have to apply to a court," Paul said thoughtfully. "And only three of us have any cause for complaint. No – amend that. All seven would have to apply. And if all seven agreed to do that, you wouldn't have to go to court – we'd merely swap vouchers."

"Oh, you're useless."

"Sadly, yes."

"We three have the grievance."

"Two," said Ada, having sat quietly for too long. "What that girl used to sing. Kay serrah serrah. You remember."

"One," corrected Paul.

Esmeralda turned on him. "Don't you feel aggrieved? Furious? *Anything*?"

"Not a bit. I won something. It's the luck – as I said –

of the draw. That concourse was packed with people who won nothing."

Esmeralda got to her feet. "You two," she said smartly, "are no use to man nor beast. I'll go ahead on my own if I have to." She snatched up her shoulder bag and marched out.

Paul gazed at Ada's empty glass. "Another?"

"Don't mind if I do."

"What're you going to do with your lawnmower?"

"Me'n my friends, Connie and Floss, we're goin' to have a lawn. At the back."

"Can I come and see?"

"You can, laddie. You can."

Ada was sure Connie and Floss would like Paul. Paul thought he'd found a new friend. They walked contentedly back towards Ada's house. As far as they were concerned, it was all finished.

During the following week it began to build up. Arthur Moreton's son, now Arthur also, took possession of the Escort, assisted by a starlet who smiled emptily at him for the cameras and crawled all over him for her own satisfaction, so that Arthur's – the new one's – married life was nearly wrecked. The car, too. It proved to be quite a handful. As had the starlet.

Nobody was fooled by this. They knew who'd really copped for the Escort. Arthur – the genuine product – received his first threatening letter by Tuesday. By Saturday there were seventeen.

The statue of Prince Albert on a horse in the round square was painted red on Tuesday night, though what he'd got to do with it nobody could say.

On that Tuesday night, too, when Lucifer Hartington was sound asleep, his barge was quietly towed away, a couple of miles into nowhere. There wasn't a pub in sight when he awoke. It was just as well he'd taken Charlie's advice, he thought.

Thursday night was exciting. The stand at the north end of the Cutters' football pitch, which was named The Slasher Harris Stand, was burned to the ground.

And by that time Charlie Pierce himself had been threatened in the street. After all, he was number three. But it was no good threatening Charlie, he just wasn't having it. Four reckless youths were admitted to the casualty ward.

It was Charlie who discovered Lucifer on Wednesday, placidly waiting on his barge for something to happen. What happened was very close to a miracle because Charlie had used his brain. Finding a gap where the barge had been he'd reasoned that it had been towed away. None of Lucifer's friends at the Buckled Arrow, where their friendship had withstood the press of history, knew anything about it. Charlie then worked out that Lucifer wouldn't have gone through the nearby lock in the night, so he must have gone the other way. So Charlie walked the towpath, and there he was, the soft old bugger, not caring a jot that he was in the middle of great empty expanses of fields and trees and things, all of which made Charlie uneasy.

"Knew you'd be along, son."

"Where's the bike, pop?" asked Charlie anxiously, not having spotted it.

"Took your advice and rented that shed in the pub yard."

"Yeah. You see – you didn't know what a bike like that deserves."

"Coming round to that, Charlie."

Then Charlie, unable to see any assistance in any direction, and happier with the barge and Lucifer and the bike all together and within reach, decided to tow the barge back to the Buckled Arrow. Lucifer was doubtful. Usually it required six beer-primed men. Charlie said, "Nuts to that."

The snag was that it had to be towed backwards which was tricky work for the helmsman. As Lucifer pointed out, "All you've gotta do is pull. I've got to think backwards."

So Charlie pulled. It took all day. Fortunately Lucifer was well supplied with food and cans of beer. They progressed, but slowly; and clearly, at the end, even Charlie was flagging. In fact, he sat down on the towpath at the bottom of the ramp up to the Buckled Arrow, and frankly, as Lucifer put it, looked knackered.

Fortunately the pub wasn't shut. They had a clear hour. At the end of this Charlie felt better, but not normal.

"Tell you what," said Lucifer. "You use the bike. Just to get home."

Charlie wasn't *that* tired. He could still walk. But he'd already felt the throb of the bike beneath him. It was Charlie who'd driven it from the shop to the canal.

He hadn't been able to resist watching the handover, which was similarly endowed with cameras as had been the car. But this was a different and somewhat less experienced starlet. She'd been confused by Lucifer's enthusiasm. "Cheeky devil," she'd said.

It was then that Charlie discovered that Lucifer didn't know how to ride a motorcycle. Charlie hadn't known that such people existed. Lucifer hadn't even ridden a pedal cycle, not even a scooter. He hadn't driven a car, either. "Could never understand why they stick the steering wheel over on one side. All that car sticking out on your left! Daft, that is. Why don't they put it in the middle, then they wouldn't have all that fuss when they want to sell 'em abroad."

So Charlie had ridden it back to the canal, Lucifer taking a bus. Now he was being offered a completely unfettered ride, all on his own.

"How d'you know I won't nick it?" he asked, suspicious

of such magnanimity, though he didn't put it like that to himself.

"You won't."

"I could just ride it off into the sunset."

"Too late for that and you'd run out of petrol in no time. Then you'd have to push *that* back."

Charlie laughed. He borrowed Lucifer's crash helmet and drove the bike home. Not a yard further, no diversions, straight home. His mother screamed at him that he'd stolen it and she was going to fetch the police. Charlie laughed. He'd ridden it as though it'd been his own and the fever was in him.

In the morning he rode it back. They went and bought another crash helmet and he began to teach Lucifer the rudiments of riding. In other words, on the pillion. That day they covered 287 miles and returned drunk with elation.

On that day Madge typed two chapters of her book in Lucinda's room, working from her scribbles. It was wonderful, wonderful. On that day, Kenny Scott sprung his trap, and Arthur paid another, evening, visit to the mayor. And on that day Paul Catterick took a day from his leave and spent it lifting blue bricks, while Esmeralda Greene, having two free periods, went into town on the bus and consulted a solicitor. By coincidence this solicitor was Ephraim Potts, the coincidence being that he was also Lucinda's and Lucifer's solicitor.

On Friday the superintendent called a conference. Matters were beginning to look serious. Present were Inspector Masters (Traffic) and Inspector Arkwright (Riot Control), along with Inspector Ralph Tomkins (CID), though there was nothing as yet to detect. But Detective Inspector Tomkins had had all his men out on the streets and was able to report that the general mood was ugly. The concerted public opinion was that something had been snatched from their secure life of isolationism and fair play, that something evil had come to the town. Already, Tomkins had a twenty-four hour watch on the mayor's home. You never knew.

They discussed whether the Harris family – Bert and Tina and their Collie, Francis – shouldn't be smuggled away to a safe house. They discussed the coming Saturday, but Masters reminded them that it was an away match and sighs of relief were sighed. The superintendent decided to alert nearby towns that they might very well need reinforcements, at any time and in a hurry.

On Friday, Paul nearly finished clearing the blue bricks from the three back yards. There was, after all, earth beneath. They'd taken down the intervening fences between Ada's and Floss's place and Ada's and Connie's. They were about to fall down, anyway, having supported fifty years of leaning over and gossiping on. It was sad to see these go but the three ladies didn't complain. The difficulty was in getting rid of the bricks, but Paul, who knew his onions, refused to throw them into the canal at the back and instead phoned around a few builders, so that a lorry came and collected them, and a surprising amount of money was handed over to Ada, Floss and Connie. They'd have danced on the naked soil but Paul pointed out that it had to be flat for a lawn, not pitted with their great, galumphing feet. He'd got the seed down that day. So where, they asked, were they going to hang their laundry? Paul told them they'd have to store their underwear until the seed germinated and the grass was strong enough. "Next spring." Then, laughing, which for Paul was going it a bit, he left them, and, still laughing, encountered Esmeralda in the Plucked Goose.

"This your local?" she asked.

"No. But if you're coming here again, it will be."

Thus they thrust aside their differences. Paul, having been demolishing fences all day, was glad to be able to mend one.

"And how's it doing?" asked Paul, bringing her a gin and lime.

"I've seen a solicitor. Ephraim Potts."

"And?"

"He's going to get a barrister's opinion."

"Yes. They do that. One gets the impression they spend all those years studying to get qualified, when all it needs is to know which barrister does what."

She smiled thinly. This was very rare. It was thin from lack of nourishment. "And you?"

"I've been helping Ada and her friends to create a lawn for their lawnmower."

"Which is where? She's collected it, you mean?"

"Yes, she's got it. It now sits in pride of place in her front room, between the settee with the antimacassars and the wedding present from Uncle Jack, which is a brass coal scuttle with accompanying tools."

"Sometimes," she said, "when you make the effort, you can be very amusing."

"When *you* make the effort," he pointed out gently. "Hello, it's chucking-out time. May I walk you home?"

Esmeralda stood, smoothing her skirt. It went against all her principles. A modern woman does not need to be accompanied home. She straightened her back. "Thank you, I'd like that. But it's quite a way out of town."

"I do a lot of walking."

"A lot of women to be walked home?"

"Alone. Pondering the ills of the world."

While they were walking home, so was Arthur Moreton. His Rover had failed to start, and his son had the Escort. Fuming, Arthur walked all the way to Agincourt Avenue to see the mayor. If that were not enough, he'd had to run the gauntlet of one very tough PC and a tougher WPC, who'd pounced on him at the gate.

"You again," said Bert wearily.

"Sign that," Arthur told him briskly, slapping a piece of paper on the chair's arm, slapping a pen into Bert's palm.

"What is it?" Bert, at that stage, wouldn't have been surprised to be handed an extradition order. Worriedly, he signed it.

"It's your application for membership to the 57 Club. Ellington is on his way out." Arthur plucked the paper from Bert's fingers, blew on the signature as though it'd been a fountain pen, whipped back his ballpoint . . . and waited.

Bert gaped. It was his heart's desire. "You mean it?"

"I'm going to put this up for consideration," Arthur promised. "We've already discussed it. You'll be the first person in history to be blackballed fifty-seven times. It'll be," he said with pleasure, "in the papers. Is this a record? We'll put it in the *Guinness Book of Records*. We'll get it on the radio, TV, nationwide network—"

"Stop!" croaked Bert.

"Shall I tell you why? Shall I?"

"If you must."

So Arthur told him. Kenny Scott had sprung his trap. Three days before. They'd taken that long, hammering at it.

Kenny had pointed out that one of his ladies on the shopfloor had been robbed by Arthur's filching of those other five tickets. Rubbish, said Arthur. Kenny said they'd been right next to the forty-five of his ladies' tickets. Not in the drum, said Arthur, they wouldn't be. You can't prove it, Kenny pointed out indisputably, it could've been next to one of them and nudged it over. Arthur declared that the odds would still have been the same. Kenny said nevertheless his ladies wanted another go at it. Another go? asked Arthur. Produce the car and we'll raffle it off again, Kenny proposed. Then, Kenny not seeming ready to leave, Arthur had grabbed his hat and gone home.

The next day, Kenny pressed his point. His ladies were ready to walk out. Arthur asked for time. He phoned a mathematics professor friend of his at Birmingham University to confirm. Three hours later, spent pounding his computer, the man phoned back, having ascertained that 97,641 tickets had been in the draw, and told Arthur the odds *with* Arthur's tickets in would've been 97,641 against one of his ladies copping the prize – in Birmingham they share the same slang. *Without* Arthur's tickets the odds would have been reduced to 97,636 to one. Arthur told him he'd already done that in his head, thus losing a friend.

Defeated, he agreed with Kenny that he would supply one Ford Escort XR3i, brand new, for raffling amongst his ladies. He would, personally, stand out for the £10,000 involved. Kenny said this was a *new* raffle, wasn't it? Arthur, his defences low, agreed that it was. Therefore, said Kenny, the men would walk out if *they* weren't in it too. Arthur said they'd had their chance. Kenny said they hadn't been given one. They were. Weren't. Were, then. Not officially, Kenny said. Not one with the shop steward officially handling it.

They both went home.

The next day, Kenny sensing blood, pressed his luck too far. He came up with the grand idea that the men should have a separate raffle, and as there were twice as many men as women, for *two* Escorts, to keep it fair. Arthur told him he could stuff his Escorts right up his exhaust pipe. They would have come to blows if Cynthia, Arthur's personal and very private secretary, hadn't intervened. She pointed out that the office staff hadn't been invited to enter the first raffle, so what about them? Kenny said he'd have the men out if the staff was included. The personal and private secretary said she'd have the office staff out if they weren't, and Arthur said if he had to lash out £40,000 they'd *all* be bloody well out.

Then they all went home, Arthur's Rover refused to start, and there the situation stood when he went to visit Bert Harris.

The next day was Saturday, so that he was free of Kenny Scott for two days. Charlie took Lucifer to the coast and back. Madge visited Lucinda in hospital. Paul and Esmeralda went to a cat show at the NEC and had a flaming row because Paul insisted on paying for their lunches. Arthur Moreton prowled his empty factory, idly kicking machines and skips of swarf, and Ada sat at the window with her friends Connie and Floss, watching for the grass seed to germinate.

The home supporters decided not to go to the away match. Instead, they wrecked the south stand of the Ockam Cutters.

And on Sunday night the seven Ockam razors, in their case, were stolen.

Chapter Five

Sunday, 24 September

After the chaos at the football pitch and the subsequent running street battles, the town was calm on Sunday. Suspiciously calm. The police were busy, though, quietly and behind the scenes charging those they'd managed to pick up, and because of this, possibly, there were less men on patrol. It encouraged a quieter but equally insidious operation: the graffiti artists were out in force.

With the sudden decrease in availability of spray cans, and with commendable respect for the environment, recourse was made to the good old-fashioned paintbrush. This makes for a longer job, if you don't want those unpleasant paint runs defacing your efforts. It was all high-quality work and showed the first trend towards hatred moving away from the mayor.

Most of the graffiti was now directed towards the winners in the raffle. Particularly the No.1 winner, Arthur Moreton. There was still an odd: DOWN WITH MAYOR HARRIS, but it was feeble. No heart in it. What were now beginning to predominate were efforts like:

The Seven Razors of Ockam

ARTHUR MORETON IS A CHEAT

and

THE 57 CLUB SAYS DOWN WITH MORETON

and

WHO DUZ MORTON TINK HE IS?

These selections were discovered on walls scattered throughout the town. Across the top windows of the fifteen-storey office block known as Rimfire Tower in the main pedestrian concourse was discovered, in six-feet-high letters done with whitewash:

WHO NEEDS ARTHUR MORETON?

They took in, and later charged, the man who did their window cleaning, as he was the only one who'd have had the nerve to do it. They made him clean it off, and without remuneration.

But Lucifer Hartington also came in for his share. On the side of his barge was discovered:

LUCIFER OUGHT TO BE SET ALIGHT

Lucifer liked that one. Done, he suggested to Charlie, by a very old soldier. Charlie, not getting it, obediently laughed, but quietly he was worried. He'd had one himself, but it didn't worry him particularly, as it seemed to be on his side.

CHARLIE PIERCE WILL GET HIS

This was painted across the window of the shop that had supplied – or would have supplied – the £2,000 worth of kitchen equipment, if Charlie had utilised his voucher.

In practice, Charlie had tried, a few days before, to trade it in for cash. But oh dear me, that wouldn't do at all. The advertisement value would disappear at once, he'd been told. The idea was that before and after photographs would be taken and printed in the local papers, and perhaps in *Woman and Home*. Maybe *The Lady*. The proprietor had then gone to Charlie's place, had agreed that Charlie's mother wasn't exactly what they'd had in mind for the photos and that Charlie's mother's kitchen not really the sort of before that presented any possibility of being transformed into an acceptable after. The photographer had to admit that if he got the camera in, then he himself wouldn't have been able to edge inside.

At this stage, bargaining began to take place. To start with the value to the shop was the wholesale value, and the £2,000 also included £473 worth of installation work. That came to, they told Charlie, £1,207 less £473, equals £734, give or take the few pence. And as the advertisement value was at least £1,000, give or take the odd hundred, in practice Charlie, if he handed in his voucher, would owe them about £266. Charlie left it at that. He'd got some thinking to do.

Detective Inspector Ralph Tomkins, trying to detect the authorship of: CHARLIE PIERCE WILL GET HIS, put his money on Charlie himself, trying to press the issue.

Charlie, having failed to persuade the shop it was worth £500 to them if he simply tore up the voucher, failed also to convince Tomkins of his innocence.

So he advertised it in the evening paper, on Lucifer's advice, and got £1,000 for it from a lady in Agincourt Drive who'd always wanted £2,000 worth of kitchen equipment for £1,000 in order to put out of joint the nose of that Tina Harris, who'd been putting on airs since Bert had been mayor. It would, she decided, take that smirk off her face.

Charlie, with £1,000 cash in the pocket of his jeans, told Lucifer he was now in a position to buy the drinks and the petrol for the bike. They went and had a drink to celebrate.

At 11.20 that Sunday night, the crash of breaking glass, immediately followed by the outbreak of clamour from the council offices' alarm system, alerted the chief security officer and his two men.

Inside five minutes the ground-floor man had found the broken window in the ladies' toilet at the rear, glass all over the floor and a large brick in the middle of it. Two minutes later the chief, his concern for the regalia on the upper walkway, discovered the smashed glass in the top of the display case. All three men had hand radios, and the third man was instructed to phone the police.

A police car was there in another three minutes, four more shortly afterwards. Later, not one of these officers could say he or she had seen a soul in the surrounding streets.

Detective Sergeant Andrew Spinks, out on the town hoping to haul in a graffiti artist caught in the act, was alerted by radio, and, reluctantly dragged from an interesting example in Urdu, ran for his car and was round at the council offices exactly seventeen minutes after the first alarm.

Spinks was an experienced officer, not lacking in self-confidence. He stared at the plundered regalia display with interest. There was the mace, there the mayoral chain, there the two gold-plated axe heads. But there was no case of seven Ockam razors. It was possible that the stuff left behind, if carefully dismantled and melted down, would have been worth something. But he was quite certain that any of those items would've posed a problem when it came to getting from the smashed window to the cabinet, making a quick snatch and running all the way back to the smashed window before the guard presented a trap.

In fact, he couldn't see how it had been done, even with the lighter case of razors. Spinks used a younger man to test it. Starting from the smashed window and using the shortest routes, the constable managed the trip through the building and up to the cabinet, touching it and running back, in three minutes and twenty-nine seconds.

The chief security officer said he'd lay his job on the line if it could've been done without his men spotting this manoeuvre.

"All right," said Spinks. "So assume he could've *got* here, dodging you three stalwarts—" He slapped the side of the display cabinet.

"I don't even accept that."

"But assume it," said Spinks briskly, not being a man who liked being contradicted. "Then . . . he must be still here."

"In the building?"

"Yes," said Spinks heavily.

So they sealed the building and did a room by room search. Nothing.

"So," said Spinks, "he's still here. He's hidden the razors, but he's here – and not hiding." He looked round significantly.

"Here?" demanded the chief security officer heavily.

"In our midst." Spinks nodded. "And as there are no civilians present—" He shrugged.

"Now you see here, young Andy," said the chief security officer, who was his uncle, and as such could indulge in a little finger pointing, "if you're saying . . ." He stopped, having been smitten by a thought. "And anyway, *you're* the only one around here not in uniform."

Before this could erupt into physical violence and the splitting of the family into warring factions, Llewellyn Pugh said from behind them, "Not the only civilian, Chief."

They all turned and stared at him. He was in pyjama top, grey slacks and slip-on casual shoes.

"I have a line from the security alarm to my flat," he explained. "Will somebody please tell me what the trouble is?"

"This young idiot here—" began the chief.

"This dotty old fool—" said Spinks, overlapping.

Pugh held up his hand, and there was silence. Pugh was good at this sort of thing, having had plenty of practice in the council chamber. "Show me, please."

Spinks knew when he was beaten. He shrugged. He took Pugh over to the display cabinet.

The space where the case of seven razors had been was obvious, not only because the black velvet bed had become faded around it, after more than thirty years of its presence, but also because the scattered pieces of glass neatly surrounded it.

"Now why?" asked Pugh, "would anybody want to steal our seven razors?" It was rhetorical. Nobody answered. "Symbolical, perhaps? Maybe political?"

"Political?" asked Spinks brightly, who knew a clue when he saw one, but couldn't see one at the moment so kept his options open.

"Perhaps symbolical and political together."

"Don't get you," Spinks admitted.

"The razors are symbolical of the spirit of the town, as you know. Occam's Razor. Symbolical. And the concept is one involving deeply radical ideas."

"Are you saying," demanded Spinks, "that this is the work of Commies?"

Pugh allowed a tiny, superior smile to flex his lips. "Quite the opposite, I would have thought. Though of course . . ." he brightened, ". . . it could be much simpler than that."

"Somebody who needed a shave?" asked Spinks, who was good at heavy sarcasm.

Pugh rose above it. "Shall we just say, somebody who needed a razor. For what purpose, I wouldn't like to offer any suggestions."

At this point Detective Inspector Ralph Tomkins, who'd been difficult to locate because he'd been spending the night at his woman friend's flat, arrived, looking just a little flustered. Wishing to get back before she locked the door on him for ever, he made a rapid decision.

"Can't do much tonight, Sergeant. Put men on to guard the display case and men to guard the broken window."

"May I suggest WPCs, Inspector?"

"What?"

"The window's to the ladies' loo."

"I can't see, if we're sealing it off . . . oh, please yourself, man. Please yourself. I'll get the team here first thing in the morning, and then we'll see." He nodded. He hurried away.

But already too late, alas. She'd locked him out.

Chapter Six

Monday, 25 September (part)

Arthur Moreton, walking from the bus to his factory, his usual half hour earlier than the rest of them, was confronted by a spread of graffiti across his entrance gate. It hadn't been there before.

WATCH YOUR THROAT MORETON

As there'd been a guard in the gate hut all night, Arthur enquired, reasonably politely in the circumstances, why hadn't it been observed during its application. The guard, hurt, went outside to look at it, and observed that it had been brush-painted and therefore would have been a silent operation, and that he, the guard, had been inside the closed gate, not outside. He offered, although he was due off in less than half an hour, to clean it off. Get some thinners . . .

"No," said Arthur. "Leave it alone. Guard it, in fact, with your life."

He stamped up to his office and phoned the police. They said they'd send someone round. Detective Constable Tony Finch, informed at the station what to expect, brought along an instamatic camera so that he was able to take to the meeting, later that day, something to put beneath the superintendent's nose.

Tony Finch, only recently transferred to the CID, was

twenty-three, a slim, dark and saturnine young man, who was determined to succeed, but was having to fight a desperate battle against his inheritance. He was therefore serious in aspect, but not always able to control a natural independence.

His interview with Arthur Moreton was short. There wasn't really much to discuss. The message on the gate said it all. Tony was later able to report not much more than that Arthur Moreton had seemed under stress.

Arthur was, in fact, very near the end of whatever tether had been restraining him. It just was not fair. He hadn't intended any harm in buying those tickets, but here he was, his factory's existence threatened, fifty-six of the club clearly looking for a way of asking him politely for his resignation, and now there were direct threats whistling round his ears – or very close to his ears, he thought, swallowing.

Kenny Scott, therefore, showed a lack of sensitivity by arriving in Arthur's office only three minutes after nine, before Arthur had even had time to scan the production figures for the previous Friday. He showed an even worse instinct for strategy by bouncing in, a grin all over his face, and shouting out, "Still with us, then?"

Arthur didn't lift his head. He reached out and pressed a key on his intercom. "Cynthia, my dear, there's an unpleasant odour in my office."

"I'm sorry, Mr Moreton. He just—"

"Then just creep in here gently, because I have a headache, and waft it away."

The door opened in two seconds flat, Cynthia recognising that heavily-repressed tone in her boss's voice. Kenny stood back, both hands raised in defence.

"Easy, easy. It won't take a minute."

"What won't?" demanded Arthur.

"If you've brought your cheque book—?" Kenny left it as a question, his eyebrows raised.

Cynthia stood hesitant. Kenny Scott was a little large for wafting, and she was only five feet two. She caught Arthur's eye. He nodded. She opened the door again but he caught her in mid-close.

"We are not to be disturbed," Arthur said ponderously, like a punch-drunk boxer. "Not for anything, Cynthia. Anything. If the place is burning down, we are not to be disturbed. Is that understood?"

Cynthia, a sensible girl, nodded, and slid out smartly.

Arthur walked round his desk. He eyed Kenny up and down with interest. He pointed a finger. "Sit." He was indicating the only chair.

"Now Arthur—"

"Sit!"

Kenny sat. There had been, throughout the weekend, the warm realisation that he'd got Arthur by the short and curlies, and though he might not be able to con him for four Ford Escorts, he ought to be softened enough for two.

But Arthur hadn't softened one teeny-weeny bit. Like a sapling in a gale, he had bent. It had been unpleasant. Now he sprung back.

"I have given the matter deep thought, Mr Scott," he said, his voice so quiet that Kenny had to strain his ears. "As I recall the situation as it stood the last time we met, I was expected to fork out the cash for anything up to *four* Ford Escorts . . . no, say nothing. Nothing. I . . . had . . . not . . . finished."

Here his voice was rising, as Kenny had shifted uneasily and had moistened his lips. Kenny was silent. Arthur nodded. He began to pace the floor.

"This," cried Arthur, passion in his voice, "arose because I was unfortunate enough . . . yes, unfortunate, that's the mildest word I can use for it . . . to win a blasted car, which I haven't even reached out and touched."

73

"Please," said Kenny, raising a supplicating palm. "We can come to some arrangement."

"Arrangement! We've been coming to sodding arrangements all the week. You seem to have the idea . . . yes you have, don't deny it . . . the idea that I'm going to produce forty thousand pounds out of my own pocket. Poor Arthur – but he can afford it! But this is my company, Mr Scott. Mine. My money is the company's. And there is not a spare forty thousand pounds hanging around. It's known as liquidity. *We* can't afford it. We'd be out of cash and nobody'd get paid. Not you, not the shop floor, not my suppliers, who'd stop supplying at once, not the wages staff themselves."

"Some arrangement—"

Arthur ignored him. "But, you will say, if we don't have a new raffle you'll have 'em all out on strike, and we'd go bust. If you *do* have four Ford Escorts, we'd go bust, but you'd at least have transport to the unemployment office. So, Mr Scott, I've come to a decision. As four, three, two or one Escort would bring us all to ruin one way or another, I've decided. D'you want to know what? Go on – have a guess."

Kenny Scott, not at all happy to be viewing all those bare teeth at the same time, procrastinated. "I'll need time."

"Ah – but there *is* no time. This is power-sharing, Mr Scott, this is what I'm offering you. You can make the decision. How many Escorts do you think I ought to supply? Go on, your turn for decisions."

Kenny, sensing a hidden trap, smiled ingratiatingly. "No. You're the boss. You decide."

"Well, thank you. Well said. I'll tell you what I've decided. None, that's what. Not one. None at all. Do I make myself clear?"

"None? But you can't—"

"Oh, but I can. It's my cheque book. I don't have to use it."

"But promises have been made," said Kenny. "See sense," he added, making a mistake.

"Sense! Tcha! I've seen it. If you call 'em out now, at least I'll be better off by forty thousand. Isn't *that* sense? None, Scott, and you can do your little bit of power-sharing by going down to your shopfloor and telling 'em so. D'you feel that vibration under your feet, Scott? That's the machines. If it stops I'll know what you've decided. Don't worry about me. I'll lock up after you."

Kenny got to his feet. He wiped his palms down the seat of his overalls. He knew when to retrench. "You did say – you agreed, and it's been promised. One car for my shopfloor ladies—"

And Arthur laughed. Actual, genuine laughter, this was. "But Scott, that was before. Ha! Before you started upping the kitty. Ha! Ha! But look at it now. Look at it. You've argued yourself into a position where we can't do that any more. Or you'll have the men out. Ha! Ha-bloomin'-ha!"

"Only if I tell 'em to."

"But you can't back out now. It's as good as promised. You said that."

"But . . ." Kenny prodded a finger into the air. "But that was between you an' me. For-sake-of-argument sort of thing, that was. Just you an' me. In here."

"Was it?" Arthur cried in delight. He whirled on his heel and shouted at the intercom on his desk. "Are you getting this, Cynthia?"

"Yes, Mr Moreton."

"And," he went on to Kenny, still shouting, "she always gets it. All the time. Isn't that so, Cynthia?"

"Yes, Mr Moreton."

"So they know, Kenny old sport. Ha! Ha! *Everybody* knows. And you've gone and lost an Escort we could've raffled to your ladies. Ha! Ha! Ha! And it's all your fault.

Ha! Oh, you're killing me! Do get out, Kenny, it's giving me a pain."

"But you promised!" Kenny shouted.

"No – *you* promised. Oh, isn't this beautiful! Laugh, Kenny, it's so bloody funny. Go and tell your ladies they're not getting it. But Kenny – oh, I can't stand it! – Kenny, keep well clear of the ladies' rest room down there."

Kenny Scott, furious, held the door in slamming position.

"And the men's!" shouted Arthur. "And the office staff's! Oh . . . are you going?"

Then he leaned back against his desk, gasping and holding his side. Beneath his feet, the floor continued its satisfying vibrations.

Which was all very well, but the buoyant mood continued too long. It was still with him when he left that evening – first in, last out – so that he was off his guard and saw very little because he was walking from the light into the dark yard.

Half an hour before this, the superintendent had closed his meeting. It had been a long one, not because of the complexities involved, but because his was a lonely life and he loved his meetings. He had, however, a tendency to wander from the point. Two issues were for discussion: the outbreak of graffiti in the town and the theft of the seven razors of Ockam. Present were all his inspectors, though Arkwright (Riots) didn't seem to have any professional interest in these matters. He was just nosy.

Also present were five sergeants, Andy Spinks rather taking pride of place because the razor theft was in some way his, and five CID constables. Of these, Tony Finch was the only one who raised his voice. The others, two men and two women, were sufficiently experienced to know that it would be over so much quicker if they kept their mouths shut.

The superintendent's office was therefore rather crowded. The temperature began to build up.

"Two issues," said the super, looking up from his notes. "I'm unhappy about the graffiti, but it might be better than the rowdyism if it means we've seen the end of it. Any thoughts on that, Inspector Tomkins?"

Ralph Tomkins wasn't pleased at having to plunge straight in like this. But he was prepared. "There's a significant difference in the objectives. The violence seemed to be centred on Bert Harris and the raffle in general, but the graffiti's pointing more towards the winners. Arthur Moreton gets pride of place, with several efforts spread around the town, and one, on his own factory gate, definitely a threat. Lucifer Hartington, who got the second prize – he's had his barge disfigured, and towed away, I hear."

"Barge?"

"He lives in it, sir."

"Is that legal?"

"I don't know." And he didn't care.

"If it's not, we could have him in. Protective custody, sort of."

Tomkins sighed. "He doesn't seem concerned about his safety."

"A toughie, eh?"

"No sir. A quiet man of around sixty-five. But he's got Charlie Pierce to look after him."

"This Pierce . . . he's the—" He shuffled papers on his desk, without visible progress.

"Yes sir. The third prize winner."

"And *he's* a toughie?"

"Not exactly. Let's say I wouldn't go to arrest him without two officers in support."

"Not *that* tough, surely?"

"He's already been physically threatened, sir. There were four of them, two of whom are still in hospital."

"Ah!" The super thought about this, tapping his teeth. He made a decision. "Better take three officers, then."

"You want him arrested?"

"No, no. Indeed not. I meant, if the occasion arises."

"I'll bear it in mind, sir. But this Pierce is the one I suspect for the message across the shop's window. This was the one, sir – you have my report – which was an apparent threat to Pierce himself, but this was the place supplying *his* prize, a complete kitchen. And Pierce wanted the money instead. It's possible he was pressuring the people into upping their offer."

"Ah! A subtle man, this Pierce."

"I wouldn't say so. Subtle as a plank."

"How did it all come out?"

"He sold his voucher."

"Ah!"

"And bought his mother an electric kettle."

"I see. Is all this relevant?"

"I don't know, sir."

The super frowned. He didn't like his inspectors not knowing. He liked even less hearing them admitting it. "Anything else?"

"Yes sir. I've had a handwriting expert on it. Took him round in my car—"

"Handwriting? What's this? I've heard nothing about threatening letters."

"For the graffiti, sir. And anyway, I hear Mr Moreton's had unpleasant communications."

"And what did your expert say about the graffiti?"

"That most are from the same person's hand. The ones most directly threatening."

"Interesting. And now we have the theft of the seven razors. Connected, do you think, or an entirely separate issue?" Blank faces waited. "My own impression is that they're connected." Blank faces took on life and heads were nodded. He smiled in gratification, linking his hands on his blotter. Silently, they all sighed.

"But I understand there's a bit of a mystery involved here. I'm not keen on mysteries. We don't want to waste time detecting things, do we?" Several emphatic nods of agreement. "But nevertheless, there's the slight mystery of how it was done. Sergeant, I believe it was you who conducted the experiment."

Sergeant Andy Spinks jerked awake. He'd been on all night. "I did, sir. At once. When it became evident there was a time element. It would've been almost impossible to break the window, get to the showcase, break that glass – with the hammer we later found tossed away in a corner."

"Ah yes. The hammer. No prints, I understand."

"Wiped clean, sir. As I was saying, he might've managed to get there, pinch the box of razors, toss away the hammer he'd brought with him—"

"It's not a hammer," put in Inspector Tomkins, thinking Spinks was hogging too much of the limelight.

"Not?" asked the super. It was on his desk. He picked it up. "Looks like a hammer to me. Or a mallet."

"It's a gavel, sir. The things people use for banging on tables and the like."

"Interesting. I'm sure you're right."

"But not any old gavel, sir. It's from the council chamber. It wasn't brought to the council offices. It was hunted out there. You can see what that means."

The super cleared his throat. He was never quite on top of things unless he was himself talking. For a second he was nonplussed.

Constable Tony Finch, a thoughtful and basically kind young man, hated to see his super embarrassed, so he helped him out.

"It was an inside job, sir."

Cheeky young devil, thought the inspector. He'd been keeping that for himself. "Perhaps DC Finch would care to enlarge on that."

Everybody turned and stared at Tony. He went pink. His face, smooth and very young, was ideal for blushing. He'd been practising, but it still did it. "No . . . really—"

The super, inclined to look kindly on this young man, who knew when to step in and with whom it was best to ingratiate himself, nodded. "Go ahead, Constable."

"Well," said Tony, aware of a murderous stare from Sergeant Spinks. "I mean – if it was somebody who couldn't have broken in, because there wasn't time for that, particularly if he had to get hold of the gavel, then he must've hidden away inside until the place was deserted."

"Since Friday night?" Andy Spinks demanded, sneering.

"Yes," Tony agreed diplomatically, "of course. You've got a point there, Sergeant. I can see that."

There was a short silence. Feet shuffled. Everybody stared at him. In the end, Inspector Tomkins broke in. "See what?"

"I'd forgotten about the graffiti, sir. Sorry. If he also did that, he couldn't have got himself stuck inside since Friday."

"Yes," said Tomkins.

"Y'see," Spinks remarked to the room in general.

"So he'd have had to have a key. I'm probably wrong, sir. It was just a thought." Tony tugged at his right ear.

"Are you," demanded Spinks, "accusing my uncle?"

Tony turned sideways and stared at him blankly. "Has he got a key, Sergeant?"

"You know damn well he has."

"No . . . really . . . I didn't."

Spinks glared at him angrily. Tony shrugged. The super looked round the group, not certain now exactly where they were. And who the hell was the fool's uncle?

"Do I take it then," he asked, "that we're agreed?" They didn't seem to take anything. What a dull lot, he thought. No spark in them, that was the trouble.

"On what, sir?" Tomkins ventured.

"That they're connected. The threats and the razors. Connected. But . . ." He leaned forward and waved a finger warningly. "We mustn't fall into the trap of assuming it. The razor snatch could be nothing more than symbolical. Perhaps related to the town's motto."

"The town clerk suggested that, sir," Spinks piped up brightly.

"Did he?" The super's eyes lit up. He'd anticipated this aspect of the matter. He had notes written on his blotter. "And did he quote the original to you? In Latin."

"Not exactly, sir."

"The town's motto."

"That's what he said, sir."

"Which of course you know, Sergeant," said the super gently, not too keen on being showered with sirs.

"No, sir."

"Anybody know?" asked the super brightly, casting his gaze around.

Lord, we're back at school, thought Tomkins. If that young idiot Finch opens his mouth I'll kill him. But Tony, who did know, said nothing.

"Right. Well, it's *Entia non sunt multiplicanda praeter necessitatum.* It translates as: Entities are not to be multiplied without necessity. Does anybody know what *that* means?"

Still they retained a tactful silence.

"It's why it's called Occam's Razor. It cuts straight through to essentials. So perhaps somebody wants them in order to do just that. To cut through to essentials, the entities being divided. We've got seven razors and seven entities, the prizewinners. Am I making myself clear?"

They stared at him blankly. Detective Inspector Tomkins, the embarrassing silence niggling at him, suggested tentatively, "A nutter, sir? I quite agree."

"You could put it like that, I suppose."

"Maybe even one of the seven winners, resenting somebody who's got his or her prize."

"That too is a possibility." The super beamed at them paternally. "But I do feel it means we've got to brace ourselves for something unpleasant. Those razors, I'll remind you, ladies and gentlemen . . ." he nodded to himself, ". . . are symbolical. The spirit of Ockam. And I'll remind you that all over the world people are killing each other over symbols. Now . . ." He half rose from his seat. "Is there anything else?"

Nobody dared to do anything but shake a head.

"Thank you all."

They went about their respective duties, Andy Spinks to his bed.

Half an hour later the phone on Detective Inspector Tomkins's desk rang. Pale and shaken he replaced it. Already, it had begun.

Chapter Seven

Monday, 25 September (cont.)

Had it not been for the fact that Arthur Moreton's car was out of order, and the fact that he'd unloaded the Escort onto his son, he would have turned from the side door directly to his parking slot. He might even have done this instinctively if he hadn't noticed it was now raining and he was about to get wet waiting for a bus. Consequently, he turned right without hesitation as he slammed the door behind him. His parking slot was clearly indicated. His assailant therefore had no excuse as there wasn't a car waiting there.

But he'd clearly expected Arthur to turn left and had therefore waited in the deep shadows to the right of the door, this being the approved position for throat-cutting with open razors. It is infinitely more practical to reach across from behind, over the right shoulder.

It was not like that. Arthur turned to the right and abruptly they were face-to-face, or rather, face to ski-mask. The assailant was at once at a disadvantage. Face-to-face required an entirely revised grip on the razor, as the double-sided guard had to be held out of the way. Also, Arthur had been a promising middleweight in his youth. He reacted.

There was something metal in that shadow's hand, he realised. It caught orange gleams from the lamp across the street. It was scarifying, so Arthur raised one defensive arm and another offensive fist. In a panic now, the assailant slashed away, cutting slices of wet air out of the night. Arthur cried out. The assailant cried out. The two sounds were very similar. The guard, fifty yards away in his gate hut, heard two distinct cries of, "Yurk!"

Then it was over and the attacker was scuttling away to the dark distance of the furthest corner of the factory grounds, and Arthur, thoroughly roused, was shouting, "Heh you, Kenny, come back here, you cowardly bastard."

This error is excusable in the circumstances, but in fact Kenny was at that moment round at the Workingperson's Club, fixing up a party for his forty-five shopfloor ladies, who hadn't really taken him seriously for one moment about another Escort, but were not averse to a bit of a do.

The guard came running, helped a red-faced Arthur into his hut and phoned the police. By the time the patrol car arrived, Arthur was rather more white than red, grey even. He had realised what he had seen glinting in the light from the streetlamp.

"A razor!" he babbled. "A bloody razor."

Then he took another sip of the magic water produced by the guard, which was brought regularly from Eire by a daughter who'd married an Irishman against her father's wishes, her father now being all in favour once he'd realised what was in those litre bottles labelled Natural Spring Water. Arthur also was now in favour. By the time Detective Inspector Tomkins arrived, he knew why that graffiti on the gate had failed to alert the guard, in fact felt himself approving.

Tomkins came with DC Tony Finch. They extracted a reasonably coherent story from Arthur and Tony almost at once discovered the razor, tossed aside as the assailant galloped away. It lay against one wall of the office block.

Tony got down on his knees to get a closer look. He had a powerful torch from the inspector's car. The razor had a bone handle, now matured to a pleasant cream shade, which was in two parts so that the blade, when folded into safety position, would lie between them. There had been an attempt to close the blade into the handle, because trapped between the two of them was what looked like a paper handkerchief. Tony crouched with his eye close to the ground. He could just make out the lettering engraved into the thick rear edge of the blade: MONDAY.

Five minutes later, the two patrol car men, who'd been sent by Tomkins in an abortive scout round the factory grounds, returned to say there was a gap in the bottom corner of the wire-mesh fence. Probably children, they said. It had a well-worn appearance.

The forensic team arrived and later the superintendent. There was no actual damage to Arthur, apart from the effects of the poteen, no blood anywhere – not on the razor or the piece of tissue – yet the super felt it to be an important case. It had, as he put it to the inspector, begun something.

There were also no fingermarks on the razor – not even Bert Harris's, who handled them most every day – this fact being explained by the presence of the tissue.

Arthur was driven home, more doleful now than joyous. There was a nervous twitch in the corner of his eye. Shock was setting in. He'd been told that the weapon had indeed been an open, old-fashioned cut-throat razor.

No clues emerged from a long and protracted search. All they found were two buttons, sliced cleanly from Arthur's coat.

Later that evening, the superintendent sat in his office with DI Tomkins.

"I'm pleased there were no fingermarks," said the super.

"Pleased, sir?" Tomkins could see no reason for pleasure in any direction.

"I'd been thinking about Bert Harris."

"Oh!"

They both thought about Bert Harris for a few moments, until Tomkins said, "I don't see what you mean."

"I mean," said the super heavily, "that Bert, as mayor, handles those damned razors – used to handle, I suppose – nearly every day. Showing off the town's treasures to groups of visitors. So Bert Harris, if he'd done it, would've been the one person who wouldn't need to wipe his fingermarks off the razor."

There was a fallacy in that reasoning, thought Tomkins, but he couldn't see exactly what it was. Surely Bert Harris . . . but why the devil would Bert Harris be considered as a possible suspect?

"Bert Harris?" he asked.

"The mayor, Inspector."

"I know, sir. But were you seriously suspecting—"

"Yes, I was. Look at the situation. He's been harried from all directions for a week. He must be near to going clean round the bend, poor old Bert. Maybe he got the idea that the only way to settle it would be to remove all the prizewinners, then there'd be nobody left to complain."

Tomkins considered idly whether Bert Harris was the one who'd gone off his head. He therefore spoke gently. "But if that'd been his intention, sir, he'd surely have started – logically, even for a nutter – with the one who had the biggest grievance."

"Ah yes!" The super waved a finger in maddening condescension. "But you're forgetting, he drew the raffle backwards. Harris is a man who *thinks* backwards, Inspector. I know him. We were at school together."

Tomkins groaned. Everybody was always at school with any person who became famous. The classrooms must've been packed to suffocation when Bert Harris was a child. Slasher Harris! Was there any significance in that?

"Were you, sir?" he asked.

"Oh dear me, yes. I remember . . . when the bell went

for the end of playtime, Bert was the first off the mark, but always the last in."

"Why was that, sir?"

"He always did a last lap of the playground. Keep-fit Harris, the teacher called him."

"Not Slasher, sir?"

"That came later, in his teens, he having the ability . . . but that's beside the point."

"Not from his footballing?"

"Long before then. But I remember, even on the pitch he was always doing things backwards. He'd take a pass, with a clear run all down the left sideline, and he'd take the ball into the middle. Or he'd turn around and head for his own goal, luring all the other team after him. Clever! But . . ."

Here he leaned forward confidentially, though it was rumoured his office was checked for bugs twice a week. Tomkins found himself also leaning forward.

"I'll tell you this, Inspector. That cup final, Slasher Harris took the ball . . . you know we won three-two? Of course. The whole world knows. Slasher got the ball. Second half, this was. It was one all. And he did one of his funnies, taking it the wrong way, to fool the opposition. Then he put it through his own goal. Not many remember that. It was ten minutes to full time, and he went wild. Tied 'em up in knots. Oh, it was beautiful to see. And in those ten minutes he put in two first-class goals."

"Through the other side's goal?"

"Of course."

"He'd worked out where it was, then?"

"Inspector, I'm trying to explain his strangely inverted thinking."

"Of course, sir. I get your point. If the mayor got it into his head to remove the winners, and in that way clear his conscience, then he might possibly start from the wrong end."

"Exactly."

"And after all, he *has* got a key to that regalia show-case."

"I expect he has."

"So . . . thinking the way he does . . . he'd of course smash the glass."

"If you say so, Inspector."

"And, as a cover up, because he's probably got a key to some secret door for mayors to sneak in by, he'd pretend to break in by way of a loo window."

"Bert might do that, I suppose."

"And with that same funny mind of his, he'd choose the ladies instead of the gents."

"I think we've had enough of this, don't you! As I said . . . a point that you seem determined to ignore . . . there're seven prizewinners and seven razors. Must be a link there."

"Yes, sir." Tomkins sighed himself to silence.

"So I think we'll keep it in the family, so to speak."

"I thought so, too, sir. But – you *did* say you intended to have a word with Bert Harris?" He waited for the inclined head, his own face expressionless. "So no doubt you'll mention those points to him. It'll cheer him up no end, especially if you remind him of the goal into his own net."

"No doubt it will. Now – can we explore the possibilities thrown up by the seven razors and the seven winners?"

"You mean, if it's one of them?" Tomkins slid deeper into his chair. They'd at last come round to what he wanted to discuss. "They are," he said lugubriously, "infinite."

"Come now. Not that bad, surely. The seventh prizewinner would resent the first. As simple as that."

"Or the sixth resent the second, or the fifth resent the third. Or all of them resent the fourth because he – no, it was a woman – she is the only one who hasn't got a gripe or a cheer to worry about. She's piggy in the middle, and would've got the fourth prize whichever way it was drawn."

"It is not necessary—"

"Or . . ." went on Tomkins remorsely, "the seventh could resent *all* the other six, the sixth resent *all* the other five, and right on down the scale, or *all* of them resent the first, and all but one the second, and right on up the scale—"

"Surely you're—"

"Or – assuming it's a raving nutter amongst them – the first could resent the seventh for being so far removed from the aggro."

"But that's Moreton, and he's—"

"Unmarked, yes. Apart from two buttons sliced from his shortie overcoat."

"You're not saying—"

"Or the second resent the third for being that much further from the aggro, and the third the fourth, and so on – and back to everybody resenting the fourth, who's sitting there, not caring a tupenny cuss—"

"You've been overdoing things, Inspector."

"I'm *always* overdoing things, sir. My entities are always being multiplied, and nobody questions the necessity. You can tell your friend William of Occam that." Then, his hands not too steady, he lit a cigarette.

After a few moments, the super gestured gently. "You wished to make a point, Inspector?"

"Yes, sir. All we're sure about is that somebody has started on Monday with the Monday razor. It's Tuesday tomorrow. I need more men, sir, borrowed from the uniformed branch. I'll have to put a watch on all of those seven, a special one on Lucifer Hartington, who won the number two prize. And on Esmeralda Greene who won the number six prize and has, I understand, been expressing strong opinions about not winning the motorcycle. And, as

a back-up, the others as well. Especially Paul Catterick, who
won the booby prize and you'd expect to be the one most
resenting Arthur Moreton winning the first prize. *That* is my
point. I need men, sir." And a bit of rest, he prayed, but the
super never gave him any of that.

"Very well. I'll see what I can do. You'll be wanting to
have Catterick in for questioning?"

"I'll certainly want to know where he was at ten past six,
which was the time Moreton was attacked – and where he's
been since."

"Logical," conceded the super. "Logical."

In practice, Paul had been with Esmeralda at six o'clock.
He was with her as the two policemen were speaking
about him, in fact a darned sight later than that. But,
as the inspector put it to himself, a wife is no alibi for
her husband, and vice versa, and after all that time at
her flat they must surely be as good as man and wife
by now.

But this was really pique, the inspector's lady friend still
barring him from her portals. And it was very far from
the truth.

Esmeralda had Made A Special Effort. She had fought
against it, but instinct had thrust her into washing her hair
and afterwards teasing it into a reasonable style. Not too
feminine, but presentable. She also searched her wardrobe
for a suitable dress, though the general trend was towards
tweed. Plenty of slacks, plenty of Fair Isle jumpers and
cardies, plenty of shirts but few blouses. There was, however, one blouse with a broderie anglaise collar, which was
not too revoltingly frilly, and a skirt she couldn't for the life
of her remember buying, which was in a material described
as 'tweed weave', but, being polyester or something, had
blessedly failed to achieve that effect. It did something
to her hips. She wasn't sure what. Nothing, she realised,
wondering why it should annoy her, could do much for those

hips. But it did something. And there was a pair of slippers, disgustingly elegant, that had a hint of heel. No make-up, of course. Perhaps just a touch of rouge to the cheeks, a touch of powder to the nose.

Paul rang her doorbell precisely at six. At that time Arthur Moreton was reaching for his hat. Paul had been pacing the street since a quarter to. It was a quiet street, lined with Georgian houses, now mostly divided into flats. Pike Avenue. Her flat was on the second floor.

No special effort from Paul, either. His best slacks were pressed to a knife edge crease, with the hacking jacket he'd bought during a holiday in Dresden, brown loafers, a crystal white shirt and a subdued tie. But he did, she thought, wear his clothes with a certain panache.

They eyed each other with guarded approval.

"You're on time."

"Yes. A Civil Service habit."

"My father used to say, any fool can be early, a bigger fool can be late."

"Very true," agreed Paul.

"He was late for his own funeral. The hearse—" She bit her lip. Nervous idiot, she thought.

Paul smiled. "I'm sure they'd have waited for him."

"Who?"

"Where he was going."

"Oh."

A short silence ensued. Paul looked round, moving a little, not having been asked to sit. A pleasant flat, he thought. Practical. Lived in. Why do people say that: lived in? Everywhere was lived in, unless it was empty. Say something, you fool.

"I was pleased—"

"I'm sure you realise—"

They stopped. Paul laughed. She smiled. "You first," he said.

"I was going to say that I thought I'd give you a meal here, seeing that I owe you for a lunch."

"A splendid idea. Cosy. More intimate than a restaurant. But I shan't be able to reciprocate."

"How d'you mean?"

"I live with my brother and his wife."

"Oh dear."

"Exactly. Don't know why I stay there. You ought to meet her."

"Ought I?"

"A terror, she is. You'd see what marriage does to a woman."

"Yes." Her lips tightened.

He realised he'd made a mistake. Relax, you fool. "Nice place you've got here. I like your pictures. Bags of colour. I always go for colour."

"Do you? I'm flattered."

"Are you?"

"I painted them."

"You did? Well, that's great."

He had difficulty envisaging her swapping a hockey stick for a paintbrush.

"A woman has to have a hobby. Have you got a hobby, Paul?"

"I walk the streets. I watch humanity in all its guises."

"Fascinating."

"Depressing, rather."

"But sit down. Can I get you a sherry?"

"Fine. Another of my hobbies."

"Drinking?"

"Wines."

"Ah."

He sat in one corner of the settee, she in the far one. It was a two-seater settee, but there'd have been room for Bert Harris in the middle.

92

"I had a job reaching you," she said. "They wanted to know my case number, whatever that is. And then – all that noise in the background—"

"My section. Twelve girls, as I told you."

"Do they always make that much noise?"

"Not always. But I never get personal calls from ladies. They were – shall we say, intrigued."

"The shouting?"

"Who is she, sir? What's she like, Paul? And rude comments I cannot repeat."

"Not in the presence of a lady?"

"Oh, sorry. I forgot. You don't like being treated as a lady."

Oh, but she did, she did.

"In the presence, then," he amended, "of a young woman."

She smiled past her glass. "And I," she told him, "had to use the public phone in the school hall. Public means, in this context, surrounded by a crowd of screaming gels."

"I thought—"

"They, too, wanted to know. Who is he, miss? What's he like?"

"And other comments?"

"Positively," she told him, sipping her sherry, "obscene."

Then he laughed, and she smiled, and a little sherry got spilled, and if her cheeks were flushed it wasn't the sherry, either that inside or that on the carpet.

"I thought," she said, "we'd eat in the kitchen. If you don't mind."

"Of course not."

"Very simple," she admitted. "I'm no cook. I hope you like steak and kidney pie."

"Love it."

"And I've done a bread and butter pudding."

"Haven't had that for years. By heaven, lead me to it."

"And you can choose the wine."

"May I?"

"Certainly. A red plonk from the superstore, or nothing."

He relaxed, she relaxed. They knew where they were now. The meal progressed, the pie was just right, the pudding was just right. He laughed. She laughed. She wasn't used to wine with her meals. All the same, wine-induced or not, she laughed, and he was very pleased to see it.

Afterwards, she introduced him to her hi-fi set and indicated her collection of CDs. He tended towards jazz, she towards orchestral music. But she had a few big-band discs from the forties and fifties. The Duke and the Count, and Benny Goodman and a rip-roaring Stan Kenton, and the Dorseys and a sweet caress from Glenn Miller, which simply shouted out to be danced to. Which they did, but neither could dance and the wall-to-wall carpet was inhibiting and the furniture got in the way, and it's very difficult when you each have a glass of something in one hand. So they finished up, gasping and giggling, on the settee, still in each other's arms, and what with one thing and another . . .

Somehow, he seemed to be kissing her eyes and her cheeks and her lips, and somehow the top buttons of that blouse became unfastened, and somehow he just couldn't find the fastener of her bra, and he must have taken so long on it . . . Giggling, not caring, was Paul. They'd got all night, hadn't they, and the bloody fastener had to be somewhere, and where the hell had his other hand gone . . .

Esmeralda was abruptly aware of the location of that second hand. And it was Too Much. She wasn't prepared . . . not ready . . . She wasn't something, but whatever it was she was struggling free in a fine old panic that she hadn't encountered in fifteen years. And it was just the same. Like a bike. Once you could do it, you never forgot. And once . . . many times . . . she hadn't been able to do it.

So she fought herself free and slapped his face, over and

94

over because the damned fool wouldn't take it away. But then he did. Stood over her. "All right. Sorry. I won't—"

"Get out!" she screamed. "Out!"

Paul scooped his tie from the carpet, slipped his shoes on, and went. Commendably, he closed the door gently. On his way home, he found himself too late to indulge in his favourite pursuit of studying humanity. His mood was not receptive, the humanity more than usually lacking uplift.

"Got the time, love?"

"It's too bloody late." That was his mood.

To cap it all, Hilda, his brother's wife, had waited up for him.

"Where have you been, Paul? Have you *seen* the time?"

Had he been in a more receptive mood, and considered her with his usual grave understanding, he might have observed the worry in her eyes. As it was, he merely pushed past, muttering, "Mind your own damned business, Hilda." Hell! She was his brother's wife, not Paul's.

Then he climbed the stairs to his room, not realising he'd left a second woman in tears.

At the flat, Esmeralda wept and wept, and punched walloping great dents into the back of the settee, whose fault it wasn't. Or perhaps was.

Chapter Eight

Tuesday, 26 September

Early in the morning, Detective Inspector Tomkins sat at his desk and eyed DC Tony Finch cautiously. The lad had done well the previous evening, barely needing instructions, and he'd taken a rise out of DS Andy Spinks. Now Tomkins had a tricky assignment for him and nearly everybody was already allocated.

"How're you on tact, son?" He was trying not to be too official.

"Too bad to admit it, sir, too good to claim it in the circumstances."

Guessed correctly, thought Tomkins. I've got something right at last.

"You'll do. I want you to go round all the prizewinners, except Arthur Moreton, who already knows, and drop just a hint to them that they could be in danger. You see where the tact comes in?"

"Yes, sir. I could be talking to the one they're in danger from."

"Yes, that too. I hadn't thought of that. But come to think of it, it wouldn't hurt if he—"

"Or she?"

"Well yes, I suppose. It could've been a woman. After all, she . . . he . . . it managed to miss Arthur Moreton, and there's a lot of him. So – to get back to it – there'd be no harm if our tricky customer got a little tip-off that we're going to be protecting everybody. And protecting them by watching them. You get my point?"

"Clearly, sir. Works both ways. He'd have to avoid his own watchers *and* the next victim's watchers."

"Good lad." Blast him, thought Tomkins, I do believe he's ahead of me.

"And I'd have to be careful not to lay on the warnings too heavily, in case it scared somebody into running away."

Tomkins sighed. "Exactly. We'd have to run after him in order to guard him."

"Will that be all then, sir?"

"No. One more point. Later in the day I'll be seeing Catterick myself—"

"Regarding his alibi? Yes, I suppose you will."

"So I'd like you—" Through his teeth, that was, which gave the young fool time to get in again.

"Not to queer your pitch. I can see that."

"I'm pleased you can."

"Though if he does drop anything out, casually sort of thing, sir, I'll let you know."

"Thank you."

"It'll be a pleasure."

"And *that* is all."

"Thank you, sir." Tony turned away.

"Oh, one thing."

"Sir?"

"You wouldn't like to take over my job, by any chance?"

"Oh no, sir. All that paperwork!"

And Tony left, not overly pleased with his own performance. It was all very well presenting a brisk and efficient personality, but it didn't mean he had to take the michael a bit with his boss. Nerves, that was the trouble. He'd gone in, wondering whether he was in for a bit of rollicking over his performance at the meeting, only to discover he was to have his own assignment. Reaction. Better watch that, he decided.

But he spent all his life watching it, hoping to beat his mother in spotting the faults and weaknesses in his personality. The trouble was that his father had Taken Bad Ways. Taken other things, too, because he'd been killed in a getaway car after a jewellery theft. His mother had promptly switched back to her maiden name and dedicated the rest of her life to ensuring that Tony didn't Take After That Man. Hence his enlistment in the police force. He was Making Amends. He was Justifying His Existence. But he had to Watch Himself for the first onset of the disease known as Sliding Back Into Those Terrible Ways.

It was enough to make anyone a nervous wreck, but Tony had a cheerful and friendly disposition – he got that from his father – and an optimistic and devil-may-care outlook – also from his father. All he really inherited from his mother was a tendency to think in capitals, but he was working on that.

One other legacy had his father left him. Tony was well-known throughout the local criminal fraternity, in spite of the surname change, as his father's son. And trusted. It was a huge advantage to a CID officer. This fact was known to his superiors. They, too, Kept An Eye On Him. It could work both ways.

But with this assignment he was going to be interviewing non-criminals. This was a slasher. Something strictly personal was involved. The criminal fraternity would frown most heavily on such activities. So Tony felt free and untrammelled from any suggestion of divided loyalties. He was going to enjoy himself.

It was therefore with a light heart that he set out on his

assignment. Having heard Arthur Moreton's account of the affray, it had seemed clear to him that they were not dealing with a slasher with any serious intentions. A frightener, that's all he was; a stirrer-up.

He collected his Fiesta from the station yard, examined his list of names and addresses and decided to take them in order. Lucifer Hartington was number two prizewinner. Canal boat, the Buckled Arrow. Two miles out on the road to Dowsing, that was. It was a fine and clear morning, mild, the rain gone but the road surfaces still wet. He hummed as he drove.

There was a plain car parked out on the road, just beyond the Buckled Arrow. Two men were sitting in it. Tony didn't even glance at them but turned straight into the pub's car park. Empty. It was too early for opening time. He got out and had a look over the low wall. Below him was the canal proceeding in a straight line into vaguely misty distance to his left, coming to an abrupt halt at the lock a hundred yards to his right. He walked out of the car park, down the muddy ramp to the towpath and sharply back on himself towards the longboat, moored twenty yards in that direction.

Here, he was on the very edge of his district. The main spread of town had been left behind and the countryside was beginning to assert itself. The Buckled Arrow had been strictly a bargemen's pub.

Two men were seated on the deck of the barge, beneath a canvas awning, their backs against the cabin. One his own age, one older. He stopped.

"Permission to come aboard, skipper?"

"Permission granted," said Lucifer, which gave Tony the clue he wanted.

He stepped over and squatted down. "You'll be Mr Hartington?" he asked.

"Always have been."

"I'm from the police. I'd just like a few words, if I may."

"There y'are," Charlie told his friend. "Knew they'd get y'. All them little girls you keep chasin'—"

"I deny it, officer. They can run faster'n me."

"If I could have words with you privately, Mr Hartington," Tony said, keeping his face straight.

"Charlie," said Lucifer, "would you care to take a little walk?"

"I'm comfy here, thanks."

"Charlie?" Tony looked from one to the other. "Would that be Charlie Pierce?"

"It would," agreed Charlie. "An' you'll have a job takin' us both in."

"Fortunately, that's not why I'm here. But . . . this is just great. Saves me no end of time, this does. Two for the price of one."

Charlie and Lucifer looked at each other. "Nutters," said Charlie.

"He surely is," Lucifer agreed.

"Haven't you heard what happened last night?"

"No."

"No."

"Arthur Moreton was attacked with an open razor, one out of a set stolen from the Town Hall on Sunday night."

Lucifer relit his pipe. Charlie closed his hand into a fist and stared at it.

"Moreton?" asked Lucifer. "That the one who won first prize?"

"That's him."

"Got them, have you?"

"Them? Oh no. He wasn't really hurt but a razor was waved around. And there was only one assailant."

"Assailant," said Lucifer. "Hear that, Charlie? Good old-fashioned copper language. Did you come all this way to tell us that, son?"

"Sort of. I thought you might be interested. I mean – these razors, they're engraved for the days of the week. One a day, seven razors. Seven prizes. Yesterday was Monday, and Monday's razor was used."

"He's trying to tell us something, Charlie."

"Yeah. Reckon he must be."

"Today's Tuesday," Tony reminded them. "Mr Moreton got first prize, and first go at the razors, you could say. You're second prize, Mr Hartington." He shrugged.

"Y' know," said Charlie, who'd been thinking it over, "he's telling y' you're next for the razor treatment."

"Seems so," Lucifer agreed. "Tonight."

"I was told," Tony admitted, "to be tactful."

"And you've done a grand job. Hasn't he, Charlie?"

"Reckon so."

"And it'll be your turn on Wednesday, Mr Pierce," Tony told him.

Charlie looked startled. Nobody ever called him Mr Pierce. It was as though he'd been dignified with a title in view of his forthcoming demise.

"There'll be no danger," Tony assured them. "We'll have men guarding you, Mr Hartington."

"That's very good of you, son. But Charlie'll be here. He'll stay the night. Can you do that, Charlie?"

"O' course."

"And he can stay the next night, too, and then I can guard *him*."

"Good idea," agreed Tony. "If you're still here, of course."

They looked at each other for a moment. Then they got it. Tact, Tony had said. This was his tact. They laughed. He laughed.

"Mind you . . ." Tony said. "What I'd do if it was me . . ."

"Yes?"

"I'd borrow a horse and tow this thing a mile or two away. He'd never find you then."

Lucifer punched Charlie's shoulder. "I've got me a horse."

"Or better still," Tony enlarged, "I'd tow it into that lock-up there, and let all the water out. That'd fool him."

"Nah!" said Lucifer. "How'd we get out when they open?" He jerked his head towards the pub.

"After they're shut, then."

"Charlie couldn't tow a plastic duck at that time."

"I can see," said Tony, "that we'll have to double our guard."

It went on like this for some time, Tony establishing public relations, and the day might have been spent very pleasantly there. Except that Tony had a thought.

"Where's this bike you won, anyway? I didn't notice it."

"In the shed in the car park," Lucifer told him.

"Can I see it?"

There is no better way to endear oneself to a motorcyclist than to show an interest in his machine. They trooped out to the car park and Lucifer unlocked the shed door. Then Charlie wheeled it out, propped it up on its stand and they all stood and stared at it. Tony walked round it. Several times.

"It's beautiful," he whispered. "Sheer unadulterated beauty."

"You're right, son."

"Sure is," agreed Charlie.

"Can I . . ." Tony took a deep breath, " . . . try it?"

They looked at each other. "You ever ridden a bike?" asked Charlie suspiciously.

"Sure. Only a two-fifty, though. Nothing like this."

They looked at each other again. "Why not?" said Lucifer at last. "Scratch it," grumbled Charlie, "an' I'll screw your head off."

"Insurance?" Tony asked.

"Any driver," Lucifer assured him.

"I'll need a crash helmet."

"Lend you mine," Lucifer offered and while he went to fetch it, Charlie, with Tony now astride it, gave the necessary briefing. Clutch grabbed a bit. Not run in yet. Gears a bit notchy, but they'd improve. Shaft drive, so watch it on bends. And so on.

It was therefore a very different Tony who drove out of the pub car park from the one who'd driven in. Unrecognisable. He turned away from town, seeking open roads, and thus passed the plain car with the two anonymous shapes inside.

These two officers, having done their homework, were already aware that Lucifer's helmet was red and Charlie's black. They therefore saw Lucifer driving out and heading towards the next county. After a brief comment that Lucifer, for a learner, was pushing his luck a bit, they radioed in for instructions.

Tony, in an aura of bliss, rode on, taking highways and byways as the mood seized him, unaware that he'd stirred up the forces of two counties and provoked action. He was, unwittingly, using an evasion technique that must have come with his genes. His dad would've been proud. The BMW devoured the road surface. Radio waves crackled backwards and forwards, until, having turned around in the general direction of the Buckled Arrow, working by the sun, he found himself confronted by a three-car road trap on the county border.

Eventually they sorted it out. Tony, red-faced and waving his ID, used language which his mother would have called Lowering The Tone. He was allowed to proceed back to the Buckled Arrow, one car behind, one in front.

Lucifer and Charlie watched him come. Their attention went first to the bike. *That* was okay. So he'd been speeding. Somewhat in awe, they watched the cars drive away and the original one again take up its position.

103

"I suppose the speedo's accurate?" asked Tony casually, now he'd recovered.

"Sure is," said Charlie.

"They said I was doing over the ton, and it was only ninety-five on the clock."

"Come'n have a drink, son," said Lucifer. "They're open."

Two pints later and with two sandwiches inside him, Tony, having decided that it would be unwise to return to the Station just for a while, thought it was about time he continued with his list.

He'd seen numbers two and three, which in effect meant he'd saved a little time, so four was next, but there was nobody in at Lucinda Porter's flat. So he went on to number five: Ada Follett, 17 Chamois St, Tanner's Reek.

She wasn't there. Nobody in, either side, whom he might ask. A woman across the road, watching his antics, shouted for him to try the Plucked Goose. He did and there they were, in their corner of the bar, nursing their milk stouts until three, when they would be thrown out.

"It's a copper," said Floss, who'd got that instinct.

"Do I look like one?" asked Tony, hurt, because he'd always thought of himself as anonymous.

They considered him critically for a few moments. "Looks like that Ed Phillips," decided Connie.

"My dad, that was."

"And now you're a copper?" Ada asked.

"I admit it. Mind if I join you?"

"If you're buyin'," agreed Ada.

"I'm buying."

He put three glasses before them, and his own pint, then his ID.

"If you're Ed Phillips's son," said Connie suspiciously, "why're you called Anthony Finch?"

"Undercover." Tony took down half his pint. He'd need it, he had decided. "Which one of you's Ada Follett?"

"It's her," the other two said, pointing at her. "What y' been doing, Ada?"

"Not what she's been doing," said Tony in a voice of doom, having worked out how to handle them, "but what's likely to be done to her."

"Eee!" screamed Connie. "You're in luck, Ada."

Then they all collapsed into howls of laughter, while Tony clenched his fists and waited. When there was comparative silence, he told them about the razors. They listened with awe and a few indrawn breaths. He explained that, even if the slasher was working his way right through the list of winners, she, being number five, wouldn't be for it until Friday.

"Thursday," said Floss firmly. "Sunday's the first day of the week. Look on any calendar."

"He was busy pinching 'em on Sunday."

"P'haps he's an atheist," suggested Ada. "His week starts on Monday."

"Your Eric's week started on a Monday, too," Connie reminded her. "An' he wasn't an atheist."

"My Eric," said Ada severely, "always stuck with brown ale. Swore by it."

"Well then—" said Floss.

"In any event," put in Tony, forcing a word in edgeways, "Thursday or Friday, you've still got time to flee the country."

"I'm not leaving my place, and that's flat," Ada told him, waving her empty glass beneath his nose. "Let me tell you, my Eric carried me over that front door step over fifty years ago, and when I leave it I'll be carried over that same step in the opposite direction."

"That," Tony promised, "could possibly be arranged," and he went to get them in again. "But," he said, banging the glasses down in front of them, "you don't have to worry, because we'll have men guarding you. *Every* night," he promised, exceeding his brief wildly.

"Heh!" said Ada. "We don't want no police cars outside our places. You wanta shame us, laddie? Never once, since my Eric carried me over that step—"

"Nobody'll know they're there."

"I'll know, Floss'll know, an' Connie'll know."

"If that's all—"

"An' we'd have to warn the others," Ada said firmly, setting her shoulders back and her lips forward, her fists in her lap resolutely.

Tony finished his beer. "My duty is done," he told them in his official voice. "You have been duly warned. But frankly," he went on, falling back on his own, "if I'd got a whole barrow-load of open razors, I wouldn't dare come near you three."

Then he bought another round to keep them going until chucking-out time, flicked the hair out of his eyes in salute and left to a patter of applause.

"Just like his dad," said Ada. "There was a lovely man for you."

"Too nice to be in the police," Floss agreed.

Connie put down her glass. "They'll break him, you'll see, break his spirit."

Tony, realising that he'd better steer clear of pubs for a while, tried 3C, Foundry St again, but still there was nobody at home. So he had only two more to look for, Esmeralda Greene and Paul Catterick.

Logically, these two, the last two in the list of prize-winners, would be the least likely to have attracted enmity from the slasher. But the inspector had said all, so all it would be. He had addresses, but other information too. Both were workers, Catterick at the unemployment office, and Ms Greene at the girls' school on Crécy Heights. Catterick's employers would not wish his labours to be interrupted, but a school suggested the possibility of free periods. Didn't they have such things? He decided to go and find out.

Crécy Manor, residential school for gently nurtured young ladies, was on the site of the original monastery. Remains of this were still visible, though the present building had been built in the 1700s. The original monastery had been founded in 1414 by French deserters, grizzled old warriors whose fathers had been grizzled young warriors at Crécy. They thus had warning of what heinous crimes the *bâtards* in England might get up to, and had twigged the trick of the bolthead switch. Not wishing to face the longbow experts, and having seen with their own eyes six arrows in the air at the same time from a single bow, they had traded in their crossbows and founded the monastery at Crécy Grange, as it was then called, dedicated to the production of a murderous liqueur they called Benedictine, thus infringing international agreements. The complete establishment died out in the plagues of the 1600s, their constitutions undermined by their deadly brew.

Now Tony, standing at the sideline of the hockey pitch, realised that they'd been replaced by even more deadly warriors. The Headmistress, a gentle little woman with a soul of iron, had told him that Ms Greene would be free of duties after the hockey session. Ms Greene was training the first team in tactics and the second team while she was at it, in case she ran out of gels.

Esmeralda Greene was in a foul mood. She was in there with them, switching sides erratically as she instilled in them the rudiments, and some of the advanced techniques, of dirty play. She just dared them to tackle her. They were falling like flies.

Tony was enjoying it. He was in no doubt as to which one was Ms Greene. She was older, more developed, clearly a mature woman, though she wore the same as the rest, the dark green short skirt and the white knicks, which were traditional. Not that there was any criticism to make on the rest of them when it came to the question of development.

It was clearly a girls' school, not a boys'. One other factor distinguished Ms Greene from the girls. She was the only one not limping.

So there he was, waiting, as they trooped off, dazed and shattered. At the sight of him they were at once enlivened.

"Is this him, miss?"

"He's only a chee-ild!"

"Can I have him, miss, when you've finished with him?"

Bravely, a credit to the force, he faced them. Ms Greene waved her hockey stick, and they dispersed. Tony, sensing that formality would be the natural trend here, produced his ID.

"Detective Constable Finch, ma'am." Which infuriated her. "Can we have a word somewhere?"

"What's the matter with here?"

"You'll perhaps have heard about last night?"

"It's all round the school."

"Then you'll realise, ma'am, that you yourself might be in danger."

"You," she said, "will be in danger if you call me ma'am again."

"My apologies. May I have your guidance there?"

"Ms Greene will do."

"Thank you."

"And if," she told him, thrusting the operative end of her hockey stick under his nose, "anybody comes near me, razor or not, they'll deserve what they'll get."

"We will have men on duty—"

"Not near me you won't. I can deal with them, too."

"I'm sure you can, Ms Greene. I'll take no more of your time. You'll no doubt be anxious to get to the showers. Good day to you."

With dignity, he withdrew, his nose indelicately sniffing.

On the way back into town he decided to call in at number 3, Foundry St, Link Green – which was in no way green – but once again 3C was empty. He was not particularly disappointed as he hoped to catch Paul Catterick as he left his office, which should be at five o'clock.

He was therefore waiting outside, chatting to the commissionaire, who had worked with his father, when Paul emerged. "That's him, Tony lad. Get in there, boy."

Tony saw a tall, gangling man very close to forty, from either direction, with the look of doom on his face that one might expect from a slasher who'd missed his target. And, being a civil servant, he would hate to have to do the same job twice.

"On my way home," Paul muttered, trying to push past as Tony asked if he could have a word.

"It won't take a minute."

"Miss my bus—"

"I'm from the police. I'll give you a lift in my car."

Paul shot him a startled look, then glanced away quickly. "That thing parked on the double yellows?"

"That's it."

"Then let's get going before she nabs you."

Tony climbed inside and watched Paul slump beside him. "It's about last night."

Paul moved in the seat. "You know about that ruddy fiasco?"

"Yes. Do you?"

"Of course I bloody do. I was there, wasn't I!"

"Were you?"

"Bloody farce, that was."

Tony took an island very, very carefully. "Pretty close, though."

"Makes it worse, don't it! Heh! How'd you know which way to go? How d'you know about last night?"

"Police. We know everything."

"Ah!" Paul sat back, staring morosely through the windscreen. "She's put your lot on me, has she?"

By this time Tony had decided that Paul wasn't their man, that they were talking about different incidents and if he didn't look what he was doing he'd have them both in hospital. So he grunted non-committally and decided to leave it hanging around. Paul was silent. A miasma of depair spread through the car. Tony was glad to reach their objective, a semi-detached three-bedroomed villa in the district of Bowmen's Fields.

Hilda had the door open before Paul's key reached the lock.

"So there you are!" she cried, as though his being early had quite unhinged her. "Coming home with the police! I knew it. Had to happen some day. What you been doing, you dirty bugger, you?"

Tony took exception to having his identity penetrated so easily. "That is not a police car, ma'am."

"D'you think I don't know a policeman when I see one! You're just like the rest. What's he been doing?" She drew back into the hall, partly so that she could view them both in full perspective, partly as though withdrawing from a fatal contamination. Then she lifted her head and her voice. "Dennis, your brother's home. Brought disgrace to our house. Didn't I warn you?"

Up to this moment, Tony had assumed this was Paul's wife. Now it seemed not. "If we could—" He didn't know what to suggest.

"And don't try hiding it from me," she said. "I'm ready for the worst."

"Chrissake, Hilda!" A similarly tall, similarly shambling man as Paul, in slacks and shirt sleeves, had come from the rear, a younger man, even less characterful than his brother. "So he was late last night—"

"Late! Two in the morning. I suppose that's not late! Philandering, that's what."

Tony, not sure whether philandering was included as a misdemeanour in his police manuals, put in, "If we could just go somewhere – Mr Catterick?" Meaning Dennis. "Somewhere quiet."

"And shut me out!" cried Hilda. "Typical."

"Somewhere," said Tony heavily, "where all four of us can sit down. It'll take only a minute."

Hilda eyed him suspiciously. Clearly, a minute wouldn't be enough to cover all Paul's sins. But she nodded. "In here."

The front room had not been reserved for visitors and was clearly used. The telly was in there. This always indicated *the* room. The set-up confirmed Tony's impression that Paul was really a lodger there. He wondered idly why, in that case, Paul hadn't packed it in long before. Perhaps he was too indolent; perhaps his brother needed moral support. Tony wandered in, allowed them to settle and seated himself on a pouffe. The seating capacity was, otherwise, a settee and an easy chair. He leaned forward.

"It's about last night."

"Not in till two," Hilda said, nodding, her black hair flopping over her eyes.

"It's obvious that not one of you three has heard what happened."

Three pairs of eyes impaled him.

"Mr Arthur Moreton, who won the first prize in that raffle you entered, Mr Catterick . . ." he nodded to Paul, "was attacked with an open razor. This was one from a box of seven stolen from the Town Hall on Sunday night. Yesterday was Monday and that razor had Monday engraved on it. Now . . . it's possible this hadn't got anything to do with the raffle—"

"It wasn't Paul," put in Hilda, now white-faced and switching sides nimbly.

"I'm sure it wasn't," Tony told her pacifyingly, because he wasn't. "The point is, the razor used was engraved Monday. And if the intention is to work through the prizewinners, so to speak—"

"Then I'll only have to wait till Sunday," put in Paul with ghoulish pleasure.

"Paul!" Hilda protested.

"When did this happen?" asked Dennis, more practically.

"Yesterday, a little after six. Mr Moreton was just leaving his factory."

"Paul wasn't here," Hilda said flatly. "Missed his evening dinner. Good food going to waste!"

"It doesn't matter where he was," Tony told her. "I don't care a tuppenny cuss where he was." Which, he thought, was about as tactful as anybody could get in probing for an alibi.

"Well I do," said Hilda.

Dennis touched her arm. "It's none of our business, my love."

"It is, when good food—"

"At six," said Paul, as though from the grave, "I was tapping on the door of a lady friend. At midnight, I was hoofed out. Sorry, Hilda, I rather forgot to warn you."

"Right!" Tony slapped his knees and got to his feet. "That's it, then. I just wanted to tell you to keep an eye open, Mr Catterick. Of course, we'll have people watching—"

"Police cars!" cried Hilda. "In *our* street."

"A discreet watch, I can assure you."

"I'll see you to the door," said Paul wearily.

So Tony drove away quite contentedly, aware that all in all he'd done a good job. Now – if only that Lucinda Porter was home, he could run that in on his way back to the Station.

Bowmen's Fields, from which he was driving, was to the north of the town, and the district of Link Green was to the east, on the same canal as Lucifer was using for his longboat. In Link Green they had forged their chains and as they needed plenty of water they'd done so in the canal. At least they had done so from the time Telford drove his canal through, on its way to Wales. Prior to that there had been a village with its village green and its village pond, complete with ducks. In this pond they had doused their chains, much to the dismay of the ducks. Now, in fact for 100 years, the district had been part of the town. You couldn't tell when you left one and entered the other. You could tell, though, when you were actually in Link Green, because there was the foundry which had replaced the original individualists. Here the fumes had been strong and lung-catching, the average life-span short. Better lately, though. The foundry was silent.

Now the tall, ancient red buildings, which had been homes for the foundry workers, were mostly shops on the ground floors and either offices or flats above. Tiny, almost unnoticeable doorways crouched between the shop fronts. Driving past, Tony saw at a glance that number 3C, Foundry St was showing a light. Way up there, under the eaves, it was.

He had to park at the superstore, no easy task just before six, with the shoppers doing a bit of last-minuteing. He walked back, found the door he'd already used twice and marched up two narrow, dim flights of stairs. He knocked. There was encouraging movement. Then a young woman opened the door.

The light on the landing was poor but Tony could see at once that this was the high spot of the day. This was no hockey player – far too delicate. She was no teacher – far too reticent. Nor was she a milk stout quaffer – far too fastidious.

"Are you Lucinda Porter?" he asked.

"No," she replied.

Chapter Nine

Tuesday, 26 September (cont.)

Tony took a step back and had another look at the door. "But this *is* 3C?"

"Yes."

"And you're not Lucinda Porter?"

She had been backing away, so that he could now see her more clearly. He followed her into the room. Nice eyes, he thought, but a little red and swollen; good, wide mouth, he liked girls with generous mouths. Good teeth. Five feet . . . what? Four?

She laughed marginally, a laugh that hadn't been exercised lately. "No. I'm Madge Fenwick, from the room below. 3B," she added, in case he might need that information. "And who are you?"

"Oh, sorry. Tony Finch. Detective Constable." He produced his ID.

Solemnly, she inspected the photo it displayed, walking round him with it in her hand. "You're taller than you look here."

"It's only head and shoulders."

"True. But it shows. And you're not as red as this picture. You're pink."

"I am not—"

"*Now* you're red."

"Blast," he said. "I always look better pink."

There was a short silence. He used it to look past her — which was a good idea just at that time. Well furnished, he thought, for this district. Some nice stuff. Top-class hi-fi.

"And if this isn't your place," he asked reasonably, "why are you here?"

"Lucy's my friend. She lets me come here to use her new typewriter."

"The one she won in the raffle?"

"Yes. There it is, over there."

He went to look at it. He was a complete duffer with typewriters, able just to use two fingers and one thumb on the ancient machines they had in the CID room.

"Looks good."

"Oh, it is. It's got a memory, too."

"A good one?"

"Better than mine. You can pick out your typing errors."

"I bet you don't make many mistakes."

"Oh, but I do. I keep missing out the Es."

He thought about that for a minute or so, aware that a good detective, Holmes say, would understand in a flash. "I don't understand."

"My own machine, downstairs, hasn't got an E. So I trained myself not to use it. Now I have to go back just the same because I can't get out of it. But at least I can put 'em in with the machine now, instead of by hand."

"I can see why you work up here. What're you typing?"

"If you came to see Lucy—"

"I did."

"She's not here."

"So I see. Where is she, then?"

"In St Mary's Hospital."

"Oh," he said. "I'm sorry," he said. His mind registered: should be easy to guard her there.

"And she's going to die." This was a whisper.

"I'm really sorry to hear that."

"Yes," she said, and to his horror she burst into tears, then plumped down into a winged chair and dabbed at her face with a fistful of soggy tissue.

There was nothing about this in his instruction manual. Perhaps it was assumed that any respectable copper would know what to do about women in tears. You collected them in your arms and said, "There, there." But Tony's father had collected too many tearless females into his arms. In the family it had been known as his Sex Fantasies. Tony had to admit that something masculine was stirring inside him, urging him to Get On With It, Son. But he was suspicious of this. He went, instead, to the window, noticed that a shadow had withdrawn into a narrow alleyway opposite, a pink face uplifted, and was pleased to observe that the watch was already in place. Unnecessarily, perhaps, but there. In this he was incorrect.

He turned. She was watching him, sideways in the chair. "I told them she could have one of mine – a kidney – but they did tests and it didn't match. Incom-something."

"Incompatible," he told her. "Like divorcees."

"Yes. That."

"Perhaps they could use one of mine," he offered, anything to stop those tears. "If I could get the time off," he shaded it a little.

"Oh . . . you idiot!" And she was up out of that chair and in his arms in a second, her head against his chest. "There, there," he said, patting her back.

After a while she drew away from him and wouldn't meet his eyes.

"What're you typing, anyway?" he asked, to take her mind off it.

"Oh . . ." She gave a vague, mock-modest wave of her hand. "It's a novel."

"You're a secretary?"

"No, no. It's mine."

"Really?"

"Oh yes."

"What's it about?"

She looked down at the traffic outside. "It's about a young woman who meets this simply gorgeous policeman—"

"No such thing."

"And falls for him."

"Waste of her time. We're always on duty."

"But she never meets him again, because he's always on duty."

"No, no. That's unreal. If he was stupid she wouldn't want him, and if not he'd come visiting."

"I'll have to change it all." She sighed.

"You've just made it up," he accused her. "There's probably a law about that."

Then she laughed, a delightful tinkle, which she suppressed abruptly, because she was basically very unhappy.

"What *is* it about, then?"

"It's supposed to be funny."

"There you are, then. There's nothing funny involving the police."

"I suppose not."

"Unless something nasty happens, we're not interested."

"Then I can't use a policeman," she decided.

"Unless he insists on calling."

"Yes."

"With a warrant, say."

"Charging what?"

"I dunno. That he gets only one laugh per visit."

Smiling, she turned away. "Can I make you a cup of tea?"

"Heavens, I'm on duty, and I've wasted too much—"

"Wasted?"

"My inspector would call it that."

117

"Oh yes. You came for something . . . official, was it?"

"Yes."

"It's about the raffle, isn't it?"

My, she was quick. "It is."

"What?"

"Well – there was an attack last night on one of the winners. Number one."

"Mr Moreton?"

"Yes. So we're going round warning all the others. But your friend's in hospital, so we can protect her there. Not that she's in any danger . . . but you have to, sort of—"

"You're getting yourself all tied up," she told him kindly.

He drew a breath. "Put it like this, then. It's conceivable that any of the last three might be dead furious about the top three, and have a go at 'em."

"A go?"

"Yes. It was an open razor. As I was saying, *that* possibility you can accept. Or, I suppose, that any of the top three, scared of what might happen, might have a go at the bottom three. But *nobody* will want to have a go at number four, who'd have been number four however they'd been drawn. So your friend's in no danger, really."

"I'm so pleased."

"But we're doing this warning bit."

"What a fascinating life you do lead."

"Yes," he agreed. "We meet interesting people. Look – I'd better be off. Duty calls."

"Just like that book."

"Which was imaginary."

"I could be imagining this, now. This very second."

"Then I'll have to pop up again in the next chapter."

On this, he was out of the door in a flash, recognising a good exit line when he heard himself saying one.

118

It was therefore with a buoyant bounce to his step that he swept into the inspector's office.

"So there you are!" snarled Tomkins.

"Sir."

"And take that smirk off your face, stand to attention when I'm talking to you and tell me what the hell you think you've been doing."

"Had a successful day, sir."

"Successful!" Tomkins ran a palm over his face.

"Establishing a rapport—"

"I didn't ask you a question."

"Sir."

"In what way successful?"

"I have been establishing a rapport with the persons involved, sir." The brooding, murderous eyes told him nothing encouraging. "It's known as public relations, sir."

"Ha!" barked Tomkins derisively.

"They talked to me, sir, as man to man."

"Even the women?"

Tony thought about that. "Yes, sir. Except Lucinda Porter, and she's in St Mary's Hospital. You'd better put a guard on—"

"Will you allow *me* to make the decisions?"

"Certainly, sir."

"I am now making a decision. Are you hearing me? Don't answer that." He pointed a finger menacingly. "You will now go off duty."

"Thank you, sir."

"For one hour. Go home and get some food in you, get a good thick coat to your back and tell your mother you'll see her with the dawn. Understand? You can continue your rapport with your friends on the barge, but you will not be seen – not by anybody. And you will watch, through the hours of the night, and you will do so sitting on one of the gates of the lock, so that if you fall asleep you'll fall somewhere that'll wake you up. I am putting you, Finch, in a position of danger. It could well be that *you* will be called on to place yourself between an attacker and his intended victim, Lucifer Hartington. And I do not expect him to receive one scratch. Do I make myself crystal clear?"

"You do indeed, sir."

"Then get on with it. One hour."

"Permission to speak, sir."

"Speak."

"Catterick has an alibi."

"He has?"

"He was with a woman from six to midnight."

"How very original. What woman?"

"He didn't say, sir."

"And so," said Tomkins, his voice sinking to a whisper, awed as he was by the extent of his own control, "I'm to accept that you've warned him off, that no visit of mine could possibly be successful. Because you couldn't help yourself asking—"

"Oh no, sir. I didn't ask him. I told him I didn't want to know."

"*You* didn't want to know?"

"Exactly, sir. So he naturally—"

"Finch—"

"Sir?"

"Leave this room. Say not one more word. Turn about and leave, not even saying sir. Now!"

Tony turned and left. No gratitude, he thought. The man hadn't the faintest idea of how to run a section.

Fortunately, his mother had a beef stew that'd been maturing all day. Unfortunately, she insisted he should wear his huge, thick greatcoat with two cardies and his jacket beneath it, about three yards of muffler and the woolly hat she'd knitted in the lonely hours. Trussed up, he complained, "But I might have to *run*!"

"Where?" she challenged.

"Away."

"Good lad. You don't want to Put Your Nose Into Other People's Troubles."

Then she thrust him out into the night.

He had difficulty bending enough to get in his car, but eventually managed to trundle off towards the Buckled Arrow. He noted the dark shape of a car just inside a farmer's gate, a hundred yards short of the pub, and another one way back in the other direction. A cigarette, not too expertly couched in a palm, glowed briefly from a corner of the car park as he drew into the only empty slot, and when he looked over the low wall he thought he saw another dark shadow, strangely shaped, like a courting couple, on the bank the other side of the canal.

That, he decided, was probably DS Andy Spinks and WDC Ethel Parker, who wasn't too particular. It was no doubt a good cover, but it didn't seem it could be maintained throughout the night. He dumped most of his upper wear on the back seat of the car and went in for a drink. Another hour until chucking-out time. How better than this to keep an eye on them?

And there they were, Lucifer and Charlie, amongst a crowd of laughing mates.

"Here he is now," cried Lucifer and when Tony joined them he explained, "Was just telling 'em about this afternoon."

They gave a little cheer and slapped him on the back. Good cover, this, he thought. Couldn't be watching 'em closer. But it had to finish some time, though they were the last out. They said their goodnights. He got in his car and drove away, then turned around and drifted back, so quietly and gently that he caught sight of another crafty drag of another poorly-handled cigarette.

He clothed himself for the night, though not so securely

as his mother had intended. Then quietly he moved along the towpath away from the barge until he reached the lock. There, not accepting the inspector's suggestion, he sat down with his back against the square lever of one of the gates and became no more than a lump of darkness. It is movement that's so revealing. He moved nothing, as the mist began to rise from the canal and the chill of it spread into his bones.

The light inside the barge cabin remained on for a while. Lucifer would be using Calor gas and mantles, Tony decided. Then, a little after eleven-thirty, it fell to a dim and nearly indiscernible glow.

The really difficult part of the night had now begun.

Inside the cabin, Lucifer had reached up and turned the mantle down to a bare minimum. He knew the danger, in such close confines, of moving around in the dark. He, in pyjamas, and Charlie, still in his T-shirt and jeans, were lying on bunks, one each side. But Charlie seemed restless. Lucifer could hear him stirring.

"What's up, son?"

"Can't sleep."

"What's crabbing you?"

"Dunno. Yes I do. I forgot to tell Ma I was stayin' here."

"Will she worry?"

"You'd never guess."

"There's a phone box just down the road."

"Y' don't think we've got a phone!"

"No. Perhaps not."

"And . . . the bike. There's that."

"We locked it up."

"Hah! I don't mean that." Charlie levered himself onto an elbow. "D'you think he was kiddin', that copper?"

"What about?"

"Said he was doing close to the ton. An' it's not run in yet."

"Of course he was kidding."

"I dunno. The engine sounded a bit rough to me."

Lucifer, who usually put his head down and remembered no more, was, by this time, showing distinct signs of impatience. "Then I'll tell you what you do. You cover both things in one go."

"How's that?"

"You take the bike and go and tell your mother what's on, and when you come back you don't make any sound at all, 'cause I'll be asleep. Not a sound."

Charlie was off the bunk in a second. "Like a mouse."

"The keys're on that nail."

"I know. Thanks Pop."

True to his honest intention, and practising on the way out, Charlie moved with soft caution. Tony saw a minimal variation in the light as the door opened and shut. He heard nothing. He decided he'd imagined it, but nevertheless a shadow did move up the ramp. Alert now, he sat more upright. It could be one of them going to patronise the outside gents in the pub yard. The shadow moved in that direction, so it seemed it could be a good guess. The requisite interval occurred, then the night was split apart by the sudden burst into life of the BMW's engine and the blinding glare as the headlight shot across the car park.

"Hell!" he said, now on his feet.

There was only one person on the bike, of that he was certain. It swooped out onto the road and turned in the direction of the town.

"Bloody hell!" said Tony.

The engines of the two cars out on the road burst into life and their lights flashed on. A red spark flew across a corner of the car park and one of the watchers ran to scramble into the second of the cars. The shape on the far side of the canal disentangled itself and began to scramble, there being no towpath that side of the canal, in opposite

123

directions. There was a splash and a scream. The other half of the shape returned and there was an interchange of urgent and violent dialogue.

Then the night was still. Tony stood, motionless, wondering what move to make. He put his radio to his ear and pressed the receive button.

". . . which one, you damned fool?"

"It's him, sir."

"Which him?" Tomkins croaked.

"The one with the bike."

"Keep with him. Are you getting this, Beta Seven?"

Tony switched off. The one with the bike? That was a great help.

In the cabin, Lucifer, Ethel's scream having penetrated his dreams, sat up in his bunk. He reached and turned up his mantle. Tony began to move along the towpath.

Charlie, leading the motorcade, was becoming aware that two police cars were pursuing him and that a third had shot from a side road, nearly ditching the other two. Charlie took exception to such treatment. He hadn't done anything. What the hell did they think they were playing at? A sensible man would have stopped and demanded an answer to this question, but this was Charlie. Assuming that his mother could wait a few more minutes, Charlie decided to give them a run for their money and began to take evasive action. A BMW bike can leave most patrol cars standing. It can, too, take narrow side turnings and winding lanes at a speed that would leave most car drivers stranded in ditches. This he did, and this they did.

But Tomkins, furious that somebody he was trying to protect was evading his attentions, called in cars from all directions. The night was cleft by flashing blue lights and screaming sirens, with, somewhere ahead and never where he was expected to be, Charlie checking Tony's statement that he'd almost broken the ton. In the distance, the night was hideous with the noise. Along the canal it was silent, with WDC Ethel Parker weeping on the wet grass and DS Andy Spinks trying to get his radio to work.

But Tony, sticking strictly to his brief, was slowly easing himself along the towpath towards the barge. One person had left it, therefore one person remained behind. There was, as far as he could see it, no reason for relaxing his concentration on the job in hand. The barge was now fully lit, but nobody had emerged. With his eyes on it, he moved into the deeper shadows where the ramp rose at his left shoulder.

Afterwards, he said that he remembered movement. There was also an impression that a shape was wearing a ski mask, but by that time he was too late to do anything about it. Something very hard hit him on the forehead, just above his left eye, and with a groan he collapsed on the towpath. Two seconds later there was a glare of light as the cabin door opened, then it was gone as it closed.

Andy Spinks raised his head. Later, he swore there had been a shout of, "You!" Then shadows chased across the side windows of the cabin. There was a howl of pain and thumping sounds. The trouble was that Andy was the wrong side of the canal, which meant he had to run along to the lock in order to cross over, then back down the opposite towpath. He found that his torch worked, switched it on and scrambled past Ethel Parker, who sensed rather than heard that something was happening and stumbled after him. The torch revealed Tony just before Andy tripped over him. He didn't pause, but made a leap onto the barge, where he flung open the cabin door.

He stopped. The torch fell out of his hand. He tried to tell Ethel to stay away but he was too late. Her screams echoed out into the night. Andy groaned, and his legs gave way.

On the towpath, Tony stirred.

Chapter Ten

Wednesday, 27 September

The superintendent massaged his forehead wearily. "Let's go through it again. There must be something we missed."

Tomkins groaned. This botch-up was going to be recorded against him and he knew it. He was in no mood for placid and detailed discussion, but wanted to go somewhere and thump somebody. He had a long list in his mind and it would take him some time before he worked through it.

"The attack was savage, sir. Brutal. Hartington was dead before Sergeant Spinks even reached the barge and there was nothing he could do. Wisely, I think, he didn't even enter the cabin. I mean – it was obvious, with blood everywhere."

"The assailant, then, covered in blood – he must have been – managed to evade a complete net of cars—"

"I had them back there in minutes, sir."

"—and leave not one trace—"

"He left the razor, sir."

"And you find that in some way encouraging? You surprise me. Your men have found no traces of blood anywhere outside the barge—"

"Still looking, sir."

"*Anywhere* off the barge! Not a trace. So the assumption is that he jumped into the canal and waded across, or along, until he could get ashore and creep away. To somewhere he had a car so deeply hidden that nobody spotted it or can find a trace of it."

Tomkins drew a breath. "I *did* explain, sir. That field the other side of the canal – climb the slope and down the other side, and there's a lane—"

"Yes, yes," cut in the super impatiently. "But you're missing the point, Inspector. If our man used the canal in order to get clear, why the devil didn't he take his damned razor with him? We'd never have found it in the canal."

The razor, bearing the engraved day Tuesday, had been found inside the cabin, wiped clean and with a piece of bloodstained tissue around it. The attack had been timed, both by Tony Finch and Andy Spinks, as a few minutes before midnight.

Tomkins made no attempt to answer. He'd thrashed his mind almost to unconscious submission and had come up with nothing.

"Damn it all, Inspector!" the super burst out. "There's a man, knowing he had only seconds to work in . . . he'd seen the cars withdrawn, but he must've been waiting there a long while and seen there was other observation."

"I shall be having words with the sergeant, sir."

"As I say," continued the super heavily, not interested what the inspector did to Sergeant Spinks so long as it was painful, "he was working to seconds, and yet he took time out to wipe the razor clean of prints when he could've simply taken it with him. Why? Answer me that, Inspector."

"I've got no answer, I'm afraid."

"Hmm! Catterick?"

"Spent the evening wandering the streets and getting generally canned, then he went home."

"Stayed there?"

"I had a man in the street and one at the rear."

"Hmph!" The super had lost all faith in the inspector's men. "That Greene woman?"

"Not a woman's crime, surely, sir."

"I understand she's a strong and purposeful woman – and she was the one who'd have won the bike if the raffle had been run as any sane man would run it."

Tomkins was tired, tired of arguing, even tired of sighing. So he didn't sigh. "She spent the evening in the Plucked Goose with Ada Follett and her friends who saw her home afterwards. I'm informed she was in no condition to go out again that evening."

"Yes . . . well . . . This Ada Follett?"

"An elderly lady, sir. Quite harmless."

"It doesn't follow. My mother-in-law . . . never mind. I just hope you're right."

"I am, sir."

The super suppressed an inclination to comment that it would be the first time. "And the others?"

"Lucinda Porter is seriously ill in hospital."

"Well, well. The only one who had nothing to gain or lose from the balls-up of the raffle – and she happens to be tucked-away in hospital."

"She's not, sir, what you'd call a serious contender."

The super frowned. "And the others?"

"There *are* no others."

"There's Arthur Moreton."

"But he's been attacked himself!"

"Well now!" The super smiled thinly. "Has he? That's the point. No blood, Inspector. Two buttons cut from his coat and a clean razor left behind. He could've done that himself. Nobody saw anything except himself. Think about it."

"But he, of all of them, would have no motive."

"And there, you see, you're wrong. That raffle win has landed him in no end of trouble. I don't think he's out of it yet, either."

The inspector sat back and shook his head stubbornly. The man was insane. "All the same—"

"No motive, you say, when we've clearly been looking for somebody who's stark, raving bonkers! *He's* about reached that."

"I'm not having it."

"Are you not, Inspector? If I remember rightly, I and not you am the one to have it or not to have it. So – you will consider it. Understand?"

"Sir."

"And the other one?"

"*What* other one, for—"

"Bert Harris."

"The mayor! But he *did* the blasted draw."

"Exactly. And no doubt, at this very moment, he's wishing he hadn't. And perhaps he's trying to wipe out all evidence of it."

The inspector was a stolid man, set irremovably in the cogs of a machine. He was not imaginative, not given to flights of fancy. In his experience, even the nuttiest of fruitcakes had *some* underlying motive, even if it was only sex and all its ramifications. As far as he was concerned, the super himself was proving to be just about as nutty as they come. And . . . *his* motive? To make life miserable for his only able officer – Detective Inspector Tomkins himself. One person who needed watching was the super! Tomkins narrowed his eyes and smoothly agreed. Always agree with them.

"Of course, sir. Excellent idea. I'll put it all in train at once."

"Hmph!" said the super suspiciously. "Yes. You do that. But . . ." He held up a palm. "Don't upset poor old Bert."

"Of course not, sir."

This task, had they but known it, was being planned for them, and efficiently, by Llewellyn Pugh, at that very moment.

"And, oh . . . one more thing," said the super. "Don't

forget – it's Wednesday, and if our friend the slasher keeps to routine, Wednesday's razor's on the cards for this evening. And *that*, I believe, is Charles Pierce. I don't have to tell you, we'll need a close watch on him. Sit right inside his pockets if necessary."

The inspector looked through him, nodded, and left. Charlie Pierce was going to be a problem.

The previous night, more accurately early that Wednesday morning, because it was then after midnight, Charlie had been having the time of his life. Once into the centre of town, he could demonstrate to the full the advantages of a motorcycle.

At that time the streets were virtually deserted, the shopping precincts brooding and silent. Nothing could have suited Charlie better. Pedestrians only, it was, during the day, when it would've been thronged. Now it presented itself as empty and irresistible.

This portion of the town was the oldest. Here, on the sight now occupied by the Rimfire Tower, was originally a collection of forges and blacksmiths. In those days there were none of these nicely checkered paving slabs that Charlie could weave his patterns around. Narrow alleys, or folds, there were – and these had remained. They made neat short cuts from one precinct to the next. Four feet wide they were, too, in places. This meant not tackling them too slowly in case you got a bit of a wobble. Charlie took them fast whilst behind him the police cars practised their 180° sliding turns, which required an expert use of the handbrake and a rapid rotation of the steering wheel. Really, there was room for only one car at a time for this sort of thing, when in general there were three at a time. Charlie learned to estimate this by the sound of impacts from behind him.

But they cornered him at the Temperance Fountain, its name relating not to abstinence – with which the town would have no truck at all – but to the practice, originally on this very spot, of tempering steel in a second bath, the formula of which was a deadly secret. Charlie's naive thought was that three cars would circulate behind him indefinitely, but he hadn't counted on three others joining the roundabout in the opposite direction.

He stopped. They all got out and stood and stared at him. It was unnerving, but their instructions had been to keep him under observation, which they were now doing. That he turned out to be Charlie Pierce and not Lucifer Hartington made not one whit's difference to the situation. They observed him. Menacingly, perhaps, but with no movement towards violence.

The situation remained static for some moments, until all the car radios began to crackle together, incomprehensibly to Charlie, but policemen seem to be able to understand this crackle-speak. They all dived for their cars, leaving Charlie shouting, "Heh! What gives?"

The last one out shouted, "The barge," and Charlie did his own bit of diving.

He'd passed the tailing car before they reached the square, was up with the leaders by the time they were blasting past the new frontage of the brewery, and, whatever they tried, was in the lead long before they hit the first tree-lined road.

Fortunately, two cars from the opposite direction were already at the canal. The four occupants eventually managed to restrain Charlie, but not before he'd fought his way to the barge and had seen what was there. Then he let out a terrible howl at the sky and after that was like a limp baby.

They had him, mumbling, in the back of one of the cars for an hour. The attending police doctor jabbed him with something that put him three-quarters asleep, and because he seemed distressed about the bike they went and locked it in its shed and clamped the keys inside his fist, not at all pleased that he should be showing more concern for the bike than for Lucifer.

But nobody ever understood Charlie. This was his contact with his friend. He'd never had a friend, not one he could relax with, talk to and depend on. Now, half conscious, he was realising it worked both ways. Now it was Lucifer who was depending on Charlie, to root out the lousy, stinking bastard who'd done that to him, and tear his arms out as a starter. So Charlie clutched at the keys like a lifeline. Something of Lucifer.

They took him home in the bleak, damp dawn. His mother, roused from her bed and in a panic, kept saying, "What's he done? What's he done?"

"Nothing, Mrs Pierce," said one of the drivers, commendably in view of the damage to his car. "He's had a shock. Just needs rest. He's all right."

But Charlie wasn't all right. He slept a restless hour in the old, broken easy chair, which was the most comfortable in the house, put down a huge breakfast at ten o'clock, and was out on the town at eleven. He had to think. He thought best when moving. He had to work out how he was going to catch that slime, that stinking . . . And only filthy words would come to him. He trembled all over with suppressed violence and with nowhere to release it. Then, strangely for him, he found he had to look for places he could sit down from time to time.

Tony spotted him, sitting on one of the benches around the square. Tony himself wasn't a hundred per cent. The police doctor had examined him, put a plaster on his forehead, checked his eyes and put a stopper to his activities. Sick leave. Take it easy for a couple of days or so. See his own doctor if he got giddy spells.

So Tony, too, was on the streets, mainly because he was fed up with being told it Just Served Him Right. And that violence was In His Blood.

In the square he spotted Charlie, on the bench in front of Prince Albert's statue, the horse still with a pink nose, and at once went to sit with him. They had something in common: they had failed to protect Lucifer.

"Hi!"

"Hi!"

Together, for two minutes, they sat silent, then, as though triggered by the same emotional impulse, they spoke together.

"If it hadn't been for me—"

"I ought've known better—"

They stopped and looked at each other. Tony said, "How about a coffee?"

"Nar! Not coffee."

Tony knew what was good for shock. "Brandy?"

"Nar! Not brandy."

"Then what?"

"Nothin'. Don't want nothin'."

They sat on. Then Charlie began talking and Tony sat and listened. Charlie's sense of guilt was stronger than Tony's and he had to unload it.

"Left him! I bloody well left him on his own—"

And so on. And on. Charlie, whatever his former failings and delinquencies, had never felt any guilt. He'd not even felt guilty about not feeling guilt. It had always been outside circumstance that had intervened in his life. This was the first time that he, and he alone, had to take responsibility, and the experience was shattering because the end result had been shattering.

Tony listened in silence. Wisely, he made no attempt to dispute Charlie's self-criticism, instinct telling him that he'd be asking for a fist in the face. So he waited until Charlie mumbled to a stop, then asked:

"Do I take it you'd like to get your hands on this slasher?"

133

"You ain't bin listenin'!"

"Oh yes I have. Every word. And you're forgetting something, Charlie. Something I've already told you."

"Oh no I ain't."

"It's Wednesday, Charlie. That's you. The man who was Wednesday."

Charlie, not having even heard of G.K. Chesterton, stared at him.

"This madman," explained Tony, "seems to be working his way through the list of prizewinners of that raffle. Using razors, Charlie, that've got the days engraved on the back edges. Monday's razor for Arthur Moreton, Tuesday's for Lucifer. You're number three. And it's Wednesday. Think about it."

Charlie's brain stirred. Then he got it. "You mean – me – tonight?"

"He'll be coming for you, Charlie, probably after dark."

Charlie curled his hand into a huge fist and stared at it. "Well . . . what d'you know!"

"So you wait, and he'll come to you. And I'll be there—"

"He's mine!"

Tony pointed to his forehead. "I got a bit, too."

Charlie considered this. "Then you can watch."

"Sure, Charlie. Watch fair play. No in-fighting, now. Good, clean stuff. No hitting below the belt, no butting."

"You kiddin'?" Charlie stared at him. "Yeah, you're kiddin'." And he grinned. "Partners?"

Tony eyed the extended hand suspiciously. It was Charlie's only method of sealing bargains. He took it gingerly. Charlie squeezed gently.

"Tonight," they said together. Then they went for that coffee.

The sacrifice, for Tony, had been severe. He'd had in mind the possibility of visiting Madge that evening, and, being off-duty, continuing with chapter two in a more leisurely and protracted manner.

As it happened, he'd have missed her anyway, as Madge was at the hospital all that evening, her friend Lucinda having taken a turn for the worse, and she didn't return to her room until very late. So that the watcher in the alley opposite saw nothing but two dark windows all the evening, and when one of them eventually lit up it was the wrong one.

That afternoon, Wednesday being a slack day for the town clerk, Llewellyn Pugh gave himself a half day off and drove out to visit the absent mayor. Whatever his views on the mayor's mental equipment, the fact that he *was* the mayor required that he should be kept in touch. Lurking behind the concern was the thought that, properly handled, Bert (Slasher) Harris might be persuaded to tender his resignation.

Tina showed him into the sun room. No sun in it now, no cheerful rays. Bert sat slumped in his swivel recliner, a sturdy table at his right hand, and was working his way through a bottle of Amontillado.

"And try to cheer him up," she instructed Pugh, not really understanding the situation.

"Oh, it's you," said Bert.

"You look peaky."

"Pull up a chair and a glass and join me," offered Bert.

Pugh did so. He preferred his sherry sweeter, but never mind.

Here, in this more relaxed atmosphere, they could talk as intimates, if not actually friends. Formality melted away. It was Bert and Clow, which was as close as Bert could get to the back-of-the-throat Llew.

"I tell you what," said Bert, after he'd been brought up-to-date with mayoral business, "I've been thinking of leaving the district."

"You can't do that, Bert. Not now."

"Why not, pray?"

"The police wouldn't let you."

"Why the hell—"

"Now look at it. Don't go off half-cocked. Look at it. You're a suspect."

"A what?" Bert coughed on a throat full of sherry.

"There is a theory that you, having made such a monumental cock-up of the raffle, might want to remove every one of those innocent prizewinners."

The recliner thumped as Bert tried to sit up. "Where'd you get this?"

"It's impossible to function as a town clerk without knowing what goes on. I've got my contacts. This is my town, Bert. Yes, mine! And I love it. So . . . I have to know."

"It's not fair."

"What isn't?"

"Picking on me."

"Bert . . ." Llew sighed. "It wasn't fair, the way you drew that raffle."

Bert was silent. He stared sightlessly out at his bedraggled shrubs. "Listen," he said at last. "I'll tell you a secret. I didn't *draw* them backwards, I only *called* them backwards. For the suspense, for the build-up."

"You got a build-up right enough. And I don't know what you mean."

"Me'n Tina – the wife – we did it together. That drum full of screwed-up tickets was here the night before. In this house. That was when we drew 'em, and carefully noted the winners and put secret little marks on them. Then, on the day, she'd got 'em in her left hand and only *pretended* to take 'em out of the drum. Moreton *was* drawn first, and Hartington second, and so on. It was all legal and above-board."

136

Pugh clutched at his head, then reached over and tossed down his sherry, reached over again and refilled his glass. Then he crashed his fist on the table with a terrible and shattering bang and shouted out, "You bloody fool! You doddering, stupid unmitigated idiot!"

"It's bad, isn't it? And don't smash the table, for God's sake!"

"D'you realise—"

"Completely."

"We can't even make it public. They wouldn't believe it. Nobody's going to believe it. They'd probably tear you apart – the police, I mean – but nobody'd ever believe it."

"That's why I thought of leaving. Canada, perhaps—"

"Oh no you don't. We've got a lunatic around with a box of razors, and you know you can't reason with *them*—"

"Not my fault."

"Of course it's your bloody fault. You triggered him. You set him off."

"That's not fair."

"Lord help me! Fair! It's not a matter of fair, you double-dyed goon. There's been one attack and one murder, so far. Do I have to tell you that?"

"Murder . . ." whispered Bert. "Come on now, Llew—"

"Hartington was virtually slashed to death last night."

"Not to do with the raffle," Bert jabbered. "Something personal. Somebody didn't like him."

"It was the Tuesday razor, Bert."

Bert swallowed. "A nutter, then. A plain, raving nutter."

"If so, you turned him on. Oh sure, probably crazy, but even the really wild ones've got something behind it, in their heads. Something. All you've done is touched a chord, and he's off on his pilgrimage."

"I wish you wouldn't—"

"And I *know* this!" cried Pugh, thumping the table again for emphasis.

"Don't *do* that. And what've you got there? It can't be a normal hand."

"No," agreed Pugh, whipping the glove from his right hand.

Bert stared, eyes protruding, at a hand of clean, shining steel. The shape of a hand, it was, but with only the thumb operative.

"How the devil—"

"I'll tell you," said Pugh. "I'm proud of this. Proud. You and the Fifty-Seven Club! Oh yes, I heard about that too. Fifty-seven black balls. Ha! But there's another and much more secret club than that. Exclusive. Membership's been hereditory since about 1720. And I'm in it. Six of us, and I'm one of 'em. D'you want to hear? If you hear this, and whisper one word, we'll have you in the boiling oil tank at the factory."

Bert paled but he nodded.

"It's like the Benedictines," explained Pugh, leaning back with his glass in his good hand. "Not that lot up at Crécy Manor – the real ones. You know . . . the secret components known only to half a dozen or so monks, one for each ingredient, in the formula for their special liqueur. They pass it on to the next one on their deathbeds and nobody's supposed to know the complete formula. Well – that's how it was with Ockam steel. A special tempering bath. You know how it's done. Red-hot, then into water to harden it, then red-hot and into a tempering bath. That's oil, but Ockam steel had a special additive. Six special additives. Still has. Only Ockam steel achieves that special fine edge to a razor. And each bit was known only to one man, who passed it on to his eldest son, and so on. Are you with me?"

"Fascinating," said Bert, who couldn't see what the fuss was about.

"And then, about 1950 it was, we had one of those crazy murderers on the loose. This one used a shotgun, though, and he couldn't aim straight to save his life, but he did a good amount of damage while he was at it. And every one of the victims was the eldest son of the members of Club Six, as it's always been called. Only the members knew this, because it's a secret club."

"You said that."

"And *they* worked out who was doing it, and stopped him by confiscating his shotgun. To this day the police think it was a madman, but the members of Club Six knew who it was. He committed suicide later."

"Poor chap. They told you this?"

"And *they* knew the motive."

"Is it a club secret?"

"To you, Bert, no," said Pugh, who'd put down more than he'd realised of the sherry. "It was my grandad."

Bert stared at him.

"My grandad, you see, hadn't got an eldest son to pass it on to. He hadn't got any sons at all. Two hundred years it'd been going on and he was the first to break the pattern. Only had one child, a girl. My mother. And Grandad couldn't stand the shame, so he thought he'd even things out by removing all the other eldest sons . . . as simple as that. Poor Grandma, she wasn't much good at having sons. One daughter. My mother." He unwisely refilled his glass. "Plenty of Grandad's sons around the village, of course, but they didn't count. The Pughs have always been highly sexed." He raised his glass and toasted himself.

"Of course, Grandad was disgraced," he went on, when it was obvious Bert wasn't going to comment. "Dismissed from Club Six. And my mother said, what about me? Meaning me, not her, of course, though between you'n me, she'd have done it herself like a shot. So Grandad took me along and I was elected. Died happy after that, he did, poor old bugger. But me, I was only twelve, because we'd jumped a generation. An' it was a man's job. Every month, first minute of the month we did it . . . do it. One minute after midnight. I'll tell you. It's a secret. We bring along – each of us – a gallon of our own secret formula. I don't know what it is that any of the others bring. Everybody knows mine."

He seemed about to weep over this. Bert eyed him cautiously.

"I don't really want to know, Llew."

"No, no . . . but we're friends. Bosom friends. What I haveta do is go into a pub and take in eight or nine pints. My only secret is the brand of the beer. A gallon, and one pint in reserve, sort of. Then we all stand round the tempering tank – it's set in the floor, see – an' they all pour their own gallons in, an' nobody knows what they are. Then I put my gallon in – and everybody knows. It's not damn fair. Not fair at all, I say."

"The hand, Llew. Get to the hand."

"Yes. At the beginning. There was me, a little boy, Bert, a little scrawny lad. An' I hadda get down eight pints. Eight, Bert. Not fair. So they let me do it one pint at a time. Y' know, drink a bit, wait a bit—"

"Must have taken ages."

"Oh it did, it did. An' the very first time . . . that last pint . . . Y'know, Bert, I was just a little tiddly. Never a beer man, I wasn't. Wine. I'm a wine man." He beamed at his newly full glass. "An' I fell in that bloody tank, an' they got the crane, an' something happened 'cause it's always been a happy crowd, Bert – an' somehow I lost a hand. Y' see. You can cry if you like. Little Llew, he lost his hand! So they made me a steel one. Big honour that was, Bert, an' they kept on doing it till I was all growed up, and there it is, before your very eyes."

"Why couldn't you have got a proper artificial one?" Bert grumbled.

"Because this is a steel town, Bert. Because I'm its town clerk, and proud of it. And proud of this hand."

"Well . . . cover it up, Llew, there's a good chap."

Llew put the glove back on over it. As though this action marked a significant point in the proceedings, he rose to his feet to leave. Paused. Bent over Bert.

"But you see the significance, Bert?" On his feet he'd become quite eloquent and fluent again.

"No."

"We've got another one here. Somebody's got something on his mind. So if you come out with the truth of the raffle, then it's all going to stop. And the police'll have nothing to go on, no trap they can set, nothing. And a murderer'll be wandering around loose. No Bert, you keep quiet, me old mate. Besides, you'd get skinned alive. Ha! Ha! Ha!"

Then he left. Bert was no happier than when he'd arrived.

Chapter Eleven

Wednesday, 27 September (cont.)

As an evening, it was a flop. Virtually nothing happened, except that Paul Catterick left home, or rather was persuaded to leave. And Charlie Pierce spent the evening and half the night baying filthy names at the moon, and not succeeding in drawing out the recipient of them. Tony shadowed him, in sight, in sound being too distant, as Charlie had a loud voice. Ada and her friends collected carriers full of bottles of stout, and spent the evening breaking them – after they were empty, of course – and therefore were not at the Plucked Goose when Esmeralda arrived and began to drink herself into a stupor. A lady alone in such a pub, and gradually becoming more and more newted, is an obvious beckoning beacon to the male patrons. Esmeralda, however, was not what she seemed. She fought. Two very kind but weary young men in dark blue uniforms collected her and she spent the night in a cell at the Station.

And Madge's second chapter progressed not at all, only in her mind, because she was at St Mary's Hospital from seven o'clock that evening onwards.

Paul arrived home, as he always thought of it, at his usual time of six o'clock, having caught his usual bus at his usual stop in the same old round square. Life, he was beginning to realise, was one continuous drawn-out bore. Strange that he hadn't really noticed that before . . .

Hilda was not there to welcome him, as had been the practice, in the hall or more usually emerging from the kitchen with a teacloth or the like, to frown at him. But Dennis was. This was unusual, as Dennis worked in an estate agency's office in Birmingham, which meant a protracted and wearying drive home at peak hour.

"Dennis?"

"Hello."

"Got the push, have you?"

Dennis didn't even smile. Now, that was very much more unusual. Dennis, two years younger than Paul, had absorbed his personality from childhood. They understood each other completely. Such a remark, straightfaced from Paul, would have produced, normally, an easy and confident grin from Dennis, he being that much more outgoing. Now he just nodded and said, "Come in the front room a minute."

"Hilda? Where's Hilda?"

"Lying down."

"Is she all right?"

"Yes, yes. Come in here and sit down, Paul."

Paul sat uneasily on the edge of a chair. "What is it?"

Dennis shook his head and stared at his feet. "It's difficult—"

"She's been strange lately," Paul remembered.

"Paul," said Dennis, grabbing the lead with both hands and hanging on, "you're a real fool, you know. We all love you, but you never see anything until you trip over it."

"She's going to have a baby! Well . . . that's just great."

"She's not going to have a baby. You could say she's already got somebody to take all her time up, all her thoughts and plans . . . oh Christ!"

"What's this?"

"You, Paul, blast it. And you just sail through everything

143

and never see. You! It was you she always wanted, you damn fool. I've been the substitute. No . . ." He held up his hand. "I'm sorry, mate, but it's gone too far. She could've shouted it in your face and you wouldn't have heard. And now . . . out till after midnight with some woman, it's brought it all to a head."

Paul was staring blankly at him, the blood slowly draining from his face. "No . . . Denny lad—"

"She's in love with you, Paul. No getting round it. And she can't live with it – and I can't. One smile from you, one beckoning glance, and you could walk out of here with her on your arm . . . that's what it's come to."

"I can't stay here. Denny, I'll have to leave."

"You've saved me asking." He raised a tiny smile. "Saved me throwing you out – and you're bigger'n me."

"I'll go and pack." Paul was on his feet.

"No rush, Paul, no rush."

"I'll pack a bag. Collect the bigger stuff later. You know. I'll keep in touch. I'll just go'n pack. Lord, I never guessed! Won't take me long, Denny. Just pack one bag." He paused with his hand on the door. Dennis was staring at his feet again. "D'you think I'd better put my head in? Like."

"You *are* a fool, Paul. No. I'll tell her."

Then Dennis simply sat, looking down into the future, which was somewhere down and not up. Somewhere very deep that'd take a hell of a while to haul up.

Paul put his head in. "I'll be off, then. I'll phone you at the office. Okay?"

"Yeah, yeah. Sure. Look after yourself."

Paul, carrying one case, not really certain what he'd tossed into it, walked to the bus stop and journeyed back into town. There, at the Cannon Inn, he booked a room, not sure how long he would be able to afford it. There, too, he got a meal, more from a consideration of stoking up the personal boiler than from any possibility of enjoying it. His brain wouldn't settle, couldn't accept it, was searching round for some explanation of how Hilda could possibly be interested in him, when she had Denny.

Afterwards, in the bar, he sat at a table and discovered a discarded evening paper. As something to occupy his mind, he glanced through the 'flats and apartments to let' column. His intention that evening, he recalled, had been to wander along to the Plucked Goose, just in case Esmeralda had remembered his remark about its becoming his local.

It was the address that caught his eye. 'Desirable ground-floor flat. Suit professional gentleman. Conveniently situated near shopping centre. 3A Foundry Street, Link Green.'

Foundry St, Link Green? Where had he come across that before? Near shopping centre? That was a laugh. It was right in the middle of one of the crummiest districts he could imagine. Nevertheless, it was worth looking at . . . but of course! One of the winners. Lucinda something. Hadn't *that* been number three?

There seemed to be a portent about this coincidence. Fate was tossing him around that evening, so he decided to go along with the trend and go to have a look at it. Why not? Probably no landlord around at this time, but he could look, couldn't he?

This he proceeded to do. Link Green was a mile out of town, but he wanted to walk . . . walk . . . walk.

Through the square, he just missed Charlie, who'd already embarked on his plan. Paul walked on. The district gradually began to deteriorate. There was a short section where they'd begun to renovate the old Georgian terraces. Could be pleasant there, he decided. Further along, they were destroying the terraces that nothing short of this would improve. Then there was a district of high-rise flats. No doubt the council could find him something there, but he hated the idea. In this, he and Madge were of a like mind.

Link Green was shortly for the ball and chain and the

JCB. He stood on the other side of the street and stared across at number three Foundry St 3C, that'd been the address, he suddenly recalled, of that Lucinda woman. Well ... maybe it wouldn't be too bad, up there and well away from it all. But ... 3A. Oh no! There, he would get the full effect of the constant flow of traffic, the consequently always filthy windows and the courting couples mumbling and fumbling on the steps of the deserted basement. Up there, now ... he'd just go and have a look. There was no light in the window of 3C, but one at 3B. He could enquire there.

When he'd climbed the five outside steps, he realised there was a dim light in the entrance hall. He put a hand to the huge knob in the centre of the door and pushed. It opened. He walked on to the checkered tile floor. There was another light in the back, so the basement wasn't entirely deserted. Probably the landlord, or lady, lived in the back, wisely.

He pressed a switch. A dusky light came on at the head of the stairs, these being carpeted, but only just, by a sliver of ancient, possibly green, sacking-like material. At the landing facing him was a door labelled 3B. He walked to it and knocked.

Inside, Madge was preparing herself. She liked to look neat for the hospital, but she needed to call from somewhere the necessary psychological attitude required to face it. The smile, she knew from practice, she could produce at the last moment. It was the attitude of mind that took a long while.

The tap on the door startled her. It just had to be that lovely pink policeman! She swept open the door.

"Oh!" she said.

Not so long ago there had been no male object in sight. Now they were queuing up. Tall and weary, this one was, with quiet and gentle eyes.

"I'm sorry to intrude," he said, half recognising her.

"Oh, you've come . . ." decided Madge, recognising him from the unemployment office.

"Weren't you at the raffle draw—"

"I really couldn't discuss—"

They stopped, staring at each other. Then he smiled a soft smile and suggested, "Shall we start again?"

"Come in for a minute."

But he didn't manage to edge one foot inside. Two shadows appeared, one at each shoulder, in unison put a hand on his arm and another on his shoulder and hauled him back onto the landing.

"Gotcha!" said one of them.

"In the act," said the other.

"Eek!" said Madge. Now there were too many men around.

"Here," said one of them, "you're Paul Catterick, aren't you?"

"Yes."

"There you are then," said the other. "Come'n have a word with the inspector."

"Goodnight, miss," they both said together.

Then they were gone, and Madge closed the door. That, she thought, could well be the shortest love affair on record. Then she giggled, and because there was something nervous in it she realised that Tony Finch's theory about number four prizewinner being safe might not be valid. All the same it was a good story to tell Lucinda. No it wasn't. Lucinda didn't need to know anything at all about the slasher. She'd got enough of her own worries.

Inspector Tomkins was a very tired man, and had been thinking of sneaking off home for an hour or two. But Charlie Pierce was out on the town and things could well be happening at any moment. He was stuck at his desk, phone near his hand and the arrival of Paul Catterick was at least something new.

"What's he done?"

They told him what Paul had done. It was true that he had no folded cut-throat razor anywhere on his person, but Tomkins was nevertheless pleased. Very pleased.

"Now . . ." he said. "You had no alibi for the period from six onwards on Monday night. On that evening Arthur Moreton was attacked."

"Aren't you supposed to charge me or something?" Paul was trying to be aggressive, but he wasn't very good at it.

"We are talking. You needn't say a word, if you don't want to. The moment I believe I can level a charge at you, I'll warn you that anything you say may be taken down, etcetera . . . Until then, we're talking. Do you object to giving me the name and address of the woman you were with?"

"I most certainly do object."

"Very well. And the following evening you got home drunk and went to your room."

"Yes." Paul thought about that. "Not completely crawling drunk. Just not quite merry."

"Very well. But your room, I understand, overlooks an outhouse, and you may not have been as drunk as you claim, so that it would've been possible to climb out, and cross a number of gardens—"

"Inspector, I went to bed."

"And it was reported to me that allegations as to your moral behaviour and sexual activities were made by a lady at the house where you live."

"I'm not there now."

"You're not?"

"I was turfed out this evening."

"Why was that?" Tomkins leaned forward with interest.

And Paul, who'd decided this had to be a joke, said, "Because of my moral behaviour and my sexual proclivities, Inspector. A better word, that, than activities. Don't you think?"

"Don't try to be funny—"

"Though in this case the better word *could* well be activities. Or rather, the lack of them."

"—with me, Catterick."

"Believe me, it's difficult to take you seriously."

"Then I'd advise you to make the effort. Shall I tell you why? You're going to hear, anyway. You have no satisfactory alibi for Monday night's attack on Arthur Moreton, and no satisfactory alibi for the killing of Lucifer Hartington last night."

"He's dead?" Paul stared at him with shocked horror.

"It's all round the town. It's in the evening paper."

"I looked only at the To Let column."

"To let?"

"I told you. I don't live there any more. I'm one of your homeless strays. So I looked in the paper and there it was: to let – at 3A Foundry Street. That's why I was there."

"But," said Tomkins, as smooth as a chrome-plated bear trap, "you *weren't* there."

"And I wasn't at 3C either."

"Ah yes. You know the critical flat number, I notice. How clever of you! What a splendid memory, for anyone who's supposed to be ignorant and innocent."

"Not supposed to be – am."

"Mr Catterick, I am very tired. It's been a hard day. I've a good mind to put you away for the night in one of our cells and start again tomorrow."

"That's a splendid idea. Just let me phone the Cannon Inn and cancel my room. It'll save me a night's money."

Tomkins leaned back in his chair. "Why," he demanded, taking another bite at it, "were you lurking in Foundry Street?"

"I've told you, and I was not lurking."

"Tell me again. Starting with that imaginary evening in a woman's flat."

"Yes, you're right there. This whole thing's come about because of that, when you come to think of it."

"So all we need's a name and address."

"No."

"Start," said Tomkins emptily, "at the beginning again."

And so on. And on. So that eventually Paul was released and came down the stairs two minutes after Esmeralda, charged at the desk with causing a public nuisance, was taken down the stairs to the cells, where the hefty WPC in charge of the female section thought she recognised a kindred soul, slipped into the cell to try it out and retired with a black eye and teeth marks on her hand.

All of which Inspector Tomkins was unaware. He was staring morosely at a report.

The forensic team had very nearly separated the barge into its individual planks. They'd put the results on paper. It didn't please the inspector.

Not one clue as to the slasher's identity had been found. Nothing. Negative. Zero. What had been found, in a set of drawers and a stunted sort of wardrobe, was a pile of initialled Y-fronts, seven silk shirts and nine cotton ones, forty-three ties, some of them bearing the colours of colleges or clubs, forty or so pairs of cotton socks, and six Savile Row suits in fine worsted materials. There were seven pairs of hand-lasted leather shoes. Lucifer Hartington was a mystery man and that mystery had to be solved, even though it probably had nothing at all to do with his death.

Nothing? Andy Spinks had heard the shouted word: You! But this need not have been a cry of recognition. It could have been the preface to a descriptive adjective, though a gentleman so adequately equipped with expensive clothing was unlikely to have used anything stronger than: rotten devil.

But it was enough to necessitate a painstaking journey into the past. It could, after all have been: Hugh.

In a small drawer, which contained expensive cuff links and other sundries, there had been a piece of notepaper. The short paragraph was dated the same evening as his death, and read:

> To Ephraim Potts, Solicitor.
> If anything should happen to me, I want my motorcycle to go to my friend, Charles Pierce. As to the rest, my will to remain as it is.

This was legally binding, the inspector had confirmed. It was signed by Lucifer Hartington above the signatures of two witnesses, since traced as being pub friends. The transaction had taken place during one of Charlie's absences in the gents.

But Ephraim Potts, they'd said when he'd phoned his office, was not available. There, they'd sounded a little cagey. In fact, he was at home, considerably shaken up by a near accident the previous evening, a car having nearly run him down when he'd been taking his after-dinner stroll.

Charlie had not been informed of this development. That would be the duty of Ephraim Potts. But the codicil, as it had to be considered, to Lucifer's will was sent round to Potts's office to await his attention.

Charlie, more than likely, would not have absorbed the information, anyway. He was concentrating on one objective.

Having displayed himself for most of the day on the bench in the square, he had returned there with the falling of darkness, and when Tony found him again he still sat there, but now with a significant difference. Across his chest he had a piece of cardboard dangling on a length of string. On it was crudely lettered:

I AM CHARLIE PIERCE

151

Passers-by, Tony observed, had a tendency to comment, "So what?" Or, "Well, who'd have guessed!"

Tony sat beside him. "You're wasting your time, you know."

"Gerraway from me."

"He's not going to come to you here, Charlie."

"Y' think I'm stoopid? Of course he ain't. But he could see me, couldn't he. An' follow. Then I'll get him."

"That's really clever, Charlie."

"So you bugger off, eh! D'you want him to see you with me?"

"I would not. Think of my reputation."

He got up and strolled away, leaving Charlie to another half an hour of his vigil.

By this time it was as dark as it was going to be. Charlie got to his feet, stretched, tossed his placard into a litter bin and began his tour through the town. From time to time he threw his head back. "I'm Charlie Pierce," he howled. "Where are y'? Come on out." And similar remarks. It was quite clear that he was disturbing the peace, but it would have been counter-productive to arrest him. Six shadows moved with him, not too near, not too far away. Tony was the seventh. He kept his eyes both on Charlie and on the protecting guards. It had occurred to him that one of *them* could be the slasher. Unlikely, perhaps, but there was another possibility; that one of them could be quietly removed in a conveniently dark entrance-way, and the slasher take his place. Everything was possible.

But the most likely was that the slasher, observing the situation, would decide to postpone the event until a later date. It'd be a pity. Wednesday's razor was due that evening. Did they have to watch Charlie right through the next week?

Charlie, too, was becoming adept at evasion techniques. He was combining two advantages in one action, by diving suddenly down narrow and dark alleyways, where his watchers had a tendency to trip over each other in silent pursuit and where the slasher would have the advantage of darkness.

But nothing happened. Charlie tried another tactic. He would fling open the doors of public bars and shout out, "It's Charlie Pierce. Come on out, you bastard."

They didn't care who he was, but there were usually one or two who had doubts as to their paternity and the evening was thus enlivened. After mopping up, Charlie would move on to the next pub.

But even he tired of this, and his footsteps were dragging by the time the beer pumps were covered. By eleven-thirty, he had the streets to himself and silent, apart from his team, who stuck to him stubbornly. At midnight he reached his home, fell into the collapsing chair and croaked for sustenance.

The six watchers went off duty. Six more took up their positions around the house. But it was now after midnight, too late for the Wednesday razor. Tony went home.

In Chamois St, Tanner's Reek, Ada and her two friends had had a busy evening. Not only was there the necessity of first emptying the bottles, but then there was the matter of breaking them.

They sat on the floor in Ada's sitting room, a house brick on the rug between them, one of the blue ones that the builder had missed, holding successive bottles in their right hands by the neck, and smashing them.

The trick was to remove the base end in order to leave a jagged edge, but the difficulty was that these were stout bottles and small. It didn't, as Ada put it, leave you much reach.

Their objective was to produce three perfect specimens, one each, with the necks unharmed to form a good grip and the other end sufficiently off-putting.

"Wine bottles," said Floss eventually.

153

They were sitting around a pile of shattered glass. Ada remarked that the vacuum cleaner would never suck that lot up.

"What about 'em?" asked Connie.

"Got better necks, an' they're bigger."

"We ought to've thought of that," said Ada. "But no. How'd we empty all that wine down us?"

"Empties," Floss explained. "Bill Fisher'll have plenty of empties." Floss was the practical one.

So they trekked back to the Plucked Goose and returned to Ada's to start again.

By the time they had three perfect specimens, the multi-coloured glass fragments on the rug made a very pretty show. Ada hefted a bottle. "I dunno," she said doubtfully.

"Dunno what?" Floss demanded.

"I wouldn't like to use it, not really. It could make a nasty wound, this could."

"We're talkin' about a razor slasher," Connie reminded her.

Ada shook her head. "I think I'll stick to my rasp."

"What rasp?" they both said.

Ada went and fetched it from the knife drawer in the kitchen. "Eric give me this, for when I was at home at night on me own."

"When was you ever at home at night without Eric?" Floss demanded.

"That's it, you see. I never was. So I never used it."

It was a 12 inch steel rasp with a wooden handle on its tang.

"That's a file," Connie told her, nodding.

"No. Files are for steel, so the teeth are tiny. Rasps are for wood, so the teeth are big. Eric told me that."

"What did Eric know about wood?"

"Nothin'. But he knew about rasps. Said they don't like the teeth goin' at 'em."

"Can't say I blame 'em, either," Connie agreed.

So Ada settled for her rasp and the other two on wine bottles. Then all three gathered up the rug and emptied it into the dustbin.

"G'night."

"G'night."

"G'night."

And Chamois Street was silent.

At about the same time Madge was walking home. She was very tired. It had been a long session at the hospital, where they'd moved Lucinda into the Intensive Care ward. Her mind was miles away when she came opposite number 3 Foundry Street, so far away that she nearly walked past it. When a man in a shop doorway spoke to her, she barely jumped.

"Goodnight," he said.

"Oh yes. Goodnight."

He watched her enter the house. Watched until he saw the light go on in 3B, then he turned away and walked the two streets to where he'd left his car.

It had been an uneventful evening all round.

Chapter Twelve

Thursday, 28 September

The day opened mistily. The canal, which had been testing the atmosphere, decided this was just right, and the empty barge at the Buckled Arrow was soon invisible. The River Penk, which, on its way to join the Severn, made a diversion in order to loop around Ockam, was soon shrouded. Lights were on all through the day in the town centre. The evening promised to be ideal for muggers and slashers and the like. Not so good for the evening's indecent exposers, though, as the fog obscured detail.

Just what I needed, thought Detective Inspector Tomkins moodily. First light had produced Detective Chief Superintendent Merryweather from HQ. He'd brought his own weather with him, but it was far from merry.

HQ had decided to send their top CID man to take over. The local superintendent was not pleased, but his protests over the phone had been uninspired. After all, he had the rest of the force in his town to worry about and Tomkins wasn't exactly proving himself to be wonderfully successful.

Tomkins, however, didn't even have the chance to protest. There was the chief super, a great bull of a man, brooding in the office they'd lent him and muttering over the reports he'd been studying. Tomkins sat watching him and waited. It was 10 a.m., and previous attacks had been later, in the evening or night. But he feared that fog out there.

Merryweather pushed aside the reports and raised his head. Thick eyebrows sprouted out all over the place, hair stuck out from his ears and nostrils, and he was quite bald. It was, to say the least, unsettling.

"What's all this cods with lists of prizewinners and bloody engraved razors?" he asked heavily, wearily.

Tomkins tried to explain about the significance of the Ockam razors and their philosophical connection with the spirit of the town, which had been upset by the inverted raffle draw. And how the seven winners were clearly linked with the days of the week, and how . . .

Merryweather held up a palm. He'd worked throughout the county, in a large number of towns, and every one of them had claimed a special distinction. All were better than the others. Every one had something more different from all the other differences. To Merryweather they were all the same, filled with the same percentage of villains and perverts and nutters in general. He had no time for all this theoretical clap-trap. He therefore held up his hairy hand, almost blanking off the window.

"Stop."

"Sir?"

"We're not going to waste time on prissy psychology. We catch him, we ask him why he's done it. Then we try him and he gets sent to a mental crew to look at, and in the end they let him out again. It's pure routine."

"If you'd allow me—"

"This is what you do. You put a protective net round every one of them—"

"Tried it, sir. They won't keep still."

"Then arrest 'em, and put 'em into protective custody."

"I'd have a riot—"

"Not you. You'd just let the Riot Squad worry about it. They're always sitting round on their fannies anyway, waiting for riots. Wouldn't surprise me if they started a few of their own."

"I'd prefer to protect—"

"Then why raise objections? It's what I said. How many have you got left?"

"Five, sir."

"That many? Oh well . . . let's go through 'em. This Pierce. Charles."

"I'd prefer him wandering around loose, sir. Atracting our man, sort of."

"Wandering loose! Good God, that's asking for trouble. No. Put a guard on his house. If he's got one. Now . . . let's see . . . Ada Follett."

"An elderly lady, sir."

"Too dangerous. Protective custody. When is she due, according to your wonderful pattern?"

"Friday, sir. Tomorrow."

"Then we take her in. Got a nice, cosy cell, have you? Good. And put in a WPC as a substitute. One you can trust. Karate and that sort of thing."

"Ada Follett, sir, is five foot three and seventy-two. I've no WPC to fit that description."

"You *do* raise the most absurd objections, Inspector. Then you'll have to surround the house."

"Front and back, sir. There aren't any sides."

Merryweather stared at him. He did believe the man was being obstructive. He looked down at his notes.

"Lucinda Porter. Due today."

"In St Mary's hospital, sir. I understand she's in the Intensive Care ward."

"Ah, then it's to be hoped she doesn't beat him to it. Ha! Ha!"

Tomkins decided he hated this man. He was the sort of

person for whom dogs ran across busy streets in order to get a bite at. "I will surround the whole hospital complex, sir. Lucinda Porter, as you so neatly expressed it, is due today. We'll have every one of the seventeen entrances covered, men and women officers in the corridors, and, if you advise it, sir, one under her bed."

"Let me tell you something, Inspector—"

"And the other two . . . Esmeralda Greene and Paul Catterick are due, respectively, for Saturday and Sunday, but nevertheless I'll have people in Catterick's office watching his every move, maybe even helping here and there, licking the odd envelope, say. And I could send a whole team, eleven would be a good figure, to the school where Ms Greene is sports mistress. They could disguise themselves as a visiting hockey team. Or even, one or two of them, as schoolgirls. At a pinch."

"Inspector," Merryweather observed, "how long is it since you were walking the streets?"

"Years and years, sir. It's all cars now."

"I know it's cars now. I meant walking the streets as a civilian."

"Twenty years at least, sir. And in all my time I've never met—"

"That'll be all, Inspector. Just get on with it."

Tomkins, walking stiffly, reciting a nursery rhyme to himself to steady his nerves, went to get on with it. Mary had a little lamb . . .

He did this from his Operations Room, having already laid on most of what Merryweather had suggested. But he'd be damned if he would confine citizens of Ockam to one place. It did not fit the Ockam spirit of personal dignity. They might get themselves killed, but they had a perfect right to do it in their own time and where they chose. His feet as black as soot . . .

Using his radio link-up he got in touch with the two

men sitting, miserable and cold, in a car outside Charlie
Pierce's home.

"I have instructions," he said, "that you're to stop him
going anywhere."

A pause. "Sir—"

"I know. But try. It's that or protective custody."

Then he contacted the car outside Ada Follett's. "I have
instructions that you are to confine Mrs Follett to her
house."

"Sir—"

"I know. It's opening time in an hour. But try."

He got in touch with the car outside the unemployment
office. "I've been instructed that you are not to take your
eyes from Mr Catterick."

"But sir—"

"I know. It's a public office. But try." And into Mary's
cup of milk . . .

He contacted the car sitting in the drive of Crécy Manor.
"A senior officer from HQ has instructed that you should
keep Ms Greene under observation every second."

"They're in the changing room, sir."

"That's WPC Carter, isn't it?"

"Yes, sir."

"Who's with you?"

"WPC Enfield, sir."

"Then I suggest you proceed to the changing room,
change, and grab a hockey stick. All right?"

There was silence. Smiling, he switched off, handed the
microphone to the PC on duty, and sat to wait things out.
His sooty foot he put . . .

He had two officers at the hospital. They could see the
appropriate bed through the glass doors. They were very
depressed, but alert.

Charlie Pierce, undaunted by a complete failure the previous evening, stirred himself at around eleven and went

outside to look at the weather. Charlie had been thinking. It had brought on a headache but produced an idea. Because ideas were apt to escape if he didn't concentrate on them, he was doing this when two police officers approached him at the space where there'd been a front gate and asked him where he thought he was going. As this was Charlie's own and personal idea, he resented interference.

"Get stuffed," he said.

"I must ask you—" A hand was placed on his left arm, one on his right. Charlie looked at these two hands, then he lashed out. The two men lay down, and he walked away.

Two or three minutes later they were using the car radio. "We've got him, sir."

"Who? Pierce? How d'you mean – got?"

"A valid charge against him, sir. Assaulting a police officer in the course of his duties. Two officers. You can charge him, sir."

"Can I?"

"And put him inside."

"I'm very pleased," said Tomkins, his voice grating. "Bring him in then."

"He got away, sir."

"Well, well. Fancy that. Your instructions are to continue to watch the house."

But if he expected to pick up Charlie easily and put another half dozen tails on him, he was to be disappointed. There were no more cries into the fog to attract the slasher. Charlie slid, as well as anyone his size could slide, from one dim and foggy street to the next, silently, purposefully. It wasn't his day. Wednesday had been his day and it had passed. But Charlie had retrieved last Saturday's evening paper from his mother's pile – she always kept them to 'read later' and never read a word – and studied the list of prizewinners. It was quite correct, what he'd heard. Monday for Mr Moreton, Tuesday for Lucifer and Wednesday for himself. But he'd scared him off. Four to go. So Charlie would protect those four.

In 3C, Foundry Street, Madge was dispiritedly tapping out another chapter. This was so that she could read it to Lucinda from the actual typed sheets, this to indicate she was making use of the Olivetti. But she didn't really want to do this, and, as is always the case in such circumstances, the task suddenly became a heavy burden. What she wanted to do was to get on with the other story, which was stuck in Chapter Two, the one involving the perfectly dishy pink policeman. What she was having to do was continue with the story she and Lucinda had conspired together to perpetrate, and strangely it didn't seem at all amusing any more.

So there she was, tapping away, beginning at least to get every E when they cropped up. She had the light on because the daylight was so dim, but it wasn't visible from the street. Very little was. Certainly not Charlie. A large front door knob was pushed, a door opened, it closed. That was Charlie.

The tap on the door produced two Es in the word 'passionately'. She nearly jumped out of the chair, her cheeks suddenly flaming. This would not *do*. She took two or three deep breaths, put her shoulders back and went to open the door.

Another one! Fate had really gone crazy. How could she fit all these men into her plot?

"Oh," she said.

This one was big, bigger even than Tony. Broad with it, bulky with it, with a huge and knobbly face. Strictly speaking, she thought, she ought to be frightened. But there was nothing about this lump of humanity that was frightening, especially the way he pushed the hair out of his eyes with a huge ham of a hand and grinned in embarrassment.

"I'm Charlie Pierce," he said.

"Are you?"

"Yes."

This one, he thought, wouldn't take much protecting. He could tuck her under one arm and leave one fist free.

"I'm Madge Fenwick," she told him.

"Ain't you Lucinda Porter?"

"No. Sorry." Nobody, she thought, ever came looking for her. "It's her flat, but I'm using her typewriter."

He spent a few moments frowning over this. During this time, Madge realised she could well be talking to the slasher himself, but it was a casual thought, not in any way serious. He wouldn't have asked – he'd have acted and run.

"Then where is she?" he asked.

"Somewhere safe. In hospital."

"Ah," he said. "Yes."

"Don't just stand there. Shut the door and tell me what you want."

He did this, unhooking the sling of the canvas bag he had over his shoulder. It was a little unnerving for Charlie, being alone with a little slip of a thing like this Madge, in a confined space. One awkward move and he might touch her, and things Charlie touched seemed to get harmed.

"It was me won the—"

"Of *course*. Charlie Pierce. The raffle." That silly raffle again!

"An' I thought . . . it's Thursday, see . . . and this Miss Porter, well, she'd be Thursday with the razor."

"You're making me shudder."

"Oh Lor'! I didn't mean—"

"No. It's all right. Just me being silly."

"No you're not. I never seem to never get nothin' right."

"I think I see what you mean."

"Things go wrong."

"I expect they do."

"Last night . . . I should've waited for him, but I scared him off."

"This slasher, you mean?"

"Yeah. It was my night, see. Wednesday."

"You'd scare anybody."

"I didn't want to frighten you," he pounced in quickly.

She laughed. "You don't frighten me, Charlie Pierce."

"I don't?"

"Not a bit."

He grinned again. Nobody ever paid him compliments like this. "If she's not here—"

"She's perfectly safe."

"I thought she'd be here, see."

"Well you would, wouldn't you."

"Heh!" A thought hit Charlie right between the eyes. "So it don't matter."

"What doesn't matter?" It was, she decided, very difficult to converse with Charlie.

"Don't matter that she isn't here."

"Why's that?"

"If I don't know, then *he* don't. The slasher."

"Don't *say* things like that. Now you *have* frightened me."

He very nearly reached out a hand to touch her. Then he snatched it back. "No," he said. "You don't have to . . . I mean, *I'll* be here."

"Here?"

"Waitin' for him."

"Oh, but you couldn't. It isn't my place—"

"Not *in* here. Out on the landing."

She bit her lip. There he was, frightening the life out of people, and offering protection at the same time. "I don't know . . . the landlady in the basement . . . you'd better ask her, hadn't you!"

He nodded. He picked up his canvas bag. Charlie knew

when he was being dismissed. "Sure," he said. "Will do. See ya." And he left.

In this way, when Madge herself left and locked up, she assumed he was down there discussing it with the landlady, when in fact he was crouched quietly in a far corner of the landing, never having had any intention of asking any land-ladies about nothing. He had enough sandwiches and canned beer in his canvas bag to last him all day and he'd found a bathroom just behind where he was. Charlie was all set.

Madge therefore made her way to the hospital, stepped over the legs of the two plainclothes police officers and went to try to cheer up Lucinda.

At three minutes to eleven that morning, it being a four-minute walk to the Plucked Goose, Ada opened her front door. Unusually for her, because she'd used the same leather handbag for fifty years – the one Eric gave her – Ada had a shoulder bag hanging from her left shoulder. Two seconds later Floss appeared from her door. One second after that Connie did the same. These two ladies also had shoulder bags.

The two officers from the car outside, which the three residents were firmly ignoring, approached.

"I'm sorry, ma'am, but I can't allow you on the streets."

"Who says so?"

"I do, ma'am." He was a pleasant, ginger-haired young man, far too young, Ada considered, to be a policeman.

"Now listen to me, sonny." Ada reached across into her bag – she'd been practising this cross-draw for hours – and produced the rasp. She put it up close to his face where he couldn't miss it. "D'you want to see my famous disappearing rasp trick?"

At the same time, Floss produced her nicely-balanced remains of a wine bottle – British Port, Ruby Style – and Connie her rather more refined one – Chateau Mouton Cadet, clean and dry without being pretentious.

The two officers glanced at each other. They stood aside. As soon as the three warriors were well clear, they dived for their car and requested instructions.

"Where are they now?"

"Walking up the street in the direction of the pub."

"Then walk after them. And stay close."

"How close, sir?"

"As close as you can without provoking actual conflict."

"Yes, sir."

Which was how they came to be sitting with Ada, Floss and Connie, buying them milk stouts and themselves pints of bitter. Couldn't be closer, they decided, and far from conflict.

Later, the three ladies assisted them back to their car.

"Didn't I tell you," said Ada. "Too young to be let out on their own."

WPCs Edna Carter and Angela Enfield encountered similar difficulties. They invaded the changing room, as per instructions, to find Esmeralda Greene already in cracking form and in her green skirt and white knicks.

"Yes?" she demanded, in a tone that would have discouraged more sensitive women.

But Edna and Angela were experienced officers, hardened by experience. "We have instructions," said Edna, "not to let you out of our sight. It's called blanket protection."

"Well now!"

Esmeralda had already had enough contact with the police. If these two were anything like that one in the cell block, it would undoubtedly be her duty to protect her tender flock from *them*. Her present lot were at that age – there were thirty of them in the 12–13 age group – when they needed to be nurtured and cosseted, and on the hockey pitch restrained in irons. Esmeralda was not in one of her softer moods. Her girls were eyeing her with apprehension.

"I don't think we need you," she told the two women.

166

"I'm afraid we must insist."

"Insist? D'you hear that, girls?"

A certain gloom of premonition had been restraining them. Sixty little ears had been straining for a particular tone in Ms's voice. Now it was there. There was a concerted groan of agreement. Eyes lit up in the shadows.

"We are instructed to remain near you," Angela Enfield insisted.

Esmeralda looked at her brood. "Not in that uniform, I think. What d'you say, girls?"

Then she stood back. Five glorious minutes later, two dazed policewomen were equipped in very tight green school strip, with even tighter white knicks, felt hockey sticks thrust into their hands, and went, in the centre of a crowd of screaming, whooping hooligans, to the fog-shrouded hockey pitch, where they learned more about combat duty in one hour than they'd have done in a year on pub duty.

Why doesn't he phone? thought Esmeralda viciously, raising her stick rather higher than regulations permitted in order to sweep Edna's feet from beneath her. She'd been trying to get away. Why does he have to be such a stubborn pig? Hacking vigorously at Angela's ankles.

He didn't phone because he didn't want her to be embarrassed by a call at the school, and when it came to the time when she could possibly be at home he was in a police cell.

He'd got to the office peaceably enough, but the counters had barely opened before he was called to the manager's office.

Two uniformed officers, after having discussed how it was to be done, had joined the queues inside, standing in the one marked P, for policemen. But if, thought the young woman behind the protective glass, they were in uniform, how could they be unemployed? She requested assistance from her supervisor, who requested assistance from the manager, with the result that Paul was called in, to find them there in the office.

"Clearly," said the manager, "we can't have this. I'll not enquire as to your activities, Mr Catterick, but I suggest you take the rest of the day off, and the following ones until I get in touch with you."

"I'm at the Cannon Inn, Mr Bigelow."

"Hmm! Very well. Get off with you, and take these two gentlemen with you."

Paul therefore grabbed his hat and coat, much to the consternation of his section, and marched out.

He walked the town. They were at his heels. He went for a coffee. They were two stools away along the counter. He went into a phone booth but they leaned against it.

Eventually, he struck somebody, for the first time in his life. They were standing by the Temperance Fountain, whose spray disappeared up into the fog. Suddenly, to Paul, it seemed the most terrible imposition that he should not be standing there, in the fog, with Esmeralda. It was because the bearded one clearly wasn't Esmeralda that he poked him in the nose. And because the moustached one said something impolite, he hit him in the stomach, and the ridiculous man fell into the fountain.

They took him to the Station. Inspector Tomkins, who privately thought it was a bit of a laugh, nevertheless had to keep the chief super in touch and was instructed to lock him up. No charge. Let him cool down.

So Paul, who was his usual cool self, in fact very cool indeed, spent a night in the cells and they wouldn't let him use the phone.

Esmeralda brooded the evening away in her flat, whilst Charlie's bones set themselves into rock, Ada and her friends had a grand time with relays of young and fresh policemen and Madge returned late in the evening, went to bed at once – and was jolted upright by thumps and bangs from above.

Terrified, she ran out on to the landing, found the switch for the light on the landing above and illuminated Charlie and Tony knocking hell out of each other.

"You!" said Tony.

"Y' damned idiot!" said Charlie.

Then all three returned to Madge's flat where she brewed tea for them and fed them as best she could; she'd never felt as safe in her life.

It was only later, somewhere around two, when they'd left, that she realised that strictly speaking she ought not to have felt safe. In some strange way, that was an insult.

But Thursday was over and there had been, as Tony had so confidently predicted, no move, no sign, no shadow of the slasher.

Smiling to herself, Madge decided that perhaps what she had felt was threatened but safe. Then she slept.

Chapter Thirteen

Friday, 29 September

At ten o'clock on Friday morning Inspector Tomkins was sitting facing Ephraim Potts in the solicitor's office. It was not an inspiring office. The general dispersion of dust indicated that nothing had moved for a number of years, including Potts. He was a thin, gangling man, when standing, in his seventies but not yet flagging. His tired old skin, though, had the ancient parchment texture of a man incarcerated all his life within four walls, along with a battery of radiators.

Tomkins was there by invitation and therefore assumed that Potts wished to discuss the will of Lucifer Hartington. He sat and waited. Nothing happened so Tomkins, faced by a slightly smiling and patient mask, led in, "Lucifer Hartington, Mr Potts—"

"Oh no!" Potts shook his head. "Definitely not Mr Hartington."

"Pardon?"

"I reported the first one to a junior officer at your Station, Inspector. I thought the second one deserved reporting at your level. But it certainly couldn't have been Hartington."

Tomkins went along with him. He'd met Potts in court often. "What deserved reporting, Mr Potts?"

"There was another attempt last night."

"Indeed?"

"The night before last was a motor vehicle. It's just as well I'm nippy on my feet."

"It certainly is."

"Last night . . . you understand that I walk home from the office?"

"I can appreciate you'd need to stretch your legs."

"It's barely two miles. A lung opener, no more. And I was standing at the pedestrian crossing in Bullet Street, the lights against me . . . I'm sure you'll recall how foggy it was."

"I do. Yes."

"And I felt someone push me into the path of an oncoming bus."

Prickles of interest stirred inside Tomkins. "But you obviously avoided it."

"I skipped under its nose, Inspector, and across to the other side at some danger to life and limb."

"It sounds harrowing. Do you know anybody who'd want you out of the way, sir?" Tomkins was gently polite.

Potts smiled thinly, the parchment cracking open. "I have made enemies in the courtroom, certainly, but mainly members of your own force, Inspector."

Tomkins shrugged. "Win some, lose some. With due respect, sir, we might win a few more without you around, but not enough to justify violent action."

"Thank you. I'm relieved to hear it. Perhaps you will . . . er . . . institute enquiries."

"Of course. Now . . . can I discuss Lucifer Hartington with you?"

"By all means."

"You could help, perhaps. We're getting nowhere with identification. He's simply a person. Nothing on that longboat of his leads back to a relative anywhere. His suits

. . . the firm who tailored them has gone out of business and records were not kept. He was obviously wealthy, at some time."

"Ah yes."

"You know something?"

"Only a comment he made to me, when I drew up his will. He went into liquidation. A private limited company. He rescued what he could, apparently, and lived since then as simply as possible."

"His will?"

Potts smiled. "Normally, I would refuse to reveal its contents. But . . ." He raised his palms. "It will tell you nothing. All of which he died possessed – which is the barge *Celeste* and its contents, plus about £1,800 in the bank, to go to Oxfam. So simple, and no help to you at all, I'm afraid. I see that."

"Hmm!" said Tomkins, knowing that he couldn't leave it at that. Records couldn't tell him anything from the fingerprints. It meant they'd have to scour the missing persons files, but they didn't know how long he'd been missing, or even whether he'd been reported as missing. The Registrar of Companies might tell them something.

"Is it so important, Inspector?" Potts asked. "Surely the killing was the work of a maniac."

"The snag is that Hartington possibly recognised his assailant. Perhaps if he hadn't, this attack wouldn't have been a murderous one. A voice was heard shouting out 'You' or 'Hugh'. It's unlikely our maniac, as we'll call him, would shout out anything, even if he recognised Hartington. But . . . if Hartington knew *him*, then we need to know who Hartington really is, so that we can probe for people he might have known. One of them, perhaps, named Hugh."

Potts pursed his lips. "Police work seems very vague and hit-and-miss. I didn't realise that. I'm sorry I can't help you."

Tomkins recognised the sincerity in this remark, but when he got to his feet and shook hands with the solicitor, he saw that those old eyes were in no way faded. They were still blue and they twinkled. The old devil knew something, Tomkins guessed. He hoped it wasn't something that could cost him his life.

He was somewhat disappointed, as he'd hoped to be able to throw at Merryweather something that would halt him in full flight. But there was nothing. Merryweather was in no way impressed.

"So," he sneered, as expected, "there's no connection that helps to uncover his background. But you still maintain that the shout heard as 'You' could well have been in recognition?"

"It's possible."

"But damn it, man, the coincidence! *If* you're still saying the razor attacks are linked with the raffle draw."

"I do, sir." Tomkins could feel his cheeks were white, the skin drawn taut.

"Man alive! You must be stupid."

"If you say so, sir."

"I do say so. If this madman has been activated by the raffle draw, it'd be thousands to one against the possibility of one of the winners knowing him."

"It could," said Tomkins, his voice stretched out thin, "have been *because* of the raffle draw that the attack was made on Hartington. If Hartington's an unknown man, but known to the slasher, and has no fixed address, then the raffle draw would've revealed where he was located. And . . ." he went on quickly, watching the flush rise on Merryweather's face, ". . . the attack would perhaps be intended to be hidden away amongst the other attacks, when he gets round to them. It'd *look* like a madman's work, when it had a definite objective."

He'd been determined to get it out. It was the only

plausible idea that had presented itself so far. Merryweather had to hear it. He could do what he liked with it.

"What other attacks?" he demanded. "You haven't got any. One man with buttons cut off his coat. Then Hartington. Then nothing. Nothing on Wednesday, nothing yesterday. Probably nothing today."

"I'm relieved to hear you agree with me, sir."

"What?" Merryweather's eyebrows shot up. He *never* agreed with anybody.

"That it isn't a simple nutter we're after, sir."

"*You* said—"

"No sir." Oh, how lovely it was to be able to cut him off like this! "*You* said it was too big a coincidence if the attacker was a simple nutcase. So it had to be a deliberate and personal attack on Hartington."

"I didn't say—"

"But we'll soon know," went on Tomkins, his voice now smoothly comforting, and feeling he had an edge. "There wasn't one on Wednesday because Charlie Pierce frightened him off."

"A man with a razor—"

"I would not attack Pierce with a sub-machine gun, Mr Merryweather. And there wasn't one on Thursday because that was number four."

"What in heaven's name—"

"*Nobody* could take offence at number four's win, because it would've been the same whichever way the tickets were drawn. That was why number four was missed."

Merryweather leaned back in his chair and somewhere inside that untidy bundle of face there lurked a smile. "Mr Tomkins," he said heavily. "Inspector. I've allowed you to run on because it's amused me to hear you digging your own grave with your big mouth. You now maintain that because of very thin evidence relating to one word of dialogue – You – it was a personal matter of killing Hartington. And

174

that the series of murderous attacks has therefore ceased. Now let—"

"Sir."

"You wished to comment? Please do so."

"I would like to say that it could well have been planned to use the raffle draw as a cover-up for a personal crime, but such series murderers . . . well, imagine it. Your resolution would fizzle out once you'd killed the one you were really after. It'd become too much of a strain, too much effort."

"Good point! Good point! As I said, you're very confident that the series has now ended. No. That was what you said. I shall record it very carefully in my notes. And because you're so certain there will be no attack on Ada Follett this evening, I intend to act on your advice. No, no. Allow me to finish. I am now instructing you, Inspector, to call in all your men from their various watches, and place them on duties they ought to have been given long before this. I want . . . no, *you* want, because you have now remembered this aspect . . . to have everybody you can put your hands on out on the town, bringing in all your nutters and weirdos and sex maniacs and the like. Every one, Inspector. And of course, as you're so certain the so-called series of attacks has now come to an end, so that Ada Follett is quite safe, you will withdraw your blanket observation teams—"

"All?"

"Well . . ." Merryweather waggled a palm. "Perhaps spare a couple of men. I'll put *that* in my report, too. That I insisted on two men. And if an attack *is* made . . . oh dear me, what trouble you'll be in."

"If I could . . ."

"I suggest you get on with it."

". . . make a suggestion . . ."

"Now, Inspector. Now."

Tomkins went back to his own office and brooded on it. The bastard had got him trapped. It was, he decided, unwise to challenge Fate when it came to a question of coincidences.

It was perhaps coincidence that both Esmeralda and Paul realised at almost the same time that their watchers had disappeared. It was certainly a coincidence that they both decided to visit the park to inspect the geese. There was, however, no dramatic face-to-face confrontation involved because there was a whole pool between them.

Esmeralda had dutifully turned up at Crécy Manor that morning, aware that once again she was being escorted. The headmistress, recognising a battle-light in her eyes, and the way she bit off the lines of 'Onward Christian Soldiers' in assembly, asked Esmeralda to meet her in her study. The headmistress was seriously concerned about the number of girls queuing at the school clinic. It just would not do. She suggested that Esmeralda should go home and relax until Monday. Not arguing, Esmeralda complied. What she'd had in mind for her two watchers that day was scarcely practical, anyway. She caught a bus at the gates and it was when she reached town that she realised she was no longer being watched. So she celebrated by going for a walk round the park and perhaps look in on the ducks.

Paul, released from his cell before breakfast – if they called a mug of grey tea and two slices of buttered toast breakfast – went back to the Cannon Inn and got a proper one, went up to his room for a bath and a shave and accordingly didn't get out into the streets until after his watchers had been withdrawn. It was in some way disappointing. He'd wanted to spend a pleasant morning giving them a run for their money. It was, even without them, still a pleasant morning, cool but sunny, so he decided to have a look at the geese.

And these, poor things, divided between one human on the west side of the pool and one on the east, were undecided what to do. Neither of these humans bore any indication of having brought food anyway. They splashed away in the middle and honked indignantly.

It is not possible to conduct a conversation across a large park pool, especially one full of honking geese. One cannot say, "I don't wish to speak to you." One cannot reply, "I had no intention of speaking." Suppressed outrage and cool dignity are delicate emotions, not easily projected across water.

Esmeralda turned north, as Paul turned north. She stopped. He, assuming she wished to avoid him, politely turned on his heel and headed south as she turned south and immediately reversed to north. And Paul, not knowing where the hell he was going, turned north. Then they jigged and jogged in both directions, until both set off at a run, exasperated at such childish behaviour by the other, each heading south. There, they at once became shrouded from one another by a rather splendid yew hedge and inevitably ran smack-bang into each other's arms.

"Clumsy oaf—"

"Ridiculous woman—"

They stood back and looked at each other. "I forgot," she whispered, "to bring anything for the ducks."

"They're geese."

"Are they?"

"It's traditional. Goose feathers, you see, that they used to use for arrow flights in the old days."

"How interesting."

"Hence the Plucked Goose."

"I did wonder—"

"Terribly chilly for the poor geese, of course."

They turned and began to stroll together, as though engaged in advanced philosophical discussion. After a moment or two of thought, Esmeralda commented, "And they wouldn't be able to fly."

"I hadn't thought of that." He noticed her hand had slipped beneath his arm. "Shall we go and buy a white loaf each?"

"I rather prefer brown."

"Brown if you wish, but with white we could stand one each side of the pool and hurl it at each other."

"And the ducks could catch it in the middle! But why white?"

"Geese," he corrected, making the most of this infinitesimal item of knowledge. "It would be a matter," he explained, "of throwing our white around."

"Brown for me, then. I couldn't associate with perpetrating such a terrible pun."

"Brown it will be. And we could pop into the Copper Kettle, and I'll treat you to a coffee." He glanced sideways. "As long as you're paying, of course."

"All right. You can pay next time."

"Certainly. We must keep a record."

She didn't reply. Hesitating in her step, she caught him off balance. They stopped. She said, "We're assuming too much, Paul."

"Are we?"

"Where can we sit?" she asked, looking round. "The benches are all wet."

Carefully, he suggested, "At the Copper Kettle."

"No. This has to be private."

He frowned in portentous concentration. "There's the conservatory, but it's right the other end."

"Isn't it shut?"

"After tomorrow, yes."

Taking it slowly, chatting casually but avoiding all mention of razors, they circled the park, which was remarkably deserted. "It's like our private estate," Paul remarked.

"Yes. We're going to consult our head gardener."

The conservatory was open, but no attendant was visible.

There was a faint sibilance of moving water, a creeping sound of tropical plants settling down for the winter.

"It's cold in here," he said.

"Is it?"

When he glanced at her she was biting her lip. "Not really, I suppose," he agreed.

"There's something I have to tell you, Paul."

"No need—"

"But there *is*. I've been married. I'm a divorced woman."

"Oh dear."

"Don't *laugh* at me!"

"Sorry. But it is rather common, you know."

"The marriage," she said dully, "was said to have broken down. Or not even begun, I suppose, would be more correct. A month. Then he went."

"Hmm!"

"What the devil does *that* mean?"

She was on edge. He realised he had to take it carefully. "Frankly, I couldn't think of anything else. I was lost for words."

"You, Paul? You surprise me. But if you don't want to hear—"

"Of course I do. You were saying?"

She took a deep breath to steady herself and stared at a nasty thing all covered with spikes. "It was a matter of non-consummation, they called it."

"Ah! Poor chap."

"Trust you to take another man's side."

"No. It can be rather upsetting, I understand. There's a word for it. Begins with im—"

"That's impotent."

"I was thinking of impatient."

"*That* was you, Paul, damn you. This was something else. Different. It wasn't his fault – it was mine."

179

He said nothing. He was staring at something with leaves that were apparently covered with bruises.

She said quietly, breathlessly, "He sued me for divorce on the grounds that I refused to consummate the marriage."

He remained pensive. She touched his arm.

"I think," he decided at last, "the word's annul. Not divorce."

"You *do* know it all!" she declared tartly.

"I must admit to enjoying the correct choice of a word."

"So *you'd* have been all right! You'd have known just what to do. All the correct legal procedures."

"Oh, I know nothing about the law, Esmeralda. But I'd have known what to do."

"You would?"

"Well . . . look at me. I'm a big chap."

"I can't see that *that* would've helped. On the contrary, in those circumstances."

"I meant, I've got more than my fair share of blood."

"Heavens, haven't you been listening?"

"I've heard every word. No . . . I meant that with all that blood I reckon I'd have been warm enough for two."

She smiled. "You're very self-confident."

"No. Confident of you. Shall we go for that coffee?"

It meant nothing to a mournful frog, who watched them leave, nothing at all when it heard her say, "Then you can pay."

It meant a lot to Paul.

At about the same time, Charlie Pierce was climbing the stairs to the office of Ephraim Potts. It had taken him that long to work up enough nerve to face it. Anything remotely involving the law was a constant threat to Charlie's existence.

He'd slept well on the top landing, having sneaked back after Tony had left. His mother seemed unaware he'd been away all night. Over his breakfast he examined the letter he'd received from Potts. It was all very puzzling.

To start with, it was addressed to Charles Pierce Esq. What was an Esq? he wondered. And the actual wording was very puzzling. 'Dear Sir,' it began, and he hadn't known he was a Sir. 'In re the will of Lucifer Hartington, it is my duty to inform you that you are a minor beneficiary . . .' Minor, he thought, wasn't that something about being under eighteen? And he wasn't. And what was a bene-whatsit? He read on. '. . . and under the terms of my duties as his solicitor and executor . . .' Executor? Damn it all, they didn't execute people, these days. Did they? '. . . I would like to discuss this with you. I would be pleased, therefore, if you could call at my office at your earliest convenience.' Convenience? Wasn't that a posh word for gents? 'I am, sir, your obedient servant, E. Potts.' My servant? He must be crazy.

Nevertheless, he went.

Potts saw at once that he had to avoid long words with Charlie. But Potts – give the dry old stick his due – rather enjoyed this part of his work and therefore prolonged it as far as possible. He explained that a recent change in Lucifer's will meant that Charlie was to have the BMW.

Only one sentence, but he stretched it out to ten minutes, ending with the warning that it would take a little time before Charlie could actually call it his own. Strong men like Charlie do not of course cry and if Potts noticed the strange moisture on Charlie's cheek he put it down to the annoying delay involved.

Charlie shook hands and mumbled something, then stumbled down to the street. Anybody out there, ordinary normal citizens, similarly suddenly presented with £5,000 worth of motorcycle, would no doubt have run cheering through the town. But Charlie moodily plodded around, kicking things. Tyres, walls, stones, benches. Charlie wasn't like normal citizens. To him, it only made things worse that Lucifer should have been killed so that Charlie might get his heart's desire. Because he couldn't share the joy with Lucifer.

Nearly bursting with a bitter fury against the person who had inflicted all this on him – the loss and the gain disturbingly reacting together as an explosive mixture – he gradually worked his way round to a decision. If he could not, himself, personally and with his own hands, take the slasher out of circulation, he didn't deserve to own Lucifer's bike. Only in those circumstances could he agree to accept it.

So who was next? Ada Follett. No old lady, however nimble, was going to get out of Charlie's sight.

In the afternoon, Detective Inspector Tomkins went to visit Tony at his home. This was very unofficial behaviour, but his visit was unofficial, anyway. Tony, fortunately, was at home. His mother nearly had one of her turns when she heard who was visiting. She put them in the living room with a tray of tea things and went to sit in the kitchen, her heart palpitating. What'd he been up to? He'd get a Piece Of Her Mind or She'd Know The Reason Why.

"This is unofficial," said Tomkins. "You're on sick leave, Finch."

"I was coming in tomorrow."

"I need you tonight."

"Then I'll come in tonight."

"But still on sick leave."

"I don't understand, sir," said Tony.

"They've sent us a chief super from DHQ to take charge. We do not see eye to eye, Finch. He's stuck on the idea that we've got an ordinary loony here, who's been sparked into action because of all the violence from the raffle draw."

"Oh, I wouldn't say that."

"You wouldn't. I wouldn't. But he does. And he's taken everybody off surveillance to bring in all the crazies and question them."

"All?" Tony was deeply concerned.

"And I'm allowed only two officers to guard Ada Follett. No more. But you, being on sick leave, don't count."

"Thank you, sir."

"So I'm asking you to help out."

Tony decided not to mention that he'd intended to be there anyway. "Who else have you got, sir?"

"Sergeant Spinks and Constable Cartwright."

"Terry's all right."

"But not Spinks?"

"I suppose he won't go into a huddle with Terry."

"What's *that* mean?"

"Nothing, sir," said Tony blandly.

"I'm asking you to go on this job unofficially, Finch. Just think, you'd be boosting the tactical force by fifty per cent."

"It's tempting," agreed Tony. "But what if I get caught at it?"

"Then you're off sick leave and I take the blame for deploying three men instead of two."

"Ah, sir. I see." Tony could see trouble. Inspector Tomkins taking blame would be something new, anyway.

"You agree?"

"Of course, sir."

"Then . . . report to Sergeant Spinks at six-thirty, at the north end of Chamois Street."

"Ada'll be in the Plucked Goose by then."

"Nevertheless—"

"If I might make a suggestion . . . she already knows me. I could report to Ada Follett in the pub at two minutes past six, and Spinks'll know where to find me."

"Excellent idea!" Tomkins hid his smile. Spinks had thought the pub would be his beat. How disappointing for him!

Then he took his leave and hurried off to try to intercept his lady friend, who would be leaving her employment – Lloyd's Bank – very shortly. But she still wasn't speaking. Tony sat smiling to himself, then went out to find Charlie.

Chapter Fourteen

Friday, 29 September (cont.)

On the face of it, Ada Follett's house, in the centre of a straight run of terraced houses, presented no difficulty when it came to observation. Look at it: a house with just two entrances, front door opening directly onto the street, and rear door opening on a narrow yard, which, further down, after it'd passed the kitchen, the coalhouse and the outside lavatory, opened out on to what had been an expanse of blue bricks. The removal of these had left Floss and Connie, each side, with a two-foot wide blue brick path along the outer edges of their rear yards, but Ada had sacrificed this facility for the lawn, which had, disappointingly, indicated no intention so far of turning green.

Along the back of the whole street ran a stretch of canal, with a towpath this side. It was possible to walk along from either end of the street to the rears of any of the houses. Possible, too, to approach in a canoe or some such vessel, but the street was on a slope, so that there were two locks in its run. In recent years the bit behind Ada's place had become an unpleasant and stagnant stretch of water. So much rubbish had been dumped in it that it might, indeed, have been possible to walk across it from the other side without wetting more than your ankles.

Therefore . . . front door and rear door to watch. Simple. Nothing could possibly go wrong.

But it was Ada's day. Allowances had to be made for the character of Ada. Regrettably, they were not. Far from terrified by the possibility of confronting an open razor this side of midnight, Ada was, even before the evening's opening time, treating the whole thing as a bit of a lark, and in fact held a council of war with her two friends. They limbered up in Ada's living room, in preparation, stabbing and thrusting with their chosen weapons and shouting: "Hi-yah!" and "Ah-kay!" These they considered to be Japanese combat cries.

Really, they should not have been allowed out on the streets. But promptly at three minutes to six Ada popped out of her front door – a murderer could have set his watch by her – a minute later Floss and Connie appeared at her side, and they set off down the street, arms linked, already in fact a bit tiddly with the excitement of it.

They settled into their corner seats. By now the bar was filling up. Everybody knew it was Ada for the razor that evening. It was unlikely it would happen actually in the bar, but this was going to be an evening to remember. A wake in advance, one might say.

At five minutes past six Tony appeared in the doorway, lifting his head and looking round for them. He should have known. It was *their* corner.

"Hey!" shouted Ada. "It's my tame copper. Come over here, lad." Tony approached.

"You still undercover, lad?" Ada screamed and everybody had a good laugh.

Tony sat at their table. He grinned at them. "Not now I'm not. What're you drinking?"

"Have a guess," Floss offered.

So he went and got them in. It was, he realised, going to be heavy work controlling these three.

Sergeant Andy Spinks had decided that, if any approach was going to be made to the house, it would not be at the front. A mouse could not have reached that front door without being observed. He therefore stationed Detective Constable Terry Cartwright at the front, hidden across the street in one of the narrow alleyways which, that side, led to the rear accesses to those houses. Terry was a good man, tough and reliable, but not vastly imaginative. It needed, Spinks realised, a man with a penetrating analytical mind at the rear, so he stationed himself there.

At the rear it was very dark. The night was clear but there was no moon. The streetlights at the front were shrouded by the houses, and from across the canal very little light came from the nearest street in that direction, which was across the other side of the wasteland where the factories had been. The Slags, they called it round there.

Spinks stationed himself on the towpath. Not actually on it, but just inside the remnants of the ancient low fence that separated the yards from the towpath, and in the shadow of the equally ancient but still noxious outside lavatory. He could, if desperate, nip into there for a quick drag from time to time, without the glow being visible.

But Charlie had beaten him to it. If Charlie had an attribute, it was stubborn patience, and he and Tony had worked out this arrangement. He had been *in situ* as soon as it was dark enough to take up the position, and was sitting with his back against the wall with his head just below the sill of Connie's kitchen window. From this position, he faced Ada's kitchen window across the width of two back yards. The lights were on in these kitchen windows, a lifelong precaution against burglars, the theory being that it looked as though somebody was home. The result was that Charlie was in deep shadow, made deeper by the window above him, the light from Ada's just not quite reaching his feet.

He'd worked out his actual position himself, which was

187

really going it for Charlie's brain. But he was forcing it, concentrating every effort on his one objective. This position, too, he realised once he'd settled in, had an added advantage in that he was protected from approach from the rear by the projecting block of kitchen, coalhouse and more modern and actually flushing outside toilet. Yet he still had a direct view of Ada's rear door.

Andy Spinks ought to have thought of this but he lacked Charlie's driving incentive.

Esmeralda and Paul were enjoying a relaxing meal at the Trocadero, which was neutral territory and within walking distance. Neither owned a motor vehicle; neither had ever found need for one. They were at the stage of probing each of their past lives, yet still in the delicate position of having to reach gently so as not to brush against any tender abrasions.

"Don't you find that life has been a complete bore?" she asked him.

"Wasted years." He raised his wineglass, smiled past it, and toasted her silently. In this light – the Trocadero favoured dim, red table lamps – it seemed to him that she was softer, more vulnerable. Was that the word he wanted? No. Accessible. That was it.

"Isn't it infuriating," she said, "when you really get down to it . . . the *years* I've spent at that blasted school, trying to hammer maths and physical culture into a crowd of useless hobbledehoys! When I could've been *doing* something."

"Such as?"

"Hell, I don't know. Exploring, climbing mountains, learning to fly."

"I've always wanted to try gliding," he admitted.

"And why haven't you?"

He shrugged. "Inertia, I suppose. You get into a groove. It's appalling. It takes over."

"We must take arms against it."

"We must."

"Enrol tomorrow."

"In what?" he asked.

"A glider course."

"They don't do it in winter."

"You're so damned literal, Paul. Anything. Scuba diving."

"Take it easy, now."

"Something wintry, then."

"You're so damned physical. I suppose you're off to Austria every winter for the skiing?"

"Not yet. But why not? Come on, Paul, stick your neck out."

"I will if you will."

"You're on."

The relationship was developing in a satisfactory manner. Too fast, if anything. Neither of them had dared to face the major problem, which would have to be surmounted some time. After brushing over it briefly in the park, they had ignored it. What the devil did they expect to come from their present situation? Ask either of them at that time and you'd have got a shaken head.

But for the moment, all was contentment.

They walked back into town. It was nine o'clock. Paul was telling her about the forthcoming lawn behind Ada's house. Esmeralda, in fact, apart from a skirmish to the Plucked Goose, and a revisit or two because Paul might have been there, had no extensive knowledge of that part of town. She had been protected by her background which had always seemed to involve gracious expanses of countryside and spacious houses. She did not, therefore, appreciate fully what a lawn could mean to Ada. But she was in a receptive mood.

"I'd like to see that."

"You shall. We'll take a small diversion—"

"We go to see a patch of bare earth in the dark?" she asked.

"We go to see Ada and her friends. We'll no doubt be invited to a garden party in the spring."

"I'll swear it's natural!"

"What is?"

"You say the most absurd things. I assumed you were trying to show off, but you just can't help it."

"You're right, I suppose. But life *is* absurd. Very amusing, really. And as a matter of fact I meant it quite seriously. Ada's just the sort of person to do exactly that – throw a garden party. Probably with a gondola on the canal and a hired tenor singing 'O Sole Mio'."

"Idiot!"

"You'll see. But I bet . . . mention it to her, and she'd go all out for it. Ada's like that. I understand her. She understands me."

"And I," she murmured, "am a complete mystery to her?"

"Don't you believe it. She might scream her head off in the bar, shout ribald jokes, do ridiculous dances when she's a bit far gone, but there's a shrewd head screwed on those shoulders. I bet she knows you inside out."

"I shudder to think—"

"What she'll come out with?"

"Yes."

"Then we'll give the Plucked Goose a miss."

"Oh no. Anybody who's faced my girls . . ." it hadn't been gels for ages, he noticed, ". . . on a hockey pitch, ought to be able to face an old lady."

"And give as good as you take?"

"That too. If necessary."

So that they arrived at the Plucked Goose as things were warming up nicely. Very nicely indeed. Ada, Connie and Floss were doing an exhibition dance, that adjective carefully chosen, to the roared chorus of 'Knees Up Mother Brown'. It was afterwards, recovering her breath and when the cheering and whistling had abated, that Ada spotted them on the outskirts, trying to find a way through.

"Here they are!" she shouted. "My friends. Let 'em through, lads. Come on, you two. Move up, Tony lad. Make room."

Paul and Esmeralda moved through the gap that appeared. For some reason there was sudden silence. Everybody already knew why Ada was livening things up. It was Friday. Ada was Friday. But these two were strangers.

Ada held up both hands. "Ladies and gentlemen, I introduce you to Saturday and Sunday. If he's here tonight – all three of us together! Let's have a cheer, boys. Let's hear y'!"

They cheered. They thumped Paul's shoulders. It was a great honour to meet the man for the razor on Sunday. But Esmeralda was the prize. She was Saturday, and Saturday was tomorrow, and a great number of pints had already been consumed, and they might not get another chance to meet her, and quite frankly, when they came to think about it, if it'd been them in the same position they'd have been off and away, visiting auntie in Yorkshire.

So Esmeralda, before she realised this indignity was to be thrust on her, was hoisted onto hefty shoulders – kick though she might, shout as she did, red-faced and quite discomposed – and marched around to cheers and shouts of encouragement. When she caught Paul's eye he winked and nodded, strangely it suddenly became part of an exciting evening and she threw back her head and laughed.

Then they put her down in front of Ada's table and she turned and kissed her supporters, to more cheers and shouted ribald suggestions, as Ada called for gin and lime for the lady. Bill Fisher, behind the bar, a man of vast experience, had anticipated this and had a good memory, so there they were, all lined up on the bar. Inside two minutes she had eight sitting in front of her, even before she'd regained her breath.

"I'll kill you for this, Paul," she said.

"You'll thank me. Come on, drink up."

He watched her fondly. He leaned sideways towards Tony and whispered, "Anything?"

"We don't even know what he looks like. Keep out of this, Paul."

"Sure. I will."

Out of what? he thought. Try getting out of this. Because it was clear that Ada had engineered all of it, surrounding herself with friends and allies, her safety being in numbers.

This went on until closing time at eleven, by which time one or two had already passed out and the rest had reached a peak of happiness and were trying to hold it there as long as possible. Bill Fisher called time and when the hoots of derision had died down Ada invited everybody along to her place to continue the festivities.

Tony glanced at Paul. Both had been deliberately going easy on the beer all evening, and were still alert. Both appreciated Ada's tactics. But it was unlikely that even Ada recognised everybody there that evening, and it was possible she would be inviting the slasher amongst them. There was a roar of approval at Ada's offer and in the final precious seconds much trade was done by Bill Fisher in six-packs and bottles of gin.

Then they all flooded down the street to Ada's place, Bill Fisher along with them, bringing his own contribution in a wheelbarrow. Terry Cartwright, seeing them approaching, very nearly radioed for Inspector Arkwright and his Riot Squad. He did inform Andy Spinks, who told him to hold the fort. So Terry did nothing.

Fifty-odd people were really a bit much for Ada's thin slice of house. Back door and front door were necessarily left open for the overflow, but Ada made it quite clear, on pain of an introduction to her rasp, that nobody was going beyond the lavatory in the yard, because from there on it was their lawn. Floss and Connie joined in by throwing their houses open to the mob, too, so that very soon there were lights on in every window of all three houses, and neighbours, awoken, ceased to complain and drew on trousers or ancient dressing gowns over their pyjamas and came to see what could be rescued before that lot finished it all off.

It was some time before Charlie realised what was going on. But when all the lights went on in Connie's place he became suddenly visible, the living room light spilling onto his legs. Yet he was reluctant to move. There, right in front of him was Ada's back door, and by heaven he wasn't going to take his eyes off it. In practice, though, nobody thought to patronise Connie's outside lavatory, or they'd have tripped over his legs. Plenty used Ada's. All this noise and excitement was very unsettling to Charlie when he'd expected silence and stealth.

Sergeant Andy Spinks, sweating from the tension and the abruptly increased responsibility, clung firmly to the conviction that the attack, when and if it came, would be from the rear. His vigilance was intensified, but he lost touch with the movements of the toilet visitors.

As did Charlie, because Paul and Esmeralda came out, so that Paul could show her the expanse of black earth out there, now that bedroom lights just illuminated it. Charlie's concentration slipped because he was trying to remember where he'd seen them before. But he had . . . he had.

Paul was saying, "The canal's over there, just the other side of the fence. See it? The light just reaches it."

"I'm sorry I missed the canal." She giggled. "But I can sense it's there."

"We could get to it if we went out into the street and back

through Connie's or Floss's. See it too from either bedroom window, I suppose."

"I wouldn't want to do that. We're Ada's guests."

"True. It would not be proper to trespass on either of her friends."

"I would've liked to see the canal, if only dimly," she told him solemnly.

"There's a lock bridge only a few yards away. Just like Venice."

Surprisingly, she laughed shrilly. "I'd *love* to see that." A pause. "Could we see that from Ada's bedroom window?"

"It is just possible."

Then they turned and went back inside. Charlie sighed. They could well have spotted him there. And why anybody would want to see the lock bridge he couldn't imagine.

By a quarter to twelve the three-house party was getting a little out of hand. Ada was wondering whether to start chucking them out. But it was her turn for the outside lavatory and she proceeded there at a fair pace. Charlie recognised her. He sat very still.

The shadow that had been standing just round the corner of the extension – illegally on Ada's portion of the lawn – moved round, so gently, so quietly, that Charlie missed him, for a moment distracted by a man lurching from the back door, but, as it turned out, going no further than the kitchen drain. When Charlie switched his eyes back, it had happened.

From inside, Ada heard a sound. To be sure, there was plenty of sound hanging around out there, but the shadow had made the mistake of allowing some part of himself to brush against the door. If it'd been a heavy knock and a shout, "Hurry up, you daft old fool," she'd have understood. A gentle sound . . . heavens, everybody had long since abandoned the gentle stage. So Ada, who hadn't forgotten her rasp even in these circumstances, jerked open the door and took a pace forward into the open, where she could at least find room for her operative arm. Or rather, she tried to take a pace, but her knickers were still round her knees, and the pace became a stumble.

This saved her. Something that winked in the light flashed sideways at her throat, but on her stumble it went above her head. By now she was screaming, the reality being vastly different from her over-romanticised imaginings. And there is something much more piercing, much more arresting, in a scream of terror than one of beer-primed joy. She straightened because she dared not go down in front of him, and in blind terror, and forgetting her stabbing practice, she lashed out frantically with her rasp.

It was a long while since the tang of that rasp had been tapped into the handle. The wood had dried, had shrunk, had cracked, so that the rasp flew from it and spun through the air within an inch of her assailant's head. That, along with a roar of outrage from Charlie, who'd seen every move of it in those two seconds but had stiffened up and could barely get to his feet, were enough to send the assailant into a quick spin and then a sprint across Ada's lawn towards the canal. At the same time the lower portion of Ada's bedroom window slammed up and Paul, taking one look at the situation, jumped out, without thought for his ankles.

Ada was going on and on, gulping in deep breaths for the next batch of screams. At the window above, Esmeralda's head and part of her bare upper half appeared in the opening, and she added her own scream. "Paul!"

But Paul was in full limp, Charlie ahead of him like a bull elephant on the rampage, ahead of him the fleeing slasher, and ahead of all of them the rasp, still spinning, and travelling at a fair speed.

Andy Spinks walked out of his concealment into the assailant's path. Masterly, he thought. I've got him cut off. Then the rasp spun past his head, taking a neat section of skin from his left cheek as he gave his own little personal scream and pressed his hands over his eyes, under the impression he'd been blinded. The assailant ran right over him, Charlie following, and it was Paul who limped up to help him to his feet. He hadn't a handkerchief to offer to Spinks as he was in pants and shirt and socks.

The slasher, now a scuttling shadow, had plunged straight into the canal. It was barely two feet deep at its best, with the household rejects here and there making it less. It was a matter of luck where you put your feet. Even though he didn't deserve any, the luck was now with the pursued, and he made it to the other side. Charlie, the pursuer, made a great leap, and plunged one foot through the spokes of an old cycle wheel. Thus hampered, he stumbled and fumbled, struggling to the other side much too late.

Out in the Slags it was dark and both men had no difficulty in getting themselves completely lost.

At the upstairs window Esmeralda wept silently. Ada, now with her clothing tidy, stood at the edge of her blue bricks and shouted for the stupid, clumsy oafs to keep their stupid great feet off her bloody lawn. She waved the rasp handle in fury.

It quite took the bite out of the party and everybody went home.

Paul returned to the bedroom and they soberly dressed. The marriage had very nearly become comsummated before the ceremony. They were silent until she said, "You didn't have to interfere, Paul."

"It was a reaction."

"And in your stockinged feet!"

"Didn't think." He glanced at her. "I'll walk you home."

"Not tonight, Paul. Really. Walk me to the taxi stand in Rimfire Street, and I'll pick one up."

"As you wish."

But that was to be a long while later because Tomkins

196

and about a hundred men descended on Chamois Street, and there were questions . . . questions . . .

Paul and Esmeralda sat side by side on Ada's settee and though they held hands they barely exchanged a word. They were now aware that the threat to both of them was once more very much alive.

Chapter Fifteen

Saturday, 30 September

Detective Inspector Tomkins sat facing the chief super. The temptation was to say, "I told you so." But Tomkins knew where he was heading, which was hopefully for promotion and diplomacy was called for.

"It does seem you were correct in assuming we've got a nutter here, sir, but I think you'll agree that his obsession is centred on the raffle prizewinners." He'd rehearsed that.

"Maybe, maybe.' The chief super was intending to go down fighting.

"Three razors used now, and each on the day engraved on the rear edge. Monday, Tuesday and Friday."

In fact, the razor used for Ada had been found on the towpath, again wiped clean and with the tissue round it, although it had not drawn blood. But – and this was the strange point – the detailed search that night had not discovered it, and it was not until nearly nine in the morning, and fully light, that it was spotted. This was by a neighbour, six doors up the hill, who hadn't been able to resist just walking along in order to stare at Ada's outside lavatory, although it differed in no way from his own. Tomkins couldn't understand how his men had missed it. The only possible explanation was that the slasher must have sneaked back in the early dawn in order to leave it there. But that was a purely pointless action, surely.

Tomkins decided not to clutter the chief super's head with details, and carefully omitted to mention this.

As Tomkins didn't seem to intend to carry on, but simply sat there brightly attentive, Merryweather was forced into asking, "Your thoughts on it, then, Inspector?"

Tomkins plunged in happily. "I think the original intention had to be to work his way through the prizewinners. One of your fruitcakes who's been roused by the disturbances we'd had in the previous week. I mean – why steal the Ockam razors, unless the engraved days on them had some significance? And he started with Monday – Arthur Moreton, followed by Tuesday – Lucifer Hartington. Then he met a snag called Charlie Pierce, who was just begging to be tackled, but would've been too much of a problem at that time. Believe me, sir, Pierce would walk right through a waving razor, probably break off the hand holding it and go on to tear him apart."

"I must meet this Pierce of yours."

"I wouldn't advise it, sir. But assume he was unacceptable as a target, then number four would've been next, and she's in hospital."

"Access to hospitals—"

"I know, I know, sir. Put on a white gown, hang a stethoscope round your neck and you can go anywhere in hospitals. But we have to assume the razor is a vital necessity to our man. A must. And though he might look like a surgeon if he carried a scalpel, I think an open razor would be looked at askance." Tomkins was bland, his face innocent.

"Inspector . . . facetiousness—"

"And he could hardly be posing as the official barber in a woman's ward, sir."

"Don't try to be funny with me."

Tomkins sighed. "He might know her address, but she hasn't been there. Perhaps he doesn't know that. Believe me . . . the risks he's been taking with the others . . . he'd not hesitate where a hospital's involved. So I'm arguing he doesn't know where she is."

"This 'she' you mention, being . . ." The chief super glanced at his notes. "Lucinda Porter."

"Yes, sir."

"Still seriously ill?"

"No change."

"Very well. Carry on."

"So he had to skip Wednesday and Thursday, and he's picked up with Friday. Ada Follett. Who decided to throw a party. We had, sir, insufficient men to cover the movements of everybody – and don't forget, sir, he could've been one of the party guests."

"Hmm!" said Merryweather. He brightened. "But at least we've been able to establish that he isn't one of your normal gang of loonies. We know that, because we had 'em all here at the Station when all that was going on."

"Sort of throwing your own party, sir?"

"You could say that." He scratched his nose. "So now we come to Saturday. Today."

"Esmeralda Greene. Yes." Tomkins waited. The man was paid for taking responsibilities, so let him take this one.

"We could spirit her away to some secret place," Merryweather mused. He was very much more quiet today, treading carefully.

"It wouldn't be secret for long. You'd hear her howls of outrage from a mile away."

"Protective detention?"

"Not without her agreement and I can't see her giving that."

Merryweather frowned. "Then – damn it – we'll have to be crafty, Inspector. It'll have to be done with circumspection."

200

Tomkins smiled. He'd been keeping this back. "Difficult, sir. The news media are on to it."

"They are? Hell and damnation."

"The local evening paper's been covering it, but now it's leaked back to London and we've got reporters and commentators flooding reception downstairs, and two TV vans out in the street."

"Ah," said the chief super. "Yes. We'll have to be very cunning, I can see. This Esmeralda Greene – where will she be located?"

"I should imagine, after last night's experience, that she won't move out of her flat."

"Which is?"

"About a mile out of town. A Georgian detached house converted into four flats. Quiet and secluded. A six-foot wall at the front, no gates, but a wide entrance. Hedges each side and at the rear. A perfect target for an intruder."

"So you're suggesting?"

"I was requesting instructions, sir."

Again the chief super frowned. "First of all, then, we don't want any of the press to find out her address."

"They can get that easily. Names and addresses of the prizewinners were printed in the *Ockam Observer*."

Merryweather drummed his fingers. He knew how it'd be, if that lot got involved. The place floodlit from all directions for the TV cameras, the walls lined with seated reporters, mikes sprouting like foetid fungi, and the BBC news, in a flurry of grammatical fervour, announcing that: "Rooves have been requisitioned for marksmen to completely cover the house approaches."

"We can get round that, I think. Something non-committal."

"You'll have a word with them, sir?"

"They like to hear from the man in charge." It would be

covered adequately with, 'enquiries are proceeding'. He could do that with massive confidence.

"And we, sir?"

"We shall be covering the house. Complete cover. Secretly and quietly. Even she is not to know."

"What if she wants to go out, sir?"

"She will be told not to."

"So she'll know what's going on."

"All right! So she'll guess. But to anybody else it'll be a quiet house with nobody around. I want a good team. I want a man – or a woman if they like that sort of thing – at intervals of eight feet all round. And one cough, one cigarette lit, and by God they'll have me to deal with. Understood?"

"We cannot control—"

"You *will* control. Every movement, every approach made to the house. Take up positions as soon as it's dark – and no cars in the area – walking from a mile away if necessary. They *can* walk, I suppose? Singly. Spaced. This time, Inspector, there're to be no mistakes. Anything more?"

"I wanted to say that I'm convinced our man deliberately returned to the scene of last night's attack, just on purpose to leave the razor."

"You think the razors—"

"And the tissue, sir. Deliberately left. To confuse the issue."

"And in what way are you confused, Inspector?"

"I can't make any sense of it."

"Ah . . . you see! That's where you make your mistake. Do not be misled by confusing clues. It's facts we want. It's somebody with a copper's hand on his collar we want. Clear, is that?"

"As crystal, sir."

Tomkins went to his office to fix it all up. He phoned Esmeralda at her flat and informed her she was not to leave it that day for any reason whatsoever. He nearly said, on pain of death, but resisted.

At once she contacted Paul at the Cannon Inn.

"Damn cheek," he agreed, when he could slip in a word.

"I was so looking forward—"

"We meet as arranged," he told her firmly. "The only difference will be that we'll come back to my room and eat at the restaurant here. Then if we don't go out, he'll never know where to find us." He didn't specify which 'he' he meant, the inspector now being as large a threat as the slasher.

"How clever of you. I'll grab my bag and be right along. Meet you at the Temperance Fountain."

Which she did and they spent the morning in pleasurable excitement around the town, first visiting the holiday booking offices to fix up a skiing holiday in January, and then getting fully kitted-up for it.

"You can hire the stuff there," he pointed out.

"And miss half the fun? No . . . you have to have your own boots and your own skis and ski sticks and gloves and masks and the rest. Then you can make yourself an absolute nuisance by pushing into buses and trains with it all draped round you, and everybody thinks you're a downhill racer or something – and you feel just great."

It was a mood he hadn't previously encountered in her. He could now understand her affinity with her girls. "Then we'll do that."

The result was that they made their first impact in the Cannon Inn, where they half-filled the lobby, and had to make three journeys out of reaching his room, so that there was not one member of the staff who didn't know she was spending the day up there with him in what was really a single room with a single bed.

It was eleven-thirty that night before Paul suggested he might walk her home. Both of them had deliberately tried to forget that she, and after midnight he, could be in danger.

They had not noticed Charlie. He had decided to play safe and not lose sight of Esmeralda for the whole day. Just because the other attacks had been after dark, it didn't mean they all would. Charlie's brain, flexing its muscles, was improving all the while. His patience and energy could hardly have been improved anyway. So he watched her from her house to the bus, was on the same one, he upstairs while she was downstairs, and watched her meet Paul – nodding his approval – then tailed them all round town, and marvelled at their purchases. He had to force himself not to go and help to carry them.

Therefore he was outside the hotel all day, one end of the street or the other. But always near. He even saw the room light go on, though he didn't know it was Paul's. What worried Charlie, insofar as he could worry, was that he had not, for the whole day, seen a sign of any other watcher, and he'd expected the police to be on it. Damn it all, they'd watched *him* closely enough. Not even Tony. He'd expected Tony around, some time or other. He was a mate, wasn't he!

But Tony, stretching his sick leave a little further than he would normally have done, was pursuing his own interests. In any event, he reckoned he would be unwelcome round at the Station after his pitiful efforts the night before.

"I'd got my hands full in Ada's kitchen," he explained to Madge.

He'd found her in her own room for once, she wondering what had gone wrong with Chapter Two of the saga.

"But you're never here!" he complained.

"I've been at the hospital a lot."

"It's not doing you any good at all," he told her, eyeing her critically. She was pale, her eyes tired, her mouth droopy.

"I don't go there to do myself good."

"No. I suppose not. Bad, is she?"

"They don't think . . . oh, damn it all, Tony, why does it have to be like this?"

He was now a master of the 'there, there' technique, but this time it came naturally. She wept copiously on his shirt. Her hair smelt of iodoform and was untidy.

She sniffed herself to silence, then ventured, "They don't expect her to live another week."

"I'm sorry." How inadequate that sounded!

She took a seat and shook herself free of it. "And you? Tell me what's been happening."

So he told her about Ada's party, presenting it as the gay old time it's been, until the end.

"I couldn't very well follow Ada out to the lav, could I?" he asked.

"Oh no." Her eyes were huge.

"Which of course I should have done. But I was in the kitchen, by the kitchen door, when Ada started screaming . . . Lordy me, those two, Floss and Connie, they pounced on their damned bottles – and I didn't even know they'd got 'em – and I just *had* to stop 'em getting involved. You make a split-second decision. That was mine. And just try restraining two women waving broken bottles in your face! By the time I got outside, it was all over."

"Bar the shouting."

"There was enough of that."

"So it's all still going on?"

"It seems so." He tilted his head, guessing what she was thinking. "But don't worry, your friend's safe where she is."

"Safe? Oh yes. She's safe enough." But she said it with bitter regret. Lucinda, unsafe but alive and well in her flat, was better than Lucinda where she was now.

"I'm afraid I can't stay," he told her, equally regretful.

"You can't?"

205

"Got to find out what's going on."

"Oh yes. Of course." When she'd been hoping he'd take her out. Out to lunch. Anywhere out . . . away from it for a while.

"Just time for a bit of lunch first," he told her, getting to his feet. "I suppose you're off to the hospital?"

"No. Not yet. This afternoon."

"Then climb into a coat or whatever, and we'll see what we can get. Come on, girl, make a move. Don't just sit there."

Chapter Two was on its way. Chapter Three was showing form.

Tony, it will be noted, had betrayed a woeful, even naive, ignorance. He had admitted to a certain amount of urgency, when everybody knows you don't ask any young woman over the age of twelve to 'climb into a coat', and expect it to take less than a quarter of an hour. He should, in fact, as he'd been there that long, have entered the door with those words on his lips, so that the dialogue could have proceeded during the climbing.

He had a lot to learn, but it didn't start just then. You'd almost think she'd anticipated it. She was into a short woollen jacket, kicked off one pair of shoes and jumped into another, and was locking her door behind her in one minute and seven seconds.

Link Green is not a district that offers anything approaching *haute cuisine*. Tony took her to Ethel's Eatery, which was a vastly inflated claim. It was not possible to believe one was eating, in the accepted sense of any enjoyment, if one's mind was on the job. Fortunately, theirs were not.

Afterwards, Tony so far forgot his already-mentioned urgency as to walk her to the hospital. Only to the entrance. He hated hospitals, though he would admit to a growing liking for hair smelling of iodoform.

It was all very well, too, that he should have claimed he

had to find out what was going on, but he had no idea of how this was to be done. Clearly, if he was to claim he was still incapacitated when he could no longer feel any pain, he couldn't enquire at the Station. He needed a free run at it. So he stood there after Madge had gone from sight and gave it some thought. Thus thinking, he saw, coming round a corner of the building, from the direction of the car park, the figure of Ephraim Potts.

He knew the solicitor, having lost a couple of cases to him in court. Potts never forgot a face. He stopped.

"Hello, young man. You're part of the standing guard, I take it."

"No, sir. I've no doubt there is—" He stopped. "You know who we're talking about, then?"

"Of course. Lucinda Porter."

"She's your client? Oh, I'm sorry. It's none of my business."

Potts smiled. How pleasant to meet a polite policeman, he thought, though he had to admit that, as his acquaintance with policemen had been almost entirely with them in witness boxes, it was hardly likely they would have been chatty. "Not at all," he said pleasantly. "Yes, she's my client. And my duty today is not a happy one."

"No? Well, it couldn't be, could it?"

"One does one's best. Well . . . mustn't stand here gossiping. I'm sure you're very busy."

"I was having a little ponder, Mr Potts."

"Always desirable. People should use more thought before they act."

"True. But that would surely put you out of business, I'd have thought."

Potts nodded, smiled, and walked up the steps into the hospital.

Tony continued to ponder. It was Saturday. It was Esmeralda's day. Therefore, he had to find Esmeralda.

And to discover himself to be one of a couple of dozen of his workmates? No. It needed something more special than that, something subtle.

The attacks, so far, had been at 6.10 p.m. (Arthur Moreton), 11.40 p.m. (Lucifer Hartington) and 11.50 p.m. (Ada Follett). The attacker preferred darkness; he preferred late darkness. He would strike, therefore, at Esmeralda Greene's residence late this approaching evening. As Tony knew her address, that she was in Flat 3 of the building, and that there was the likelihood she would be there some time this evening, he decided to wait for her there.

He was outside the Georgian house long before daylight failed, weighing up the prospects. He could see that there was a panel bearing four buttons and a microphone beside the door that was inside a deep porch, so he knew he wasn't going to be let in by anybody unless he had a good reason. But he hadn't got one. Yes he had. He pushed button number one.

"Yes?"

"Police, madam. May I come in and have a word?"

There was a pause, then a click, and the door opened at his touch.

He was in a square tiled hall, with one or two old and handsome pieces of furniture in it. Ahead was a wide staircase, beside it two dark recesses leading to rear premises. Number one was to his left.

The elderly lady who opened the door to him seemed agitated. He hadn't wanted to upset anybody.

"Is it the television? The man's been and I've paid him."

"No, no." And he spun a brisk and impromptu account of a car accident in town, one of the drivers having recognised, he thought, a witness. This very woman.

"Oh no," she assured him. "No, no. We haven't been into town for months. Ask my husband."

"No need," Tony told her, smiling. "It was clearly a mistake. I'm sorry to have troubled you."

He stood back. She closed the door. He was free to take his time in discovering some secret place where he could hide on the upper floor. But he'd omitted to prepare himself with food and drink, and it was going to be a long wait, especially as Ethel's eateries were already proving to have no lasting effect at all. It was then 4 p.m.

At seven o'clock Tomkins began to despatch his team, four at a time. They were to park their vehicles well clear and walk, quietly and singly, to the house. They'd each been allocated a waiting spot, with a cross on the little maps he'd supplied. He himself would be there at nine. Last man in. Then silence was to reign supreme.

Terry Cartwright, who'd been around the town all day, reported that he'd seen Ms Greene out shopping with Paul Catterick. Later, he reported that she was at that time in Catterick's room at the Cannon Inn. It was to be assumed that she would go home some time, though they could well decide to remain there for the next day or two. Tomkins allowed his squad to guard a house empty of Esmeralda. He couldn't think what else to do.

At this time Tomkins was operating strictly on Merry-weather's instructions. His mind had locked on to them. Had this not been so, he might had perceived the possibility that the slasher might also know that Esmeralda was at the Cannon Inn. But Tomkins was playing it cannily – protecting his own neck as a priority.

But nothing happened at the Cannon Inn, nothing, that is, of any interest to anyone lacking a salacious mind. So it need only be said that both of them were without visible wounds when they left the inn at 11.30 p.m., and clearly, because they were chatting happily, without psychological ones, either.

Paul had timed this exactly. The walk was a half hour

one, if carefully judged. The evening was fine – crisp and clear – so that there was nothing to disturb the timetable, and he reckoned that she'd be safe after midnight, at which time they would reach the house.

He was carrying her skis over his right shoulder and a large floppy bag on a strap over his left. This contained sundry articles of warm and/or waterproof clothing. Her boots were dangling from his left hand. She was carrying, over her shoulder like a rifle, the two ski sticks and she wore the woolly hat with the bobble, for no other reason than that she felt in a wild and mad mood, so that she could barely restrain from shouting out a load of nonsense to the nearly-deserted streets.

But very soon they were in completely deserted streets, with the street lamps still hiding their heads in the leaves of the chestnuts, which hadn't yet begun to discard them. Here it was dim and silent, and if any streets had ever been planned for clandestine and dirty deeds, these were they.

Behind them, Charlie began to close the gap. He didn't like this at all. Every tree trunk cast a huge and menacing shadow. The houses were set well back behind their own greenery. Damn it, didn't they *realise* . . .

No, they didn't. Esmeralda was teaching Paul the words and the tune of a rather risqué version of the school anthem which she'd heard the girls singing. A solitary pedestrian, walking his old and incontinent dog, crossed to the other side of the street.

Trailing along at the rear, Terry Cartwright sweated.

Tomkins had expected her to be home long before this. He'd been going by the time of the last bus. Damn it all, if she left it too late she wouldn't give the slasher time to get at her before midnight.

At 11.55 they reached the gateway. Tomkins whispered into his radio. Forty-eight men tensed. Paul put a hand on her arm. They paused. Midnight, he'd timed it for, at the front door. One minute to walk up to it . . . they'd got three to four minutes to spare, and how better to utilise it than to make a spectacle of themselves, there in the gateway! Asking for trouble, they were.

"Time," said Paul softly.

"Already?" she whispered.

"I'm afraid so."

They walked to the door. It was 11.58.

She slid her key into the lock. The door opened away from her. Paul, with his load, stood just behind her shoulder. A dark shape in a black ski-mask moved from the darkness just to one side in the hall and she gave a little gasp.

There was time for no more. His hand slashed sideways as she stepped back on Paul's toe and stumbled. The razor neatly sliced the bobble from her hat and just missed her nose. Then at last she screamed and brought up her ski sticks, points going for his face. One more slash slid the razor down the length of the sticks, there being a flash of white, later thought to be the tissue already round it. Moving down the sticks, it could not avoid her hands. Her scream became one of terror and distress and she dropped the sticks at her feet.

By this time Paul had reacted. He brought the skis down just past her shoulder, aimed at the attacker's head. He didn't know he was roaring at the top of his voice. But the dark shape was already thrusting past her and behind him Tony was coming down the dark stairs three at a time. Silent, Tony was, a menacing silence. Behind Paul, Charlie was at full speed, his head down. Silent, too, except for a growling sound.

The trouble with Paul was that his instinct was to reach for Esmeralda, who was trying to clutch one bleeding hand over the other bleeding hand. He missed with the skis and dropped them. The dark shape tripped over them, then kicked them ahead of him. Tony, who hadn't mapped-out the hall too accurately in his mind, hit the hall surface with his right foot and discovered that there was a rug there, which slid from beneath him into the fine old grandfather clock against a side wall, which just managed to get out the first stroke of midnight before collapsing with a scattering clang.

At that moment Paul heard Esmeralda whisper, "Get him, Paul."

Turning, undecided, Paul . . .

Chapter Sixteen

Sunday, 1 October

. . . sprang down the steps, where he could see the attacker was on his hands and knees. Wildly, he ran at him, got one foot through the strap of the canvas bag and went flying face downwards into the drive. When he rolled over he found himself looking up into the masked face, with the razor again moving. He jerked his head sideways and felt the hot searing slash down his left cheek.

It was one minute past midnight.

In a second, the dark figure was on its feet again. But, though it might be thought that Esmeralda and Paul were now out of it, this was not so. Esmeralda had seen. She whipped up the ski sticks again, though with blood streaming from her hands she could not be expected to do much with them, but it was a miracle that she could do anything at all. She threw them, like spears, having done a little javelin throwing in her younger days. But her aim was poor.

Behind her, thrusting through, came Tony, scooping up the skis where Paul had dropped them and hurling them, one after the other, at the assailant. Paul had now rolled free, his hands to his face. The shadow raised his head, ducked beneath the skis, and turned to run.

Charlie, rumbling at full speed like a rhino, was too close. Terry, lighter built, was coming up fast. Tony, frantic for

213

more light on the scene, scrambled around with his hand just inside the doorway for the hall switch.

The shadow ducked beneath the skis. Charlie, who was good at this sort of thing, managed to get his legs tangled in them and did a spectacular somersault to land on his back with a grunt. Terry Cartwright fell face down on top of him.

Around them there were shouts. "The front! The front!" Tomkins was now wishing they had the TV cameras there. Lights were what he needed. Until the light came on in the hall there was nothing, and when it did it only showed, in black silhouette, the assailant taking advantage of it to run past the crouching Esmeralda and the baffled Tony – what a daft place to put switches! – and running into the dark depths of the house, where there was sure to be a back door.

Tony, certain the rear would be covered, turned his attention to Esmeralda and Paul. But those who should have been behind were now in front, and those in front were also there, so that there was a tangled mass of galloping humanity where it wasn't needed, while the attacker was away towards the greenery at the rear . . .

Closely followed by Charlie, who, not having the equipment for rapid thinking, kept his mind firmly on the main objective. He had seen his enemy disappearing into the depths of the house. Whatever chaos might be erupting around him, he ignored it, and charged in pursuit. He heard ahead of him the slamming of a door, so he ran until he banged into a door, opened it, and plunged outside.

A shape was disappearing into the dark mass of the shrubbery facing him. There was an orange glow beyond the shrubbery, which indicated a street over there somewhere. Bursting through it, he found himself in somebody's garden, beyond that a street and in the street the sound of a car engine roaring into life, then the scream of overstressed tyres.

When he reached the street there was no sign of anything.

Listlessly and in baffled frustration he returned the way he'd come.

By this time, everybody was in the act. The media, unprimed, nevertheless seemed to spring from the ground beneath. Vehicles rushed in all directions until there was barely room for the ambulance when it arrived, or for the chief superintendent's car. He thrust through a growth of waving mikes, snarling and snapping, found Inspector Tomkins, and stood there, hands in his pocket, and simply glared. Later, Tomkins said it was like a flamethrower pointed at him.

Esmeralda and Paul were taken away in the same ambulance. Paul was barely able to speak – barely to breathe with his mouth full of blood. Esmeralda whimpered herself into unconsciousness as they'd given her an injection. In Emergency, they lay on adjoining stretchers, but were separated almost at once and rushed away for treatment.

It was daylight before everything had settled down, when the cars and vans had departed and all that was left behind at the house was the team searching the grounds for clues. There was nothing. The two razors were found almost at once, one in the hall (Saturday) and one on the rear path (Sunday). As before, they'd been wiped clean and left, accompanied by their wiping tissues.

The local superintendent had made a brief statement to the media, carefully worded to convey nothing specific. Frankly, he knew no more about it than they did. Loonies, he could understand, perverts and rapists he knew how to tackle, but an obvious nutcase who took appalling risks in order to satisfy his personal fantasies was something he preferred not to think about.

After breakfast, though they were both exhausted, Chief Superintendent Merryweather got down to business with Detective Inspector Tomkins.

Merryweather was exercising severe control over his

emotions. That headache was back, the one the consultant had warned him about. Stress and tension, he'd said, avoid them. It was, indeed, more stressful to control himself now than it would be to take Tomkins in his bare hands and tear him into pieces. His voice was heavy but toneless.

"Right," he said. "I'll say nothing about last night's fiasco, except to tell you that it's all going down in a report, which you'll be able to see before it goes in. As of now, you're still on duty. Understand? Good. Now . . . your thoughts on it."

Tomkins raised his head. He'd assumed he'd get no chance to say a word. But his voice, too, was colourless as he felt completely punch-drunk, wanting only to go somewhere, curl up, and pass out.

"Seven razors were stolen, sir. To our man, they're related to the winners of the raffle. Don't ask me why. And he's absolutely determined – obsessed – with the idea of using each and every one. All he's got unused are the Wednesday and Thursday razors, which relate to Charlie Pierce and Lucinda Porter. It's tightening the objective, or objectives. It makes it easier for us, with only two people to watch."

Beady eyes stared at him. The chief super was motionless, apart from his head, which nodded.

"We know something about his personality now, sir. He isn't decisive, you might say. Anybody with an open razor, you'd think, would go right in and finish it off. But no – he seems to flinch away from anything too violent."

"Hartington!" rumbled the chief super.

"A special case, I'm sure, sir. They knew each other. I'm convinced that all there's ever intended is an attack. In each case. After all, Ada Follett wasn't harmed at all, nor Moreton. I think, in fact, that he made a later decision about Ada. In every other case he's found time to wipe clean and discard his razor. I suspect he hung on to that one, wondering whether to have another go at Ada. And, as you know, the razor was brought back and left in the morning. He'd made up his mind. He'd made an attack – it was enough – so he surrendered his razor. Sort of."

Merrywether grumbled again. "Fanciful. Too fanciful, man."

"Perhaps, sir. But my point is that violence isn't natural to this man. He flinches away from it. With Hartington, it seems it was a matter of complete panic. Wild and frantic. But behind it all there's been some quick thinking. Had to be, the way he's snatched his opportunities for attack and for escape. Very quick. I mean – consider the Ms Greene and Mr Catterick attacks."

Merryweather had no wish to consider them. He growled, "What about them?" Was there something he'd missed?

"He managed to attack Ms Greene at one minute before midnight. Fine. Just managed to get it in on Saturday. That obsession again. But then . . . Catterick was to hand. Midnight had struck – I heard it myself from the clock in the hall. So he dealt with Catterick, and with the Sunday razor! Now . . . how's that for quick work? It's almost unbelievable. There were only a few seconds between the attacks, but Catterick's was after midnight. With a different razor! And *that* had to have been thought out like a shot. In a split second. He couldn't have anticipated it, you see, because he must've been waiting in that house since early in the afternoon, so he wouldn't even know they were together."

"Why d'you say he must've been there early?"

"Because," said Tomkins smugly, "I had a man in there myself that afternoon, so our razor expert must have got in first."

"Then your man wasn't very effective."

Tomkins shrugged. He couldn't very well blame Tony for failing in his duty, when he hadn't even been on duty. The chief super tapped the table surface in irritation, using a finger like a tent peg. It was time for decisions.

"Very well," he decided. "If all our reasoning is valid, then we can assume we've got a bit of a break until Wednesday, as there's only Wednesday's and Thursday's razors to come. I'll get a team in from DHQ, to supplement what you can get out on the streets, and we start a blanket check. We know he got home after Saturday midnight. A neighbour might have seen something. This time, he must've been covered with blood, with no canal he could jump in around there. Something else to look for. Traces of blood in his car. Heavens, Inspector, it's all routine stuff. Pursue every lead. Tie every possibility up tight. Get things moving – I'm off to my bed."

Tomkins had the same idea, but he knew it wasn't to be. He was about dead on his feet and if his lady friend were to open the door to him now he'd be able to do no more than fall inside.

One thing about it, he realised. One less dark spot, if not exactly bright, was that the media had left them alone at the Station. They were all round at the hospital.

Esmeralda and Paul, having been stitched up and supplied with a replacement of blood, were in the women's and men's wards respectively, the women's on the second floor, the men's on the third. For two or three hours the Ward Sisters had managed to fend off the invasion of microphones and video cameras, but they couldn't very well refuse access to personal friends. And these were multitudinous. It had been on the radio news that morning and the facts spread like fire through the town.

Paul's section from the office swarmed in to comfort him. "Don't make him laugh," the Staff Nurse said severely. He could barely whisper, with half his face sewn together. But *they* laughed, exercising their imaginations as to how he'd look when he returned to work, and inventing reasons he could muster in order to excuse his new looks. They then, because this was really what they'd come for, went downstairs to Esmeralda, to see this woman of his and to discover whether she was good enough for him.

There they found a whole swarm of girls from the school who were discussing whether Esmeralda would ever again wield a hockey stick, or even manage to chalk up mathematical propositions on what now had to be called the chalkboard. These girls were shooed away by the headmistress, who'd intended to be very severe with Esmeralda for bringing adverse publicity to the school, and distressingly found herself undermined by an attack of tears.

Paul's young ladies waited until it was clear, then they went to give Esmeralda a look-over and grudging approval. And no end of advice on how to treat him. Esmeralda smiled. She knew.

Esmeralda's mob went to see Paul, were disappointed they were not even supposed to kiss his good cheek, and advised him to claim it to be a duelling scar. It was generally agreed he'd look thoroughly evil when it healed. He reached for his pad, wrote a couple of words and held it up. They did so and for some time there was peace.

But then the media got through. In spite of the fact that he could not speak, they nevertheless shot questions at him, like a barrage of bullets. "What did you think when you saw the razor coming at you?" "Can you tell our readers your feelings about this monster?"

Fortunately, he hadn't destroyed the message on his pad. He held it up for the cameras. They departed.

Esmeralda, though, could speak. It was a coincidence that she used the same two words. They gave it up and went in a flood to the Station, which they found to be strangely quiet and deserted. It was, they decided, a dead loss, and dispersed to the various local pubs.

Tony came. He was still, he assumed, on sick leave, though he felt a hundred per cent. "Christ, mate, I'm sorry. I never guessed the bastard'd be there before me.

Don't try to cuss me, just nod if you agree that I'm a useless slob."

Paul nodded. His eyes signalled. Tony grinned.

"I've seen her. She's all right. In full voice. She'll be able to talk for both of you. It's both hands. Not many stitches, but they're not sure about her grip when it heals up. Tendons or something. I'm instructed to go back and tell her how you are."

Paul wrote: 'Tell her – can't talk – but otherwise fine.'

Tony nodded, forgetting for a second that he could speak. Reached for the pad and wrote, 'Will do.'

In the afternoon Ada and her two friends came to disrupt both wards. "Can't stand hospitals," said Ada to Esmeralda. "You're lookin' grand, I must say. Brought a blush to your cheeks, it has."

Then, liking hospitals or not, she and her friends proceeded to spread joy and dispel despondency throughout the ward – and later through Paul's – by visiting the rest of the patients, fluffing up pillows that didn't need it, running errands that didn't require consummation and feeding everybody vast quantities of a fortifying liquid they claimed was orange juice.

Two staffs consulted and decided that after all a bit of a laugh didn't hurt anybody, before they finally sent them packing.

Later in the evening, after dark because he wasn't yet certain he was safe outside his own four walls, Bert (Slasher) Harris came. He had confronted himself in the mirror and told himself he'd got to face it. These were the only two injured, except for Lucifer Hartington, and he couldn't apologise to him. So he came to do exactly that to Esmeralda and Paul.

"Don't be a damned fool," said Esmeralda. "It wasn't you with the razor, was it?"

"No."

"Well then."

"It was my fault."

"You made a mistake. So what? Haven't you ever made a mistake before?"

He blushed and looked down at his hands. "I put a ball through our own goal – and in a cup final, at that."

She looked serious. "Good Lord. How terrible. This is nothing in comparison. Nothing."

He toddled away happily. Heavens, she thought, I'm catching it from Paul.

Bert went to see Paul with the same apology.

Paul thought. He wrote: 'Don't do it again, then.'

Poor Bert, not getting the reactions he'd expected, and vaguely realising he'd have felt better after a good rollicking, went away somewhat confused. But at the same time relieved and revitalised.

On the steps outside he met Charlie who was hanging around and looking lost. They did not exactly recognise each other for what they were in this situation, but Charlie remembered his idol, and thought this man was he, and Bert thought he remembered this young thug ploughing his way towards him through the crowd on the concourse.

They faced each other, hesitant.

"You're Slasher Harris, ain't y'?" said Charlie, who wouldn't have been able to tell he was the mayor. Charlie looked on mayors as high-ups, who wore a chain round their necks.

"That is true," said Bert, warmed to be recognised as a somebody. "And who're you?"

"Charlie Pierce."

"Ah yes. I remember. You won—"

"Won nothing. We're all soddin' losers, strikes me. But I'll get 'im. You can bet on that."

In the light from the entrance hall, Bert Harris considered him. There was plenty of Charlie to consider and what he saw pleased Bert. "Yes," he said. "I've heard about you. You've been asking for it, young man, that's what you've been doing."

"He'll come for me, then I'll get him. Here . . . can I ask y' something?"

"Ask away."

"You was before my time, see. I never saw you play. But dad told me and I tried to do it. You know that swerve – when y' get the ball on the outside of y' right foot and swerve left . . . I never did get that right. I mean, you've gotta scoop it up, sort of—"

"You've played?" Bert was eager.

"Yeah. But I was no good. Couldn't get rid o' the ball. Even put it through me own goal."

"You didn't!"

"I did."

Bert clapped him on the shoulder. "Me too!"

Then they laughed together and walked round for a while, discussing football and how it'd changed, until Bert asked, "And what're you doing here?"

"Come to see a couple of me friends. They copped it last night."

"Then go on in."

"Can I?"

"Why not?"

Because Charlie's mother had put the fear of damnation in him with respect to hospitals, that was why not. Only the very last moments of your life were ever spent in hospitals. Go in there and you never came out again. And the screams . . . enough to drive anybody mad.

"Don't like to," admitted Charlie. "An' I ain't got a pass."

"Nonsense. Go in. Second floor for Esmeralda, third for Paul. And say you're a friend. All right?"

"I'll tell 'em Slasher Harris sent me."

"Do that. See what it gets you." And chuckling, Bert Harris headed for his car.

It was this minor and insignificant meeting that eventually led to the downfall of the slasher, but to each of them it was no more than a congenial interlude.

Charlie had really encountered Esmeralda and Paul only in those few moments of the attack the previous night. He couldn't have explained his motivation for visiting; something to do with keeping in contact with what was going on, something to do with having let them down. Neither had been in any condition to remember him from that incident.

The meetings were therefore embarrassing and mainly silent. Paul was patient. He wasn't going anywhere. He gathered enough to realise that this vast young man was intending to avenge the attack, so he simply wrote, 'Come again', and Charlie went off to see Esmeralda.

Charlie quietly and politely asked permission whenever he encountered a nurse. They smiled wearily. They'd had a day of it, and one more, especially a patently healthy lump of humanity, wasn't going to do much harm.

Esmeralda terrified Charlie. She didn't know who he was and why, and he didn't seem able to explain himself. Eventually she realised that she knew him as somebody who'd tried to help. Then she said, "Get him for me, Charlie. Get him."

"Yes ma'am."

She beckoned him close, as though to whisper, and kissed him on the lips. This horrified him. She was quite obviously not one of those females whom it was dangerous to touch for fear of them falling apart. In that second, Charlie learned a lot about women, though it was a long while before he could adjust his thinking to accept it.

Two important encounters for Charlie that evening! Esmeralda was about to launch at him the third one.

223

"Go up and see Paul for me, will you?"

"Just seen him."

"See him again then, and pass it on."

"Pass what on?"

"That kiss," she said.

Charlie left the ward in a daze. He didn't know what the world was coming to, and that was a fact. But because she'd entrusted it to him, he headed up the stairs to Paul's ward, though not being able to see any possible way of accomplishing his task.

In the corridor he met Madge. A friendly face!

"Hello," he said.

"Hello yourself."

"What're you doing here?" they both said together. Whispered, rather. It was very quiet in the wards at this time.

Madge, even in the seclusion of the Intensive Care ward, had heard all the news and knew that the slasher had been at it again. And, being intelligent, she understood Charlie long before Charlie understood her. By this time, Madge was well known to all the staff, and was allowed a free rein. She took Charlie in to see Paul.

Paul was very nearly a stranger to her. Their only encounter had lasted ten seconds. But she felt an affinity for him. To Paul, she was a strangely taut and exhausted girl who'd come to stare at him, and who lived in 3B.

"I seen her," said Charlie.

Paul lifted an eyebrow.

Charlie explained. "That woman you was with, she sent you a message."

Paul nodded, wincing delicately.

And Charlie, emboldened by his recent discovery, and determined to pass on his message and check on his new-found confidence, turned and kissed Madge on the lips – and if he could ever come across any girl looking more delicate he'd give up beer, that he would.

224

"She sent that to you," he said to Paul.

Madge, pouting and smiling at the same time, leaned over and kissed Paul on the corner of his mouth, the least painful corner.

To any other three people, this would have been a paltry incident, even slightly mawkish. To these three it was a vastly important one.

Madge and Charlie went out into the corridor. They stood together.

"She's asleep," said Madge.

"Yes," said Charlie. "Who?"

"Lucinda. I've been sitting with her."

"Yes."

"I'm going home now."

"I'll walk with you. Okay?"

"Lovely."

She put her hand in his arm and he walked her home.

Chapter Seventeen

Monday, 2 October

The town clerk, Llewellyn Pugh, walked into the mayor's parlour at a quarter to nine on Monday morning, not expecting to find anybody there. It was a matter of habit, of routine, to check that the desk had been polished and the ornate inkstand dusted, the inkwells filled, the pens laid out. He had never known a mayor who used either the pens or the ink, but it was a question of pride that they should be ready. Indeed, in a lower drawer there were half a dozen very old quill pens, and if Pugh had his way these too would be laid out, *and* used. Always assuming any of them could write.

Bert Harris was there, at the window, gazing at what had been the uninspiring frontage opposite, now the collapsed frontage, with barriers all round it. It didn't look any worse than it had before.

"You here, Mr Harris?"

"I'm here, yes Mr Pugh."

Pugh managed a thin smile. "I've nothing laid on for today, not expecting you, you see."

"I thought it time I showed myself. And . . ." He hesitated. "And there was something I wanted to ask you."

"Oh yes?" Pugh looked suspicious of requests. Then, as the mayor hesitated, "What is it? Anything within my duties—" He stood waiting with a hesitant smile.

"You married, Llew?"

"What? I mean . . . why d'you ask?"

Bert was clearly embarrassed. Charlie had given his self-confidence a boost, but Bert hated things becoming too personal. "Sorry. Nosy, that's me. No, it's not that. You've never mentioned your wife."

"No. I haven't."

It was difficult, and Llew wasn't helping. Bert wondered how to go on. "Children? Have you got any kids, Llew?"

"No. Not really." Hell, he thought, what a stupid thing to say. "No. I haven't."

"Then how," Bert demanded," are *you* going to manage?"

"I'm managing."

"I mean, if you don't *have* any."

"I suppose you do. Can you please explain." Pugh was shaking his head. "Are you all right, Bert?"

"Just a thought, that's all. I had a thought."

"I'm sure it was very exciting."

"That Six Club of yours—"

"Club Six."

"That story you told me – your grandfather not having any son to pass it on to . . ." Bert cocked his head. Pugh had gone rigid, his face set, his eyes bleak. "You know. If you've got no sons, how're you going to be able to pass on your membership?"

"Are you saying . . ." Pugh took a deep breath, then he laughed thinly. "I'm not doing what my grandad did, if that's what you mean. Doesn't fit, does it?"

"What doesn't fit?"

"There isn't an eldest son in the lot." He stared at Bert, but met a blankness. "This slasher . . . you can't be suggesting—"

"Hell no. Don't be damned ridiculous, Llew. I'm only asking – what're you going to do when you retire from the club? Eh?"

227

Pugh relaxed, managed to shrug. "I'm not exactly intending to retire. Not just yet."

"But . . . when you do."

"Oh . . ." Pugh waved his left hand vaguely, the right being clamped on a coloured file cover. "My fault, I suppose. I gave you the wrong impression. It's changed a lot since my grandad's time. More informal, you could say. We simply propose somebody."

"That's what I meant." Bert was clearly satisfied.

"Did you?" He cocked his head. "Is there a point in this, Bert?"

Bert felt that his face was hot. It wasn't often he asked a favour, but now he was very close to having to plead. "You said it was exclusive. Only six of you."

"That's why it's called Club 6."

"I thought you might like to propose me, Llew. Eh?"

"What! Oh, come on now . . . here, you mean it, don't you?"

"Yes. I mean it."

"But you're older than me."

"Not all that much, Llew. And I can hold my drink. Ask anybody. Nine pints, you said. I can manage that."

"There's more to it." Pugh sighed. "It's not all over when we've primed the tank. No. I told you, less formal, more a social thing now. We go on from there. Pile in our cars and drive out to somewhere we've booked. Make a day of it, like. Maybe a few ladies—"

"What! *You*, Mr Pugh?"

"Unlike you, Bert, I've got no wife to comfort me."

Bert Harris nearly said he hadn't, either. Things with Tina had been a little strained and lacking in courtesy lately. "Are you implying I'm not the man I used to be?"

"As I don't know the man you used to be, I can't very well say," Pugh pointed out, clearly now having had enough of the subject. "But what you weren't, and what is

228

an absolute must, is a steelman. You have to have worked in a factory."

"But I did! Before going pro with the football."

Pugh became more terse. The man was persistent! "But in any event, as I said, I'm not yet ready to retire."

To Bert, this seemed to be no more than stubborn rejection, lacking in anything approaching interest in the feelings of a man who'd been blackballed fifty-seven times by the 57 Club. Bert therefore said something that he should not have done, just catching Pugh as he turned away towards the door.

"A little bird tells me that you might not get the chance of retiring."

Pugh stopped. He spun on his heel. "What little bird? What did you hear?"

"That you were late for this month's ceremony. Half an hour late."

Pugh was very still. He licked his lips. "Who told you that?"

Bert felt he'd been snubbed. No little twit like Pugh was going to condescend to Bert Harris, especially when his confidence was returning so satisfactorily. He smiled, pleased to have shaken Pugh. "One of your six."

"Who?"

"Does it matter?"

"Of course it bloody well matters."

These were strong words from the town clerk. Bert jerked out, "I believe he's your present president."

"Moreton! That blasted blatherer!" Then he recovered quickly, but his smile wasn't what you could call sincere. "But in any event, Bert, if I should retire – or even resign – we'd need a younger man. Wouldn't you say! Somebody we could rely on. You get my point, Mr Mayor?"

It was a direct slap in the face. Bert drew himself up, all dignity and without the chain to help him. "Very well. I'm

sorry I mentioned it. But . . ." he got in his own dig,
". . . assuming you *will* be asked to resign – and I might just
have another word with Moreton – I'll suggest somebody to
him. To take your place. Oh no, not me. I'm too old! But I
have a young man in mind. Absolutely reliable, I can assure
you. Oh yes. A good lad. Strong and fit. Good for a number
of years yet." He stopped, nodding to himself as though he'd
made a satisfactory decision.

"Who?"

"I have my secrets, Mr Pugh." Teasing, that's what it
was.

"I have a right—"

"Have you? Very well, it's a very minor point. His name
is Charles Pierce. Known as Charlie."

Bert swore the man looked right through him as though
he wasn't there. Pugh's lips opened but nothing emerged.
He simply turned on his heel and went out, leaving Bert
wondering why he couldn't keep his silly mouth shut.

After a few minutes, Bert made up his mind, reached for
his phone, and made a call to Arthur Moreton. It would be
as well to let him know that he, Bert, had betrayed what had
been a private and very personal word in his ear, Arthur
having realised how upset Bert had been about the 57 Club
business, and slipping in a hopeful hint.

But Arthur Moreton wasn't in a receptive mood that
morning. In fact, at the time Bert called he was sitting at
his desk and rereading the letter he'd received from the 57
Club that morning.

"Well – thank you, Bert!" said Arthur bitterly. "You've
just landed me right in it." Then he hung up gently, put his
head in his hands, and groaned.

Just when he'd got Kenny Scott eating out of his hand,
this had to happen! He might have guessed he'd finish up
taking the blame for the mental deficiences of Bert Harris.
He'd been Chairman of the raffle committee; he therefore

carried the can for the fiasco. It was all very well to threaten Bert with fifty-seven black balls, but Bert didn't finish up any worse than he'd been before. It was infinitely more harrowing for Arthur, who now looked as though he was about to be expelled from the 57 Club.

The letter was without any frills or embellishments. He was called before a sub-committee of nine fellow members, that same evening, to attempt to satisfy them on the question of why, when it had been specifically forbidden, he should have bought tickets in his own name in the raffle.

That in itself was bad enough. The really galling point was that the letter was signed by the appointed chairman of that sub-committee, Llewellyn Pugh.

For a long while he sat there thinking about it before he decided he had only one chance of stalling a request for his resignation.

Kenny Scott would have laughed his head off, but fortunately he need never find out. Arthur reached for his cheque book.

By this time the teams were out and around the town, conducting their random questioning. Regrettably, Tony had no faith in these measures. It was unlikely that anyone would've seen a car after midnight, on a Saturday night of all nights, acting strangely. They all did. The man they were after would take care to act normally and go about his usual life without any indication of stress or strain. Consequently, Tony centred his actions that day on Foundry Street, Link Green, more specifically on number three. Madge had to come home some time, hadn't she?

As she didn't, not while he was around, he sought out his friends at the Plucked Goose – Ada, Connie and Floss – reaching there a little after six.

They were discussing the party they would have when Paul and Esmeralda came out of hospital.

"A bit early for that, isn't it?" Tony asked. "I'd have said a month."

"What!" cried Floss. "Not our Esmeralda. A week. I give her a week. She won't stay a minute longer than that. You'll see."

"And Paul?"

"He'll look horrible, but he'll be with her," Ada decided.

"You're probably right."

"My Fred," said Connie, "looked horrible. But that was natural."

"You coulda done better," Floss agreed. "My Harry wasn't exactly Ramon Navarro."

"Who?" asked Tony.

"Before your time, luv," Ada told him. "Film star. Didn't fancy him myself."

"You'd better hadn't," Floss observed, her lips curving sourly. "Your Eric would've cut up rough."

"Eric," said Ada, "was gentle as a lamb. Wish we had him here now. He'd soon have settled that slasher. Took him apart, he would."

"Doesn't sound all that gentle to me," Tony observed.

"With ordinary people," Ada said severely. "Get him really riled and he was a terror."

"I know a chap like that."

"Oh yes?"

"Charlie Pierce. He was the one who got the prize you would've had."

"Then why haven't you brought him to show me?"

"I'll do that. I'll do that as soon as I can."

He got to his feet. "Must be going. I'm officially on duty. If I see him, I'll bring him along."

It was no more than a vague promise. At that time it seemed to have no relevance to the case at all, so it was sheer chance that he did meet Charlie, and only as an afterthought that he took him along to meet the three old ladies.

Naturally, his first call was to number 3, Foundry Street, and the sight of a light in 3B sent him running up the stairs. He knew that Madge no longer had any reason for going up to 3C. There was no more story to type up and read out to Lucinda, as that was the one they'd worked on together. And the other story . . . wasn't there another? She'd said something. It would, in any event, be far from her thoughts now.

He banged on her door, impatient, arranging a cheerful face. She opened the door and her smile was painful. The silly creature, she was making herself ill. He followed her into the room, and Charlie levered himself halfway from the tatty easy chair, which had collapsed just a little more since his arrival.

"Hello," said Madge emptily. She did not actually tell him to go away, but the welcome was certainly not as warm as he'd expected. It came from rehearsing it in his mind. Whatever he'd planned to say, and it varied greatly to encompass all possibilities, he had always imagined her face with a smile, possibly forced but nevertheless there.

"You here, Charlie?" Tony asked, trying to keep all challenge out of his voice.

"Sure am," agreed Charlie, who wasn't bright enough to catch all the nuances. He sat down again.

Madge said, "I'll make some more tea," because it was all she could summon up from the back of her mind.

"No, no," protested Tony and then he moved a hand vaguely, conveying agreement with whatever suited her best.

Madge therefore retired into her tiny, cramped kitchen, in which there was no flat surface large enough to accept all the trappings of three cups of tea. She didn't want one herself, having been almost living on hospital tea and hospital sandwiches, but she didn't want to seem impolite by failing to join them.

It would be incorrect to say she had her mind on the job, incorrect even to suggest that she had any control at all over her mind. Images and impressions flashed through but they made no emotional impact. She had lost touch with the progress of time, could have told you it was evening because it was dark outside, but if challenged she would have to admit it was perhaps early morning. Which day, she could not have said. Only the mechanical actions, instilled from numerous repetitions, could she perform. Tea she could make. In practice, the water wasn't really boiling when she poured it into the pot and when she emerged her tiny tin tray was rattling in her hands.

Tony absently took it from her and put it down on her small table in the window, next to the Royal. She sat, knees together, on a kitchen chair so wobbly she'd forbidden Charlie to go near it, and stared at them. They were part of her life, she knew, two men friends who'd involved themselves in her existence. Beyond that, she had no feelings about it. After they'd left, she might lie down for a while. Then she would get up, perform a rather perfunctory cleansing operation, and return to the hospital.

"Glad I've found you," Tony was saying, meaning Charlie. "I wanted to check something with you."

"Sure," said Charlie, who was, Tony casually noted, rather more relaxed than before, not so nervous, less deferential. Charlie was, in fact, taking Madge's acceptance of his presence for granted. "Not as I know much," Charlie said.

"What you saw – up at that house – Saturday night."

"Rff!" Charlie said, a kind of laugh sound. "All I did was run like hell and trip over them bleedin' skis."

"Think though, Charlie. There was this character – the slasher. He'd already had a go at Esmeralda—"

"That Esmeralda! Heh, there's a smasher for you!"

Tony stared at him with his head on one side. He decided not to pursue this point. "Well, whatever she is, he'd already

234

had a go at her. Then, about five seconds later, he was having a go at Paul. Went for his face. Remember that?"

"Sort of. I was on me back, though, tryin' to get me breath back."

"Right," said Tony. "But concentrate. Did you see him get that second razor out of his pocket – or somewhere like that – and put the other one away? I mean, the razors had Saturday and Sunday on them. In practice, he'd managed, by about two seconds, to get Esmeralda with the Saturday one. Then it was midnight and at about three seconds past – so that it was technically Sunday – he was carving up Paul. And both razors were found, and *not* on the drive. The point is, and as far as I know nobody's thought of this, when did he switch razors? When did he put one away and get the other one out? Y'get my point? He'd only got seconds. Did *you* see anything, Charlie?"

"No. Not me. I didn't see anythin' like that."

"I didn't either. You see what it means?"

"No."

Tony turned to Madge. "But you see, Madge, don't you?"

"What?" She seemed to jerk into consciousness.

Tony looked at her more carefully, but equally careful not to make it obvious. He turned away quickly, shocked by her empty eyes and the drawn greyness round her mouth, the tattered remnants of chewed lipstick, the pitiful attempt to colour cheeks that were white and pinched.

"Charlie," he said, "we'd better get out of here. Let you get some rest, Madge."

"No!" she cried sharply, rather to her surprise, when rest was what her whole body cried out for. "I don't want to be alone," she whispered.

"You're about asleep on your feet," Tony told her, despite the fact that she wasn't on them, and knew it already. "Why don't you get your head down for a bit?"

"I can't!" There was a trace of panic in her voice. "I've got to get back."

"Tonight?"

"What time is it?"

"Just after eight."

"What day?"

"Monday," he told her gently. "Night," he added, just to be certain.

"I promised. I've got to get back. Did you know . . ." Her voice set itself into a drone, an almost toneless mutter, as though it came from way back, where the horrors were lurking. The very lack of emphasis impressed the two men more than hysteria would, Tony perhaps more than Charlie, because he'd spoken to men who'd been out on motorway multiple pile-ups. Lifting her chin, making an effort, she went on tonelessly.

"She's in this ward, see. Where they die. Usually. Waiting for them to die. But oh . . . they do work hard to keep them alive. They run. I've seen them running down the ward. Why? That's what I ask myself. Why do they keep them alive, suffering so? Why don't they just let them go? But she's determined, see. She's told me. What day is it? She's always asking that. Don't know why, and I have to ask a nurse. What day is it? One more day, one more night. I suppose it's a kind of pride. I've lived through another night. Sort of. It always seems to happen in the night, you know. Two or three in the morning, I suppose. You can always tell. When they're expecting it, I mean. They move the bed up the ward, closer to the doors. I've seen them do it. And then . . . then, when it gets to the last, they go round the ward pulling the curtains round all the other beds. It's so cruel, I think. It tells everybody that there's another one going. And you wait. Then they draw the curtains back – and there's an empty bed nearest the doors."

She stopped. It simply tailed off as she stared emptily at it and allowed it to drain away.

The two men said nothing. Barely breathed. Dared say nothing.

"I've got to be back at two," she whispered. "Promised. Myself," she explained.

Tony realised she was afraid of falling asleep in case she awoke too late. "You in a hurry, Charlie?" he asked.

Charlie, his senses highly tuned for once, got it in a flash. "Nowhere particular to go."

"So you," Tony said to Madge, "can get your head down on your little bed, and we'll wake you around one-thirty."

Her eyes looked startled. "Oh . . . I couldn't."

He grinned. "One man here, that'd be improper. Two, and it's okay."

This he said with such conviction that she accepted it without any thought. It meant to her that she could relax. Oh, glorious chance! She drew in her lower lip for a second, said, "I'll just pop—", and waved her hand vaguely, then she disappeared out onto the landing.

Her bed was behind a curtain at one end of the room. She returned, some colour in her cheeks, said something about not changing, and the creak of the springs came a few seconds later. Tony gave it two minutes, then he peeped. She was fast asleep. He gently drew the overlay across her and returned to Charlie. He drew the chair closer, so that they could whisper.

"You see what I mean, Charlie?"

"Huh?"

"About the razors. The Saturday and Sunday razors. You haven't been listening!"

"I have then."

"Well?"

"Well what?"

"Don't you *see*! I'm saying he didn't *use* both razors,

because he didn't have time. He used the Saturday razor on both of 'em, but he dropped that one in front of the house, and the Sunday one at the back, both wiped, both with their tissues. Y' see – he couldn't have expected both of them together, and exactly on midnight. It was fortuitous—"

"It was what?"

"A bit of luck for him. He managed, by sheer chance, to use up his Saturday razor on Saturday and the Sunday one on Sunday."

Charlie frowned heavily. "Yeah. Sure. Lucky."

"Or unlucky, Charlie, that's the point. You see, he made a mistake. His first, by the look of things. A mistake, Charlie."

"All right, a bleedin' mistake." Charlie's tone appended a 'so what?'

"It tells us something."

"It don't tell me nothin'."

"Because you're not thinking, Charlie."

"Ain't in the mood." Charlie was thinking, but it was worry about Madge.

"You see, he wouldn't go round with a pocketful of razors. One night, one job, one razor. But this time he was carrying two. Just by chance? I don't believe it. And not in the same pocket, you can be sure of that. He'd want to grab Saturday's razor when he wanted Saturday's. But he'd got Sunday's with him so he dropped that too, even though he hadn't actually used it. But . . . *why* had he got Sunday's with him? That's the point."

Charlie grunted.

"You're not listening."

Charlie grunted again, so Tony carried the idea along in his head.

It had to mean that the slasher had intended to need both razors, but not both the same night. So he was carrying Sunday's in anticipation of an attack on Paul Catterick at

238

a later time on Sunday, probably Sunday evening. Which surely had to mean that he hadn't expected, that Sunday, to have access to the place he had the razors hidden, which was probably his home.

Yes. That was reasonably valid. It didn't prove anything, it didn't lead anywhere, but it was a detail to be levelled against the unknown assailant.

Charlie had gone to sleep, he having the chair he could lean back in. Tony got to his feet and went to stand at the window, with the lights off in the room. There was sufficient light from the street lamps. He lit a cigarette. There was something strange about the tissues, too, but he couldn't reason through it. Not that they'd been used to wipe them clean, though it would've been easier and safer to wear gloves, but that they'd been left with the razors. Why leave the razors anyway? Why – even more so – leave the tissues with them? Why – even stranger – in Ada's case, go to the trouble to sneak back in the morning after in order to leave the razor *and* the tissue it'd been wiped with?

For one fleeting second he thought he'd captured an idea, but then it slipped away when he was distracted by a shadow moving, down there in the street. It was near midnight now and there was no police surveillance on the house, Lucinda being in hospital. He saw a pink, uplifted face.

Quietly he went down and out of the front door, but he could find nothing. He decided he'd imagined it.

At the same time Arthur Moreton was standing at his bedroom window, staring out at nothing. He had a glass of brandy in one hand, a lighted cigar in the other. Behind him his wife was fast asleep. In the morning there'd be the devil's own game about the stale cigar smell in the bedroom, but what the hell! Arthur felt a warm comfort flowing through him, the comfort of success.

As far as he could see, he'd now eased his way round all the obstacles and no pitfalls lay ahead. Mind you, it'd cost money, but it was well spent. Even Kenny Scott could no longer pester him.

It had been disconcerting to face the sub-committee, in the Ruby room at the club, beneath the chandelier and facing the grim painting of the club's founder. And facing, too, the equally grim chairman, Llewellyn Pugh.

Pugh was using his most official and sombre voice, though he was unable to call forward any force or magisterial criticism. The case against Arthur was simple. He had bought five tickets for the raffle. Worse, he had come up with the winning ticket. That was the inexcusible fact.

Yet behind Pugh's eyes, Arthur could detect the restraint. If Pugh pushed too hard, then Arthur wouldn't hesitate to boot Llew himself out of a much-more-treasured membership, that of Club 6. It all became very amusing and Arthur allowed it to go on for a while, listening to those rumbling and plaintive voices making points that were never less than obscure. In the end, taking pity on them, he produced the cheque and put an end to it all.

"I thought," he said, "that if I made a contribution to the fund, to the amount I understand is around what I won, it would clear the matter."

Then he tossed the cheque for £10,000 onto the long table, beneath Pugh's nose.

The atmosphere changed. The members recalled that Arthur was a very popular and valued member of the 57 Club. Murmurs as to his past generosity were heard. He smiled modestly.

Then, everything cleared to everybody's satisfaction, they retired to the bar where Arthur called up the drinks.

Pugh was at his elbow. "Very generous, Arthur," he said quietly.

"Thank you, Llew. I'm obliged by your fair presentation against me. Very fair." He took a sip of his brandy. "Oh, and those rumours . . . all those silly rumours I've

240

heard about you resigning from Club 6 . . . Unfounded, I trust?"

"Completely, Arthur, completely."

Arthur took another sip of his brandy, but this one at his own bedroom window. No harm had been done. Very satisfactory.

Chapter Eighteen

Tuesday, 3 October

At one-thirty Tony gently woke Madge. She'd been muttering in her sleep. Then he woke Charlie, who'd frankly been
snoring.

Madge seemed dazed when she emerged from behind her
curtain, not certain what they were doing there. But she
disappeared out to the bathroom while Tony brewed tea – he
could find no food in her cupboard – and Charlie lumbered
around the room, complaining he'd lost the use of his right
leg. Madge returned, some colour in her cheeks now that
she'd washed away the traces of make-up. She disappeared
behind the curtain in order to change into fresh jeans and
a checked cotton shirt, then she shuffled into her coat and
was ready to leave, protesting when Charlie said he'd just
rinse the cups and saucers.

Then they went with her to the hospital, a tiny girl between
two big men, through the mist-threaded and deserted streets.
Strangely she chattered. Strangely she spoke not one word
about Lucinda or the hospital. It was only when she left them
at the double swing doors of the ward that her mind switched
on to encompass what was ahead. It was two in the morning.
The danger hour. Her eyes, Tony noted, went at once to a
certain bed, halfway along the ward on the left.

The curtains were open. The patient still lay beneath her

242

tangle of drip tubes. The ward was silent, the lights on dim. At a table in the middle a nurse sat with a small desk lamp and a book. Swotting for her exams, no doubt. The silence was oppressive. When Madge pushed open one of the doors, the sound of the minimally disturbed air reached the nurse's ears. She lifted her head, saw who it was, smiled, and returned to her book.

Madge had forgotten them. She didn't look back. Charlie said quietly, "Better be gettin' home."

"Right," agreed Tony.

In the corridor, two uniformed officers, now in plain clothes, were gently napping. Tony didn't disturb them. The danger to Lucinda was entirely beyond those doors, until Thursday.

Charlie and Tony separated before they reached the centre of the town. They each knew intimately the side roads and short-cuts to their respective homes.

At the Station, Detective Inspector Tomkins was still on duty. He'd lost touch with when he'd last seen his own bed. Asked abruptly, he'd have had difficulty in remembering his wife's name. Certainly, he couldn't have told you when he'd last slept with her.

Nothing had come from the house-to-house enquiries. Nobody had spotted a blood-stained driver arriving home very early on Sunday morning.

Forensic were sending in reports on the only clues they had to examine – the razors and their respective tissues. The razors for Monday and Friday (Arthur Moreton and Ada Follett) naturally bore no traces of blood. But nevertheless the tissues had been left with them. That for Tuesday (Lucifer Hartington) and those for Saturday and Sunday (Esmeralda and Paul) all showed blood residues. Also naturally. The tissues bore bloodstains of the same blood group as their appropriate razors.

Nothing, thought Tomkins in disgust. The only strange

thing was that the tissues had been left with their razors. Clearly, their man wasn't aware that fingermarks could be lifted, these days, even from tissues, using all kinds of esoteric wizardry. Unfortunately for Tomkins, no traces had yet been found.

Chief Superintendent Merryweather, confident now that the razors were related to the days on which they were used, and aware that only the Wednesday and Thursday razors were still at large, had decided to bank everything on an all-out protection of Charlie and Lucinda, when the time came, and had nipped off back to DHQ in order, he said, to keep in touch.

The obvious thing to do, thought Tomkins, would be to take Charlie into protective custody. But that would only stall off the evil hour. How many more Wednesdays would Charlie have to be invited inside for the day? But . . . were they justified in allowing him to run around loose, putting his life on the line?

Or rather, would they be able to prevent him from doing so?

At a little after nine o'clock, realising that he'd read a complete report without being able to recall a single detail, he signed himself out and went for some breakfast at the café where his lady friend worked. A mistake, this was. His bacon was overfried, his egg watery, the tea weak. Mournfully, he decided to go home and see how his wife was getting along, whether in fact she was still there.

He couldn't remember where he'd left his car, so he walked. Good to stretch his legs. The centre of the town was very busy at this time, the traffic heavy. The benches round the statue, this being October and none too warm, were not heavily patronised. Only one, heavily by Charlie. The inspector walked past, not wishing to become involved with anything remotely official.

Charlie was simply sitting. His life, he thought morosely,

seemed to consist, these days, mostly of sitting. Round at Madge's place, he'd sat. Back at home, it'd been another short kip in another collapsing chair. And here he was, sitting again. But it was the only way he knew to contact Tony. In the back of his mind there was stirring the idea that he and Tony were together in this. Twin souls, meeting as one. As Charlie's mind wasn't up to much, that would be one and a quarter. He acknowledged this with a rueful smile at himself.

When someone approached him from his left and sat beside him, Charlie simply assumed it was Tony, and without turning said, "How's it going?"

"Reasonably well, thank you."

Then Charlie turned. He saw a slim man of around fifty, though Charlie was useless at guessing ages, in an anorak and a tweed hat, who was smiling thinly at him as though having discovered a lost treasure.

"You're Charles Pierce, if I don't miss my guess."

"Charlie," said Charlie, who thought Charles was a bit of a snooty name. "How'd you know?"

"You're becoming famous. Who else goes marching through town shouting out challenges? I admire your spirit. We all do."

"We? Who's we?"

"At the town hall. I'm the town clerk. Llewellyn Pugh."

Lordy, thought Charlie. What's this, then? They don't want me for mayor, do they!

"Your name has been mentioned to me. By the mayor. A very strong recommendation for membership."

"I ain't interested."

"How d'you know that, before—"

"They ask y' for fees and things."

"No, no. You don't understand. This is for Club 6."

"Oh ar?"

"A very secret society."

"Never heard of it," Charlie told him. He was always chary of people offering something for nothing.

"Of course you haven't heard of it. It's secret, with only six of us in it. The club's been going for over two hundred years."

"It'll manage without me, then." Charlie stared at his feet. Secret societies had a special sound. As a youngster he'd been in dozens. "What'd they do, then?"

"Meet once a month."

"Doin' what?"

"That's the secret."

Charlie said, "Ain't interested." It all sounded very suspicious to him.

"I'm thinking of retiring," Pugh confided. "It's my job to propose somebody to take my place."

"Don't see why—"

"Mr Harris seemed to think I'd pick him. But no. Oh no. But he recommended you and the mayor's word carries a lot of weight."

"Harris?" said Charlie. "Slasher Harris?" He began to take an interest. He hadn't realised Slasher Harris was the mayor.

"I believe that's what they call him," said Pugh disparagingly. "But of course, he's out of the question for this. We need – I need – somebody I can be proud of. Somebody . . . well . . . distinguished, shall we say."

"Me?" said Charlie.

"Why not? You're well known in the town. You're big and you're young. You could do it, too, I'm sure."

"Do what?"

"Your own special, personal task."

"What's that then?"

"To drink nine pints of draught bitter and stand up long enough to get rid of them."

"Eh?"

246

"To drink—"

"I heard y'. Sounds crazy to me."

"It's a very great responsibility. This – this duty – has been in my family, and passed on, for nearly two hundred years. This is the first time we've had to appoint a successor. It's a great honour, Charlie."

"Well . . . I dunno . . . can I—"

"Where can I pick you up? Here? This bench? Very well. Tomorrow evening, shall we say? Around seven. I'll introduce you to the other five members, and if they like you, then you have to swear a solemn oath . . . and if you don't want to, you simply forget all about it. It's so damned secret, Charlie."

Charlie stared at his hands. "If it don't take long."

"Half an hour at most."

That sounded all right. He could be back and trying the same thing again, shouting his challenge at the night, and there'd be plenty of that left.

"All right then," he conceded.

"Fine. Grand." The town clerk got to his feet. He wasn't very much to look at, thought Charlie. Scrawny, even.

"Can you do it?" he asked.

"What?"

"Drink nine pints."

"It's taken practice, Charlie, practice." Then Pugh walked away.

Charlie, though no great thinker, was not exactly stupid. In his mother's fond phrase for him, not as green as he was cabbage-looking. It was all very strange, this being presented to him, and at a time when he, when the whole town, was in the middle of a bit of a fuss-up. But names had been bandied about. Slasher Harris had been mentioned and he knew Slasher. He'd spoken to him. The mayor! All the same, it didn't smell right. So Charlie wandered off for a cup of tea and a beefburger, sitting always making him feel peckish.

247

It wasn't until eleven that Tony came along, to find him back on the bench.

"Been looking for you," Tony said. "Where've you been?"

"Here," said Charlie, patting the seat. "Might've popped off for a minute or two."

"Yeah. Well, come on, I want you to meet somebody."

"I'm always meetin' people."

"Somebody special, Charlie. Come on."

"Where?" Charlie was being awkward. Everybody seemed to want him to do something or go somewhere.

"The Plucked Goose. Lady wants to see you."

Charlie fell into step with him. "Lady? They ain't let her out, have they?"

"What're you talking about?" Tony asked, half laughing, now knowing Charlie's general conversational quirks.

"That Esmeralda."

"Oh no, not her. You can always visit her. Any time."

"Can I?"

"This is an older lady."

"Yeah."

They walked a hundred yards, then Charlie said, "You ever heard of Club 6, Tony?"

"No. What is it?"

"Can't tell you. It's a secret."

"If it's secret, what's the good of asking me?" Tony asked reasonably.

"Dunno. I've been asked to join."

"Who by?"

"The town clerk."

"Then you probably have to put on funny clothes and walk in processions."

"Oh." Charlie thought about that. "With nine pints in me?"

"Nine pints?" Tony glanced sideways, his interest roused.

"Shouldn't't've said that. It's secret."

"All right. I won't say another word."

Which wasn't what Charlie wanted, but as he wasn't certain what he did want he couldn't protest. They walked on in silence for a while. At last Tony said, "You'll like her."

"Who?"

"Ada Follett. She's the one who nearly got cut up on Friday night. You were watching, remember? And she's the one who'd have got your prize if the draw had been done properly."

"She's welcome to it," said Charlie. "A bloody kitchen of stuff. All posh. I sold it for a thousand quid."

"There you are then," said Tony, as though he didn't already know.

"She can have halfa that, if she likes. Only fair, that'd be."

Tony said nothing. He glanced again at his friend. Unpredictable, that was Charlie.

"I got the bike, see," Charlie told him. "Lucifer left me the bike."

"Well now!"

"An' *that's* a secret," said Charlie fiercely. "Anyway, I don't want it till I've got me hands on that slasher. *Then* it'll be mine."

Tony walked a few more yards. "Yes. I can understand that."

"Well," said Charlie. "All right then." It was a tone that hinted he didn't want to hear another word about it.

Ada and her two friends were predictably in their corner. Tony automatically paused at the bar to order the necessary nourishment from Bill Fisher, so that Charlie was left, somewhat embarrassed, staring at the interested three women and rubbing his palms down the seat of his jeans.

"This is Charlie Pierce," said Tony, coming up at his

shoulder. "Charlie, this is Ada, and her friends Connie and Floss."

"How d'you do."

"Pleased to meet you, I'm sure."

"Oh, he's a big 'un ain't he!"

Charlie tried to smile. The one called Ada, now he got a clear look at her, reminded him of their next-door neighbour, Poppy Leach. She and his mother hated each other with a consuming hatred that left nothing to spare, thereby conferring a huge benefit on the rest of the community.

"Let's see y', lad!" cried Ada, beckoning him. "Heh! This one ain't undercover, is he? You couldn't hide him behind a number seven bus."

Yes, thought Charlie, just like Poppy Leach. Coarse, his mother called her. Lacking in lady-like comportment. Not in those exact words. Charlie grinned. Ada said, "Sit here, lad. Between me'n Floss. There y'are. Hodge up, Connie, y' great lump."

Charlie gently lowered himself to the seat. He gratefully buried his face in a pint glass.

Tony sat opposite. "Seen any green yet, Ada?"

"Nah! Them great hulkin' feet all over the lawn! We hadda rake it level again."

"I'll tell Paul when I see him."

"Already told him. He wrote somethin' on his pad. What was it? Yes, I remember. Down on y'r knees. What's that mean, d'you think?"

Tony thought about it. "What he means is you've got to get right down so's you're looking along the surface. Try it, Ada. Some time."

"We'll haveta do that." Ada nodded. Tony had a vision of three rumps jutting up as they squinted along the surface and took a quick swallow of his beer.

"*You've* got a lot to say for yourself, I must say," observed Ada, digging Charlie in the ribs. "Cat got your tongue?"

"Couldn't get a word in."

"We'll sit quiet," Connie offered.

"As a lamb," Floss agreed.

"Get in there, Charlie," said Tony. "You've got seconds, no more."

He was correct there. The clamour died down though, and Charlie put in, "You ever heard of Club 6?"

It was what kept popping up to the forefront of his mind. The existence of such a club seemed very unlikely.

"Club 6!" cried Ada. "That I have, laddie. My Eric was in it."

Charlie looked blank.

"Her husband," Tony amplified. "The famous Eric Follett."

"Oh ah?" said Charlie.

"That one night a month," said Ada. "Midnight . . . he hadda be there, my Eric. Took a gallon can with him. Daft, I call it. Useta fill it from the canal out the back."

Tony stared at her. Charlie looked interested. Connie said, "He didn't drink it, you can be certain of that. Drank somethin', but not that."

"Poor dear," said Ada in remote nostalgia. "I always hadda help him to bed." She stared at Charlie. "Why?" she demanded.

"I've been asked if I wanta join."

"There!" Ada cried. "Now ain't that somethin'! You'll do 'em proud, lad, that you will. Who asked you? I knew 'em all, you know."

"I thought it was secret," Charlie protested stoutly. He was finding it difficult to handle the situation.

"Secret! Sure it was. But Eric told me. He would, wouldn't he. Who was it, lad?"

"Mr Pugh."

"Llew Pugh!" For some reason Ada became convulsed with laughter, slapping her thigh and gasping out parts of words to her two friends.

251

"What's funny?" asked Tony on Charlie's behalf, observing that Charlie seemed lost.

"Llew!" she gasped. "He was the only one who didn't have to take his lot in a can. Poor old devil – young devil then, o' course. Loaded it inside himself first."

"No!" said Connie.

"I never!" said Floss.

"An' Eric said . . ." Ada was again convulsed, in the end clamping a hand to her side and fighting for control. "Said Pugh hadda do it left-handed!" Then, while she still had a bit of breath left, she leaned across Charlie, so that the three heads came together somewhere close to his breast pocket, and she whispered hurriedly. Then they all collapsed in such screams of laughter that even Bill Fisher looked concerned.

Charlie sat motionless. He wasn't sure whether they were laughing at him, the club, or Mr Pugh. He didn't dare venture a word, having overheard what they were laughing about and feeling it was a little indelicate for three elderly ladies to converse about it in public. Charlie's mother still called his Y-fronts his underthings.

Tony watched it all with quiet amusement. When it had all died down, when they were all patting their chests, Ada lifting her skirt to wipe her eyes, he said, "What's funny?"

"It's . . . it's Pugh . . ." gasped Ada. "His right hand. It's . . . it's . . . you tell him, Floss."

Floss gulped. "It's artificial," she said huskily. "His hand. It . . . it *clamps*. Can y' imagine—"

They could and were off again, but it was like a deflating tyre now, with nearly all the air gone. In abrupt unison they each sat still, gripped the table, and nodded themselves into propriety.

"Artificial?" murmured Tony,

"Let's have a look at your hands, lad," Ada said to Charlie.

Reluctantly he produced them. The three ladies examined them with sudden and serious contemplation.

"Yeah," they decided. "Good strong hands."

"You'll do," said Ada. "Grab the chance, laddie."

"The chance!" screamed Connie, which set them off again.

Tony went to get in another round and said to Bill Fisher, "I'd call the police in if I wasn't a policeman."

"Don't *you* start."

"Charlie," explained Tony to them, when he got back, and deliberately changing the subject, "won the prize you would've had, Ada."

"Good luck to him." Ada sucked in stout. "Kitchen stuff, weren't it?"

"Yeah," said Charlie, who was still wondering whether they'd been laughing at him. "Sold it, though."

"Wouldna been much good to me, anyways up."

"The money would," Charlie told her. "I got a thousand quid for it."

"You never!" said Connie.

"It's right," Charlie said. He lumbered to his feet so that he could reach into his back pocket. It was trapped in there, flat against his buttocks. He sat down again and slapped it on the table. "It's all there."

It was in fifties, twenty of them. Tony reached out a finger and moved it around experimentally. "You carry it around?"

"What else?" Charlie demanded.

"There're people who can cut that pocket out as clean as a whistle."

"The slasher? Just let him try." Charlie was rapidly recovering his composure. "Anyway, I don't want it all. Here," he said to Ada, "you can have half of it." And he slid across ten of them.

Charlie had never possessed something he could give

253

away. It was one of the pleasures in life of which he'd been deprived. He was not, therefore, exactly *au fait* with social conventions, which, in any event, he'd have attributed to a class different from his own. All he knew was that he felt warm about something. His big round face was red with it. Ada, too, was uncertain. Nobody had ever given her anything – not counting the thousands of stouts she'd been treated to and not counting the years of Eric's devotion – so she didn't really know what to do. How to refuse it politely without offending the great sloppy lump?

With a careful finger she reached out and slid it back towards him. Her face was puckering with wavering emotion.

"Buy y' girlfriend a present, Charlie."

"Haven't got one."

Which provided the relief of a change of subject. The three women pounced on it.

"Gerraway!"

"Of course you 'ave."

"A big healthy lad like you!"

Charlie stared at his big, healthy and clumsy hands. "No. I break things."

"Girls?" asked Tony, fascinated.

"Nah, you clown!" Charlie grinned. "Things. Daren't touch girls."

"Certainly not," agreed Tony. "Breaking girls'd be a criminal offence."

"He's off his crump," Ada decided.

"Who?" asked Tony. "Me?"

"Him there." She jerked a thumb at Charlie, who was lost again, partly in a tumult involving his emotions, which didn't want to settle down to anything he could comprehend, and partly with the difficulty of understanding these three women. When were they serious, when not? An instinct told him not to ask. In any event, they wouldn't know.

"My Eric," said Ada, "was as big as you. Stronger,

254

though. Betcha! He could've tucked me under his arm and walked away as though I was a handbag."

Charlie had a brief flash of memory. Tuck under arm . . . of course . . . Madge.

"An' he never hurt me. Not once."

"Scared of y', he was, Ada," Connie said.

"That too," agreed Ada. "Gentle, was Eric. Oh yes. But he could've held you down with one hand, young Charlie."

"I bet," said Tony.

"It's true," said Floss, nodding with proprietorial pride.

"An' did he," asked Charlie, for once intruding his own thought, "pass it on to his son? Your son, Ada."

"What? Oh . . . you still on about Club 6, are y'? No. No sons. Three daughters. All great big girls, they are. There, Charlie, one of them would've done for you. But they're married."

"Oh," said Charlie. "Pity." Getting the general mood right at last. "Made a luvly ma-in-law, you would."

"The youngest's forty-eight," said Ada. "But you're a polite lad. You can get 'em in." As a special concession.

Which Charlie did. While he was at the bar, Tony asked, "Who'd he pass it on to, then, Ada? His membership I mean. Your Eric."

"It's a secret."

"Don't tell me then."

"Arthur Moreton."

Tony nodded. There had been a niggle in his mind about this Club 6 business but that just about settled it. Pugh and Moreton were responsible citizens. It might, though, he thought, be a good idea just to check it with Moreton.

In the end it was Tony who had to break up the meeting, because Merryweather was back at the Station and had called a conference for that afternoon. It was for sergeants and above, but Tony knew the rest of his mates would have to hang around, waiting for instructions, so it would be a good idea to be there. He wasn't, in any event, quite certain whether or not he was officially back on duty.

He and Charlie left before closing time so that the £500 was still sitting there on the table as Charlie got to his feet. Ada cleared the air by picking it up, folding it deftly and the three of them made a bit of fun out of forcing it into the back pocket of Charlie's jeans. The two men walked out, hearing Ada say, "Here, they never got 'em in."

They parted in the square. Tony signed himself in, discovered he was already far too late for the meeting, but that Detective Sergeant Spinks had his duties all lined up for him in the morning.

It was again to be a blanket cover of Charlie, but this time it was more detailed. No skulking groups shadowing him and hiding round corners. No. They were to be ordinary citizens, who just happened to be going along with their lives. They would be drunken groups of louts (Andy Spinks in charge of this lot) or courting couples (pick your favourite WPC), the odd person here and there with a pushbike, the married couples with prams, the late shoppers borrowing a store's trolley to get the shopping home. That sort of thing, nothing suggestive of surveillance at all. Clever stuff, this. Merryweather was very pleased with it.

Nothing else happened that day, except that Tomkins had to visit Ephraim Potts in hospital. He'd been attacked with a heavy, blunt instrument as he left his office late the previous evening, solicitors being able to choose their own working hours.

It was a wasted journey for Tomkins. Potts was still unconscious, and there was talk of possible concussion and a hairline fracture of the skull. The inspector would have to wait for tomorrow before he could be questioned. Tomkins wondered whether this was connected with the two previous attempts on his life that Potts had reported.

256

Probably it was. But there were more important matters to be attended to. Two more razors to go.

Regrettably, his mind being packed full of organisational plans, he forgot about Potts. Anything not related to the slasher had very little relevance at that time.

Tony, finding himself at a loose end, and inactivity making him nervous, decided to call in at Moreton Milling and have a word with Arthur Moreton. Cynthia told him her boss was in a good mood, so just knock on the door and walk in. Tony put his head in first.

"Come in, son. What can I do for you?"

Tony explained that he was back on routine duty, making general enquiries about anything unusual that anybody might have seen on Saturday night to Sunday morning. It didn't do to plunge straight in with details.

Arthur put his fingers together and openly grinned. As Pugh had already explained to Bert Harris, Arthur, as President of Club 6, had been otherwise engaged, and later in no fit state to observe anything.

"Out of town mainly," he said. "Sorry."

"How was that then?"

Moreton peered at him, his tented fingers hiding a small smile. "If you'll recall, officer, it was I who was attacked first."

"I wasn't suggesting—"

"Of course not."

"Just asking." Tony waited.

"It's kind of secret."

Tony said, "Then I don't want to hear it." After all, it'd worked well enough every time he'd tried it.

"I'll tell you. It's a ridiculous thing, though, a tradition. You know what I mean, something going on year after year, just because it's always been done, and in spite of the fact that it's no longer any use at all. To tell you the truth . . ." he leaned forward, ". . . it's an excuse for getting a day off from the missus. Just a midnight ceremony, then we make a day of it."

"You're talking about Club 6?"

"You knew! Really, you shouldn't have let me go on."

"Sorry. But there's something you can confirm for me. Something I couldn't line up in my mind."

"Yes?"

"Eric Follett. He was one of your six. Ada says he was never away from her. Not one day. Certainly not a night and a day."

"Ah!" Moreton laughed. "I see. Eric was a special case. He couldn't have a day off in case the factory closed down. And we couldn't let him bring Ada, could we? He wouldn't go anywhere without Ada."

"So it wouldn't get him drummed out of the club?"

"Not for that. The midnight ceremony, one minute into the next day – that's sacred. Daren't miss that. Oh no."

"And no one ever has?"

Moreton didn't say anything. He sat and thought. Then, "I can't answer that, unless it's got something to do with your investigation."

"I doubt it, sir." Then he changed his mind. "Unless it happened this last time, which was midnight on Saturday."

"Hmm!"

"You mean it did?"

"I don't want to go on with this."

"Of course not, sir. I'll simply assume you're telling me it did."

"We'll say no more," said Arthur flatly.

"I'm wasting your time. Sorry, Mr Moreton. But you'll have heard about the other attacks we've had?"

"I have. It's very shocking."

"They were at midnight on Saturday," Tony pointed out quietly. "Which was the last day of the month."

258

Moreton stared down at his hands. Then he raised his head. "I think you'd better leave, young man."

"It wasn't you, by any chance, sir? Who was late for the ceremony, I mean."

"How dare you!"

"I know, I know. I'm exceeding my duties. The idea *has* been put forward, though. You lost only two buttons, you see—"

Then Moreton laughed. "Very clever. You now expect me, in sheer self-defence, to give you a specific name. But no. Change the subject, Constable."

Tony got to his feet. "There *is* no other subject, Mr Moreton. I thought I had a lead. It appears not."

"Definitely not."

"Ah well," said Tony after a few seconds, "then I'd better get back to it, I suppose."

"It doesn't sound very exciting, this job of yours."

"There's a hell of a lot of pure routine. Asking questions – getting nothing out of them."

"Like me? Sorry I can't help."

Tony smiled thinly. He had a feeling Moreton might have helped after all.

Chapter Nineteen

Wednesday, 4 October

Traditionally, Wednesday was the big shopping day in Ockam, because Thursday was early-closing day. Nobody seemed to notice that none of the shops closed on Thursday afternoon and hadn't been able to afford to do so for years. It was simply that Wednesday was *the* day, and the town would be half empty on Thursday.

This Wednesday the town centre was packed. There was not a police car to be seen anywhere, not a uniform, but the force had entered into the mood of it and many had brought their wives along, even their children, and did genuinely indulge in shopping. This was somewhat restricted, though, because all the activity had to be centred around Charlie Pierce who was unaware that he was the focus of attention and remained stubbornly in the square, on his same old bench, heavily patient.

He knew – they knew – that nothing was going to happen until after dark. It was all a token display, the more difficult task being ahead, when Charlie, it was confidently expected, would become active, vocally and physically.

At that later time it would not be valid to flood the town with shoppers and family groups. Life would therefore become more difficult for the police.

Tony decided that it would ruin the pattern if he did what

he would normally have done, which was to join Charlie on the seat, so he decided to visit Esmeralda and Paul in the hospital. His intructions for the day had been very vague and easily reorganised. Charlie was to be watched every inch of the way. And Tony knew *he* couldn't do that and not be spotted by Charlie. For some time he'd thought about that. Would it not be reasonable for Charlie to be seen walking with a friend, reasonable and natural? But it would scare away the slasher, and nobody was certain that this was an outcome to be desired.

In any event – the decider, this was – Tony could always hope to arrange a chance meeting with Madge at the hospital, then persuade her to take a break, perhaps. With himself.

This he failed to do. He saw Esmeralda, who was noticeably more perky, less heavily bandaged and demanding to be allowed to go to see Paul. He saw Paul, who could now speak quietly, in a ventriloquial method he'd been practising and in a manner that didn't move his lips, and thus his cheek. He managed to say that they wouldn't allow him to go to see Esmeralda.

Tony laughed. "With a bit of luck, you'll meet her halfway."

Paul didn't think it was funny. "Got him yet?"

"The slasher? No, we haven't. There's another big operation on today. Half the county force is in on it. You'll see – we'll get him."

"Young man."

Tony turned. The quiet voice had come from the old gentleman in the next bed. He had recently met Ephraim Potts outside this very hospital, but he hardly recognised him in pyjamas and in the indignity of a hospital bed. Tony hesitated.

"Mr Potts?"

"You're Constable Finch, aren't you?"

"Yes sir."

"Did Tomkins send you?" The voice was thick, as though control over the tongue was not complete and it seemed to Tony that the eyes were not focussed.

"No sir. This is merely a social visit."

"An idiot, that Tomkins. I hope you're not all that stupid."

"I hope not, sir." Then Tony realised he was not perhaps being very loyal. "I mean, I hope I can help – Mr Tomkins is very busy."

"Not," Potts grumbled, "looking for *my* assailant, I've no doubt."

"You've been attacked, sir?"

"Why d'you think I'm in this damned bed?"

"It could be anything."

"It wasn't anything, it was an attack. If I hadn't been wearing my bowler hat, I'd probably be dead now. And why hasn't anybody been to see me? I thought these things were reported."

Tony sat on the edge of Paul's bed and got out his notebook. "It has now, sir. Tell me what happened."

It was simple enough. Potts had been late leaving his office. The street had been empty. He'd felt a blow and had come round in hospital.

"Is there anyone you know, sir, who'd wish you dead?"

"Of course there is. Or rather, are." Potts was becoming tired, though. He squinted at Tony painfully. "This is the third go he's had at me."

This needed more notes and the interview was terminated when Potts simply closed his eyes and went to sleep.

"Is this what your job's like?" Paul managed to say.

"Sometimes. We get to meet a lot of people."

"Interesting." But Paul, too, was feeling the strain.

So Tony left him, so immersed in pondering the significance of the three attacks on Ephraim Potts that he quite forgot to hunt out Madge. But there was something strange about this. Potts might claim enemies, but solicitors usually do not acquire such bitter ones as to make three attempts at assault, and nearly succeed in murder with the third. It had the same feel as the slasher series, a persistence in the assailant, an intensity. And the attacks on Potts had occurred during the same time-span as the slasher's activities. Could there be a connection? Solicitors, though not attracting venomous enemies, did acquire a vast amount of information, professionally sacrosanct but potentially dangerous.

So Tony hunted out Tomkins, who was in the control room with his mind in a whirl. If there was anything Tomkins didn't want to hear about at that time it was Potts. Tony, deliberately misunderstanding Tomkins's crisp comment, went off home for a good meal and a good think. The first sent him dozing off in the chair by the fire – he was still missing a good portion of last night's sleep – so that it was very much later that he heard they'd lost Charlie.

It happened so simply that it left everybody helpless. If they'd only . . . but that's life, full of ifs.

Charlie had been sitting, one minute, on his bench. It was two minutes to seven. He was completely unaware that the stubborn passers-by, who didn't seem to want to go home, were police officers. He had taken no notice of the ragged old chap who'd sat on the next bench and begun to eat sandwiches – and was, in fact, Detective Constable Terry Cartwright – and was aware only that it was seven o'clock and nobody had turned up. It was vaguely disappointing. Charlie liked the idea of secret societies. Such as the Ku Klux Klan, he thought, though he didn't know what it was, and if he had he wouldn't have joined. His bench was directly beneath the nose of the horse in the statue behind him. Five yards to one side, separated from him by no more than pavement, the street ran, the traffic now easing. A horn pipped, a door was thrust open. Charlie got to his feet, got into the car, and it drove away.

Five seconds, that was all it had taken. Terry Cartwright was still eating.

The trouble was that nobody had expected a car. Previous attacks had been on foot, sneaky creepings in the darkness. This was a vehicle, in the full blare of the tightest cluster of streetlights in town, and there had been no secret stalking of Charlie. Charlie had gone to the man.

Man it was. Twenty officers were willing to swear that, but none could go into details. A man had picked up Charlie and the meeting had clearly been amicable. The intention might, therefore, also be amicable. But the fact remained that Tomkins had no patrol car within reach, he having scavanged the crews and persuaded them into venturing onto the streets on foot.

Twenty or more hand radios clashed their waves into Tomkins's control room. All he could make out was that Charlie had gone, in a plain, small car, make unknown, registration number unobserved. He frantically called in what patrol cars he had. He was too late.

Charlie fastened his seat belt and sat back placidly. After what he'd thought was to be a let-down, the realisation that it wasn't boosted his confidence.

"Where're we going?"

"You'll see."

"Who'll be there?"

"All of us. Six. It has to be a unanimous decision. I propose, and the others have to agree."

"Yeah," said Charlie. "Here, I've heard about these secret things, people doin' daft things to qualify. Walkin' round with one leg in a bucket or somethin'. I ain't having any of that."

Pugh took a corner abruptly. All his driving was abrupt, Charlie noticed, but it must've been a bit tricky because Pugh's right hand was gripping a nob on the steering wheel.

"No need to worry," Pugh told him placidly. "We're just ordinary people, not stupid old buffers. Mind you . . . Baker's getting on a bit, and Levinson's no chicken."

"Who're they?"

"Rupert Baker of Steel Equities and Arnold Levinson of Pressed Steel."

"Oh." Charlie wished he hadn't asked. They'd probably be in black jackets and bow ties. "Did y'know Eric Follett?"

"Eric?" Pugh darted a glance at him, taking a sharp corner dangerously at the same time. "Certainly I did. I was a youngster myself then. Now *there* was a man for you! A steelman through and through."

Charlie was relaxing more every second. "Yeah. So I hear."

"Where did you hear about Eric?"

"I was having a drink yesterday with Ada. Bit of a laugh, she is."

"How did you get to know Ada?"

"Well . . . we was both prizewinners in that raffle, see. She said she wanted to meet me."

Pugh peered ahead. The street lights out here, on the outskirts of town, were not modernised and in contrast seemed dim. "The raffle, of course. She and you. I'd nearly forgotten."

How anybody in the town could possibly have forgotten the raffle draw, with the general uproar it'd caused, Charlie could not imagine.

"Where're we goin'?" Charlie asked again, looking round for landmarks. "Looks like the Slags to me."

"It's traditional, you understand," Pugh explained. "The ceremony's still held in the same place as it's been since 1820, when they built the factory. Diamond Edge. Remember them? Famous for their steel; the keenest edge you could get. But it's closed now. We've got legal access and we've all got keys. You'll have your own key, Charlie, if they like you."

"Oh," said Charlie. "I've heard of Diamond Edge. They made razor blades and garden shears and things."

"They did. It's all moved to their main factory at Sheffield now."

"Pity." Charlie went on. "They made them old-fashioned open razors, too. Called 'em cut-throats."

"That's right." Pugh switched his lights to main beam. "We have to go through the new industrial estate."

The council had built this estate of small, almost identical, single-storey buildings for rental as factories, warehouses, business centres and the like. It was not an inspiring vision, even in the daylight, but marginally better than the bleak and shattered landscape had been. It had been a slow-starter, but more recently had become more commercially viable, now containing a large retail store and a DIY centre, and as there was plenty of parking space it was clearly going to be a winner all round. Eye-catching and glaringly colourful frontages enlivened the prospect.

In daytime, that was. Now all were deserted, with only a few scattered cars hanging around. As the street lighting was concentrated round the buildings, now closed, unlit and silent, it was all very dark and somewhat eerie.

The hard surface of the roadway ceased and they were bumping along what had been an approach road to the old factory, but pot-holed now and neglected. The factory revealed itself gradually against the faintly orange clouds, a grey and gloomy spread of buildings, which was not actually built in the concept of bricks and mortar, but constructed from steel girders and corrugated iron. What else, for a factory engaged in steel production?

Pugh was still talking. "The foundry's the higher building at the back there, Charlie. That's where they had their furnaces. One of the first Bessemers in the country, they had there. This lower building here is where they did the rolling and turning of the higher quality steels and the tempering bath is actually on the site of the original one – or rather, the one that'd been there since about 1800."

"Fancy that," said Charlie.

"It's rather splendid, really. Don't you think it's splendid, Charlie? They built the factory actually round that very site. Sentimental gesture, some would say. But I think it was only right and proper."

"I suppose so." Charlie was looking round. "Don't see any more cars."

"We must be the first. Did you know – a bit of history this is Charlie, and rather fascinating – that fountain in the shopping precinct, the one they call the Temperance Fountain, well, *that* was the site of the original tempering bath, way back in the 1600s and 1700s. There used to be a blacksmith's forge, right where the Rimfire Tower is sited now. Don't you think that's fascinating, Charlie?"

Charlie said, "Oh yeah. Ever so."

"There's a torch in that cubby-hole in front of you. Better bring it along."

"We here?" Because Pugh had drawn the car to a halt.

"Yes." Pugh opened his door. "This is the old loading bay. See, it's raised for the wagons. Come on. I've got my own torch. Up these steps. Watch yourself, they're a bit crumbly. Don't want you twisting your ankle." He gave a short bark of tense laughter. "It'd take all six of us to lift you back into the car."

Charlie was staring all round him. The streetlights were way back and seemed a hell of a long way away. "There ain't anybody coming."

"It was short notice but they'll be coming along."

Pugh stood above him on the loading bay. Charlie walked up the ten steps, his torchlight centred on his feet. Pugh swung the focus of his torch. The slatted huge up-and-over door faced on the loading bay. Beside it, inset into the corrugated-iron wall, was an ordinary door, beside which a pipe rose like a chimney into the night. Pugh flicked his light over the door.

"Somebody's already here," he said. "The padlock's unfastened."

It hung on its open hasp. Pugh lifted it from its hook, swung back the tongue and pushed the door inwards. Charlie followed him inside.

The huge building seemed to rustle and flutter in the night. Though there was no wind, somewhere a sheet of iron flapped with a mournful persistence. There was a plink of dripping water, even this tenuous sound seeming to raise echoes in the lofty roof beams. There was no light visible inside, apart from the two swept beams of their torches.

"Nobody here," said Charlie.

"You wouldn't see them. This way. Up here."

It was soon evident why they could not see their objective. Charlie had worked inside an operating factory, when it had seemed that the floor was all on one level. But that had of course been the access surface between the machines. This factory had clearly contained larger equipment than Charlie had encountered. The surface, here, through which Charlie's torch probed, was a series of huge and sometimes high platforms of concrete, still with rusting location bars protruding. They were not all the same size, not the same height. Where the presses had been there were deep square pits.

Pugh led the way, weaving and winding. Their voices hollowly echoed, their feet chased up runnels of harsh sound, thrown back viciously from all directions.

"Here," said Pugh.

He canted his torch so that it swept across the mouth of a sunken tank, whose top edge was level with the surrounding surface. It was ten feet by eight feet and when Charlie peered over the edge it seemed about seven feet deep. It was empty.

"The tempering tank, Charlie," said Pugh, in a peculiar little voice, and Charlie turned in time to see, by the light from Pugh's own torch, something bright in the strangely inflexible right hand. In that small part of a second Charlie realised how he'd been tricked, but it was too late even for that thought to mature. His left arm, holding his torch, automatically came up to protect his face and something hard struck the torch, jerking it from his hand. It fell behind him with a clatter into the tank and went out.

Pugh was screaming. A kind of terror or excitement had seized him. The torch in his left hand danced around. Mouth wide open, he was screaming as the razor slashed back on its return stroke. Charlie again raised his arm, ducking his head, poised for a charge. The blade ran down the outside of his left arm from shoulder to elbow. With something approaching wonder he felt the flesh being parted. The very nature of the seriousness of the wound produced an instant shock to the immediately surrounding nerves. He felt no pain, but felt the blade, then he was himself roaring with fury and with the anticipated pain as he moved what he thought to be forwards. But he'd been too close to the edge as he turned. His arms flew out in balance and Pugh kicked him on the right thigh. Charlie toppled backwards, and lay unconscious in the bottom of the tank.

Llewellyn Pugh laid down his torch whilst he carefully wiped the razor, dropping both razor and tissue together beside the tank. His hands were shaking as he turned and stumbled back towards the open air. His whimpers ran away into the darkness, unheard by Charlie, heard only by the old factory that had suffered the pounding of heavy machinery and constant clamour for a hundred years, yet now winced in tiny squeaks of metal and minute tings of pain, almost in sympathy.

Pugh was in an agony that was almost overpowering. His very personality was twisted and distorted by this vile necessity, as though each nerve was being wrung with the passion that flooded through him, beyond his control. He didn't know how he could go on. One more, only one more! Then maybe the pain, so much more piercing in that he dared not allow it to be observed, would leave him. Then, perhaps peace. Rest.

He sat in the car, unable to organise his mind sufficiently to start it, until he heard – or thought he heard – a distant cry for help. Then he started it and in jerky and uncoordinated distress he drove back the way he had come.

Charlie had not shouted. After regaining consciousness he lay still until his mind could grasp the situation. The pain in his arm jerked him awake. He reached over with his right hand and felt only a wet stickiness, but it had soaked the whole sleeve of his shirt and the thin jacket he had over it. He could see nothing. The blackness was a solid weight around him.

In such a situation Charlie was perhaps the type of person most likely to be able to handle it. Part of this was lack of imagination, which stifled fear to some extent, at least short of panic level. He had also a natural will for survival, an animal determination to keep going. Behind it all was a brain that would work when pressed to it, and was completely logical. He was here; how did he get out? It was as simple a conception as that.

In execution it was more difficult. The first consideration was the torch. It was down there somewhere with him, not working but not necessarily dead. He could not, at that point, find the energy to stand, nor could he crawl with only one operative hand, so he shuffled around on his behind until he felt a foot kick the torch, swivelled, and located it with his right hand. He shook it. Nothing. No rattling of broken glass, though. He thumbed the switch, which seemed to be stuck, so he applied pressure and it went over with a click – and there was light.

He shut his eyes for a moment then opened them and surveyed the prospect. It was like a room of steel. The floor was slightly sloping towards one corner where he spotted an outgo pipe. That would be necessary for draining, he realised. He also realised that Pugh had told the truth about this being the traditional tank. The residue stank of everything foul he could imagine. Strange that he could think of Pugh without blind and all-consuming fury, but in fact it was with satisfaction. Now he knew. Now he could find Pugh and destroy him.

But not yet. Get out first, though there seemed no way. In one of the corners he managed to lever himself to his feet. Reaching up with his right hand, he felt he could curl his fingers over the edge, but not grip. There was nothing to fasten on to. He tried all the way round, but there was no grip anywhere. Jumping? He made an attempt at that, but he was giddy by then, his legs weak.

Over one corner of the tank, ten feet above his head, there was an ancient standpipe with a tap. It dripped. Plop-plop. It seemed logical to Charlie that if he was losing blood, then he was losing liquid; therefore he ought to put it back. So when he decided to sit down and have a rest he did so with his back in one corner so that his right hand could catch the drips which he could then lick from his palm.

He did this a few times with the torch on, then with it off, and found he could still catch the drips in the dark, so he put out the torch altogether and laid it beside his thigh.

Now he was very tired. The accomplishment of the water drips seemed enough for one attempt. Another later. So he closed his eyes and went to sleep.

Chapter Twenty

Thursday, 5 October (part)

At a little after midnight the Station was strangely quiet. Most of the available officers were out and about, doing everything they could to find some trace of Charlie Pierce. The rest had been sent home to prepare themselves for the Thursday ahead. It was expected to be a difficult and exhausting day.

In the CID room Terry Cartwright was sitting quietly. He'd either been forgotten or Inspector Tomkins had simply kept him till last as a special treat.

Tony was facing him, sitting astraddle on a chair, backwards, and conducting his own interrogation.

"But you were *there*, Terry, for God's sake! Right there beside him. Can't you remember anything, damn it? An impression . . . wasn't anything said? A whisper—"

Terry sighed. "One second he was there, the next gone. I looked up. He wasn't there any more."

Tony got to his feet angrily, sending the chair spinning across the office. "It's been five bloody hours! I've got to see the inspector. Perhaps he'll listen—"

Terry made a crude sound with his lips. "Wish he'd listen to me, then I could get off home."

With a random kick at the desk, Tony returned to the prowling he'd been doing for the past hour. He'd asked the WPC on duty if he could see Tomkins. The response had been a flat no. "If he'd only give me a minute—"

He was interrupted by the WPC putting in her head and saying, "He'll see you now, Terry."

Tony put up a restraining palm. "I'll go."

"But you *can't*—"

"No? We'll see." Tony marched purposefully past her, she clutching uselessly at his arm. He almost ran along the corridor.

"He'll kill you," she gasped. "He's in a murderous mood."

"Me too!" Tony thrust open the inspector's door and took one pace inside.

Tomkins raised his head. "Out!" he snapped.

"I'm sorry," whispered the WPC, but Tony stolidly closed the door in her face. Then he turned to face Tomkins.

The inspector no longer knew what he was doing, where he was, what time it was. He was performing the required routine duties like a dull and stiff machine, his eyes red with strain and his face drained. Constant mugs of coffee had set his nerves jumping, but hadn't done much to steady his pounding brain.

"I sent for Cartwright," he said flatly. "Not you. Now get out of here and send him in."

"I've got to talk to you—"

"Do it. Don't argue with me. Out!"

"Please sir, I've got information. Talking to people – round and about. There's something you ought to know."

Tomkins leaned back in his chair and ran both hands over his face. "Put it in a report and send it in."

"And have it sit under that lot!" said Tony, gesturing towards the pile beneath Tomkins's eyes. "It's urgent, sir. And it all fits in—"

"Don't you come telling me what fits in and what doesn't. Put it in a blasted report. Now get out of here—"

"I know who it is, sir."

273

Tomkins flopped forward and pointed a finger. "Don't waste my time with theories, Finch. I'm warning you—"

"I can back it all up with facts, sir. Please." And to emphasise his determination he reached over for a chair, banged it down in front of the desk and sat on it purposefully. Tomkins flinched as the chair scraped.

"Say it then. Waste no words. Understand? My patience is running low, Finch. If you're here when it goes, heaven help you."

"Yes sir. Can I take it we're agreed—"

"*We* are? I don't have to agree with you."

"Agreed, sir, I meant, that this isn't a straight loony, doing it for a thrill. There's been too much effort in drawing attention to the razors and the days engraved on 'em. Always deliberately leaving them. Even, in Ada Follett's case, coming back the next morning to leave one."

"We don't know—"

"It's almost certain, sir. And the mad scramble over the Saturday and Sunday razors—"

"What about them?"

"I was there. And Charlie was there. And we agreed he couldn't have had *time* to switch the razors. He used Saturday's for both the slashings, Ms Greene's and Mr Catterick's. But he left both. Keeping to the routine, clinging on to the symbolism."

"I'm not having *that*, for a starter. Don't talk to me about lone crusaders, for Chrissake!" Tomkins was struggling for a firm attitude. He needed help, was crying out for it, but he should not have been hearing it from a mere constable. Not have been listening . . .

"Not that. Not that at all, sir. I think he's trying to make it all look symbolic, when it's not. I think everything he's done has been sort of inverted, in an attempt to make it look like what it isn't."

"Calm down, calm down. Explain that."

Tony sighed. He felt he'd forced his way over a high peak; now it was all downhill.

"The original break-in . . . it was an inside job made to look like a break-in."

"Hmph! Don't press your luck, Finch."

"And the tissues . . . the ones left with the razors. Why were they left? There had to be a reason, because it's all been so deliberate. Even with the razors that didn't even draw blood – the tissues were left. He's been *telling* us something, sir, and I believe – if we remember the faked break-in – that he was telling us the razors had been wiped."

"Well of course—"

"Exactly, sir."

"Exactly? What the hell d'you mean by exactly?"

"The first thing you said, your natural reaction – of course the razors had been wiped. *That* was what the tissues meant, that they'd been wiped."

"And why," asked Tomkins, a dangerous tone in his voice because Finch had introduced a tiny light into his dark pit of gloom, and now appeared to be about to snuff it out, "why shouldn't they have been wiped?"

"Because they didn't need to be, sir. That's my point. That's *his* point, rather. He wants us to believe he'd wiped them . . . because they weren't wiped. And he'd only need to give that impression if he couldn't leave fingerprints in the first place. 'I've wiped off my prints,' is what he's telling us. Why – unless there weren't any to be wiped off?"

Tomkins cocked his head. "Are you sure you're all right, Finch? You did get a bang on the head, after all."

"Sir—"

"Man alive, if there'd been no prints and no tissues, we'd simply have assumed he was wearing gloves."

"Which wouldn't suit him at all," Tony said patiently. "Not if he *had* to wear gloves. Or one, at least."

"He? You sound as though you—"

"Yes, sir. I've got a certain person in mind."

"You have?" Tomkins was cautious. The fool might say Merryweather.

"Imagine, sir, that you've got an artificial right hand, had it for years so that a lot of people are aware of it—"

"In *that* case," Tomkins said sharply, his brain working now, stimulated, "I'd learn to use my left one."

"Of course he would. But he wouldn't want to use that in this case. It might be remembered that he'd used his left hand and he couldn't have expected to kill all seven. In fact, his attacks have been fairly feeble."

"Feeble! What about Hartington?"

"A special case, sir. I thought the idea was that Hartington knew him personally."

"You thought . . . the idea—"

"But you do, I'm sure, sir. Accept that he knew him, I mean."

"All right. Get on with it."

"Then, if he knew him, how did he recognise him? The slasher's always been masked. I think Hartington recognised the artificial right hand. There can't have been anything else. So he had to be killed. And the attacks on Esmeralda Greene and Paul Catterick – one was a mistake because the blade ran down the ski sticks, and the other a panic reaction. So you see, sir, he had to allow for his victims to remember which hand he'd used, so he wouldn't have dared to do them left-handed. He had to give the impression that the right hand he was using was a normal one – hence the tissues." Tony breathed out slowly. "Sir," he added, for good measure.

Tomkins looked down at his blotter. The lad was making a good case. He'd given it a lot of thought. But it was all so . . . what was the word? Airy-fairy? No – ephemeral, that was the word. All theory. Nothing concrete.

"You're describing a man who's planned all this – for a purpose."

"Yes, sir."

"What purpose?"

"I believe he grabbed this chance that the raffle business has handed him. It makes it all fit a loony who's been sparked by the upset. But it doesn't quite fit, does it? It's all too . . . too positive, sir. I think his purpose has been to remove *one* person out of those seven. I think, if Charlie hadn't ruined his sequence last week, he'd still have jumped number four, who is Lucinda Porter, as you know. Thursday. I think he'd have jumped to the last of the list, Catterick, and worked back to Ms Porter. It's only a guess but that's how it's turning out. Charlie's missing. If he's dead, the attacker's left with only Thursday, Ms Porter. After all, whoever he was aiming for, that would have to be the end. He wouldn't have been able to carry on after he'd removed his genuine intended victim. That's psychological, sir," Tony added apologetically.

"Hmm!" said Tomkins, who'd said much the same to Merryweather. "It's still a lot of I believe and I think. No proof."

"Sir – there is a man in this town who has an artificial right hand. This man – and I have evidence of this – was late for an appointment at midnight on Saturday. This same appointment would have involved him with other activities all through Sunday, which would explain the fact that he was carrying both Saturday and Sunday razors when he attacked Esmeralda Greene—"

"What appointment? Where?"

"I don't know. It's to do with Club 6."

"Club 6? What the hell—"

"It's a secret society, sir."

"A secret . . . oh Christ! Don't come that game. Secret societies! And I thought—"

"Really sir . . . it's the truth."

"If it's bloody secret, how d'you know about it?" There

was a bitter tone in Tomkins's voice. He'd thought Finch
had something. Now this!

"I've heard. Talking to people."

"You talk too much, Finch."

"But sir – this man—"

"Do you expect me to go to the chief super with a lot
of crap about secret societies? What the hell do they do –
remove from our population the people they don't like?"

"It's a kind of traditional thing."

"Like bloody mistletoe at Christmas?"

"Something like that, sir. Always done – no reason for
it, really. If you like, I can find out—"

"It seems to me you've found out too much already."

"Charlie Pierce, Mr Tomkins, was approached by this
man, the man with the false hand. He was invited to join
Club 6."

"Your precious secret society?"

"That one. Yes. I know this, because Charlie told me."

"Told you. You, you, you. It's all what you've heard and
what you think. I'm rapidly losing faith in this, Finch. I'm
tired. I'm up to my eyeballs and you come here talking about
secret societies!"

"Charlie Pierce had an appointment to meet him."

"When?"

"And he *did* meet somebody, and went off with him
in a car."

"When?"

"You know when, sir. Seven o'clock, in the square."

"I mean . . . did Pierce tell you his appointment with this
man was at seven in the square?"

"No, sir. Otherwise I'd have kept an eye on it."

"There you are then. Could've been anybody who picked
him up. Some other secret society, perhaps. There could be
hundreds in this damned town."

"Sir. Listen, please."

278

"You've gone too far, Finch."

"A search warrant, sir. His house, home, whatever. His car, his office. It'll be somewhere."

"What will?"

"Thursday's razor. We've got to do *something*. Charlie could be alive—"

"Don't tell me what we've got to do."

"A search warrant."

"Don't be a damned fool. What JP would give us a warrant on that! Christ, you're making my head ache. Get out of here, Finch. Send in Cartwright."

"I have his name, sir."

Tomkins gave it a few seconds. He wasn't sure he dared to ask. In the end he asked softly, "Who?"

"Mr Llewellyn Pugh. The town clerk."

"Pugh," said Tomkins, still quietly, but managing to get it out as a hiss, though there was no S in it. "The town clerk!" Then he was on his feet, swaying with the exhaustion that still possessed him. "And you expect me to apply for a search warrant – to have Pugh in, I suppose, to grill him? The town clerk! You must be insane."

"Yes, sir." Tony felt empty. He'd got it all out, and thought he'd done it logically and sensibly. He'd unloaded it but now it looked as though he'd delivered it to the wrong address.

"And would you care to repeat this load of rubbish to the chief super?" Tomkins demanded, still uncertain, still flinching from the responsibility.

"By all means sir. Glad of the chance." Which seemed to be the only, and last, chance.

And Tomkins saw that in this way he could toss both ends of this embarrassing situation at each other without being, himself, trapped in the middle. He suddenly smiled and Tony winced.

"On your feet then, and you can do it."

279

So Tomkins took him in to Merryweather. "Constable Finch has picked up a few pointers, sir. Have you got time to listen to him?"

Without answering, Merryweather pointed a pencil at a chair. Tony sat and facing bleak cold eyes he repeated it all, without interruption or comment, without query, without encouragement.

At the end Merryweather asked, "And you'd suggest?" His voice was menacingly smooth.

"Get Pugh in, sir. I think he'll confess. He'll be near breaking point now. Search his house and his car and his office, and you'll find Thursday's razor. Today's, sir. So we haven't got much time."

"*We* haven't got much time! Did you hear that, Inspector? Right. I've listened. I'll not have it said I didn't give you a hearing. I will *not* act on spurious theories that mean nothing. You said yourself they were inverted clues. I am placing you on suspension, as of now. You will go home. In due course you will have the opportunity to defend yourself. Dereliction of duty, Finch. How else would you have found out all this interesting load of crap? Take him away, Tomkins."

Tony, pale and tense, got to his feet. "But you can't ignore . . . he knows what he did with Charlie. He's my friend! Let me—"

Merryweather rose with intense and overwhelming authority. "Be silent!" he shouted. "Go near Pugh and I'll see you dismissed from the force. Get out, damn you!"

Tomkins stood and held open the door. Because he was embarrassed, he made a ridiculous gesture, like a major-domo ushering out a treasured guest. He slammed the door with a brisk finality on Tony's heels, unfortunately, he realised, leaving himself on the same side as Merryweather, who had certain pithy remarks to make about Tomkins's blundering incompetence in allowing Tony Finch anywhere near him.

Tony ran down the stairs, his feet barely brushing them. He went to his car and walked round it a few times because he couldn't trust himself to drive with such a blinding fury obscuring his vision.

Eventually he drove away, at first purposelessly. Then, realising there was only one thing left for him to do, he stopped, did a fast U-turn, and headed out to Crécy Drive. It was nearly one in the morning.

Time, to Tony, was now only minutes that ate away at what could be left for Charlie. It did not occur to him that the rest of the town was asleep. There were things to do, a phone booth to be located, its directory to be riffled through hurriedly, Arthur Moreton's address to be located. Crécy Drive, he knew. Somewhere in that tree-shaded road. Yes – The Mount, number 63.

Ten minutes later Arthur Moreton was awakened by a continuous ringing of his doorbell and an accompanying hammering on his knocker. Somewhere in the rear his dog was barking in frenzied concern. He threw on a dressing gown. "All right, I'm coming." Switching on lights as he went.

Tony stepped into the hall. "I'm sorry, Mr Moreton. It's urgent."

"Constable Finch? The factory?"

"No, sir, no. Your help, if you will."

"Yes?"

"Club 6, sir."

"I told you, I can't discuss—"

"It's not a name. I don't want a name from you. I believe one of your members was late for the Saturday Sunday meeting. I don't need you to tell me who. My friend Charlie Pierce was invited to become a member by somebody who said he was retiring—"

"No one is retiring."

Tony ignored that, pressing on. "Charlie was picked up by

281

that same person. Charlie told me who it was going to be. That was six hours ago. At that time it was Wednesday and Charlie would've been Wednesday in the razor sequence."

Moreton was very still, his lips thin, his face drawn. Suddenly he looked very old. "What is it you want?"

"Not a name, sir. Not now. There isn't time. A place. The location of the place Charlie might have been taken to."

"It's secret—"

"For God's sake! We're not playing kids' games now. A place. Tell me, please. Somewhere I can go and look."

Moreton stared at him in agony for two more seconds, then he came to a decision.

"Wait. Two minutes. I'll get my key, throw something on. Wait."

"I didn't expect—"

But Moreton was running up the stairs. Tony sighed at the delay, his nerves crying out for movement and action. But the fact was that he had to have help. Desperately.

A red setter came sidling into the hall suspiciously, even though Master had spoken to this person who was here at such a strange hour. Tony had a way with dogs. He said, "Hello," in that special voice of pleased surprise, and the tail moved. Tony ran fingers through her ears, staring into the mild and trusting eyes. Charlie's eyes. The velvet feel calmed him. He waited for Moreton who came pounding down the stairs in pyjama top and slacks, a huge torch in his hand. He grabbed his anorak from the hall stand and they ran out to Tony's car, Moreton calling out, "Sorry, Claire," to the dog.

"It's out Steelcroft Lane way. Know it?"

"Yes, sir."

"Just Arthur will do, if you don't mind. Got a siren on this car?"

"No. A blue winker though. On the back seat. Got it? Switch it on and stick it out on the roof. Here we go."

It was full night with a slight mist, the roads clear. Tony took them at eighty into town, sixty through it, and hurled the car along Steelcroft Lane like a rally driver, on the edge of all adhesion and possible safety.

"Slow here," said Moreton. "A left turn just past—"

"Through the new industrial estate?"

"That's it. The old Diamond Edge place."

"I might've guessed," said Tony in disgust at his own lack of perception.

"No reason why you should. Watch it over here, you'll ruin your suspension. That dark shape ahead."

Tony failed to watch it, forcing the car over the uneven surface, skidding to a halt in front of the loading bay.

"It's up the steps," said Moreton. "Got a torch? Good. Where's my keys? This is it."

The padlock hung, unlocked, through the hasp.

"Somebody's been here," said Moreton softly.

"Yes," Tony agreed hoarsely. "You'd better lead the way."

They ran through the factory, both torches fanning ahead, the shapes around them like prehistoric monsters, moving ponderously as the shadows chased round them. Their feet echoed ahead. "Charlie!" roared Tony. "Charlie, where are you?" This echoed back, but unaccompanied by any reply. Moreton pounded ahead, reached the tank, stopped, and cast his torchlight downwards.

Tony came to his shoulder. Charlie was slumped into one corner, the tap above him dripping onto the side of his face. A pink mixture of blood and water dribbled away to the far corner of the tank.

"I've gotta get down there," said Tony.

"No. Me." Moreton took his arm. "You've got to get help. I can't work your radio. Help me down first."

"You shouldn't—"

"Be buggered to shouldn't. Help me." Moreton put his

283

torch away, sticking out of his pocket, and crouched down. "I'll need a hand. Come *on*."

Tony knelt beside him, taking his hands as Moreton got down with his back to the tank and reached his left foot over. "Got it?" Slowly he eased over, until Tony could take his weight and lower him so that he could jump the last three feet. Tony reached his torch forward and centred it on Charlie. Moreton knelt beside him, then raised a shocked face.

"He's very cold . . . wait . . . there's a pulse. Very weak. Yes, he's alive. Get moving, Finch, get moving."

Tony ran back, only half aware of the route but fanning his torch frantically. "He's a strong lad," he said to Moreton, though Moreton was way back out of the reach of his voice.

He called in the ambulance and the fire service, because Charlie would have to be lifted out of there somehow. He ought really, he realised, have contacted Tomkins, to save him from wasting manpower on the search for Charlie, but then he thought: bugger Tomkins. After all, Tony was on suspension. An outcast. They'd have the radio out of his car in a flash.

Then he ran back to the tank, to find that nothing was changed. Moreton had his anorak around Charlie's shoulders and was holding him tightly, to pass on as much warmth as possible. Then Tony ran back to the loading ramp, holding his lighted torch and waving it backwards and forwards to guide them in the moment the winkers and sirens began to splinter the night.

The fire service made it seem all too easy, lifting Charlie out on a stretcher so that the ambulance crew would have room to work. The arm was still slowly oozing blood and they stemmed that. They got him in the ambulance and set off slowly and tenderly over the rough bit before they reached smooth tarmac and plunged off for the hospital.

Tony and Moreton stood on the loading bay. They seemed reluctant to move, as though part of Charlie and of themselves might be left behind.

"Ruined your anorak," said Tony.

"Yes."

"I owe you thanks—"

"No. It's not often a person gets the chance—" He stopped.

"I know. I'll run you home, shall I." Not a question; they were already moving towards the car.

"I suppose," said Moreton, "they'll fetch him in now."

Tony was silent, seeming to have great difficulty in fastening his seat belt. "Who?" he asked at last in an empty voice. "My superiors will listen to nothing from me. No time for my stupid theories. I mentioned no name to you, Arthur. No name at all." He drove away.

"But you know!"

"I *know* nothing. It's all theory. Charlie's not saying anything, is he? All I can put together is ideas. Yes, Charlie said that a Mr Pugh was going to propose him to your Club 6, but not when. This attack didn't have to have anything to do with your lot. We just don't know." He hammered the palm of his hand on the steering wheel.

"Easy, young man. You'll have us off the road. And you're forgetting the padlock. Only six of us have keys."

"I haven't forgotten it. It's a fall-back he's left himself. If challenged on it, he'd say the last one out forgot to lock it and that somebody else must've used the opportunity."

Moreton was silent. After a few moments Tony glanced at him.

"Who *was* the last out, Arthur?"

"Pugh," Moreton said softly.

"You see. He only needs to deny everything – and there's no proof."

"Charlie—"

"Who might not recover consciousness," Tony cut in.

"He will. I feel he will."

"And that," said Tony, in a tone of desperate inadequacy, "gives our slasher an extra target at the hospital. My God—"

The car jigged across the road. Tony caught at it and steadied it.

"What is it?"

"He's such a clever sod! Have you realised that? Every attack he's made – even the one on you, when he'd got his retreat worked out – he's managed to wriggle out of the trap. Now he's got Lucinda Porter to aim at. She's Thursday. Today . . . tonight . . . they'll have that hospital swarming with police. He'll know that. They'll all look innocent, like hospital staff. He'll know that too. So he'll create a diversion. I can guess what that will be. He'll go for Charlie first and in the confusion he'll get to Lucinda . . . Oh Christ! And I can't do a thing."

"Why not?"

"I'm on suspension. I'm not supposed to go near."

"You have a right. You can visit a friend and sit with him. They can't stop that."

Tony suddenly threw back his head. A gurgling sound, like a choked laugh, emerged from his throat. "What a damned fool I am! Of course. They can't stop me from sitting with Charlie. They can't stop me from visiting Paul and Esmeralda and even going up to the women's intensive care ward. I've got another friend there. A young lady. I can always visit Madge."

He drew the car into Moreton's drive. At the bedroom window his wife peered out, fearing the worst – as she always did with her volatile Arthur. Who didn't seem to be in a hurry to get out of the car. Just sat there.

"Mr Moreton?"

"There's something I can do."

286

"No," said Tony flatly. "You've done enough. More than enough."

"I," said Moreton flatly, "can do more. I can meet Pugh – visit him – as a friend. We're both members of the 57 Club too. And I need never let him out of my sight."

Tony hissed through his teeth. "No . . . please no," he said quietly. "The man's gone way past some point where he could control himself. I don't want to have to worry about you, too. Please . . . keep out of it. Promise me that."

Moreton got out of the car. Just before the door shut, he put his head back in. "D'you think a promise would mean anything?"

Oh hell! thought Tony as the door slammed.

Then he drove to the hospital.

It was 5 a.m. They were very busy in Emergency, having to tend to all the casualties who'd drifted in from the car crashes in the night. They were still attending to Charlie, sewing him up while he was unconscious, transfusing a large amount of blood into him, feeding him energy with a glucose drip. Tony was able to have a word with the young doctor who was attending to him. Charlie, he said confidently, was out of danger, but he'd be out of action for a few weeks.

Don't you believe it, Tony said to himself. He went up to the fourth floor to see whether he could find Madge. She was there, but really out of contact. The next bed to Lucinda's was empty and therefore unmade. Madge had fallen back on it and was fast asleep. The nurse at the table caught his eye as he approached, raising a silencing finger, then she beckoned. Tony went over and bent low, because the nurse wished to whisper.

"She a friend of yours?"

"Yes."

"Can't you get her away from here? She's going to have a breakdown, I can see it coming on. It doesn't help—"

"Helps Ms Porter, though?"

The nurse bit her lip and nodded.

Tony whispered, "Then I'm not going to be able to shift her."

She nodded again in agreement and said nothing. It'd been a try.

"How long?" Tony asked gently.

"Lucinda Porter? We don't really . . . expect her to last through another night."

"I'll be around. *Then* I'll take Madge away."

It was all he could do, he realised, with every aspect of it – be around. Waiting and watching, hiding from Tomkins, who was sure to be around some time during the day. And now his head was buzzing from lack of sleep, the skin on his face tight and dry and rough with beard, his stomach uneasy from snatched food. He would, he decided, go home and grab an hour or two, and run the gauntlet of his mother's admonitions. A night-owler, she would call him.

So he went home and if his mother said anything his mind was too far away to notice. He ate the stew she'd kept for him. What meal was it? Breakfast or supper? He lurched to his bed, set his alarm for nine and was even deeper than Charlie into oblivion before he'd got his trousers off.

Chapter Twenty-One

Thursday, 5 October (cont.)

Bathed, changed, fed once more, his chin shaven to polished perfection, Tony drove on to the forecourt of St Mary's at ten in the morning.

A police car was parked by the front entrance, an obviously official vehicle, intended to add invisibility to the very official but anonymous officers in every possible location. Tony got out of his car as the uniformed driver did the same. It was a man he knew, with whom he'd worked.

"Sorry, Tony. I've been ordered to stop you."

"What's the charge, Frank?"

"What?"

"On what charge do you intend to hold me?" Tony asked reasonably.

"No charge."

"Well then. I'm a civilian now, you know. On suspension. Unless I'm disorderly or violent you can't touch me. Or it'd be unprovoked assault. Right?"

Frank looked uneasy. "I'd better ask—"

"You go and do that, and while you're at it . . . I've got four friends inside here, all waiting for a visit. Okay? Oh . . . and a solicitor, too."

Frank grinned. "Solicitors frighten me to death." And he stood aside.

Tony ran up the steps and into main reception, turned left, and paced along the corridor to Emergency. He was beginning to know this hospital now. It took him a few minutes to get information. "He's out of danger," they told him. "They've got him up in the men's ward."

Which suited Tony just fine. Paul was there, now Charlie was there, and also Ephraim Potts if he needed legal guidance or protection, and unless he missed his guess, Esmeralda too.

She was . . . sitting in a chair beside Paul, in rather natty pyjamas and a silk dressing gown, which her headmistress had fetched from the flat. She and Paul were in deep and intensely concentrated conversation. Tony didn't interrupt them, his eyes elsewhere. Charlie first. He was the other side of the ward, looking strangely less bulky in bed, and with only his pale grey face showing, and when he went to stand beside him Tony could see no more than a slow rise and fall where his chest would be.

He went into the office in the corner to locate the staff nurse. "Rather weak," she said. And, "No, he hasn't regained consciousness yet. He lost a lot of blood and he was suffering from hypothermia."

"But he'll be all right?"

"Yes," she told him patiently, "I said that." She twisted her lips into a strangely sardonic smile. "Another one for the young lady to worry about."

"Oh . . . yes. That'll be Madge."

"Is that her name? Hmm! If this goes on, we'll have to take her on to the permanent staff."

Tony said quickly, "No trouble, is she?"

She shrugged. "A help. No trouble, certainly, she's an intelligent girl."

He turned away, gesturing. "I've got other friends. Oh . . . has anybody informed his mother? Charlie Pierce's. D'you know?"

"He's had no outside visitors."

"Thank you."

Damn it, he thought. They might have fetched his mother. But no. Not Tomkins.

Esmeralda and Paul watched him coming with an intensity of suppressed excitement that should have warned him. "Hello, you two," he said cautiously. "How's it coming along?"

Paul was now able to speak more clearly. The dressing on his cheek had been reduced to no more than a tracery of sticking plaster. "We don't think she'll be able to handle a hockey stick again."

"I'll be glad, glad," she said quickly. "It's Paul who's upset. I can fall back on my maths."

"Of course you can."

"I can see what'll happen to me," Paul said mournfully. "They'll send me out to the counter when we get an awkward customer they want scaring off."

Tony laughed.

"But we wanted to ask you—" Paul began.

"Ask you," Esmeralda repeated.

"If you'll be best man for me."

"No! I mean yes! Oh hell, of course I will. Delighted. You're getting married?"

"What the hell d'you think we're doing?" demanded Esmeralda.

"You won't want for bridesmaids, anyway," Tony said cheerfully.

"I'm dreading it," Paul declared. "Absolutely dreading it."

"You!" she said.

"She can't hit me," Paul explained to Tony.

"Later," she told him fondly. "Later. It'll all come back."

Tony turned away. There was Madge to see, Madge to worry about. But Potts was still in the next bed, sitting up, his bedspread covered with papers, glasses perched on the end of his nose.

291

"You still here, Mr Potts?"

"Come closer, young man."

Tony bent over him. "I am," said Potts softly, "doing what we used to call skiving. They'd let me go home if I asked, but I've got business upstairs later tonight. So it's much more sensible to wait it out here."

"You're a crafty old devil," Tony whispered. "What's it worth not to tell the sister?"

"If you do so," Potts murmured, "I'll tell Tomkins I recognise you as my assailant." He winked.

Tony whispered back, "But I know who that is and I think you do too. Or you'll have guessed."

Potts pushed his spectacles back up his nose with his finger. The twinkle had gone from his eyes. "Why might I have guessed?"

"You said you have business upstairs tonight, Mr Potts. It's Thursday. I believe you have a client who's in danger, who's been in danger, who might have been killed *last* Thursday if Charlie Pierce hadn't ruined the slasher's sequence. I think you've realised this, but for some reason which you'll claim to be professional ethics you've kept quiet. It was only a guess, you would claim. Only a guess! But people have been injured because of this. Two of them behind me, one across the other side of the ward. And another one has been killed. But you guessed, Mr Potts, because you've now been attacked three times yourself. You'll have realised it's all connected. A pretty concrete guess, wouldn't you say? I'll bet you're having trouble with your conscience now – you and your ethics. Because you've known, haven't you? Known!"

"Known they're all connected? Of course."

"No, no, Mr Potts. Let's have none of your court voice and your playing with words. Known who's been responsible, I meant. And you know *that*, too."

All this had been said by Tony in an intense whisper, the

smile not leaving his face. In one way he admired this old man who stubbornly clung to a code he'd practised all his life. In another way he despised him, that he should have rejected a public duty in this way. After all, Potts was an officer of the law.

"She's safe now," Potts muttered.

"Is she? Because this place is packed with police? Is that it? But he's managed so far, getting round all the protection Tomkins has laid on. Are *you* safe? Ask yourself that. I know who's been doing it, Mr Potts. But Tomkins won't listen. Are you prepared to tell him now, before it's too late? I'll fetch Tomkins. Tell *him* what you know. Tell him what it's all been about. Tell him,' he suggested softly, "why she must be killed before midnight."

Bent over the bed, his fists digging into the bedclothes, he stared Potts challengingly in the eyes.

Potts said softly, "You speak of guesses. That was one of your own guesses."

Tony shook his head slowly.

"Then mention a name." Potts tilted his head.

"Llewellyn Pugh," Tony whispered.

For two seconds Potts was very still, then he inclined his head. It could have been a nod, but his glasses slid down his nose, and this might have been his sole intention, because he returned at once to his paperwork.

Tony wasn't sure Potts actually said anything. It could have been, "Later, young man. I must think."

Nothing can be more infuriating than a person set in his old ways, inflexible, his whole life devoted to them. They wouldn't budge. Never.

Out in the corridor, moving fast now, he met Tomkins, who stood barring his way and glaring.

"I thought I instructed you—"

"You've got no authority over me now, Mr Tomkins. Why haven't you fetched Mrs Pierce here?"

Tomkins too was set in his ways, one of them being that he didn't respond to impatient demands from junior officers. He had to force himself to patience. Finch was only on suspension – not yet dismissed. His authority still existed.

"For your information," he said with dignity, "I *did* send a car. She refused to drive in it."

"Thank you. Then I'll fetch her myself. And for *your* information, I'll be round and about all day, as an ordinary visitor. All right?"

Tomkins nodded. It could have meant that he agreed or merely that he understood. Tony marched out of the building angrily. Two stubborn fools! It was only when he got outside that he realised he didn't know exactly where Charlie lived. The district, yes. The address, no. But of course . . . the prize draw! The local paper would have it. A quick trip to their offices, a short period of illegal parking and one parking ticket later, and he was on his way.

She had the door open before he reached it, her curtains still twitching. Stolidly, she barred his way.

"Where is he? What's he done?"

"Done nothing, Mrs Pierce."

"Then why'd they sent a police car here?"

"To pick you up."

"Why would they want me, if he hasn't done anything?"

She was a smaller and more compact version of Charlie, with about ten times his amount of aggression to make up for it.

"We don't want to talk about it out here, do we?" he asked.

"You'd better come in, I suppose."

She took him in and sat him in Charlie's chair. He knew it was Charlie's because the dent was twice the size of his own behind. I'll make a detective yet, he thought. "He's in hospital, Mrs Pierce. He was attacked with a razor, but he's out of danger now. He hasn't come round yet."

She was eyeing him with her lips compressed, her eyes bleak. She nodded. "He will. You'll see."

"They sent a car to take you there."

"What! A police car! Never! I'm not going to be seen getting into a police car."

"I'll take you. The car's my own."

"Hmph! What good'd I be in a hospital? I ask you."

"Good for Charlie, perhaps, when he does come round."

"Oh lovely! The first thing he sees when he opens his eyes is this face of mine. He'll have the screamers."

"Seems all right to me," Tony said, cocking his head. "Doesn't frighten me."

"You're a good lad." She nodded at something. "I'll just get my purse."

"What'd you want—"

"If I'm there all day, I'll need a cuppa tea. Time to time. Here . . . can I get somethin' to eat? I ain't coming if I've got to starve."

"Mrs Pierce, if they starve you, they'll have to put you in a bed and force-feed you. They don't like doing that. Grab your hat or whatever, and let's go."

It seemed longer going back than it had coming. Not for one moment did she cease talking about Charlie. What a good lad he was. How he'd looked after her, ever since his dad was took. Never hurt a fly, would Charlie, and now this had to happen to him. If there was somebody up there looking after things, then all she could say was that he wasn't making a very good job of it, and when her time came she'd have something to say about it. And you could bank on that.

"You might not go there," Tony managed to fit in, as they marched up the hospital steps.

"If I don't, I'll want to know the reason. Where is he? Up

295

these stairs? What do they think we are, bloody athletes! I'll bet it's a waste of time, when we get there. Got up out of his bed and tooken the bus. You'll see. Oh, is this it? That his bed? That isn't Charlie, is it? My Charlie!"

Then she was in tears and he had to slide a chair under her, and only then did he take time to look round, and find that Madge was with Esmeralda, still there, and Paul. When he smiled, Madge came over, and it took more effort than he thought he had to spare in order to hold the smile, as she'd visibly lost weight, when she'd been nothing much in the first place, and her eyes seemed huge and empty in a strangely depleted face, the bones showing, her lips only a thin, pale line.

"For God's sake!" he whispered. "You've got to get some rest."

"I'm all right. She relies on me, though, now. They don't think . . . they think . . ." Her voice was insecure. "Think it'll be her last night, Tony."

And *then* she can rest, he thought. "Come'n meet Charlie's mother," he said, and Charlie's mother had heard every word through her tears. She turned, her head coming up.

"This is Madge," said Tony.

"Hello, Charlie's mother," said Madge, dragging up a smile from somewhere.

"D'you know my Charlie?"

"Oh yes," Madge assured her, whipping up a little verve and a tiny pleasantry. "He slept round at my place the other night." It seemed ages ago.

Mrs Pierce stared at her for a long few moments. "Yes," she said. "I reckon." Then she drew herself together in a pitifully plump attempt at primness. "It was a lot different in my time." Only a wisp of wistfulness escaped her.

There isn't much you can do, staring down at somebody unconscious in a bed. His mother took his hand but it felt so limp and unresponsive that she dropped it. Madge took it but she felt it to be so vital and responsive that she too put it down, and tucked it away.

Tony said, "I've got things to do."

Madge glanced at him quickly. "You're on duty?"

"Not at the moment. There's something, though, that I might try."

Might try? The realisation showed itself in her face, an abrupt fear darting across it. "She's safe. Really she is," he assured her quickly.

"I'm sure." But her voice was dull.

He touched her cheek, to check that it was still warm. "I'll be back."

He turned quickly and walked away. A sudden small thrill of cold fear had touched him.

Tomkins was in the corridor again. It seemed almost as though he'd been waiting for Tony. It then became clear that he had been. Tony stopped. He spoke first.

"If you could tell me what you've got arranged, I'll try not to interfere. But I've got a lot of friends here."

Tomkins spoke in a voice almost detached, as though he was relating details remote from himself. The words seemed to emerge before he had a chance to marshal them. "The chief super's in charge. We've got every possible approach covered. If you don't see anything, then it's going well. If you do, you'll ignore it."

"He could try a distraction."

"Covered."

"A disguise. So many doctors and nurses—"

"Nurses?"

"A male nurse."

"Or a soddin' female one," Tomkins grunted. "He could try any blasted trick. But it's covered. We've identified all the legitimate ones. A small red sticker . . . I won't tell you where."

"Red? A good idea. Red for blood?"

It was an arid exchange, getting nowhere. Tomkins was embarrassed, now miserably aware that perhaps he'd been wrong. He'd been too exhausted, over-stressed. But his basic professionalism had not allowed him to ignore Tony's ideas completely. He had initiated a discreet watch on Llewellyn Pugh. Now he was forced to reveal the results. But not directly, which would be too close to an apology, the very thought of which nearly choked him. He approached it in a verbal sidle.

"It's no good you going looking for him," he grumbled.

"Him?" Tony asked innocently.

Tomkins refused to be tied down. "He's not at home. Moreton was looking for him." He looked vaguely past Tony's shoulder, along the corridor. "Been there since dawn, I gather."

"Did Moreton say why he'd been there?"

"No."

"Or mention a name?"

"What name?" Tomkins countered.

Tony hesitated, then he met the mood. "Wait till Charlie comes round and he'll give you a name. Have a word with Ephraim Potts. He wants to see you, anyway, if only to complain. He knows something. He's being cagey, though. Mention the same name to him, and see what happens. Which'll probably be nothing."

"Hmph!" said Tomkins. "Well . . . I don't know. For your information, I've got a WPC in the next bed to Lucinda Porter, trying to look as though she's dying. Why do WPCs all look so damned healthy? And if you bump into somebody who looks like a priest, that'll be one of our men."

"Armed?" asked Tony blandly, lifting one eyebrow.

"Hardly. But he's got a truncheon under his cassock."

Tony stared at him blankly, then he nodded and walked away. Needed a break, that was what Tomkins needed. And where was Merryweather? Hand on the helm, steering the

298

ship through the rocks? Not him. Back in the office waiting for news, that was where he was.

The day dragged on. It was protracted misery for those involved. Officers who had been trained in silent and motionless surveillance now had to keep moving, if only to produce some appearance of being hospital staff. They bumped into each other; they walked into wards they should not have visited. Terry Cartwright almost found himself assisting with an operation.

The danger periods were the regular visiting hours, when genuine relatives and friends visited genuine patients. Keeping a watch on all these was stretching nerves to breaking point. The hospital discipline was, too, rather slack. Apart from times when patients were actually under treatment, visitors were given a reasonably free rein. It all led to confusion and frayed tempers.

Tomkins was close to collapse as the day wore on to evening. Nothing had happened. It was nine o'clock. The hospital was beginning to drift into its nightly hibernation.

Madge sat and held a cold and paper-dry hand. The curtains around Lucinda's bed were now permanently closed. Madge saw nothing of the curtains, nothing of the face in front of her, inset in a dent in the pillow. Lucinda's mouth was slightly open. More often, now, a nurse would draw aside the edge of a curtain, take a pulse, make a note on the clipboard, and leave, saying nothing.

One floor below, Ephraim Potts sat quietly on the edge of his bed. He was prepared, in dressing gown and pyjamas, but there was no point in making a move this early. At five minutes to midnight he would go up to the intensive care ward. Maybe he would be too late, but before midnight he would also be too early. So he sat and stared at Paul, who stared back at him, and neither could think of anything to say. Talking, in any event, tired Paul, and Potts, whatever he might have claimed to Tony, would not have been released to go home because he still had a splitting headache at times and occasional double vision. So they sat and communed in silence.

Across the ward at Charlie's bed there was a quiet and gentle increase in activity. Charlie had moved and groaned. A doctor had come and checked him over, spoken quietly to the duty nurse, and gone away. Charlie opened his eyes cautiously, then closed them again. His mother was no longer there to set him screaming.

At that point Tony entered the ward, as though he and Charlie had been in radio contact.

"He's coming round?"

"We'll see," the nurse said.

"Can he talk?"

"No."

Tony sat beside the bed and waited.

At a little before ten o'clock Tomkins walked in. His step was uncertain and he almost walked past the bed. Paused. Stared at Tony as though wondering who he was, then sat on the edge of the next bed.

"Anything?"

"He's been awake. Spoken. Doesn't know where he is or why."

"Asked him a name?"

"No. I don't need to."

"Damn it . . ." Tomkins was abruptly savage, then he controlled his anger. "I'll stay for a while." They might not be able to find him there.

"By all means."

"Where's his mother?"

"I took her home. She got herself convinced he's dying and she wouldn't stay."

Tomkins stared at him. "His own mother – she wouldn't stay?"

"I think she's confused. It's been a bit rough on her.

300

Nothing's ever harmed Charlie before. She said he'd either go, or he'd be home for his supper. So she's gone to get it ready."

"God!" Tomkins stared into space. "She ought to have somebody—" Then he slapped his knees. "Wasting time."

"Yes," said Tony, who'd asked WPC Angela Enfield to pop round. "Potts is over there."

"Tried him earlier. Not saying a word. Not a word."

Then he got to his feet, walked off in the wrong direction, wandered back, and out.

At a quarter past ten Charlie said, "Tony—"

Tony jerked awake. Charlie was trying to lever himself up with his good arm. Tony tried to push him back. "It's all right. Relax, Charlie."

"Wha's . . . wha's happened?"

"You got hurt. Your other arm. You've been out for a long while, Charlie. Lie back, there's a good chap."

"Whassa time?"

"After ten. Night time. The day after you went off in the car—"

"Pugh!" jerked out Charlie, falling back on his pillow.

Tony looked round. Where was Tomkins when he needed him?

"Yes," he agreed. "Pugh. We got you out of there. You're in hospital. You've got to rest."

"Gotta get the bastard."

"Not now."

Then the nurse reached them, made shushing sounds as she fought him to get Charlie's wrist, trapping it for his pulse. "I'm gettin' up," he said. "No you're not," she told him. "Gerrin' up."

Calmly, patiently, she took his pulse, raised her eyebrows, put down his arm. "Now behave, or I'll give you a jab that'll do it for you."

He glared at her. She grimaced at Tony and whispered, "Like an ox, he is. Try to keep him quiet."

"Fat chance," said Tony.

Ten minutes later Charlie was sitting with his feet on the floor, swaying and woozy, but sitting. "Arm hurts," he complained.

"More'n likely," Tony agreed. "You've got a ten-inch wound there. You've lost a lot of blood, mate. Even you can't do without blood."

"I'll have his. Where is the bugger?"

"Wish I knew. Wish I knew. You look a treat in that nightgown, I must say."

Charlie glanced down. "Where's me stuff? I can't go home in this."

"You can't go home yet, anyway. So behave. You oughta be lying down."

"Ma'll have something ready for me . . ." Charlie protested. "Jesus, I'm hungry."

Tony grinned at him. "She's been to see you."

Charlie was startled. "Ya don't say! Swore she'd never come in a hospital again. Swore it."

"When was she in hospital?"

"When she had me."

"Ah," said Tony. "I can see what's put her off."

Charlie flopped himself down again. The woozy feeling had suddenly swamped over him. "Gotta get home," he whispered. Then his eyes closed and he was silent.

The nurse came and checked him over, now that he was unresisting, and said he was sleeping naturally. So Tony gave it a few minutes then wandered up to the ward above. It was eleven o'clock, the time when everything was settling down, the lights low, and the screens on their shelves above each bed flicking their green waves above the humans they guarded, monitoring, poised to shout out at anything unusual.

Madge was sitting on a chair beside Lucinda's bed. The curtains were open on one side, a doctor, a staff nurse and the ward nurse working quietly, whispering and nodding.

Madge was not facing the bed. She sat with her knees together, her hands clenched into fists and resting on her lap. She saw Tony, raised her head slightly, but made no move to get up and come to him. He stood undecided, but realised he could not intrude at this time. He raised his hand in salute and turned away.

Nothing moved in the corridor. Ten minutes past eleven. Where were the guards? Tony remembered what Tomkins had said; if he saw nothing, then all was well. He walked slowly down the stairs. The cafeteria in the basement would have been closed and empty for hours. He bought a paper cup of coffee and stood beside the machine pensively. But there was nothing left requiring thought. Only patience.

In the men's ward, it was not so silent. Charlie was awake again and that little nap had done him the world of good. Up, was Charlie, and vociferous. Paul had got up, had come across to silence him and was searching in the bedside locker for Charlie's sneakers.

"Wants to go to the lav," he explained to Tony, who returned at exactly the right time. "Here's his bloody shoes. *You* do it. I've had it." He looked to be in pain from what had obviously been a disagreement with Charlie.

"I ain't usin' this bloody bottle," said Charlie, and then the nurse, who'd been having difficulty with Potts, came hurrying across.

"What's the trouble here?"

"He wants to go to the lav," said Tony.

Charlie had got himself to his feet, and seemed fairly steady. She said, "Then you help him. He can't do any harm to his wound."

The left arm was strapped across Charlie's chest, not

simply in a sling but completely immobilised. They'd recognised the problem he would present.

"Sit down," said Tony, prodding him in the chest. Charlie plopped down on the bed, which groaned. "Here – lift your foot. Now the other one." He fastened the laces, stood, held out a hand and pulled Charlie to his feet. "Now, arm round my shoulder. Not *all* your weight, you big oaf. Do some work for yourself, damn you. That's it. Now, one step at a time."

"We'll haveta hurry."

"All right. Clench your teeth. We'll hurry slowly."

The nurse across the ward glanced at them worriedly, but the concern could have related to Potts who was causing his own bit of trouble.

"But I've *got* to," he was protesting as Charlie and Tony disappeared round the corner.

When they returned to the ward, Potts was still protesting, with the nurse becoming more persistent. Charlie said, "I'm doin' okay now. Let's do a few laps."

Slowly, therefore, with Tony taking less and less of the weight, they moved up and down the ward.

"On me own now," said Charlie, a little out of breath.

Tony released him. Charlie moved with uncertainty, but with one stubborn foot after the other. Tony watched anxiously, poised at his shoulder. An ox, the nurse had said. More like a harried and bleeding fighting bull, head down, stubborn, moving . . . moving . . .

Then he'd had enough. "Sit down now," he said, and sat on the bed. This time it didn't groan. After he'd got his breath back he asked, "What're you doin' here, anyway?"

"Watching you, Charlie. And guarding, kind of. It's still Thursday, and she's in the ward upstairs."

"You oughta be on that landin'."

"What? Which landing?"

"Y'know. At Lucinda's place."

"She's here. I told you that. Up on the next floor."

"Yeah," said Charlie. "But does *he* know that? Pugh. Does he know she's here?"

Tony stared at him. It took a genius like Charlie to state the obvious. Where was Tomkins? Where the hell *was* he? They could trap Pugh . . .

"Officer," called out Potts from across the room. "Constable Finch."

Now what? Tony glanced at Charlie and shrugged. "Be back."

The nurse said, "He shouldn't be out of bed."

"This young man," said Potts, similarly attired as Charlie, and who was also sitting on the edge of his bed, "is a police officer. Constable, will you please instruct this young woman that she has no legal right to detain me, and that you'll arrest her for assault if she persists."

Tony risked a discreet wink at the nurse. "Where d'you want to go, Mr Potts?"

"I have a client on the floor above. I told you that. I must be with her at midnight. This nurse forbids it."

Tony spoke delicately. "Surely—"

She was doing her best, but really . . . two at the same time, both trying to do harm to themselves! "I could get a trolley here, but I can't see—"

"Can he stand?"

"Yes."

"Can he walk?"

"Just about."

"Then will it do any harm if I help him to get there? I think it's really important, you know."

She looked doubtful, recalled that he'd managed Mr Pierce, who was about four times the weight of Mr Potts. "Very well. But make him sit when he gets there – and explain to Nurse Onions."

"I'll do that. Come on, Mr Potts, let's have you."

Potts was a tough old character and when it came to it he didn't weigh too heavily on Tony. With his nightgown flapping and his hair standing out in all directions, his brief-case clutched under his free arm, he nevertheless managed to maintain his dignity. Slowly they mounted the single flight of stairs.

The intensive care ward was quiet and still. Tony couldn't see Madge anywhere, but the attention was still around Lucinda's bed. One curtain was drawn open. None of the other beds were curtained. Tony sighed. He hadn't wanted to be there when they were all closed.

A chair was already in place beside Lucinda's bed. Potts headed for it.

"Nurse Onions?" Tony asked. "This is Mr Potts."

"Thank heaven," whispered the nurse. "She's been fretting. Will you sit here, Mr Potts."

"Thank you, young man," said Potts, sitting gravely. "Thank you, nurse."

Tony took one brief look at the harrowed face on the pillow, then turned away. Where was Madge? he wondered. Hiding from it? Surely not, but in some way he hoped she was. He hurried back to Charlie, who was doing a few more laps all on his own.

"Found him?"

"Who?" Tony asked.

"Tomkins."

"No."

Charlie muttered something.

"What?"

"Did y'see Madge?"

"No. In the lav or something."

"Didn't y'check?"

"How could I—" Tony stared at him for one blank moment, then he whirled on his heel and ran out of the ward, galloped up the stairs, and burst into intensive care with his nerves twanging, forcing himself to walk quietly.

"Nurse! Please," he whispered tensely.

"Yes?"

"Where's Madge? Do you know—"

"Oh." She smiled. "Mrs Porter sent her for something. A diary, I think. Frankly—"

But he'd gone, now not caring what noise he made as he slammed out of the doors, bounded down the stairs, and crashed into the men's ward.

"She's not there, Charlie. Gone home . . . for a blasted diary. I'll have to go."

"I'm comin'."

"No you're not. Nurse—"

"Comin'," said Charlie, a dangerous rumble in his throat.

"But you can't!"

But Charlie was already thrusting him aside, using his good shoulder. Tony looked round desperately for assistance. The nurse was almost in tears. He had to decide – would he lose more time by restraining Charlie, if necessary by force, or by taking him along as a dead weight? He could, perhaps, knock him out. Do him a lot of good, that would. Probably break his own hand . . .

"Come on then!"

"You mustn't!" the nurse protested.

But Tony was already pushing one of the doors open with his shoulder. The stairs were bad, Charlie's vision clearly not being a hundred per cent. The main lobby was chaos, attendants and nurses hurrying to intercept, as the nurse had clearly rung down.

"Let us through," said Tony, in a flat voice that at least made them hesitate. Then Tony saw a man pushing a trolley, clearly supposed to be a porter, but even more clearly Terry Cartwright.

"Terry! Just the man. Grab hold of Charlie here. Hold

307

him. Okay, Charlie, relax, I'm comin' back. It's all right, Terry. Just keep him safe. Back in a sec."

He ran for his car.

The temptation was to drive like hell away from there, but Charlie was a friend. Couldn't dump him.

He skidded to a halt opposite the steps. Terry helped him get Charlie into the car. Charlie yelped as they put pressure on his left arm. Tony gasped, "Tomkins. Find him. Tell him, Pugh'll be at number three, Foundry Street. Got it?"

Then he was away in a spray of gravel.

Chapter Twenty-Two

Thursday, 5 October (end – et seq.)

Tony double-parked outside number three. There was a light on in the top window. "Stay here," he said sharply. "Stay – Charlie!"

"Get stuffed."

But the short and hectic drive had taken it out of Charlie. His voice was weak, his face pinched and grey. Tony dived out of the car, thrust open the front door and bounded up the stairs. Two flights. The urgent impulse was to shout out her name but Pugh might already be there. In any event, Madge must surely hear him.

The door was slightly ajar. He thrust it fully open and Madge was just turning from the dressing table Lucinda had managed to squeeze in. The room was scattered in clothes, with the contents of drawers she'd simply pulled out and upturned in a frantic search.

She turned, and he saw that her face was streaming with tears. "I can't find it," she whimpered.

"No," he said, his voice toneless. "I doubt there *is* a diary. She sent you away. She didn't want you there, didn't want you upset."

"But I promised! Promised myself."

"Never mind," he said, hearing himself saying it. Stupid

thing to say. "Stay here, now. Or rather, in your own room. I'll try to get Charlie—"

"Charlie's here?"

"In the car."

She at last seemed to realise that he was taut with tension and strain. He watched her expression change.

"What is it? What's all the fuss about? You come charging up here like a mad thing—"

He moved a hand casually, making light of what had been panic. "There was a chance – the slasher – you know. Lucinda's the last, and he might not have known she's in hospital. Might've come here. So . . . well, we came round, Charlie and me—"

"Silly!" She tried to laugh, but emotion choked it. "He wouldn't have hurt *me*."

"He might not know what Lucinda looks like. And . . . I mean . . . you're in her room, and there's still ten minutes left of Thursday."

"Of *course* he knows," she cried. "He's her husband."

"What!"

"We worked it out. She's told me everything. It's what it had to be, Tony. We just worked it out, on the facts."

"You mean *you* worked it out."

"I suppose. Well, yes."

"What facts?"

"It's the date of her decree absolute tomorrow. That's what Mr Potts is there for, to get her signature to the application after midnight. Then she'll be really free of him."

"Well I'll be buggered." He stared at her as though she was a wondrous treasure. "You know his name's Pugh?"

"Yes." Lower lip between her teeth. "But only today. She's been using her maiden name."

"Then let's get out of here. We've got to find Tomkins."

"Who's he?"

"Leave that mess for now. Let's go." He went to the door,

waiting for her, urging her silently, and heard a movement on the stairs. He held up his hand. "Wait," he whispered, though of course it could be Charlie.

He went out on to the top landing. The lighting out there was one weary old dust-laden forty-watt bulb, dim after the brighter room. A figure in a dark grey tracksuit and a black ski mask was slowly mounting the second flight of stairs, left hand hauling him up, one step at a time.

Pugh was very tired. The actual effort involved in slashing with an open razor might not be much, but the stress, the planning, the violent escape techniques, were all digging into his reserves. It was all he could do to mount the stairs, and it absorbed all his remaining mental poise to cling to the one final objective – that room and that woman.

Tony spoke from above him. "It's over, Pugh. Throw that razor down and stay where you are. It's finished. She isn't here."

The razor clamped in the right hand was the only bright object on the stairway. It seemed to draw light from the bulb and concentrate it. From Pugh there was a cry like an animal on which a trap had fastened. He lifted his head. Behind him, using his right hand crossed over his chest, Charlie was stubbornly mounting and had reached the landing below.

"Don't be a fool!" Tony shouted, but Pugh had searched deeply and produced from somewhere a burst of blind and frustrated energy. He thrust himself forward and upward, the blade whirling and glinting.

Tony steadied himself and kicked him on the right shoulder, even in that second thinking mainly of disarming that lethal hand. Pugh cried out again and toppled backwards, and Charlie, himself rescuing a reserve of energy and fury and charging up beneath Pugh, put his good shoulder down and his good arm up and caught Pugh in mid-air, straightened, and with a howl threw Pugh over his head, to crash down behind him on the landing.

311

Then Charlie collapsed. Behind Tony, Madge was scream-ing. He stepped back and held her tightly in his arms. He knew that Pugh offered no more danger to anyone, the way he'd been lying with his head twisted at an impossible angle.

They were still there when Tomkins arrived with a squad of men, the four of them set in a tableau. With this sort of situation, Tomkins came into his own. Two ambulances, because all four of them had the same destination, the hospital, except that Pugh's ambulance would go round the back to the morgue. And Charlie, back in his own bed and recovering fast, was fit enough to demand what the hell they meant by arrest.

"You killed somebody, Charlie," Tony explained.

"Oughta get a medal."

"I agree. But they have to charge you, and see what the top brains say. I expect it'll come out as self-defence or justifiable homicide. So don't worry."

"I ain't worryin'. How's Madge?"

"Upset, of course. Her friend died just before we got back."

"Yeah." Charlie then went very silent as he considered Madge being upset. It was Madge he was worrying about, and where was she, anyway?

Madge was with Potts, who'd borrowed the nurse's office on the floor above. He was explaining that Lucinda had not only signed the application for a decree absolute, just after midnight, but had also signed her new will.

"That's why she sent you away, my dear," he explained softly. "I had Paul and Esmeralda up to witness the signature. She left everything to you."

Madge bit her lip. She was quite wept out, suffering only from occasional shuddering attacks.

"She was determined I should have that typewriter," she said dully.

Potts smiled and cocked his head, but decided not to worry her any more at that time. He went down slowly to his own ward and there he explained to Tony and Charlie.

"Pugh apparently made a lot of money from bribery and corruption, somewhere up north. Perhaps Lucifer Hartington was involved – I don't know. But Pugh got out before they tied it down, changed his name, and put all his money into property, in his wife's name – Lucinda's. When they broke up – she left him on cruelty grounds – he realised he couldn't get it back. She got her decree nisi six weeks ago, and he knew his only chance was to kill her before midnight tonight. But she hid herself away in that room in Foundry Street and he didn't know where to find her until the raffle revealed her address. I suppose he realised he couldn't simply kill her, because he'd be the obvious suspect when he came forward to claim her estate. So he hid it all inside the raffle upset, as a madman's work."

"Property?" asked Tony. "You mentioned property."

"Well yes. In this town."

"And Madge owns it now?"

Potts smiled. "She has me to guide her. She owns an apartment block in Agincourt Road, and the Rimfire Tower in the main concourse."

Tony gaped at him. "That's—"

"Yes. She'll be quite wealthy."

Charlie whispered, "She'll need a minder."

Five months later, Tony performed his duty as best man as he'd promised to Esmeralda and Paul. He was now Detective Sergeant Finch. He stood looking out at what was a car park behind the register office, but was now a seething mass of Esmeralda's girls and Paul's young ladies. Somehow, he'd found it more difficult than facing the slasher, to keep that mob under some sort of control, especially when they'd come under the influence of Ada, Connie and Floss, who'd been Esmeralda's maids of honour and were at the moment three brilliant flashes of colour in the middle of the crowd. They showed no signs of leaving as they were all waiting for the next wedding, in which they also had an interest.

Tony held the smile left over from Esmeralda and Paul for the second car, which was bringing Madge, and also Arthur Moreton to give her away. And here she was, in a very smart pink outfit that presented her as a veritable princess, he thought. Then, drawing a deep breath, he went back inside quickly to stand beside Charlie.

It had been absolute hell and was going to get worse. There was going to be a combined reception in the conference hall on the top floor of the Rimfire Tower. Everybody, and anybody, invited.

Sometimes, life could be pure bloody murder, Tony decided, straightening his shoulders as Charlie grinned at him.

It was Tony's second go at being best man in half an hour.